Lost Tomb of Alexander

Other books by John O'Melveny Woods

Return to Treasure Island
Lost Tomb of Alexander
Jesse James Secret
The Crusaders
A Stroke of Hope

Also Available with Co-Author Frank Kelso
California Gold
Juan's Revenge

Lost Tomb of Alexander

John
O'Melveny
Woods

ISBN: 9781945190124
CSFV 16HBI

Published by

www.IntellectPublishing.com

www.LostTombofAlexander.com

Other books by the Award-Winning author:

Return to Treasure Island
www.R2TI.com

Jesse James' Secret
www.JesseJamesSecret.com

The Crusaders
www.TheCrusadersBook.com

Dedicated to those who still aspire to search for the truth...
wherever it may lead

10, 827 B.C.E.

Our ancestors made a startling and terrifying discovery. A huge, worldwide cataclysmic event would soon befall the Earth; one that could literally destroy all of humanity.

Racing against time, the world's civilizations came together and constructed monuments and repositories around the globe - high in the mountains, deep within the oceans, in the deserts and jungles… hoping against hope that somehow a few of them – us – would survive and use this knowledge to start civilization anew.

Repositories, which, to this day remain undiscovered.

They also foretold of a group in the future who would uncover and decipher the codes and clues left for us… and help rediscover our true past… a group they called

The Seekers

The libraries in Alexandria, Egypt, housed the largest repository of ancient knowledge and history ever assembled in the known world.

The destruction of this Serapeum and its contents in 1187 B.C.E. is considered one of the most significant losses in human history.

The collective libraries of Alexander, known as the Serapeum

The Lost Tomb of Alexander

Part One

All truths are easy to understand once they are discovered.
The point is to discover them.
Galileo

Chapter One

Present Day
Umbrian Region, Northern Italy

Vestiges of orange and red clung to the wooded mountains as the setting sun slowly cast its glow on the fall foliage. A chill breeze whispered through the valley while the river below gently snaked its way toward Lake Olgivere. Nestled up against the eastern walls of the remote valley were the faint outlines of an ancient monastery, its angles accentuated by deep shadows cast by the sun's final rays.

Constructed of local stone in the early thirteenth century, the entire structure appeared as one with the cliff. It was built by a group of what the church claimed were renegade monks. Brutally beaten and ostracized for their heretical beliefs, they were relegated to the annals of rumor and legend, and long since disregarded as ever having existed.

The original monks designed the monastery using a central courtyard, with labyrinthine halls and tunnels leading to various living, meeting and work areas deep underground. In the center loomed an enormous granite obelisk, its sides inscribed with Egyptian glyphs, standing as a lone sentinel guarding the seemingly deserted monastery.

A chapel bell rang out, shattering the silence and causing a flock of crows to clamor into the air and off toward the sunset.

Hooded men appeared, many carrying torches. They crossed the intricate mosaic of rose-colored marble that carpeted the courtyard, disappearing beneath a stone archway.

* * * * * * * *

"I've done nothing wrong, your Excellency," McIntyre pleaded, wringing his sweaty hands.

The cavernous chamber's shadows were abuzz in feverish whispering, finger pointing and disagreement by men whose faces were hidden beneath hooded robes. McIntyre, a tired, frail and balding man of fifty-seven, stood before three men who were seated high atop a towering court bench. Hopelessness surrounded him like static electricity.

His bewildered but gentle expression stood in stark contrast to the hard and compassionless stares of the men looking down upon him. Two elderly men, gowned in ornate, high-collared red robes flanked the tribunal judge in the center, who was clothed in royal purple. His pale unlined face belied an age which could be fifty, or then again, ninety. A large golden amulet hung from his neck, its ornate carved design repeated in gold leaf across the cedar bench before which McIntyre stood.

"Nothing wrong?" the central judge intoned. "You have broken our covenant of silence and divulged information that we, your brethren, hold sacred and most secret.

"It is because of you that people are now investigating the existence of our vast network of catacombs, seeking to learn about the knowledge they contain. Contents that *we* have sworn to protect from discovery with our very lives. What have you to say about this?"

Angry grumbling arose from the observing monks as more hooded faces emerged from the shadows. Torch lights reflected their features as the brethren nodded their agreement toward each other. McIntyre's deep-set gray eyes darted frantically from one to another, unable to make eye contact. Turning back, he straightened, took a deep breath and faced his accusers.

"I only question and search for truth." He licked the perspiration from his upper lip. "Are we so afraid of what we'll find that we stop looking for it?"

The tribunal judge leaned forward. "You have done more than question, Cardinal McIntyre. You have allowed these fanciful tales of yours to be written about as if they were authorized by the church."

"Our covenant has kept our existence secret from everyone within our order – *even his most Holy Father,"* McIntyre cried out in frustration. The monks quieted in response to the unexpected outburst.

"And while it is true we have sworn an oath to protect our flock from learning too much, too soon…" McIntyre took a deep breath, gathering strength before continuing. This was the moment he most feared, yet knew he had to face.

"Perhaps… just perhaps, they are ready to know," he challenged, wiping the perspiration from his forehead. "The knowledge we are sworn to protect may well help save humanity. We need not fear its discovery. It is inevitable that they will find out soon-"

"Enough!" roared the central figure sweeping his palm toward the audience, silencing their gasps. Turning back to McIntyre, his disdain and contempt for the monk's insolence was plain in his icy expression.

"We have heard enough. You will remain confined to your room until sentence is passed. Until then, I suggest you contemplate your egregious betrayal and pray for forgiveness. For you will surely need it."

Slamming down his gavel, he stared through McIntyre for a few moments, and then gestured to the guards.

"I will personally escort the prisoner to his quarters. You will accompany us," he said, standing.

* * * * * * * *

McIntyre stumbled as he and the judge followed two guards down a dank stone hallway. They stopped in front of a wooden door as one of the guards pushed it open.

"Why have you done this to me?" McIntyre asked in a trembling voice.

"You have done this to yourself," the judge said, throwing back his hood to reveal smooth but sharply cut features, the most pronounced being the enormity of his balding head.

"There is more to this than you are saying to the others!"

"It is of no importance now. You will remain here until the council determines the appropriate punishment." He motioned to the guards, who directed McIntyre into his room and started to close the door.

McIntyre grabbed the door's edge. "You know the time is now, your Excellency. We can wait no longer. The people must be warned. The church has a much greater role to play in this--"

Lilne turned back, pointing. "You have been warned."

"*They must* be warned!" McIntyre yelled in desperation.

A hollow ring echoed throughout the monastery's lower living quarters as the guards pushed McIntyre in and slammed the door. The grating of the turning key sealed his fate. He'd never been locked in before and knew he was trapped. His sparsely furnished ten by twelve foot room was carved from solid rock with no windows and only a metal ventilation screen atop the thick wooden door. Stumbling to his cot, he sat and slowly sank into it, lying curled on his side.

"This is it?" he whispered. "This is the result of the good works I have tried to accomplish all my life?" McIntyre knew Lilne would not tolerate his actions, and that he also controlled the tribunal. He had not planned on this happening. In fact, he had not planned on doing anything like this.

As a young boy, he had forsaken everything in his quest to learn about God, to find out the truth and source of His loving grace. He ran away from home when he was twelve and traveled for six years, learning everything from Sufism to Zoroastrianism before being led to one of the more visible orders of a certain brotherhood in Sicily. He was finally accepted into it and studied, worked and prayed diligently for over thirty years before he was sent to this secret location.

When first approached and told about the Guardians, he was unsure of what to do. He prayed about it and came to realize how important this appointment would be. Through loyalty and hard work he eventually worked his way up to the position of 'Keeper of the Knowledge'. This position allowed him unfettered access to the catacombs and indexes that listed all the treasures hidden beneath their monastery, as well as other secret locations worldwide, including the Vatican. Now, his whole life's work was thrown into doubt. What was the right way?

McIntyre rose from his cot and knelt before his primitive wooden praying pew, looking up at the statue of Jesus hanging on the cross. Reaching to light a match he flamed a red votive candle.

I must pray about this. All that is happening to me can be helped by my faith in God. No matter what may come of me, it will be my Lord's will.

Crossing himself, he placed his forehead onto his folded hands, and spoke aloud.

"My Lord, please grace me with your sacred help-"

"If you want to live to see another day you must leave, *now*!" interrupted a low voice.

Startled, McIntyre pushed away from the pew and turned toward the door. He cautiously crept toward the grated metal opening above it and peered up.

"Who is there?" he whispered, not recognizing the muffled voice.

He tiptoed to try and see through the grill. The silhouetted face of a hooded brother was barely visible in the flickering light of the torchlight.

"A friend. *Now go*."

A scraping noise caused McIntyre to look down and see a key slid under the door. Footsteps faded into the distance before McIntyre could thank him – whoever he was.

His heart pounded. *What should I do? Where would I go?* He looked over to the crucifix of Jesus who now seemed to be smiling. *Of course*, he thought, *of course*.

Calmness mixed with determination rose within him as he grabbed his backpack and began stuffing it with clothes and what little money he had. Reaching to the bookshelf for his Bible, he clumsily knocked the other books to the floor. He eyed one in particular and stooped to pick it up. The cover read 'Unexplained Archeology'. Opening it, he read the handwritten note on its inside cover:

Thank you, M. Without your help none of this would have been possible. Diandra

A small hope flickered inside him. *Maybe this will be worth it after all,* he mused, as an outrageous thought started to take hold. With reverence, he added the Bible and the book, zipping his backpack. That thought soon mushroomed into an idea; one so big, so outrageous, so unlike any idea he'd ever had before, that it both terrified and exalted him at the same time. A tingling, like an electrifying charge, erupted in his lower spine and slowly rose and shot up his back. It continued into his neck and through the crown of his head, causing him to shudder in almost painful ecstasy.

He smiled uncontrollably.

* * * * * * * *

McIntyre stealthily made his way down a dark passageway deep within the monastery, an oil lantern in hand. Crossing over to a stone alcove he gingerly moved aside the Holy Mary icon before making the sign of the cross. Nervously, he glanced around and then pushed on a particular stone that yielded easily to his touch.

The wall lazily opened to reveal a long dark stairway leading down into a haunting abyss. Once inside he pushed another stone and the door closed. One hand against the wall, McIntyre began his descent, the light from his lantern creating a golden glow as he stepped downward.

* * * * * * * * *

Above the door McIntyre had just passed through was a square recess carved deeply into the granite, which housed a camera. A red light began blinking as the lens moved slightly with a soft whirring sound.

* * * * * * * * *

McIntyre's lantern revealed the stairway's bottom step. He continued past the stone archway and entered the catacombs. Holding the light high, he surveyed the thousands of wooden crates and shelves of artifacts covered in dust and cobwebs as far as his light shone. He never failed to be awed by the immensity of these hallowed catacombs, and had never fully explored them, despite the many times he'd been down there. Oftentimes, when he thought he had found the end, he discovered another room just around the corner with more artifacts and tablets.

He set down the lantern and stretched his back, the tingling in his spine still reverberating from the experience in his room. What was it about this place that gave him such strange sensations?

Shaking it off, he pulled out a small paper tablet from his pocket and thumbed through it, stopping when he came to a particular page. Looking around he tried to get his bearings.

"I'm pretty sure it's over this way," he mumbled as he adjusted his backpack, picked up the lantern and headed in that direction.

* * * * * * * * *

A pounding on the door awoke Lilne from a fitful sleep. He fumbled for the lantern on his nightstand and turned the flame up, casting dancing shadows throughout his meticulously clean room.

"What?" he demanded irritably, rubbing his eyes.

"I am most sorry to disturb your sleep, your Excellence," a sheepish male voice echoed from behind the door.

Lilne sat up in his bed. "Get to the point."

"Cardinal McIntyre has escaped and breached the catacombs."

Lilne's eyes darted about as he digested the news.

"Terminate him," he said through clenched teeth.

* * * * * * * * *

Holding the pad with the roughly drawn map in his hands and counting his steps, McIntyre gradually made his way through the maze of boxes and crates, walking hundreds of yards by his estimate. He finally located a particular box that had Latin markings written on its side in a section of the catacombs he had never visited. Setting the lantern down, he lifted the box from its perch and placed it on the ground. Removing the lid, he began rummaging through the contents until his hand found a particular piece of a small stone tablet.

Taking off his backpack he took out the 'Unexplained Archaeology' book and turned to page 346, comparing the picture in the book to his fragment. They were the same. Smiling with relief, he replaced the book, along with the fragment into his backpack.

Exhausted, McIntyre stood up and stretched, shouldering his backpack. Picking up his lantern he noticed a metal lever protruding from the stone wall that had been hidden by the box he had just moved. Above the lever was carved a winged globe with a glyph of an enneagram beneath it. Looking around first, he gingerly placed his hand upon the lever and pushed it downward. It moved easily. Nothing happened, although he wasn't sure what he expected to occur.

Shrugging, he turned around to leave.

Then he heard a grinding noise and froze. It grew louder. He watched in disbelief as a solid wall of stone about two feet to his left started swirling on its surface. Resembling a small sandstorm, it was accompanied by a grating noise as if large boulders were rubbing against each other. As it grew louder in intensity he thought he could hear the faint sound of music.

"This cannot be!" he reasoned out loud to himself, as the sandy surface swirled faster and the grating noise grew louder. McIntyre covered his ears against the pain.

Suddenly, the noise stopped.

The sand dropped silently to the ground, revealing a doorway framed by two large slabs of stone.

Silence reigned again.

McIntyre raised his lantern, walked toward and then *through* the entrance and timidly held the lantern high.

"Oh my God."

* * * * * * * *

Far above, the stone wall within the catacomb's entryway began to open. Men in black military fatigues hurried through and down the stairs, their flashlights casting beams haphazardly against the walls. They were carrying HK-40 rifles with military night laser scopes and silencers.

* * * * * * * *

"My God," McIntyre repeated, aloud.

The room was full of artifacts; Egyptian, Sumerian, Mayan, and other civilizations that McIntyre couldn't identify. Huge statues of strange-featured deities wrought in marble, alabaster, and rare hardwoods. Gold gilded furniture lay scattered about – chairs, shelves and thrones. Golden chests inlaid with jewels sat atop low pedestals. In fact, everything looked golden. Something caught McIntyre's attention, and he slowly turned toward an even brighter golden glow.

He crept toward the light and, *Mother of God*, stopped in his tracks and just stared, gape-jawed. Before him stood a golden altar about four feet tall by six feet wide, spotlighted. He sought the light's source but could only detect a ray of light coming from somewhere high above. As his eyes adjusted he observed, in the center of the altar, a ten-inch by ten-inch book resting atop a small wooden lectern.

Stepping closer he noticed the thin wooden cover of the book was intricately carved with an enneagram similar to the one on the wall, and encrusted with precious metals and gemstones. The inside pages appeared to be made of parchment.

Staring at the book, questions raced through his mind, paralyzing him with fear. *Is it from the hand of God himself? Am I worthy to even be looking upon it? Is it a sign from my Lord that I am on the right path?*

Steeling himself, he raised his trembling hand, reached over and lifted the cover to find, written in Latin illuminated script:

'Chronicles of the Order of the Guardians'

McIntyre was slowly running his fingers over the words on the textured parchment when a noise startled him. Slamming the book closed, he spun around and crouched. Beams of lights shone through the stone doorway, arching across the ceiling and moving in his direction. He grabbed the book and leapt aside as muffled gunfire turned the wooden lectern into splinters.

Scooping up his lantern, McIntyre raced past the artifact shelves into the darkness toward the back of the catacomb. Bullets whizzed by his every move. Turning a corner he ran into a dead end. He spun around to track back and down another tunnel when he saw the flashlight beams gaining on him.

Tears welled in his eyes. "What do I do? Lord, help me, please help me!" he prayed aloud, stumbling along until he heard a clang under his feet. Beneath his feet lay a large metal grate. Lowering the lantern he gasped -- it revealed raging water surging a dozen feet below. He could hear the footsteps getting nearer, closing in. The muffled gunfire had quieted for the moment.

Setting the lantern down, he grasped the grate, heaving with all of his strength – and moved it slightly. He strained again and it budged out of its carved rock grooves. One final pull full of desperation mixed with a fifth of adrenaline moved it free. He shoved it aside using his legs for leverage, causing a loud clang to echo throughout the catacombs. The light beams crisscrossed just above his head. McIntyre picked up his backpack, tossed in the Guardian's book, made a sign of the cross with his left hand from head to chest and jumped.

A bullet tore into the fleshy part of his upper leg. Kindling erupted as bullets pinged off crates and shelves as he plunged down into the watery abyss, screaming in agony.

Hearing a shout from behind them, the armed men surrounding the grate opening turned to face Lilne as he rushed to the scene. They snapped to attention.

"Did you get him?" Lilne demanded.

"I think so, your Excellency," one of them replied.

"You *think* so?" he mockingly repeated. Lilne knelt and inspected the blood splattered around the opening before shining his flashlight on the rushing waters below. Standing again, he backhanded the armed man who had answered, flinging him against the wall. "That's not good enough."

Then, turning slowly, as if sensing something, he retraced his steps around the corner toward the golden light and approached the altar and what was left of the wooden lectern.

He froze, eyes raging.

* * * * * * * *

Amulet worn by Lilne

Chapter Two

Outside Ankara, Turkey

To say that Mali's Bar was in the wrong part of town would be like saying the ocean was wet: the entire city was the wrong part of town. Founded in 1235 during the Ottoman Empire and originally part of Constantinople, this part of Turkey had been home to the worst of the worst throughout the centuries -- smugglers, killers, and despots. And Mali's Bar was the embodiment of those present day characters.

Nestled in the middle of a crowded neighborhood that was dark even in daylight, it provided cover for clandestine meetings and deals twenty-four hours a day. Dozens of booths in a bazaar lined both sides of the dingy street, with vendors hawking their wares to everyone entering and leaving the bar. In the midst of this, three large middle-eastern looking Neanderthals with walrus mustaches pushed past the crowds as they shouldered their way into Mali's.

In a dimly lit corner at a small table sat an unshaven Pete 'Dutch' Vorhees, smoking one of his Don Quijote cigars. He glanced over his shoulder as the three men tried to enter unnoticed, then turned his gaze back at Navaro, a short, pudgy exaggerated caricature of Peter Lorre from Casablanca, who sat directly across from him.

Dutch threw a stack of digital photographs onto the table, leaned back and took a gulp of beer. Picking them up, Navaro cursorily examined the pictures of US soldiers behind barbed wire fences somewhere in a desert. One of them hung from a post, bruised and bloody. He viewed the images as if they were vacation pictures from a tropical island – completely dispassionately.

"They're all there," Dutch said.

Navaro wiped his sweaty forehead with an already damp handkerchief while continuing to look through the photos.

"Excellent, most excellent," Navaro finally said. "You took quite a risk photographing these men."

Dutch wiped his mouth with the back of his hand. "Not nearly the risk those guys took who are still alive and rotting in that POW camp in Iran."

"Do not worry, my friend. After your government sees these, they won't be there for long."

"I'm hoping not." Dutch leaned forward and jabbed his finger in Navaro's face. "You tell your *contacts* that if they wait too long, I'll be taking in my own team and getting them out. And it won't be the politically correct way, either."

Navaro eyed Dutch's Special Forces ring, acknowledging with a slight nod that if anyone could do it, Dutch would be the one. Scooping the pictures into his briefcase, he looked around as if ready to leave.

"Navaro, how long have we known each other?" Dutch asked as he put out his cigar in the ashtray by his glass.

"Almost twelve years, I think." Navarro wiped his forehead again and raised his eyebrows. "That seem right to you?"

Dutch ignored the question. "Aren't you forgetting something?"

Navaro gestured toward the three men who had walked in earlier and were now seated two tables away. They were focused on Dutch as they rose from the table.

"Now you're embarrassing me," Dutch quietly said to him, a slight grin gracing his unshaven face.

Navaro heard a gun hammer cock under the table and peered down to a see a red laser dot squarely in the middle of his crotch. He gestured frantically for his men to back off. He reached quickly into his briefcase and threw an envelope on the table. The red dot disappeared.

"Do I have to count it too?" Dutch asked.

"No need," Navaro replied, raising his shoulders. "Can't blame a man for trying, can you Dutch?"

Grabbing his hat, Navaro rose from the table, donned it, and tipped the brim, smiling.

"Always a pleasure."

Dutch raised his glass of beer. "Saluda," he toasted and took a swig. Navaro turned to leave as Dutch slammed the mug on the table.

"Make sure those pictures get to their destination, Navaro. I don't want to have to come looking for you."

"I will, my good friend, I will," he replied gesturing with his hand as he headed toward the door, the three men following in tow.

"I'm not your friend," Dutch muttered in a low voice as he drained the glass and pushed it aside.

He'd been up almost seventy-two hours and the fatigue was starting to weigh heavily. Getting those pictures had taken a lot of effort and planning; flying a motorized hang glider into Iran, taking the pictures and barely escaping with his life after it crashed and exploded in a ball of flames.

Leaving his fellow soldiers in that camp disturbed him greatly. His training in Special Forces hammered into him the motto 'no man left behind'. But that was better left now to the young Turks. He had been out of the Army for almost eight years, and who knew what would happen if he had to go in there as an independent operative?

At least with a government crew, they'd get full military support and satellite recon in real time. They have their proof – it is now up to them, not me, to deliver the goods.

Rubbing his aching eyes, he realized just how tired he was. "Man, I need some sleep," he mumbled to himself.

He grabbed the envelope and put it in his bomber jacket, got up and approached the bar. Mali waddled up and put another beer in front of him. Dutch smiled as he thought about how, after all the years he had known Mali, he still found it difficult to stifle a laugh at the seven hair comb-over attempt atop his seriously bald cranium. Mali held up a manila legal size envelope.

"Received another one this week from you know who in your New York," Mali said.

"No shit," Dutch said, taking a big gulp.

"You like I should file it with the others?"

"Might as well," Dutch replied, finishing his beer and sliding the empty mug back to Mali.

Mali unceremoniously tossed the envelope into a trashcan and refilled Dutch's glass. After chugging at it he looked around.

"That's it Mali, I'm through with this business. I've done my last freelance mission."

"Yes, yes," Mali replied as he cleaned a glass. "And I'm thinking of closing up my fine establishment here and joining the cast of your Baywatch."

Laughing to himself, he walked away and spoke in Turkish to a seedy group near the end of the bar while nodding toward Dutch. They broke out laughing.

"So they don't believe me this time either, huh?" Dutch mused to himself while lighting another one of his cigars. "Just wait."

Dutch turned around and surveyed the bar, just in case Navaro had a change of heart. No goons. *That's good*, he thought. But something did catch his eye, an obviously frightened fifty-something year old man sitting at a table nervously fingering the rim of his drink.

This guy really is in the wrong place, Dutch noted.

A young street urchin entered the bar with a load of grilled corncobs. He spoke in Turkish as he pulled on the shirts and jackets of various patrons trying to sell them his wares. Dutch eyed the young vendor as he walked over to the stranger's table and tried to strike a bargain. The man motioned that he didn't understand while trying to shoo the kid off. Dutch watched as this little Houdini expertly lifted a leather satchel from the man's knapsack and hurried out the front door.

Dutch shook his head ruefully. He exhaled a ring of cigar smoke as he put his drink down and headed out a back door.

* * * * * * * *

A black limousine crawled down Kanayra Street near Mali's Bar sporting dark tinted windows, a common way to travel in that dangerous area. Pulling up to a group of street vendors, it stopped as the front passenger window slowly disappeared, revealing a heavyset man with a large mustache and scar across his left eye. He leaned out the window and motioned for a group of peddlers to come closer while he spoke in Turkish.

"Have any of you seen this man?" he asked in Turkish, holding up a faxed copy of a photograph.

They spoke amongst themselves, and finally one of the men pointed up to the hotel directly above Mali's and motioned toward it.

Inside the limousine three other men smiled as they pulled out and cocked their silencer-equipped guns.

* * * * * * * *

The street urchin was proudly showing off the new leather satchel he had snagged to his street friends who were quite impressed. A coughing noise and bright red ember emanating from a darkened alleyway startled them, and the friends quickly ran off, leaving the little guy literally holding the bag.

An arm shot out of the shadows and pinched him by the nape of the neck. Dutch emerged, cigar in mouth, shaking his head. He pulled the little pickpocket closer, and in a surprised tone with just a hint of sarcasm asked,

"Hey kid, what've you got there?"

* * * * * * * *

Dutch re-entered Mali's with the satchel and looked around for its owner, who was nowhere to be found. He made his way to the bar and took one last hit of his stogie before stubbing it out.

"Hey, Mali, you see where that old gray haired guy over there went?" he asked, motioning with his head toward the man's former table.

Mali hooked a thumb upward.

"Room with number twenty-two."
"Got a name?"
"McIntyre, I am thinking."

* * * * * * * *

Dutch hated Mali's hotel. It was dark, dingy, and the smell almost made him throw up. "My god, how could anyone stay here?" he wondered aloud as he tried to breathe through his mouth. The noises emanating from the rooms ranged from moments of ecstasy to Saturday night wrestling matches. *This guy McIntyre sure has lowbrow taste in lodgings*, he mused.

Reaching room twenty-two he knocked on the door. No answer. He started to knock again when he heard the crashing of broken glass on the other side of the door. He stepped back instinctively and headed shoulder first into it, shattering the already flimsy lock and flinging it open.

Dutch quickly surveyed the situation. Two men were trying to kick in the bathroom door while two others were ripping into the furniture and toppling everything in search for something. *The four men from the limousine.*

Dutch held up the pouch, and with a slight smile laced with a dash of humor, asked,

"Hey, any of you guys lose a satchel?"

One of the men trashing the furniture turned toward Dutch and pulled out his gun. Dutch quickly caught his gun hand, twisted it downward and then spun his entire body around in one fluid motion, causing the man to twist upward and then smash down onto and through a wooden table, pieces of wood flying everywhere.

The other three sprang into action, charging Dutch. This was now his game. He knew he had to make a statement quickly to get them reacting, and his first stunt had worked. He waited until one of them got close enough and with a violently swift side kick pushed him through the window, splintering the wooden louvers as he plunged to the street below.

Another one jumped on Dutch's back. Charging backwards, Dutch smashed him squarely into the wall, where he slithered to the floor just as the first man was crawling from under the wreckage of the table and stood up.

Man that is one tough dude, Dutch noted to himself, narrowing his brow.

For a moment everything stopped as the two remaining goons eyed Dutch's gun, which had fallen from his holster to the floor. One of them went for it. Dutch reverse spun, whipping his leg around and connecting with the guy's forehead with a sickening thud. "I don't think so, buddy," Dutch said as he watched the man's eyes roll back as he flopped to the floor. Dutch reached down and reclaimed his .45 silver-plated Smith and Wesson.

The last man pulled out an automatic twenty-shot Glock with a silencer. He got a bead on Dutch just as Dutch pushed his laser sight and centered it on the guy's scarred left eye. A moment passed as they locked stares, each knowing that this could be the moment of their own last breath. Through his peripheral vision Dutch noticed the man's hand start to tremble -- ever so slightly. *He's blinked.*

"Whatever it is you're after," Dutch said, "it's not worth dying for."

The man looked quizzically at him. Dutch calmly repeated his message in Arabic and watched as large drops of sweat dripped across what Dutch estimated to be a five or six inch scar stretching from the top of his left eye down to the bottom of his chin.

Dutch took a breath, nodded his head toward the door and then stated in Turkish, "Walk away."

While the scarred-face man started backing up toward the door, Dutch noticed he had a small digital camera hanging around his neck. *Pretty strange for a robber*, he thought. Scarred-face craned his neck to see if he was heading in the right direction, carefully stepping over the unconscious body of one of his buddies, then turned and bolted through the door and down the hall.

Dutch breathed a huge sigh of relief. *What the heck was that all about?* He flexed his hands a couple of times to check for full movement. Nothing but a couple of scrapes. His shoulder throbbed from his heroic door smashing, while he shook off the other minor punches he had taken. *I sure hope this guy really needs whatever's in this bag,* he thought to himself while rubbing his shoulder gingerly. Walking to the bathroom door he knocked.

"You can come out now, old man, those goons are gone."

Silence.

Well, one more door won't matter, he reasoned. Backing up, he rushed forward while jumping and kicked in the door, revealing an empty bathroom, curtains blowing in the breeze. "Son of a bitch, the dude got away," Dutch lamented out loud. "Now what?" He was hoping for maybe a little reward for returning the guy's leather pouch, especially in light of his having probably just saved his life. All he was left with was the satchel.

Shrugging, he sat down on the commode and opened it. *Interesting*, he thought, a Vatican City passport. Thumbing it open he found it belonged to a Cardinal Harold McIntyre. *Hmmm. A bigwig in the church.*

Next he found some letters and papers, and a holy cross money clip with twenty Euros. Reaching in again, he felt something and lifted it out - a flat rock of some sort. It was a small right-angled piece of a stone tablet with strange glyph-like writing carved into it, maybe three by five inches. "No reward here," he mumbled to himself.

At the bottom of the leather bag was a book titled 'Unexplained Archeology'. Sticking out of the book was a folded piece of paper. He shook his head as he opened the paper and found it was written in Latin with symbols drawn across its bottom. The heading of the letter had a name and address in English:

To: Diandra Weiss - New York Museum of Natural History.

"No frigging way," Dutch said, leaning his head back against the wall and banging it a couple of times. "I can't be that unlucky."

Chapter Three

Lower Honduras, Central America

No matter what the national weather service predicted for that region, it seemed to always end up the same – oppressively hot, one hundred percent humidity and no trade winds to offset the brutal heat. Situated about eighty miles southeast of the Nicaraguan border, the archeological site was almost fifty feet below sea level. Densely covered rain forest and jungle stretched for dozens of miles in every direction. The forest canopy, which rose in some places to over two hundred feet, was like a Crockpot lid, running interference with the rising heat and refusing to offer any relief to the sweltering floor below.

And the rain. It had been pouring down relentlessly for the past four days.

Diandra Weiss had never fully adjusted to these conditions. Cold, she could handle, but her Midwest roots hadn't prepared her for the hardships that presented themselves at the various tropical digs she had been involved with during the past fifteen years. And this day was particularly difficult.

Sitting in her tent, she thought back to earlier that morning when two workmen were seriously injured. A rain-saturated wall had inexplicably collapsed within the excavation. It was only sheer luck that a large urn they had found a few moments earlier shielded them from being completely buried. It had taken almost two hours to dig them out and get them gurneyed off for the four-hour 'Mad Hatter' ride to the nearest hospital in San Paolo.

Because of the dense jungle and rain they weren't able to bring in a helicopter to ferry the men out. And all this was *before* she received a call informing her that the museum had set up an interview with Archeological Expedition magazine, with the subsequent news that the reporter would be there at any moment.

"Oh well," she mumbled. "Things could be worse." Of course she was kidding herself. With the injuries and setbacks this dig had encountered, she was easily a week behind schedule, and quickly going over budget. The museum had reluctantly agreed to fund this expedition only after an anonymous benefactor had put up the majority of the dig's budget. But her estimates had been slim right from the start, knowing what the museum could afford and what results they needed to see in order to approve it. There was no room for error.

Once the benefactor's monies had come in, it was too late to increase the budget. She was stuck and she knew it. The only thing that could top this day would be to get another call from the museum. Highly unlikely, she remembered as she smiled to herself, since her assistant, Jack Woods, had volunteered to run interference between her and the field phone that was the outside world's only communication into the site. A much needed respite from all she was going through.

As she wiped the sweat that dripped down her forehead, she tried to focus in on why she was even there in the first place. She remembered the excitement she always felt whenever something new was uncovered. Like a few days earlier when Ramos found some pottery with strange 'Grecian' style markings on them. The strata line indicated that it *could* be over nine thousand years old. She'd have to wait for the radiocarbon dating to be sure, but if it was that old, well, more fodder for her theories. But at that moment, she was hard pressed to find much more of a silver lining in the cloud of problems that seemed to be almost bursting at the seams.

Jack, a tall, handsome, mid-fifties professorial type with gold-rimmed glasses and a goatee, entered the tent, interrupting her train of thought.

"That reporter is here, Diandra," he informed her.

"Any other calls?" she asked, half expecting some additional source of bad news. He gave her a devilish smile back.

"I don't understand it," he earnestly stated. "There seems to be a lot of *static* over the phone line today. I think I received a couple of urgent calls from New York." He gestured with his shoulders and winked at her. "But who knows? I'm pretty sure the problem will clear up later today."

'Good. Hopefully by then I'll be in a better mood." She started to leave and turned back.

"Thanks for that 'static,' Jack. It's been one of those days."

"And it's only noon," he laughed. "Glad to help. Now go on out there and give that reporter heck."

Give her heck? Diandra laughed to herself.

Jack had assisted Diandra on her last four digs, including the hellish month last year in Tunisia when she was going through her marriage breakup and needed a strong shoulder to lean on. A handyman extraordinaire, he was also an accomplished paleontologist with a degree from the University of Pennsylvania. On loan from the University for this dig, Diandra inwardly credited him with saving her sanity on more than one occasion.

As she trudged through the muddy slosh toward the main tent, she started to feel tension in her belly. Stage fright. She didn't like being in the spotlight. Never had. She'd told the museum over and over she hated these types of interviews. But they insisted that donations rose whenever news stories broke about digs they had financed, and she couldn't argue with that. Still, she hated those pre-interview jitters.

She remembered feeling the same way when she gave piano recitals as a little girl in front of parents and students in the school auditorium. It always turned out the same. After playing the first note, she would do fine. It was true of these types of interviews too. After the first question she calmed herself and got down to business. She straightened her shoulders, refreshed her auburn ponytail, and tried to pull her shirt away from where it clung to her sweaty body. *Just shake it off and get in there, girl!*

Meals were cooked and meetings held in the main tent. It was really just a tarp canopy draped over a group of poles, with netting around it that afforded incomplete relief from the mosquitoes that plagued them twenty-four seven. Once inside she watched two men setting up lights and a camera. A female reporter was blotting on makeup and seemed frustrated about it. Diandra walked over to her.

"It's amazing how in the rain you can still sweat. I've never gotten used to it," she offered in support.

The reporter looked over at Diandra and smiled, dropping her makeup brush to the table and extending her hand.

"I'm Sarah Mills, from Archeological Expeditions. It's a pleasure to meet you, Doctor Weiss." Diandra grasped her hand firmly and returned the shake.

"Diandra please, Sarah. Nice of you to make the trek out here, although I'm a little surprised. We haven't made any announcements about anything of particular interest regarding this site--"

"My editor is looking for a piece about the history of this area. You know, background filler stuff about the site and all. So we… wanted to get the interview here."

"Whatever floats your boat. Give me a minute to change out of this dirty wet shirt into another clean wet shirt, will you?" She winked at Sarah and disappeared behind a partition, quickly changing her top and applying as much makeup as she dared without ending up looking like Tammy Faye Bakker after two minutes in that humidor of a jungle. She put her auburn shoulder length hair into a ponytail. At five feet eight inches she figured she was about six inches taller than the reporter, although she was unsure why that mattered. She dabbed at the smeary liner surrounding her green eyes, noticing crows' feet. Ugh. A little lipstick. She slapped the tube closed. Done.

The camera was positioned so that Diandra could stand behind a table full of shards and pottery already culled from the site. When she reappeared from behind the screen the cameraman motioned for Diandra to take her position and held up a light meter. The other man looked through and adjusted the camera. He finished with a sound check and they were ready to begin.

Diandra noticed Sarah was studiously looking over her notes and sensed that she was a little nervous too. *Good,* she thought. *We'll be on even ground.*

"Is this where you want me to stand?" Diandra motioned with her hand.

"That's fine." Sarah replied. She looked to the cameraman who adjusted the focus and gave her a thumbs-up. The soundman holding the boom also nodded in the affirmative.

"Do you think this rain will affect the sound?"' Diandra asked, wanting to make small talk and relax before the first question.

"We're fine, really," Sarah stated. "Now, I want to first go over why you're down here and then let it flow from there. Is that alright with you?"

"Sure."

"Okay then." She turned toward the cameraman, who motioned with his hand and mouthed 'rolling tape.'

"Hello, I'm Sarah Mills here in Honduras, Central America, with Doctor Diandra Weiss. We're here to… interview Doctor Weiss about her present project at the so-called Rejaunto Phantasma site, which loosely translated means the ghostly resting place or tomb.

She turned toward Diandra.

"Doctor Weiss, perhaps you could start by telling us why the New York Museum of Natural History would be interested in this Central America site in the first place?"

"Of course. But please, call me Diandra." Facing the camera, Diandra felt the tension in her stomach release. She knew her stuff and was ready to tell it.

"Well, we're actually here for two reasons. First, we are near the site of an impact crater created by a huge meteor millions of years ago in the gulf of Mexico near the Caribbean ocean; an impact that may be at least partially responsible for the extinction of the dinosaurs. It is possible that where we are digging was the site of a much smaller impact, perhaps a piece of the larger meteor. We are taking soil samples and radioactive volcanic ash readings to send to

Penn University to check it against other findings throughout the world.

"Here," she said, picking up a carved stone head, "is something believed to be sculpted from a fragment of the meteor itself…"

Suddenly, Diana's vision blurred, and she caught herself against the edge of the table, overcome with dizziness. Images flashed through her mind, people screaming, running, terrified. She gasped, dropping the stone head and staring at her trembling empty hand. *What the frig was that?*

Taking a deep breath, she looked into the faces surrounding her and recovered her composure. "Sorry, butterfingers! Only worth a couple of million!"

The group laughed with her as she stooped to place the head back on the table, quickly withdrawing her hand.

"Can we start over?" she asked in what she hoped was a professionally calm voice.

"You okay?" Sarah asked, head tilted to one side.

"Yes," Diandra replied, rubbing her hands together. "Just recovering from a bit of Dengue last week."

"Just continue where you left off."

"Okay then. Secondly," Diandra resumed, getting back in her groove, "many indigenous Indian tribes consider this one of the holiest of holy sites; a spiritual place where their gods departed this earth and ascended to the heavenly holy land to live for eternity. Their shamans have come here for thousands of years to meditate and receive visions to rejuvenate themselves and foretell the future. We are exploring what the ruins here may mean in the contextual history of the region, especially regarding ancient civilizations including the mysterious Olmecs."

"Isn't it true, Doctor Weiss," Sarah interrupted, "that your museum funded a previous expedition in 1947, headed by another archeologist named Doctor Everett Werner?"

Sarah's tone was a little more authoritative, and for a moment Diandra thought she almost detected a bit of attack mode in her mannerisms. Brushing it off as part of her earlier jitters, she cleared her throat.

"Yes, that is true," she answered, hoping the trickle of sweat running down her chest wasn't obvious. "He was excavating a tomb that, coincidently, lies almost directly below this tent. But he was unable to finish the dig due to-"

"Did he not dynamite the site after experiencing some sort of visions here himself?' Sarah interrupted again, stepping closer.

Diandra leaned back in surprised response to Sarah's aggressive tone. *Accusatory? Maybe.* Definitely more forceful than was necessary. This struck her as odd for an archeological reporter.

"You have done your homework, Sarah." She slowed her response to get some breathing room to think before responding. The museum did send this reporter, she reasoned, so she guessed they also approved her questions and assumed they wanted her to tell the truth. After all, it was reported in the newspapers back then. But a lot of the details weren't. Especially regarding the rumors of his permanent commitment to a mental hospital under a pseudonym. She decided it was better to play it close to her chest until-

"Dr. Weiss?"

"Yes?"

Diandra was jolted back to the moment and saw Sarah was looking quizzically at her, nodding for her to continue. "Yes... well, it was reported, *Sarah*, that Doctor Werner experienced some visions that told him this site should not be disturbed. He interpreted it, in our opinion, incorrectly, and took matters into his own hands. Consequently, because of the severe nature of his misguided actions we are now unable to dig for or explore this tomb below us, as part of our agreement with the government and local Indians. Our present work here is only to find out about any structures that still remain in the immediate area."

"How, then, Doctor Weiss, do you respond to the reports of supposed curses surrounding this site?"

Diandra frowned, noting the self-satisfied smile on the reporter's face, and the slight nod to the cameraman. What was going on here? This was the kind of question she would have expected to see gracing the cover of one of those so-called 'news' magazines populating the racks at supermarket checkout counters. She stiffened her spine and used what her hopefully-soon-to-be-ex used to call her 'professor voice'.

"I believe the science of archaeology has no place for entertaining religious or superstitious beliefs. We can certainly use them for guidance, but at the end of the day, we are trying to find out the truth. And as to those supposed curses? Well, let's just say I'd relegate those to the realms of talismans and magic stones. There's no basis at all-"

"This morning, Doctor Weiss," Sarah spoke over Diandra, raising her voice, "we ran into a van with two of your injured workmen going to a hospital in San Paolo. They told us they believed this site was haunted and that's why they were hurt. They also told us they weren't coming back."

"Superstitious natives and coincidence. I wouldn't give much credence to that." Diandra picked up a glass of water. "Isn't this a little off subject for this interview, Sarah?"

Sarah bit her bottom lip and ignored Diandra's question while she shuffled through her notes, focused.

Diandra caught the soundman motioning to the cameraman with his hands – flattening them to just above his head and across his neck. The cameraman turned the focus knob of the digital Beta-cam as he zoomed in to get a close up of Diandra.

The reporter reached into her briefcase and pulled out a book. The camera lighting hit Diandra's eyes and she squinted as Sarah tossed it on the table, where she could read the title: 'Unexplained Archaeology' by Dr. Karen Sue Lanier.

"Do you know anything about this book, Doctor Weiss?"

The loud drip, drip of water from a particular branch over the tarpaulin tent cover was the only sound that could be heard as they all waited for a response.

Diandra's felt herself flush from her chest to the roots of her hair. A piercing high pitch noise began ringing in her ears – echoing to the back of her head, while her heart pounded louder and more pronounced throughout her body. *Holy crap, how could they know?* she asked herself. *What am I going to do now?*

She willed herself to stand her ground, rather than running at full speed from the tent, which is what she wanted to do. Run like she'd never run before. Grabbing the table for support, she pleaded to herself. *Please god, don't let me fall!* She was as weak kneed and scared as she'd ever been in her life.

Of course she knew someone, someday, would find out. That was inevitable. But not here. Not now. Not like this. *Crap. Crap. Crap!*

"Dr. Weiss. Do you want me to repeat the question?" Sarah pressed boldly while motioning to the cameraman to get even closer.

Diandra could see that Sarah was centered, in her game. The nervousness had been a ruse, the bitch. And it had worked.

Had Sarah really contacted the museum? Was this whole interview a scam? Did the museum know about her book? If so, her career could be over, dead in the realm of conservative academia. Shit.

Sarah had stumbled on the revelation by accident while researching ancient archeology, and, sensing a big story, had contacted a major television network news outlet and worked out a deal that if she could get the story, she would get a chance to present it 'live' on one of their national television shows. Her big chance.

"I love my job," Sarah said to the cameraman, who nodded a "good job" toward her, eyebrows wiggling.

* * * * * * * *

The office suite was dark except for the light of the huge seventy-inch flat panel plasma screen, which framed the center end of the room. From the reflection of the screen's light, ancient and priceless statues, artifacts and artwork could be seen scattered throughout the office.

A man leaned back into his leather-padded wheelchair, watching the scene unfold on the TV screen – an interview on the Late Line television show featuring Dr. Diandra Weiss. They were showing the edited footage from Diandra's interview in the jungle.

"We obtained confidential documents from the publisher that shows you are the real author of this book," Sarah continued on the television screen. "A book that challenges the very foundation of archaeology as we know it today, and embraces religious myth as a legitimate tool of investigation. In light of your recent statement, would you care to comment on these revelations, Doctor Weiss?" Sarah drew out Diandra's last name for emphasis.

Using the remote control, he turned up the volume and observed Diandra's impressive poker face. She had obviously mustered every bit of her strength to reply, calmly and coolly.

"This interview is over."

She quickly walked out of the television frame while the camera jerked around and followed her dash out of the tent and into the misting rain. The camera panned back to Sarah who was smiling like a Cheshire cat. She signaled to the cameraman to cut.

The screen changed to the studio set of Late Line where Sarah sat behind the desk with the Ken-doll host.

"Were you able to get any follow up questions?" Ken-doll asked.

"No, I never spoke with her again. When I contacted the museum for any comment, my calls were never returned."

"Great job, Sarah, and welcome to our team. That was an excellent 'expose' story. We look forward to any follow up reports you have in the future. Next, we take a look at-"

The screen went static as the man in the dark room clicked the remote, rolled his wheelchair over and set it down on the highly polished mahogany desk.

* * * * * * * *

Chapter Four

Umbrian Region, Italy

Upwardly curving stone arches supporting the block ceiling were bathed in a rainbow of reflective light from the stained glass windows set within the chamber's walls. Elaborate pedestals with statues of Sumerian gods flanked along both sides of the pillars that led into the entryway.

Ten members of the Guardians were seated around a large oval table in the center of the room, the hoods from their robes partially covering their heads. The only features clearly visible were the silhouettes of their noses and chins. Two empty chairs remained, one at each end of the table. A somber mood pervaded the incense-scented chamber.

The men stood as Lilne entered the room and bowed their heads, reverently. Once he was seated at the head of the table, the group took their seats. No one spoke as Lilne slowly moved his eyes from member to member, as if assessing some internal dossier in his mind as he held his gaze momentarily upon each one. His eyes fixed and rested on the empty chair opposite of his – McIntyre's former place at the table.

Finally one of the members cleared his throat.

"Yes?" Lilne responded.

"McIntyre was spotted in Turkey by one of our operatives and nearly apprehended."

"Nearly?" he replied, tapping his fingers together.

"It seems he was helped by someone. We don't know who or how," the member added.

"We've always known this could happen," Lilne frowned, "in spite of the precautions we have taken. However, I am supremely disappointed that it was one of us that breached the sacred trust we have been given. McIntyre *must* be found. And silenced."

Brother Buscemi leaned into the light.

"Respectfully, your Eminence, McIntyre is but one man. I think you overestimate the damage he can cause us and our mission."

"If, as you say, he is but one man… then who was it that *helped him escape?"* Lilne snarled.

The group broke into a river of murmured discussion. Lilne stared at Buscemi for a moment, making a mental note to keep an eye on him. Finally, Lilne silenced them with a raised hand.

"Do we know yet what he took from the catacombs, besides the sacred book?"

Another council member opened a folder and paged nervously through a group of papers.

"One of the items we're sure about is artifact number PFC 3416. It was the key fragment to the Macedonian tablet," he informed them.

"Is this a problem?" Lilne inquired.

"I don't believe so," the member continued. "There are no known photographs that include the other half, and that part of the tablet was destroyed over sixty years ago. Without it, the fragment is virtually useless."

Clearing his throat, another man raised his hand sheepishly.

"Yes? You have something to add?" Lilne demanded.

"Your Eminence… that's not actually, completely true," the member cautiously offered.

Lilne's pale face flushed with anger and impatience.

"Tell me what *is* true - now!"

* * * * * * *

Chapter Five

Lower East Side, New York

The New York Museum of Natural History was itself an antique – founded almost two hundred years ago and relegated to remain in the shadows of its more famous cousins within the city. Located on the lower East Side, it was a great location in its heyday but an out of the way destination for present day tourists and New Yorkers alike. Pretty much the only visitors the museum currently entertained were school children on field trips a few times a year.

Heavily endowed by industrialists including Carnegie and Flagler in the late nineteenth century, the museum's basic financial needs were well taken care of. The stone façade bespoke this by the constant attention to detail and impeccable upkeep. It was a respected and revered educational institution, on a par with Chicago's Ford Museum and the Los Angeles Museum of Natural History. Its president, Mathew Chang, a former professor of archeology from Harvard, had been head of the museum for the past ten years.

Inside the top floor boardroom the tension was rapidly escalating. Diandra sat at the side of a large table before the six members of the museum's board of directors. At the head of the table sat Dr. Chang. Margaret Bishop, Diandra's immediate supervisor, sat against the back wall near the doorway.

One of the board members, Duke Overstone, threw down a supermarket tabloid on the table to make his point, his bushy gray eyebrows moving up and down emphatically.

"Have you seen the story this tabloid *rag* has written about you, *and us*, Ms. Weiss?"

"That's Doctor Weiss, and no, I haven't, but I-"

"Well we have, *Doctor* Weiss," he said, leaning toward her, elbows on the table. "They've kindly sent us an advance copy. And now it's been picked up by the national news organizations. And just this morning, we received a call from the Archeological Society licensing committee, threatening our accreditation and credentials for next summer's college excavation programs. This museum is rapidly becoming the laughing stock of the archeological community."

"It was certainly not my intention in *any* way to make this museum the laughing stock of anything. I take my work here very seriously. I only wanted to-"

"Wanted to what?" an impeccably dressed female member of the Board chimed in, abruptly interrupting her train of thought. "Your actions are now being viewed as representing some 'secret agenda' of this institution. Did you think about us for one moment when you wrote this, this dribble you call a book? Did you think of the consequences it would create, or how it will affect your entire field of study?"

"Yes, as a matter of fact, I did," Diandra replied. "As you know, I have worked long and hard for this museum, and my past research has only been to the credit of its reputation. It was to avoid any public controversy that I published this latest book under a pseudonym." She knew the Board was stacked against her, but she would get her side on record before they took any action. She paused to marshal her thoughts, then stood and began walking back and forth before turning to face them again.

"My god, I love archeology," she continued, making eye contact with each member around the table as she spoke. "It's what I've wanted to do all of my life. But after years in the field and traveling all over the world, I finally could not reconcile what I now know to be true regarding what was, and still is, going on within our field. We archeologists have been going around discovering ancient cities and unearthing incredible artifacts. And then, with almost no basis in fact other than our 'esteemed opinions', we declare them to be this, that or the other. Every one of us, like trained parrots or automatons, goes right along with this charade. And when something is discovered that contradicts these 'opinions', well, look out. You're in big trouble then."

She ignored the grumbling rising from her audience, walked back to her chair and grasped its back.

"Don't you see?" Her voice rose in volume, regaining their attention. "I wrote this book not to hurt our profession, but to wake it up! To get us out of this catatonic state and stop defending positions that we absolutely know are not true."

"The proper way to 'wake up' the profession, as you so aptly put it, is to submit for publication what you believe," an elderly male board member interjected, raising one finger in the air, "and then have it peer reviewed and submitted to the scrutiny of experts using objective science."

Diandra groaned in frustration, mystified at the others' inability to see the crux of her passion.

"Aren't you listening?" She shouted, slapping her hand down on table. "I'm talking about artifacts and monuments that are totally unexplainable within the context of what we currently accept to be historical fact! Who is there to objectively pass judgment on the validity of these anomalies? Are you suggesting that the people who put forth these dubious theories in the first place, and then based their life's work on them, are the same ones to openly embrace evidence that completely negates all that they have strived to achieve? Don't you get it?

"That's why I wrote the book using a pseudonym – if you don't toe the line and parrot back the accepted theories by our so called experts, you're ostracized; relegated to that fringe group all the major archeological societies call 'quacks', or worse. Look what happened to Velikovsky and his theories. They crucified him."

Diandra shook her head. "I only wanted to make people aware that there are things we can't explain as archeologists… mysteries that still create wonder, and to… to try and start a dialogue within the archeological community to address these issues and together find the answers. I see *that* as the true quest of the scientific community; to embrace and strive to understand the as yet unexplained. This is *your* chance! With my book and its controversy, I have given the New York Museum of Natural History an opportunity to support a new line of inquiry, a…."

Taking in the skeptical looks surrounding the table, she ground to a halt.

The board members eyed each other, while looking to Dr. Chang for direction. He picked up a folder, pulled out a paper, and reached for a silver Montblanc pen in his shirt pocket.

"You should have used the proper channels," said Dr. Chang, uncapping the pen and signing the paper with a flourish. He looked up at her. "You have put the very reputation of this institution at risk *Doctor* Weiss, and that is inexcusable. We have no choice but to put you on temporary suspension. We'll meet again later this week to decide what further actions must be taken. This meeting is adjourned." Abruptly, he stood and exited through the rear door of the boardroom.

Diandra looked over to Margaret and read support in her expression of commiseration with a subtle shake of her head. She was a beautiful African American woman in her late forties; her soft ebony features and almond shaped eyes framed by short-cropped hair.

Diandra quickly gathered her paperwork and stuffed it into her briefcase. Without another word to the rest of the board members still seated at the table, she defiantly slammed the door to the boardroom so hard the glass windows rattled in their frames.

That was childish, Diandra admonished herself, at the same time acknowledging that slamming it had felt good. *But, they're wrong, dammit. And I'll prove it to them.*

She'd hardly had a moment to think since arriving home. The day after the Honduras interview an urgent request had come from the museum to return to New York immediately. She had found out about the reporter's ruse when she called Margaret to inquire about the rush to get back. Turned out it was Margaret who was trying to call her that morning and warn her about the ambush. *Hell of a day to have Jack run interference for me*, Diandra thought ruefully. It was just Diandra's bad luck that Sarah had taped the interview with her in order to parlay it into getting a network job. Another success story for unbridled ambition.

"Diandra, wait!" Margaret ran down the hall and caught up with her. They walked together without speaking for a few steps.

"They just don't get it." Diandra finally blurted to Margaret.

"No, *you* don't get it." Margaret's voice was firm.

Diandra stopped her in her tracks and stared at Margaret. "What?"

"They consider what you did akin to being a traitor." Margaret shrugged her shoulders. and let that sink in before continuing.

"The truth is, I think they're more embarrassed than anything else. Here you are, a bestselling author, and the book is based on telling the world that most of what *they* believe may be wrong."

Margaret started to laugh. "That's pretty funny when you think about it."

Diandra tried not to give into this moment of mirth, but Margaret's laugh was infectious. She shook her head as they continued to walk toward her office.

"Look," Margaret continued. "You're a talented and devoted scientist. And, believe it or not, you do have a couple of admiring friends on the board. I'm sure, given time, this will all blow over."

Reaching her office, Diandra touched the sign that read Diandra Weiss, Ph.D., then turned and faced Margaret.

"I'm not so sure I want it to blow over at this point, Maggie. Maybe this is the right time for me to move on."

"Listen, girl, that's just you being tired that's talking. Get some rest over the weekend and I'll put in a good word for you on Monday. " She caught her eye and smiled. "And Diandra, I'm sorry this had to happen to you on your birthday. I'm sure it wasn't planned that way."

She pulled a card out from her purse and gave it to Diandra, who realized that she had completely forgotten about her own birthday. "Thanks, Maggie. This was one helluva birthday gift from the museum. You truly are a wonderful friend."

Diandra gave her a big hug. Margaret smiled and continued down the hall toward her office as Diandra entered hers.

Ebrahim 'Sam' Zahed, her twenty-something and beyond brilliant Persian assistant, wearing a Philadelphia Phillies t-shirt and baseball cap, careened around the office in her executive roller chair while bouncing a miniature rubber basketball and calling plays in his best Dick Enberg announcer voice.

"He goes left, no shot! He makes a quick right and sneaks past the guard. He spins around to take a shot for the winning game point and-"

Sam twirled around and threw the ball at the trashcan as Diandra reached over and caught it, dropping the card Margaret had given her on the floor. He blushed, then grinned at her.

"Great catch. You wanna play? We can shoot for shots down at Harry's later. Celebrate your birthday?"

She tossed the ball back to him.

"Really not in the mood, Sam. Another time."

"Figured out something new today," he said, his brain always at full bore as he picked up his smart phone with his other hand and hit a button.

"What's that?"

"All the continents on Earth start and end with the same letter."

"Fascinating."

She walked over to her cabinets and started extracting files. Thinking about it, she smiled. "That is, if you leave the North and South off of the Americas."

"But of course," he replied, setting the ball on the desk. "How'd it go up there?"

As if he needed to ask, Diandra thought to herself. She was probably the last to know the museum scuttlebutt.

"Not too bad, really," she said in a calm but ironic tone. "They're allowing me the opportunity to find my full potential elsewhere."

Sam frowned, confused.

"I think they're going to fire me," she explained.

His jaw gaped open. "You've got to be kidding."

"Nope. I'm not. I'm on temporary suspension until they make their final decision. But I think it's a *fait accompli,* as they say."

"Man, talk about simple minds at work. I can't believe their cumulative IQ even breaks three digits."

Diandra was tired and just wanted to be alone for a while. She knew when she felt like this she sometimes took it out on other people, and it wasn't very nice. *Not this time.* She sighed and reminded herself that Sam, especially, deserved some extra leeway in the patience arena.

His father had arranged for him to escape from Iran as a child after Khomeini took power, persecuting anyone intellectual or with liberal leanings. He was sent to live with an uncle in New York, and suffered in school due to his brilliance, which set him ahead academically but ostracized him from his fellow classmates. After being placed in a special program at MIT, he excelled and learned over a dozen languages, and fell in love with archeology.

"Listen, Sam. Can we talk about this later? Why don't you swing by my house and we'll have that drink."

"It's a date!" he beamed, ever hopeful in his crush on Diandra.

"No, it's a drink."

"Whatever," he responded, failing to suppress a grin. "I'll see you then. Sam almost skipped out of the office as he left, entering some keystrokes on his smart phone.

Young men, she thought. *When will his testosterone levels get back into this stratosphere again?*

Sam had spent the past couple of summers working with Diandra on various digs and as a historian of ancient languages. She was aware that his guarded feelings of loss for his own family in Iran and difficulty fitting in with his peers made his obvious crush on her, the older woman, a vulnerable and highly sensitive issue.

She sank down in the office chair Sam had just vacated and closed her eyes, resolved to have a drink with him, keep it light, and do something about this lousy mood she was in.

Maybe a couple of glasses of wine wouldn't hurt?

* * * * * * * *

Chapter Six

Location Unknown

Within the pitch black confessional, the voices of a distant choir floated gently upon the incense-laden air flowing into the small confined area. The confessional window abruptly slid open to reveal Lilne, the speckled light from the tight-woven screen creating a mosaic on his chiseled features.

"Bless you my child," he intoned as he motioned his hand in front of his face.

"It's been a long time, your Excellency," a chillingly deep raspy voice answered from the supplicant's side.

"Indeed it has. Thank you for coming on such short notice."

"Did I have a choice?"

"A serious situation has come up," Lilne said, ignoring the question. "A certain cardinal within our order, McIntyre, has vanished along with one of our more precious possessions. We had a lead on him, but it seems our operatives in Ankara failed to retrieve him or our merchandise, although the trail is not completely cold. I need you to finish the job discreetly… and correctly."

"'And when I find this McIntyre?" his voice strained to ask.

"I have no further need of him. I am only interested in getting back what he took."

The stranger's labored breathing was audible as he dispassionately contemplated what was just said.

"You say the trail is not cold?"

Another small door wide enough for Lilne's hand slid open. He passed through an envelope. Clipped on top was a security camera picture of McIntyre standing in line at an airport ticket counter. The man opened the envelope to inspect the Zurich bank passbook that showed a balance of five hundred thousand dollars. Pushing it back in the envelope he studied the photograph.

“That is McIntyre,” Lilne whispered. “He was last seen at the Istanbul Airport two days ago. We believe he might be heading for Africa, although we are not sure where.”

“Anything *else* you can tell me?”

“There is a man who may have been contacted by McIntyre… an unknown factor. One of our operatives had the good sense to shoot this picture of him.”

Lilne slid it through the opening.

The stranger picked up the picture and squinted at it in the low light. His eyebrows rose with a hint of a malevolent smile.

The photo showed Dutch in front of Mali’s, carrying McIntyre’s bag

”I will accept the assignment, your Excellency,” the stranger rasped, one hand stroking his throat.

The confessional window slammed shut as the stranger heard the outer door open and footsteps fade off into the distance. Looking back down at the photograph, he smiled.

“Not completely *unknown*, are you Mr. Vorhees.”

* * * * * * * *

Chapter Seven

Lower East Side, New York

The storm that had been drenching the entire east coast for the past few days finally dwindled down to a light mist covering the city – creating a Christmas tree effect with the flashing neon signs and billboards reflected on wet streets and framed by the night sky.

Diandra was working late rummaging through old files in the central file room, located down the hall from her office. Suddenly she heard the distant clank of another metal file drawer being slammed shut down the hall. She remembered Bert, the security guard, coming by an hour earlier to say goodnight.

Odd, she thought. *Why would he be looking in the files?* She listened and there it was again. She stuck her head out and looked down the hallway. Nothing.

"Hello? Is anybody there? Bert?"

No answer. Then she saw a flashlight's beam moving around in her office. Her office. She grabbed a replica of a small statue of Osiris and started down the hallway, stooping below her windows as she made her way for the door.

Those damn board members! she fumed. *The nerve! I should just call the police. But they're in my office. Probably thinking I've already left. I'll show them.* She took a deep breath and slowly rose in the doorway to see the silhouette of a tall, lean, but powerfully built man going through her file cabinet. She held the statue steady in one hand, reached over and turned on the light, bathing the office in fluorescent brightness.

"Don't you move or I'll-"

The man turned around, squinting his eyes.

"You!" she screamed.

"Hi there," the man in the travel-stained bomber jacket raised a hand in greeting.

She took one step forward, dropped the statue and promptly laid into his chin with a roundhouse punch – a truly automatic reaction to seeing her not-so-ex-husband, Dutch Vorhees. He reeled back into the cabinets and held his arms up in surrender with an impish grin. Diandra backed off as he massaged his chin.

"You haven't changed much, have you?" he said, bemused.

For a long moment they eyed one another - each taking some internal inventory of all that had filled in their mutual past. Diandra didn't know whether to hit him again or hug him in relief. Anger won; an anger that ached for release.

"This has got to be the perfect end to an already lousy day. What the hell are you doing in my office?" she demanded, shaking her aching right hand.

"I thought you might have left an autographed copy of your book for me. You know, for old times' sake?"

"Very funny, Vorhees. You know, speaking of autographs, have you signed the divorce papers yet?"

"I never got them." That was a bold faced lie. Her expression made it obvious that she wasn't buying it for a moment.

"I swear to god, Di. I move around a lot, you know that. Right now there's probably some *other* Dutch reading my divorce papers and wondering what he did wrong."

"Well, if he's anything like you the list is long."

"Ouch! You know, I've missed our little chats." He plopped himself into her office chair while casually putting his feet up on the desk, gesturing for her to take a seat as well.

She looked him over again, but remained standing, groaning at his nerve. *Damn. He looked good.* Ever since the first time she met him her breath seemed to shorten and tighten in her chest each time she would first lay eyes on him, and it was still the same. *Funny how you forget about those things until they happen again,* she remembered. He had this way of being totally unaware of how gorgeous he was; it was so seductive.

Wait a second. She also remembered he never did anything without a motive behind it.

"So what do you *want*, Dutch?" she asked, crossing her arms. "I don't hear from you in a year and you turn up like Mission Impossible in my office. What's your angle?"

"If it's any consolation, I'm done. I just finished my last freelance mission."

'Right. And I just finished my last dig and will be asking people soon if they want to *super size* that order."

"What is it with people," he stated, looking around at unseen listeners, "I'm being serious here, Di."

"What do *you* want?"

This conversation was going nowhere fast, and she had neither the time nor blood sugar level to deal with his banter. He reached into his pocket and handed her a small gift-wrapped box with a little purple bow on it.

"Happy birthday, Di."

Surprised, she studied it as if it might be a 'Jack-in-the-box' ready to pop open.

"It better not be another Hong Kong negligee you got a deal on. Maybe it's just me, but I like silk that the worms have finished with."

"This one's made of antediluvian stone," he answered, smiling.

She forced herself to look away from his handsomely chiseled face and shook the box. It felt heavy.

Okay, I'll play his little game. She walked over to her desk, sat down and untied the bow. She shook it again, and ripped off the wrapping paper revealing a silver box… probably from Nordstrom. Inside she found a tablet fragment and quizzically studied it, looking at both sides. She eyed Dutch, who was smiling like a kid at a candy store, then back at the fragment.

Wait a second. This looks eerily familiar. She inventoried her memories until they returned to her freshman year in grad school. A professor was speaking about discoveries that were lost, and one in particular in ancient Persia….

"What the-?" she whispered to herself in disbelief. Pushing Dutch out of her chair, she sat and turned on the desk lamp. She held it under the light, almost in disbelief, experiencing that familiar sensation of her heart revving up; the same growing excitement she felt whenever a new shard or artifact was found at one of her digs. Only this wasn't just any artifact. This was *the* artifact.

"Where, how, did you get this?" she asked wide eyed. It wasn't a question. It was a plea.

"So you like it then?" he asked, smiling with the boyish charm that always went straight to her heart.

"Like it? Dutch, this is the missing piece of the Macedonian tablet!"

"I guess it's not missing anymore."

"So where did you get it?"

"I found it," he hedged.

Abruptly, Diandra's ecstasy at her gift morphed into doubt. "Found, or stole it?"

"That hurts." he objected, playfully, both hands to his heart.

"Goddammit Dutch!" She yelled, throwing her hands up as she rose and stormed around her office. "Why do you always do this?"

She stopped, hands on hips, and almost stomped her foot in frustration.

"Tell me where you got it right now, you narcissistic jerk!"

"I'll tell you over dinner," he responded with grating equanimity. "Shall we say Francois' at eight?"

* * * * * * * *

Chapter Eight

Rabat, Morocco

"I am in great trouble, your Excellency," McIntyre said, steadying the phone in his sweaty hand.

"I am listening, my son," replied the concerned voice.

Taking a deep breath, McIntyre related the events of the last three weeks. After jumping into the drain opening in the catacombs, he had clung to his buoyant, waterproof knapsack, the turbulent water rushing through seemingly endless underground caverns. He was finally spit from the mountain and, still bleeding from his leg wound, struggled to reach the riverbank, where he passed out from pain and exhaustion.

When he awoke, it was sometime after midday. He vaguely remembered the area. Ripping off a part of his jacket he bandaged his leg, then hobbled south toward a village he hoped was less than three kilometers away.

As he had approached the village five sheepherding dogs ran toward him, barking ferociously. He froze in his tracks. The dogs surrounded him, and he slumped to the ground, no longer able to stand. Surprisingly, the dogs quieted and sat, watching him -- heads cocked, tails wagging.

After awhile, he attempted to stand again. Immediately, the dogs sprang to their feet, baring their teeth and growling. He eased back down to a sitting position. Some hours went by before a young woman arrived, having heard the barking from repeated attempts at standing.

"These are my father's dogs,' she apologetically explained, "and it took me this long to find them after they had escaped from their kennel." She noticed his wound, and his monk's collar, and immediately offered him assistance and shelter at her parents' home.

Putting his arm around her shoulder, she led him, limping, to their small house in the countryside. Afraid of letting his true situation be known to her family, McIntyre feigned that a stray hunter's bullet had caused his wound. For two weeks he stayed with the family, regaining his strength, unable to contact anyone for help.

A small gift of money from the sheepherder helped him book third class passage on a train headed to northern Turkey, where he caught a bus into Ankara. He was able to covertly communicate an urgent message to his Excellency in the Vatican regarding his location. However, limited funds had forced him to stay at Mali's hotel while he waited for help. Then his run-in with Lilne's men and escape had forced him to make his way south to a monastery where a seminary roommate of his was the monsignor. Passage was arranged aboard a container ship bound for Morocco, where he could take shelter in one of the only Greek Orthodox Coptic churches in the country, located about twenty kilometers east of Rabat. From there he was able to find an Internet café and use a Skype phone to make a call.

The sonorous voice asked, "Are you now recovered?"

"Yes, your Excellency," McIntyre replied. "Although my leg still pains me a bit. Most importantly, though," he continued, "I regret to say that my complicity in being the source for that book was uncovered. They blocked me from any outside communication and tried me as a heretic. I barely escaped with my life."

"And you are safe?"

"I believe so."

"Where are you?"

"I would rather not say," McIntyre replied. "Their tentacles run deep. Somehow they found out where I was in Ankara. If not for the actions of a benevolent stranger, I shudder to think of the consequences. I could not wait for you there."

"Contact me later in the agreed upon manner, and I will arrange for your safe return."

"Your Excellency, it has been a difficult journey but not without reward. I have additional news," McIntyre said.

"Yes?"

"I found it."

"Found what?"

"The Guardians' Chronicles."

"And you have it?"

"I do."

A silence on the other end of the line was followed by an audible sigh.

"Then it has begun."

"What shall I do, your Excellency?"

"Guard it with your life. It must not be released until arrangements have been made."

"I will do so, as I already have done."

"May the Lord be with your soul, McIntyre, for you will surely need it."

"With the Lord's help, I will be safe."

"Does anyone else know of this?"

"I do not know."

Silence greeted his response.

"I will await your sign for contact," McIntyre finally said.

"McIntyre?"

"Yes, your Excellency."

"This call never happened."

A dial tone followed as McIntyre set the Internet's Skype phone back in its cradle and slowly stared around the café, feeling someone's eyes on him. Cautiously he visually swept the area but saw no one suspicious. Satisfied, he pushed the chair back and rushed out to catch a bus back to the Coptic monastery.

* * * * * * * *

Chapter Nine

Manhattan, New York

François's was a little out-of-the-way French cafe on the lower thirties opened by a fellow named George Sheinberg. He had studied briefly in France's Le Cordon Bleu during the late eighties. Despite the undesirable location and lack of a true French chef, it came to be regarded by all the people *in the know* as the place to go for clandestine rendezvous and romantic outings. It was one of the few places Dutch liked to go for dinner whenever he was in the city, mainly because he shared George's quirky sense of humor and enjoyed popping into the kitchen to hear the latest off-color jokes.

Dutch had called ahead to reserve a table for the two of them, and when they arrived George had his favorite corner table set with a beautiful bouquet of orchids flown in from Hawaii – which not totally coincidently, was where he and Diandra had honeymooned.

Diandra wasn't sure how he had talked her into this, other than the fact he wouldn't let on to where he got the tablet fragment unless it was discussed over wine and oysters Bogalusa. That was one of the things most irritating to her. On the one hand he had more charm than all the gold in Fort Knox, yet on the other he was about as emotionally forthcoming as a parked car. Tonight was one of Dutch's golden moments. The meal was fabulous and they had shared two bottles of excellent wine, creating a comfortable atmosphere that she recognized as probably heading for trouble. Subconsciously, she tugged the scoop neck of her cream silk blouse a little higher.

Their impeccably attired waiter approached their table, setting down a dessert menu.

"And then…" Dutch noticed the waiter and motioned to Diandra.

"Hold on a moment."

He picked up the dessert menu and gave it a cursory look.

"You want to split something?" he asked her.

"I'm pretty full, thanks."

"Okay. I think I'll have the blueberry crepes with lemon sorbet. How is it tonight?"

"Nothing but compliments from everyone who's tried it."

"Good. Bring two spoons just in case."

The waiter bowed slightly and left. Diandra began to fidget.

"You were saying?" she urged.

"Oh yes. So I open the door and this old guy had jumped out of the second floor bathroom window. I kid you not. I looked out of it and thought-- holy moley -- I don't think I'd have tried that."

"Come on," she replied disbelievingly, shaking her head and smiling.

"Really. I was just trying to be the good Sumerian," winking on the last word. This cracked her up, as he knew it would.

"Looking for a reward if I know you," she quipped back and they both laughed.

Sipping her wine, Diandra took a few moments to take stock of her hopefully soon-to-be-ex. His sandy blond hair, except for a few gray strands growing in, looked as full as the day she met him, almost twenty something years ago in high school. What had started out as a summer day job sorting bones at the La Brea tar pits had resulted in her meeting the love of her life, or at least she had thought so then.

And those eyes. My god. Ice blue, and accented even more tonight by the light colored blue shirt under his double-breasted navy blue blazer. He really could put on the Ritz when he wanted to.

His chiseled features were a little softer in this light, but he was still handsome as hell and she hated that she was still attracted to him, in spite of all that had gone on. *Although it wasn't his entire fault, by any means*, she reminded herself.

She was the one who had wanted to legitimize their relationship after he left the service, tired of never knowing where she stood. It was she who was worried when he was called away for some secret *boys* mission, not hearing from him for weeks at a time. She thought that by getting married and settling down their relationship would grow. They would have a family. Live the American dream. He was the one who always wanted to keep it loose and free, seeing where it would lead. A train wreck that they both failed to fully appreciate lay perilously ahead.

But still, maybe if they had both just tried a little harder? Put in a little more effort instead of giving up. It might have worked. But she knew what she really meant was if *Dutch* had tried a little harder. Then there was that other problem.

Dutch had been reminiscing as well, only through different colored lenses. He never could get her out of his mind, no matter how hard he drank or how much he distracted himself by risking life and limb. She was always there in his thoughts. Of course he missed her. And at the same time hated her for screwing up what he thought was a perfectly good relationship. At least for him.

He had agreed to get married only because he was sure she would leave him if he didn't. Funny enough, though, she finally left anyway. So it ended up the same. And it wasn't lost on him that she had grown more attractive and sexy over the past few years than he had ever seen her – even including those private Victoria's Secret dress up nights. But what was done was done. She'd made it clear as day that she wanted the divorce and that was final. *It wasn't his fault they couldn't find him to serve the papers, was it?*

Dutch raised his hand for the waiter. Diandra went a little cold.

"Don't you think that's enough alcohol?"

"I was going to ask if George was available in the kitchen, that's all," he said, slightly offended.

She sat back in her chair. The jovial mood had definitely been shattered. Dutch tossed down his napkin on the table as he started to get up.

"If you'll excuse me a moment?"

He stormed toward the kitchen. Damn, she hated when she did that. She had promised herself she wouldn't say anything that even remotely sounded like she cared about what he did, especially his drinking. And then she'd just blurted it out. That had been one of the major problems of their married relationship. Although he seemed to handle any amount of drink in public, alone she had been privy to his sarcasm and self-deprecation. And she didn't like it for a moment.

While lost in a myriad of thoughts, she noticed his blazer draped on the back of the chair. Not really the coat, but the book sticking partway out of an inner pocket.

"Dutch? Reading? This I've got to see."

Reaching over and pulling it out she saw that it was… *her* book. He had helped her come up with the pseudonym before they… whatever. She was really touched. He had always made out like it was no big deal to him that she wrote the book. And now, here he was with a copy of it.

She opened it and viewed an inscription on the first page.

'M. Thank you for all of your help.'

It was her writing. It took a moment to remember whom she'd given the book to. And then it hit her that this may have been the 'old guy' Dutch was referring to. But that was impossible, wasn't it? He was in Italy. *This doesn't make sense at all.*

She heard Dutch laughing at one of George's jokes as he exited the kitchen. He briskly walked to the table as Diandra hid the book under it on her lap. Once he'd settled he started to say something when…

"All right, Vorehees. Cut the schmooze crap out right now. Who was that old guy who jumped out the window? If there really was an old guy or even a hotel."

Dutch was ambushed and he knew it.

"I'm telling you the truth, Di. Scout's honor," he replied crossing his fingers in boy scouts fashion.

"Did you by any chance catch his name?" she asked, leaning forward.

"I told you. He was just some old guy with gray hair. I've never seen him before. Mali said he signed in the hotel as a Mac something or other."

"McIntyre?"

"Yeah. That sounds right. How did you know?"

She brought up the book from her lap and tossed it onto the table.

"You know, just when I think you're for real, you never fail to substantiate my misgivings. Where's the letter?"

"What are you talking about?" It was not a totally convincing response.

"I know this man, Dutch. And he – and you – knew the other half of the tablet was mentioned in my book. It was clearly intended for me, and I seriously doubt he would send it without a letter. Now, where is it?"

Dutch realized that there was no wiggle room in her tone, and knew when she got like this, it was better to capitulate early. He reached into his pants pocket, pulled out the letter and tossed it across the table. For emphasis he looked around as if he didn't have a thing to do with it – Huck Finn style.

She picked up the paper and saw her name at the top. After a few moments she looked over at Dutch, who was still looking up at the ceiling, and shook her head. "You are too frigging much, Vorhees," she exclaimed while noting the letter was hand written in Latin, with strange symbols drawn below McIntyre's signature.

"I couldn't really make any sense of it," Dutch chimed in while she looked it over. "It's written in some sort of allegorical gibberish."

Diandra took a closer look, then gave him a smug smile. What he didn't know was that this *gibberish* was a code McIntyre and she had worked out to pass information to each other. Just in case anyone got hold of their communication. He was ultra paranoid about getting caught. By whom, she didn't know. She was just grateful for the inside help on Vatican artifacts and tablets that she had made a decision not to pursue the reasons why with him.

Finishing the letter, she looked up at Dutch, his boyish charm starting to wear very thin at that point.

"Why did you come back here, Dutch? Really now. No BS."

"I read your book-"

"You read my book?" she gasped in total surprise.

"Well, kinda glanced through it."

"Oh." Just as she thought. Another moment of tense silence.

"Anyway," he continued, "it says, I guess I mean you say in it that when the corner of the tablet I gave you is joined with the other piece it could possibly lead to the tomb of Alexander. That place would be a veritable treasure trove."

"Fortune and glory, hey Dutch?" She was thoroughly disgusted, as well as surprisingly disappointed.

"Doesn't sound too bad to me," he replied. "They didn't coin the phrase 'Soldier of Fortune' for nothing."

"Well, I hate to rain on your parade, but the other half of the tablet was destroyed during World War II. So I guess you'll have to seek your fortune through some other scam."

He pursed his lips into a slight grin.

"Really, Di? Judging from what I could make out of McIntyre's letter, he seems to think the other part may still exist."

She looked at him and then down at the letter. All of a sudden the kitchen door burst open with George carrying a huge cake with candles ablaze followed by all the waiters who sang:

"Happy birthday to you, happy birthday to you…"

During the serenade Dutch mouthed happy birthday to Diandra and smiled.

Damn it's hard to stay mad at this man.

* * * * * * * *

Buscemi walked alone down one of the labyrinthine hallways that wound below the monastery, distracted in thought. Out from the shadows Lilne stepped into the wavering torchlight and blocked his path. Startled, Buscemi jumped back.

"Your Eminence," Buscemi blurted, hand to heart. "You startled me."

"I am not a man to be crossed, Buscemi."

"And I would never cross you," he offered in a subordinate tone, eyes lowered.

Lilne narrowed his eyes as he assessed the monk's trustworthiness.

"Be sure of this," he said coldly. "I am watching you. I see everything and hear everything. We still don't know who gave McIntyre a key for his escape, but believe me, we will."

Buscemi licked his lips and swallowed, as the sinister undertones of that last statement sunk in. "I am not your enemy, your Eminence."

"Time makes enemies of us all."

Lilne held his gaze for another moment and turned to leave. After a step he swung half back around, pointing directly at Buscemi.

"Remember what I said. I have eyes and ears everywhere."

With that Lilne disappeared into the darkness. Buscemi breathed a sigh of relief as he straightened his robes and continued down the hallway.

* * * * * * *

Chapter Ten

Lower East Side, New York

A large to-go bag sat on the cluttered desk of the museum's forensics lab in the area where artifacts were cleaned, photographed, cataloged and then entered into the national database. Diandra sat at the computer, entering the letter and decoding the text as she had done dozens of times before with McIntyre' communications. Her attention was transfixed on the screen, while Dutch tossed a small statue up and down in an impatient way, waiting for the results.

"If you drop that you'll owe the university about fifty-thousand dollars," she stated matter-of-factly, never moving her gaze from the screen.

On that note he almost missed the next catch and gently set it down on the table. Diandra caught his stunt peripherally and smiled to herself.

"You find out anything yet?" Dutch inquired.

"Other than you're still as impatient as ever? Yes. You were right about the letter. McIntyre says the other tablet may still exist. It says we have to look through the smoke… to see beyond the flames. Look here."

She pointed to the computer screen as Dutch bent over to see.

"McIntyre keeps talking about how this information needs to get out, blah, blah. Something about a message left for us. Most of these symbols here at the bottom of the letter are completely unknown to me. I do recognize the enneagram and the winged globe. They repeat every so often – perhaps written in some other code. I just can't seem to make head or tails of them. Even screening them into our database nothing comes up."

"And by the way," she continued, looking up to him, "I had no idea you were so talented in breaking codes, especially in Latin. My compliments to you regarding my letter."

"I'm just an amateur. What we really need is a professional code-breaker." He stood up and paced around behind the desk and stopped, snapping his fingers. "And I know just the person to call."

He grabbed her coat off the chair and tossed it to her. "Let's go."

* * * * * * * *

Location Unknown

A tall, gaunt man lay on his back in a bed; a smoldering cigarette dangling from his fingers. Slowly, he exhaled the noxious blue smoke, emptying his lungs and coughing, gasping for breath. Hysterical laughter and screams of patients, male and female, filled the background, but he didn't hear them anymore.

His eyes surveyed his living area; a ten by twelve foot room with no windows. The only way out a steel door, bolted shut with a wire reinforced glass window that opened only from the outside. A stainless steel commode and sink occupied the corner. Two dual bulb fluorescent light fixtures tried to pump light down on him. However, he had managed to knock three of them out with his shoes, a feat that was not appreciated by the staff at the locked psychiatric ward.

He had used the black heel of his shoe to draw hundreds of symbols on the walls, in various shapes and sizes, all ancient in form and nature. A newspaper article was taped to the center of one of the walls about the New York Museum of Natural History. Circled in pen within the article was a picture of Dr. Diandra Weiss, along with a description of her work on a site in New Mexico.

The screaming of the patients grew louder as he slowly raised the smoldering cigarette to his lips, inhaled, and blew it out again.

* * * * * * * *

Chapter Eleven

Queens, New York

A knock on the hotel room door startled Skip from his fixation on his computer's laptop screen. He hurriedly covered it over with an empty pillowcase and turned.

"Who is it?"

"Donald Trump here with the keys to your new condo."

Pushing back from the desk, he got up and stared out the peephole. The hotel manager was standing on the other side, working on at least his fifth day of beard growth and sporting a potbelly that looked even bigger through the fish-eye lens. He was seesawing the unlit cigarette impatiently in his mouth.

"Hold on there, mate."

Skip fumbled with and finally unhooked the chain lock, and then twisted the deadbolt. The manager stood there with his hot water.

"Here ya go, your highness," he spat out through his clenched teeth. "Hope the monarchy is okay with the temperature of the water this time."

He handed Skip the plug-in coffee pot with steam billowing out. Skip grabbed the handle with a handkerchief covering his hand.

"Thank you ever so much."

"Yeah, yeah. Just pay your frickin' bill on time and I'll be just *dandy*," he replied in a mocking tone.

The manager turned and mumbled something about how ungrateful *they* were about *our* having saved *their* asses during the last big war as he started back down the stairs.

Skip clumsily relocked the door while awkwardly maintaining his grip on the pot. Smiling with anticipatory pleasure, he walked over to the flimsy table in the middle of the room, set it down and began his ritual.

Doctor Geoffrey 'Skip' Duffin loved his tea. In fact, it was more than love. A total addiction – not to the caffeine, but to the joy he received from taking that first taste of the bittersweet liquid. He'd thought many times that it might be related to when he was a little boy in Manchester. Drinking their afternoon tea was the only time his family actually sat down and talked together. But who knows? He was not a psychologist, and he really didn't care all that much.

The good news was, he had managed to find the *right* tea in almost every country he'd visited, which were too numerous to remember, over the last fifty years.

Grabbing the pot handle again with his handkerchief, he emptied the now-lukewarm cup into the bathroom sink. Pouring the new hot water into the cup, he pulled out a stopwatch and then opened his airtight canister and removed a bag of PG Tips. It was one of the new triangular bags, which he personally detested. But until his next shipment caught up with him, he'd have to make do. He gently submerged the bag in the cup now filled with steaming hot water and pressed the stopwatch, counting to himself as he watched it. Twelve seconds later he gently spooned out the bag, squeezed it along the rim of the cup and unceremoniously tossed it in the sink. He carried the cup over to the computer, smelling it as he sat down.

"If I didn't know better I'd say this is better than sex," he kiddingly told himself out loud. "But it's been so long now it's hard to remember." After he took that first taste, he settled into his zone. *The little comforts bloody well make the difference*, he liked to think.

His fleabag hotel certainly did not add to those comforts. It was one of those out of the way numbers that was certainly clean enough – even if the furnishings were probably on their last leg of allotted life and then some. No, the one major advantage to staying there as far as he was concerned was that they conveniently forget to ask you for ID when you checked in, which in his line of business was a big plus. If he had to rough it a night or two, so be it. He'd be back in a five-star Ritz soon enough.

At over thirteen stone, his five foot seven inch frame was not the most graceful. The truth was he waddled more than walked. He had combed his remaining wisp of hair down the center of his head. Frameless glasses sat atop a surprisingly long, slim nose, surrounded by an exceedingly pudgy face.

"Now, back to work," he told himself as he set his cup down. Pulling out a disinfectant wipe from the box next to the computer, he cleaned his hands, finger by finger, including a quick swipe under each nail. He then slipped the pillowcase off the computer and started typing away.

Skip, as he'd been known for most of his adult life, had segued after retirement into what's known in the spy business as an independent contractor, and one of the best in his field – cryptography. He had worked for MI6 for almost thirty-five years in the research department and finally out in the field, where he became their expert on computer encryption and counter-programming. He had been intimately involved from the very beginning in developing a lot of the computer-controlled gadgetry at the home office. He was always accused of being cut from the same cloth as the character Q from the James Bond series. *Without my sophistication or class, of course*, Skip had more than once ruefully mused to himself.

He'd left the agency almost seven years earlier, due mostly to the ineptness of the new guard whom the home office had this annoying habit of hiring. Sure, these whiz kids could operate a computer, but there was no foundation behind their actions, no elegance in their approach. "Like bulls in a china shop," he'd told them.

After a while, his constant complaining made an early retirement inevitable, and so he took the requisite gold watch and wall plaque and decided to go out on his own. He still received no small joy on those occasions the old boys on Baker Street called to ask for his help, to which he happily obliged while charging them triple his normal going rate.

Tonight, he was just honing his skills before his next job, seeing what he could do. He had met an old contemporary, an expert consultant in computer security and counter-measures, at a conference the previous week. The man had told him about his company's latest project, the Pentagon's newest anti-hacking defenses installed post 9/11.

Skip wasn't sure if it was the irritating way he bragged about it, almost taunting him about how impossible it was to penetrate, or the fact that he once stole Skip's girlfriend. Well, not exactly a girlfriend. More like a girl at a bar during a security conference in Scotland back in 1978. But at that point it didn't matter. Skip was going to get into their impenetrable system and show that twit a thing or two.

He had figured out the algorithm to the basic entry system, and had planted a Trojan horse within it a few hours earlier, hoping that someone would send some information out. And he was right. When they sent it they unknowingly also sent out a key password to him. *That's the problem with security features,* he thought. *They are so afraid of something coming in they forget to watch what's going out.*

He hacked into a less secure server, routing through it and masking the source of his ISP account. Known as a phantom account, it was a very effective way to hide your trail that he had perfected for MI6 years earlier. Bringing up the server, he laughed to himself as he forwarded his algorithm code through it. He was using a Lithuanian lingerie factory's main server, knowing it would drive them crazy when they tried to trace it. He typed in the new password he had just received.

"Bingo!" Complete access. Now this *was* better than sex. He brought up the main directory address system, hit a key, and – there it was. On the screen he saw the logo of the Pentagon and the title in large letters:

'Decoding section – Level 6 Top Secret Clearance Required.'

"Hello again, my dear," he said seductively. "Top Secret, eh? I don't know why you don't just have an open house sign on the site."

He picked up his tea and took a slow deliberate sip.

"I'm having way too much fun," he chuckled to himself.

He sat back in his chair and savored another taste of his tea, smug in the knowledge that old what's-his-name wasn't so smart after all.

Suddenly he heard a beep. Freezing like a doe in headlights, he slowly focused back at the screen – almost afraid to see what he knew was there. He set down his teacup and leaned forward. Along the bottom a new window popped up for a program he had created, alerting him if anyone tried instigating a reverse trace on his activities.

But this isn't right. He was going through another set of servers. "There's no way… unless…"

Another message flashed onscreen:

'WARNING – THIS TRANSMISSION IS BEING TRACED. ISP COMPROMISED.'

"Bloody hell," he whispered in disbelief. His right hand tugged at his ear as he stared for a moment. "What the...?"

Immediately he pulled the Internet connection out of his computer and breathed a sigh of relief. He reached for his teacup when all of a sudden he heard sirens in the distance. *No need to be overly paranoid. Probably just some – wait a second. What if ol'... what's his name?... Chuck something or other, was setting him up? Using him to test the Pentagon's system? Nah, he's not that smart. Still, those sirens seemed to be getting decidedly louder.*

Skip flipped the screen down, knocking his tea to the floor, a crime he was only too happy to overlook at that moment. He grabbed his backpack and stuffed his laptop and small satellite dish in it. The sirens grew louder as he waddled for the door then turned, dashed back to the window and exited slowly to the ledge. About five feet away was the outside wrought iron fire escape.

"Not too far," he told himself encouragingly. "You can do it, old boy! Just like that Bond character!" Turning toward the fire escape he mistakenly looked down and had to close his eyes to quell the dizzying nausea.

"Now I know how that chap Jimmy Stewart felt in Vertigo. Don't look down. Just don't look down," he whispered, reminding himself why he hated fieldwork, always preferring the sidelines, being the support, while the real 'James Bonds' took care of that spy business.

Finally reaching the fire escape, he draped a leg clumsily over it and jumped, or rather stumbled, onto the platform. He clambered down, his under exercised two hundred and sixty plus pound body unaccustomed to coordinating downward speed and steep metal steps at the same time.

He jumped the last couple of steps, hitting the asphalt like a big bowl of Jell-O. Steadying himself, he limped down the alleyway. About to cross the street, he peered around the corner and then slammed himself tightly against the brick wall, willing his rotund gut to flatten. A police cruiser with flashing lights raced by and screeched around the corner, followed by two black unmarked government-issued Crown Vic's with flashing blue lights.

Still panting, Skip heard them skid to a stop on the opposite side of the block where he perceived the hotel's entrance to be. His heart beat a million miles a minute. *You've really buggered into it this time, Mister Duffin. What to do, what to do?*

Trying not to be too obvious, he slipped around the corner and headed south down Olive street in a kind of half-gallop, half-walk. Suddenly, a black Ford Explorer screeched to a stop on the sidewalk, blocking his way. He almost ran into it, stopped and jumped back. The front driver's door opened, as Dutch poked his head out.

"Come on, Skip. Jump in."

Skip backed away. This was too much.

"Dutch?" he cried disbelievingly. "Oh no," he said, raising his hands in instinctive self-defense. "I am not going anywhere with you, chum! Not on your life, or… on my life," he amended, momentarily confused.

"I know the feeling," piped in Diandra, craning her neck from the passenger seat to look up at Skip.

Dutch looked over at her with a 'shut the heck up' look. She smiled a 'got you' right back at him. More sirens were coming toward them in the background.

"Your move, Skip," Dutch stated.

Skip looked back at the flashing lights and listened for a split second to the oncoming sirens. Shrugging, he pulled off his backpack, opened the back door and threw it in. Jumping in, he slammed the door, out of breath and sweating.

Dutch gave the throttle full pedal and squealed the car off the sidewalk and back onto the street, nearly knocking over a newspaper rack. He headed in the direction of Diandra's place. Skip looked out the back window and watched as the police and some plain clothed alphabet men ran around the corner, guns drawn. They threw a college aged young man violently against the wall, ripping off his backpack and started searching through it.

Skip turned back into his seat and slouched down a bit. "That was really quite frightening," he muttered. Looking up at the rearview mirror he saw Dutch smiling at him. But he was not sure what was worse. He'd gotten clear of the frying pan. Was he now looking at the fire?

"Forget it, Mr. Vorhees. Whatever it is you are selling, I'm not interested," Skip informed him.

"Come on, Skip. We need a quick favor. It's not like I'm asking for a lifetime commitment."

"Which I, for one, can assure you will not happen," Diandra added sarcastically, breaking a slight smile at that zinger.

"Are you anywhere near through?" Dutch shot back.

"Only getting warmed up," she answered.

"How did you find me?" Skip demanded.

"I called your Miss *Moneypenny*," Dutch said, ignoring Diandra's comment. "Old habits are hard to break."

Dutch was right. Skip let his former secretary know everywhere he went, although her name was really Kelly Havenspur. He made a mental note to take Dutch off his trusted list of friends.

"Now, Skip," Dutch continued, "Let me at least tell you about it before you-"

"In case I have not made myself crystal clear," Skip interrupted. "Let me spell it out to you. Every time you need a favor, Dutch, someone ends up hurt or dead. I, for one, prefer to avoid either of those possibilities."

"I could make a call to whatever alphabet agents are after you."

Skip squirmed in his seat at this not so veiled threat. *A bluff, no doubt.*

"You don't know anything," Skip shot back.

"I know you weren't running from your landlady back there," he said, thumbing toward the hotel.

Skip's face was getting redder by the minute. "I said I was not-"

"Stop it right now," interjected Diandra. "We don't have time for this adolescent banter." After a few moments she turned around in her seat. "Look, Skip," she said in a more reasonable tone, "we need a cryptographer. It'll only take a few hours, and Dutch tells me you are one of the best."

"Well, for once my Neanderthal friend is almost correct. Although, I am not *one* of the best; I *am* the best."

"So you'll help?" she asked.

Skip took stock of Diandra. Dutch had told him many times about her, but none of his descriptions really did justice to how poised and elegant she was. Her hair was a warm reddish brown, a beautiful color even in the pale light. *Eyes like sparkling emeralds, and quite pretty*, he told himself. In fact, she reminded him of a younger, forty-something Audrey Hepburn, but with a much less vulnerable aura about her.

Yes, Skip mused, *this would be the kind of woman Dutch would be attracted to*; *strong-willed, beautiful and with a deep sense of self.*

But that would also be the problem. Someone that smart would realize, after all the charm was used up, just how difficult getting close to Dutch would be. Skip had been around him on and off for the past seven years, Dutch had hired him for his first job after he retired from MI6. And Skip was constantly perplexed by him. In spite of his initial misgivings, he couldn't seem to resist Diandra's softer approach. *What the heck*, he finally thought, *at least she seems to sincerely need my help.*

"All right," he relented. "But I'm doing this one only for you, dearie. Anybody who was married to this man deserves all the humanity one can spare."

"Hah!" Dutch grinned at the insult. "Did I mention I've missed you too, Skip?"

* * * * * * * *

Umbria Region, Northern Italy

"Your Excellency?" The brother bowed his head respectfully, looking at the floor.

"Yes?" Lilne answered as he sat down at his desk in the monastery.

"We have just been informed of a call that was made a few hours ago."

"The point?"

"It was to a Cardinal Assanti within Vatican City."

Lilne stopped what he was doing and turned to listen, nodding for the brother to proceed.

"We are trying to recover the entire conversation. However, through voice recognition we believe it was from Cardinal McIntyre. What we did learn is that this Cardinal Assanti knows about the *other* item that he took."

Lilne assessed this news and tilted his head in thought.

"Then it is only a matter of time until he…"

Standing, he pushed the intercom button on his desk.

"I need to be in Rome within the hour."

"Yes sir," a male voice replied.

Turning his steely attention back to the brother.

"Do we know exactly where McIntyre is located?"

The brother shook his head with some trepidation. "Only that the call was routed through Switzerland. We believe it originated from an Internet provider in northern Africa. We should have the IP address soon.

"I want the entire conversation. Now!"

The man bowed as he hastily backed his way to the door and scuttled from the room.

Lilne pushed another button and waited as the phone rang.

"Yes," the barely audible raspy voice at the other answered.

"I have a new lead for our primary quarry," Lilne said. "He may be in northern Africa."

"Understood. I will have my men check it out."

* * * * * * * *

Chapter Twelve

Scarsdale, New York

The black Ford Explorer cruised silently down the street past the big leafed poplars lining the middle-class neighborhood of mid-seventies tract homes a few miles north of the city. Pulling into Diandra's driveway and stopping in front of the garage, the SUV's headlights illuminated a pile of newspapers lying scattered about.

Dutch, Skip and Diandra emerged and walked toward the front as Diandra continued her conversation with Skip.

"So it's really just the bottom of the letter that we need decoded. There are a lot of recurring symbols, most of which don't equate with any known language I am aware of, living or dead."

"Could be math-based that translates into words, being that there is a recurrence," Skip replied. "Throws a lot of people off. Seems simple enough. I'll just run a-"

Dutch suddenly stretched his arm in front of them, stopping them dead in their tracks. He had noticed a shadow waiting under the large elm by the front porch and gestured with his hands for them to be quiet and wait. Pulling his Smith and Wesson seventeen-round chrome plated .45 automatic from under his jacket, he rounded the corner, raised the gun and grabbed the lapel of-

Sam, standing there in a jacket and tie, holding a little box with a ribbon tied around it. "Holy Christ! Don't shoot," Sam screamed, nearly fainting with fright.

"Dutch!" Diandra screeched as he relaxed his grip on his quarry and slowly lowered the gun.

Diandra and Skip ran up to join them.

"What are you doing here, kid?" Dutch queried. "And why are you lurking here near the front porch?"

"It's Sam, not kid. And I wasn't *lurking*. I was waiting," he answered somewhat indignantly, while trying to regain some masculine composure. "Diandra and I have a date."

"Oh, Sam, I'm so sorry!" Diandra's hand flew to her mouth. I forgot all about your coming over."

"Well, that's apparent," Sam replied sarcastically, eyes watering. "But then again, why would you when GI Joe's back in town?"

Dutch detested that reference and Sam knew it. Diandra decided to derail their testosterone fest.

"Come on," she said, clutching her sweater closer. "Let's get inside before we all freeze to death."

Sam shook his head and shot Dutch a *'what a jerk'* look as Diandra took out her key and unlocked the door.

* * * * * * * *

The house had been the first concession to domestic living Dutch made after they were married. Prior to this Diandra had owned a small upper eastside condo conveniently located near the museum, and Dutch was living in a rental office/house setup that Diandra rather kindly referred to as 'that dump'. He hated the condo, she hated the office, so the concession was to move to the burbs, buy a neutral place and try to start a more normal family life. Dutch hadn't been too keen on the *family* part, at least not back then. But he reluctantly agreed to give the neighborhood concept a try.

In retrospect, Diandra realized this concession by both of them was the start of their downhill slide. Neither one of them was happy with the compromise. Dutch hated the yard work and the small talk that accompanied neighborhood life, and Diandra discovered rather quickly that she was no Martha Stewart. They ended up spending most of their time apart and when they did find time to get together, Dutch was always coming up with inventive ways to not stay at the place – mostly suggesting weekend trips away to tropical locales.

It was a neat, if sparsely furnished, three-bedroom two-bath tract house. Dutch had hated the small size of the rooms so he knocked a big hole for a doorway between two of the bedrooms, but had neglected to ever finish it out. The hole was still there.

* * * * * * * *

Sam stood in front of the roaring fire Dutch had just started, warming his hands. Diandra readied a kettle of water on the stove and walked out to warm herself before the fire too, standing next to Sam as she held her palms out and rubbed them together.

Sam reached into his jacket pocket and pulled out the small present he'd brought for her.

"Happy birthday, Diandra," he said sheepishly. "I hope you like it."

Diandra opened her arms, leaned over and gave Sam a big hug, which he returned gratefully while surreptitiously looking over toward Dutch and smirking a bit.

"Thank you so much, Sam. I'm sure I'll love it," she bubbled. "And I really am sorry about forgetting our drink."

"Wait a second. I get slugged and he gets hugged?" Dutch feigned being hurt. It was not entirely convincing.

Sam smiled.

"Ahem, yes," Skip interjected. "Where can I set up and get started?"

"You can use the guest bedroom over there," said Diandra pointing. "Excuse the mess," she added while looking at Dutch. "The *builder* seems to have run out on the job, like he does everything else."

Skip picked up on the dig, and to diffuse the tension went into his full British aristocracy *airs*.

"Er, Dutch, my boy," he started, "I'll be right in there. Just so you'll be able to find me, when the tea is ready?" He winked at Diandra.

"Would that be with one lump or two?" Dutch retorted.

Skip ignored him and escaped into the bedroom.

"So what's going on Diandra?" Sam inquired. "Who is that guy and what is he doing?"

"You won't *believe* me when I tell you," Diandra replied.

"Well, at least you'll know how I feel, kid," Dutch stated, half laughing.

Sam locked eyes with Dutch.

"I told you, it's not 'kid.'"

In the bedroom, Skip surveyed the work area, removed a small can of Lysol from his backpack, and sprayed everywhere he could reach. Taking a towel from the bathroom, he cleaned and rubbed the desk and chair. Finally, he pulled out a small box of antibacterial wipes and disinfected his hands, finishing each fingernail with a final swipe. Satisfied with his preparation, he set the wipes on the desk and got into action.

It took him the better part of half-an-hour to set up his computer system, including a small satellite dish pointing out one of the bedroom windows. Finally he pulled out a 'Rube Goldberg' looking silver box with dozens of little wires sticking out of it and hooked the satellite cable into it. Another cable ran from it into his laptop. He powered on the system and up popped a picture of her majesty, the Queen, as the national anthem played through the speakers.

Sam walked in with a cup of tea and set it down beside Skip, who pretended to sniff around and then sight the teacup, acting totally surprised.

"Thank you, my boy. Thought you chaps forgot about it."

"We did," Sam confessed. "Mind if I watch?'"

Skip gestured toward a nearby seat.

"No worries."

Sam sat and studied the setup while the computer was booting.

"What's that weird box you have there?" Sam asked.

"That, my boy, is the secret to my success." He furled his brow as he remembered the incident that had occurred a little earlier and wondered just how brilliant his invention actually was. But that had been different. He was up against the entire US government. *Not a fair match*, he reasoned silently.

"It is an encryption program that I wrote to bypass the normal Internet systems and fool them into giving me access to NSF web."

"NSF web?" Sam said. "I've heard of that."

"It's possible, since you are in academia. Not many people outside of it have. It's a fiber-optic infrastructure that was originally put in place worldwide a few years ago to support academia. It links all educational and government research departments with high-speed broadband connections. The idea was to create a pure Internet search engine that teachers, scientists and government types could use that would literally link together all of the world's current knowledge and research.

"Unfortunately, because of that dot-com boondoggle a few years back, government and private funds dried up, so it's not very widely known and hasn't launched as widely as they thought it would. Fortunately for us, the first thing they did was download all of the information to a host of major servers throughout the world and hyper-link it all together. You know, a build-it-and-they-will-come sort of thing."

He took a slow savory sip of tea and grimaced.

"How the Americans can drink this muck is a mystery to me," he muttered to himself, grimacing. He realized Sam heard him.

"No reflection on you, my boy. It's not your fault they kicked us Brits out two hundred years ago. They deserve this slop for that." He smiled at that thought.

Skip reached over and placed McIntyre's letter in the scanner and hit the start button. Sam tried helping him by closing the scanner door. Skip quickly pushed his hand away, using the side of his arm.

"No need to touch anything here, my boy," he said. "I will take care of it."

Sam shrugged. "Okay."

The the image appeared on his screen and Skip started typing. A box surrounded and then isolated the symbols at the bottom. He typed again and the letter disappeared while the symbols enlarged and filled up the plasma screen. He leaned closer as he studied them for a moment, shaking his head slightly.

"What's wrong?" Sam asked.

"These look like they're going to be tricky little buggers. I think I'll need a Fig Newton if I'm going to crack these."

"What's that? Some super secret computer program?" Sam asked, excitedly scooting his chair closer.

"It's a cookie. I think that's what you Americans call them."

"Huh?" Sam looked confused. "Like the information websites collect on users?"

"No, not that kind of cookie, I mean a biscuit, like perhaps a rich tea biscuit?"

Sam frowned and tilted his head to one side.

"Chocolate Hob Nob? Shortbread?" Skip pulled his glasses lower on his nose in order to peer over them, eyebrows raised.

"Ah!" Sam replied with an enlightened nod and practically sprang from his chair toward the kitchen. "I think I saw a Twinkie in one of the cabinets."

Skip rolled his eyes at this uncivilized country. "This is going to be a long night," he lamented aloud.

* * * * * * * *

As the minutes turned into hours Dutch paced endlessly about the house, popping his head in and out of the bedroom and switching between reading a book he couldn't care less about and watching the latest X-Box game that Sam played on the family room TV while texting messages. He had to step outside every time he wanted to smoke a cigar, and it was getting colder by the minute. Skip had been on the search nonstop and through umpteen cups of tea, while occasionally taking off his glasses to rub his rapidly fading eyes. Data streamed across his screen, but nothing hit of any interest.

Diandra had thrown together some cheese quesadillas for the crew a few hours earlier that they had gratefully devoured. Other than the fact that within the twenty-four hundred square foot house

Dutch and Diandra had repeatedly managed to avoid talking to each other, all seemed to be going pretty smoothly.

* * * * * * * *

It was well past four in the morning. Sam had fallen asleep in the family room in front of the latest infomercial about becoming a real estate short sale millionaire, while texting on his smart phone at the same time. Dutch came in, turned off the TV and threw a blanket over him. Diandra was mindlessly cleaning up in the kitchen.

In the bedroom, Skip was on autopilot – simply going through the motions and trying to focus. This was really perplexing him, but he was so tired he couldn't seem to clear his thoughts enough to make sense of it all. Everything he'd tried so far had resulted in zip, and he was definitely not accustomed to zip. He rubbed his eyes in frustration, hoping that some epiphany would spring forth. "Wait a second," he thought aloud, sitting up straight again and running his fingers through his sparse hair. "Maybe I'm looking in the wrong area. Maybe…"

Reflexively, he reached for another sanitary wipe and did a cursory finger clean, cracked his knuckles and scanned the letter again. Typing in another search, he hit the enter key with a hopeful, "Voila?" and-

Beep. Beep. Beep. A hit. Skip typed in a couple of keystrokes and up popped an inventory list written in Russian. At the top he clearly could see K.G.B. – Top Secret.

"Aha! There you are you little bugger." He nodded to himself in satisfaction, and sat back, his hand instinctively reaching to rub his ear lobe. "Time to come home to Papa."

* * * * * * * *

Diandra sat across the kitchen table from Dutch, watching him nurse the dregs of black coffee in his cup. Only a faint, sporadic beeping from Skip's computer in the bedroom broke the room's stillness. Whether she was tired or what, she didn't know. Biting the cuticle of one thumb, she decided that this moment seemed as good as any to bring up a long-avoided topic.

"You don't even remember that you promised to sign the papers, do you?" she asked.

Dutch looked up, quizzically.

"What are you talking about?"

"You know what papers I'm-"

"Di," he interrupted. "It's really late and I'm not in the mood-"

"You actually don't know what a promise is, do you?" she cut in. "I mean, you use the word when it suits you, but it really doesn't mean anything. To you it's just a word." She tasted blood, looked down at her hand, and spit out the hangnail while reaching for a paper napkin to wrap around her thumb.

Dutch took a gulp of his cold coffee and slammed down the cup.

"And what about you? For richer, for poorer, in sickness and in health, until I die? Sound familiar? And guess what? I'm still here!"

"That's not fair," she replied defiantly, but then her anger ebbed to a sigh, as she remembered how happy she had felt back then, picturing herself saying those very words as he gazed at her lovingly, her hands in his. She decided to change her approach.

"Why didn't you return my calls, Dutch? That really hurt."

"I called. I just never hung on long enough to talk."

She straightened up at his response.

"I knew that was you," she shouted, smiling and pointing her finger at him.

"And you doubt your mother's belief in telepathy?"

"Let's not bring her up in this, okay?" She warmed at his remembering how her mother's psychic abilities had always been a thorn in her side. She remembered how easy it had been to talk about herself to him. But, when it came to *his* opening up, well, that was a different story. Still…

This was the moment she had dreaded all evening. She was tired, her defenses were down and she didn't even want to address the fact that she still had feelings for him. But those eyes, that smile. They stared at each other for a moment while her heart started to beat a little faster.

Sam lumbered in, tired and rubbing his eyes.

"Did I miss anything?" he asked.

Diandra slumped back into her chair, deflated at the lost opportunity to finally talk with Dutch while he was trapped there in the house.

"No, nothing's happened," she replied.

Sam walked over to the refrigerator and opened the door, scanning for anything edible.

Skip popped his head into the kitchen, a little perkier than he'd been in hours and *almost*, god forbid, smiling.

"Any chance for a *good* cup of tea?" he chimed.

"Only if you fly home and get it," Dutch piped in, obviously relieved at the interruptions.

"Oh well, your version will have to do." He waggled his eyebrows.

"I know that look, Skip. Have you got something?" Dutch asked, hopefully.

Skip fumbled and looked through some pages while he came in and sat down at the table.

"Something? I guess you could call it that," he replied smugly. "I'm still running a decryption program on those symbols. That is one tough nut to crack. But what interested me more was the letter itself, and whoever wrote it-"

"McIntyre," Diandra volunteered.

"Yes, McIntyre. Well he certainly believed that the matching piece of the tablet may still exist, and that gave me an idea. What if that tablet fragment and these symbols are in some way connected? So I decided to search for information about it and guess what? It turns out that he was right."

"Whoa, wait a second," Diandra interjected. "What do you mean he was right? That's impossible. That part of the tablet was destroyed in the firebombing of Dresden in January, nineteen forty-four. It's right in my book."

"Quite right, my dear, quite right." He let that sink in a moment before continuing. "Or so we were *led* to believe."

Now that he had their attention, he held on to the silence for a few more moments. He so relished this type of drama. Standing up, he commenced pacing about the room while he searched through the pages he had printed out.

"The last recorded person to have this tablet fragment was S.S. Haupt Lieutenant Erich Stemmler, a high ranking official in the Nazi hierarchy whose main job was to catalogue all the items such as paintings and artifacts stolen from various museums and private individuals' collections during their occupations.

"Let's see, ah, yes, here it is." He fumbled to another page and quickly eyed it.

"After the war some Nazis were given sanctuary by the equivalent - back then - of Russia's KGB. So I decided to crack into their files and see what they had on this Stemmler. It turns out they had quite a lot – especially for some reason his sexual proclivities, which we can go into if you want at another time."

He looked over his glasses meaningfully at Dutch and Diandra, cutting his eyes toward Sam. Sam rolled his eyes and snorted at the implication.

"But that's not relevant right now. It seems that, in exchange for their sparing his life, he cut a deal. He turned over some of the stolen art treasures from the Dresden Museum to the Russians. As you are no doubt aware, they were very anal about their record keeping, and so I found an old document that listed all the items he gave them. And there, buried away between the listing of a Monet and a Napoleonic Russian lacquer box, was the tablet. It turns out that the Dresden Museum was bombed *after* this exchange took place."

Diandra could hardly contain herself.

"So where is it?"

"That's the irony of this whole search, Diandra. It is back in Dresden. After the war, they rebuilt the museum and moved hundreds of boxes back into it. It is in one of those boxes." he replied.

"Nice job, Skip. See, I told you he was the best," Dutch said, turning to Diandra and then back to ask, "You find out anything else?"

"Yes. It's official. I'm now wanted in one hundred and eight countries. Your government boys know they pinched the wrong chap."

* * * * * * *

Chapter Thirteen

Vatican City, Roma

Lilne burst into Cardinal Assanti's office over the objections of his frail male secretary. Assanti raised his hand to the man.

"It is alright, Brother Dowling," Assanti said. The secretary acknowledged the gesture with a slight bow and left the room, closing the door. Lilne glared at Assanti.

"To what do I owe your presence here, Lilne?" Assanti calmly asked.

"Certain information has come to my attention that I need to confirm with you," Lilne replied as he walked toward the desk.

"A phone call would not suffice?" Assanti asked, gesturing toward the handset on his desk.

"I could not trust that your phone line is secure. It seems there have been calls that may have been… monitored."

Assanti nodded and pointed to a chair in front of his desk. "What is it that you want to know?"

Lilne took a seat and tapped his fingers together, staring at Assanti, who waited patiently.

"One of the members of our order has revealed himself to be a traitor. We have discovered that he was releasing information about our archives to an outside source."

"This is a serious matter."

"Indeed," Lilne replied, continuing to hold his gaze. "We tried him before the full tribunal regarding the matter."

"Why was this done without my knowledge?" Assanti demanded. "I am the Holy Father's Cardinal *in pectore,* and-"

"You were unavailable," Lilne interrupted.

"I should have been consulted."

"I was appointed by Vatican Council. It is I who will decide such things," Lilne dismissively answered.

"I see," Assanti replied. "And where is he now?"

"He escaped. And he has added to his crimes by taking certain artifacts that were in our custody. We have operatives looking for him." Lilne paused. "It appears he is receiving help from someone within these very walls."

Assanti thought for a moment, then asked,

"Which artifacts?"

"That is irrelevant," Lilne answered, raising his voice. "Just know that I will use my considerable resources to pursue this matter."

"McIntyre must not be harmed, Lilne," Assanti said, frowning.

"Who are you to tell me what must or must not be done? Have you forgotten to whom you speak?" A vein throbbed in Lilne's forehead. "My authority shall never be questioned. I will not be ordered around like one of your church minions."

Assanti took a breath and leaned back in his chair. "Forgive me, then. May I suggest you exercise mercy and let us reform and return him back into the fold of our flock?"

Lilne's angry eyes assessed the question.

"That will depend entirely on his actions. In the meantime, do not act foolishly. Remember our covenant. And remind the Holy Father as well. It would be unwise to go around us directly to your 'flock' at this time."

Assanti nodded as Lilne stood up.

"You said you were here to confirm some information," Assanti reminded him, standing up and walking around the desk.

Lilne stared at him for a moment. "I never mentioned who the traitor was. It came from your lips."

Unfazed, Assanti raised his hand and made the sign of the cross before Lilne.

"May the lord be with you," he said.

"He is," Lilne replied tersely as he turned to leave the room. "It is you who may need *your* Lord's help."

* * * * * * *

Location Unknown

Sitting in front of his laptop in a dark corner of a non-descript room, a man known to others only as Shadow Man typed away. His flickering silhouette danced against the large blowups of McIntyre and Dutch that were pinned against the wall in front of him, a fireplace roaring behind him. Maps of northern Africa and the United States flanked their pictures on both sides.

On his screen he entered a search for 'Vorhees'. A dozen or so entries appeared. He refined the search by entering +Military +Special Forces, and tried again. On the screen, two choices appeared: Peter Vorhees and John Vorhees. He highlighted Peter and then pressed the enter key.

A picture of Dutch with a military jacket appeared. He clicked it to open and started reading.

What he read confirmed much that he already knew. Dutch joined the Army in 1990 after bouncing around from various corporate jobs for four years after college and serving in the ROTC, having graduated at the top in his class. Through a special arrangement with the Air Force, he had the choice to enter flight school, but was not guaranteed a position flying jet aircraft, so he entered Special Forces training, where he again graduated number one in his class. He learned Arabic and Turkish, quickly rising through the ranks and attaining the status of Lieutenant Colonel.

Vorhees specialized in dangerous drop missions. These involved being inserted solo into hostile zones. Once there, he would gather reconnaissance and return with ground and personnel intelligence, including pictures that would clear the way for either air and/or ground support to get in and accomplish their mission.

He'd completed twenty-six successful sorties including missions in Cambodia, Vietnam, Libya, and Afghanistan. Due to a misunderstanding with a superior officer over his wife, he was transferred to a field unit where he commanded a team that was inserted into Chechynichin. However, something had gone wrong with the mission. No details were available. The records showed only that there was a court martial, in which Vorhees testified against two fellow officers. The results of the hearing were permanently sealed and remained unavailable.

Vorhees retired shortly following this incident after eight years of service, although, interestingly, the trail of information revealed that he still kept an office at the Pentagon.

Shadow Man concluded that the retirement was in name only. He continued to refine his search and discovered a wedding announcement for the following year in the New York Times. Pulling it up, he found a portrait of Vorhees and Diandra, tastefully composed, and wondered if the marriage had any more credibility than the groom's employment status. Beneath the portrait he found a short bio on Diandra that mentioned her job at the New York Museum of Natural History.

Entering Diandra's name and New York as the location, a yellow page listing of her suburban address with a telephone number popped conveniently into view, followed by a beep, beep from his computer. Another document showed up on the screen; a photographic copy of the court filing of divorce papers by Diandra, dated over two years earlier.

He sat back, gently rubbing his chin while considering his next move. It could be a dead end and a wasted trip. Then again, she could be just the bait he needed to catch Dutch. So what if she turned out to be a dead end. Who knows? She looked like she'd be fun.

For a while, anyway.

* * * * * * *

Chapter Fourteen

Scarsdale, New York

Smoke billowed above the range as Dutch attempted to cook up a typical military breakfast – bacon and eggs. He never had gotten used to the convection burners on the Jen-air stove, and so they were inevitably either too hot or not hot enough. In this case, the bacon got the worst of it. He took out the burnt strips and threw a new batch in, causing the cast iron skillet to sizzle and smoke even more.

Diandra, Sam and Skip were poring over reference books and maps. Looking up over the crumpled piles of paper scattered everywhere on the kitchen table, Diandra surveyed her not so former husband as he hunched over the stove, curling her lips while shaking her head. *He never could cook either,* she recalled.

"Too bad we can't order out for breakfast," Diandra wryly observed loud enough for him to hear. "Looks like it'll be a while."

"I'm getting the hang of it. Just hold on there," Dutch said, waving the spatula like a conductor's baton.

"'I'm not sure I have enough porcine on hand until you do." She winked at Skip who was *almost* humored by the scene.

For the past few hours they had scoured over the dozens of books and research papers Diandra had used as references for her own book. They had been stored in her garage, since she was afraid to take them to her office and risk being discovered. In each case they found the same references and citations for the tablet – meaning that although there were literally hundreds of different publications mentioning the Macedonian tablet, they all emanated from one source. And that source appeared to be a certain Russian antiquities authority in 1947.

Diandra was most concerned by the lack of any references to the tablet before that time, especially regarding the language it was written in. Although there were no known pictures of the tablet, a couple of drawings of the tablet fragment were completed on site when it was first discovered. However, these only served as a reference point and did not accurately depict what the symbols and cuneiform type markings really looked like.

The only good news in the research so far was the discovery that they were drawn by Antoine Montfort, an artist known for his meticulous, detailed renderings. His etchings were later published by the Louvre in a compendium that included many of Jean-Leon Gerome's famous sketches from Napoleon's occupation of the Middle East.

Based on these drawings, Diandra and Sam were convinced that the symbols were either modeled on or directly descended from the Mesopotamian script, a descendant of Sumerian script. This was encouraging to them both.

Skip, in the meantime, returned to his computer with a fresh cup of tea to see what he could unearth regarding the symbols. To his dismay and at the expense of his mildly bruised ego, he still hadn't a clue as to what they meant. Finally surrendering to the olfactory lure of breakfast, he joined the others in the kitchen.

Diandra nursed another cup of cafe Americano while Sam, unable to contain his excitement, jiggled his leg, his knee tapping against the table bottom.

"Come on now. Let's not get off the point." Sam pleaded. "If the tablet is in the Dresden museum, why haven't we heard about it? For sure there would have been some sort of an announcement or something."

"I'm guessing either they don't know they have it… or they haven't figured out what it is yet," Skip offered. "After the wall came down, things turned pretty chaotic over there." He paused. "And, could you please stop bumping the table? I find it utterly annoying and it does nothing for my concentration."

"Oh, sorry," Sam said, abashed like a little boy caught picking his nose. "So," he attempted to redeem himself with the truly formidable amount of knowledge stored in his brain, "the find of the century and it's just sitting there? That's sick!"

Skip looked quizzically over at him and then Diandra for clarification. She was too excited to try to explain this foreign terminology to him. She'd made a decision and needed to sell it.

"I say we go get it," she blurted.

That got their attention. Including Dutch's, who'd been listening a little more than he should have instead of focusing his attention on his chef duties at the stove.

"Well, think about it," Diandra continued, "if we alert the local officials, or even the Archeological Society, they'll snap it up and keep it out of sight until they've deciphered it. And then who knows? Maybe they'll lock it away or keep it only for viewing by approved archeologists as they did with the Dead Sea Scrolls."

"So what you're saying is," chimed in Skip, "it's sort of a mercy mission. We'd, in fact, be liberating it rather than stealing it?"

Diandra nodded in enthusiastic agreement.

"Exactly!" she exclaimed, then she frowned as she realized Skip was yanking her chain. He winked at Dutch, who cracked up. She shot Dutch a knock it off look.

"Oh come on guys," she dared. "As Sam just said, this truly is the find of the century. Trust me…it's big."

Dutch gave up on the morning's menu and walked over to the table, retiring the checkered cook's apron that he knew looked ridiculous.

"It does seem simple enough," he started. "It's not like it's behind enemy lines or anything. And if they don't know what they have, how heavily guarded could it be? I mean, it is a museum, right?" The group nodded in agreement, except Skip. *Good*, he thought, *that's the right attitude to sell this thing.*

"And at the very least, I'm sure there would be a reward for finding it," he added in an undertone.

"That's not the point," Diandra rebutted. "This could be one of the greatest archeological discoveries of all time. And we could be the ones to make it happen. We've got to at least try to find it."

Dutch stared at Diandra while she fidgeted, waiting for his answer.

"So let's do it. Are you in?' Dutch finally asked her.

"You know I'm in!"

"If Diandra's in, I'm in," Sam volunteered.

"Well, there's a surprise." Dutch said while rolling his eyes. "This isn't a tourist vacation we're planning here. Necessary personnel only. You can wait here and guard the fort until we bring back the missing piece."

"Oh yeah. I forgot. I'm not a trained killer, just the dumb ass *kid*," he pouted. "But tell me this, Rambo. What are you going to do if you can't get the tablet? What if you get right next to it and can only look at it, huh? What are you going to do then?"

"What is he talking about?" Dutch asked Diandra.

"He's talking about translating it," Diandra nodded her understanding. "From what we can tell, it's probably written in either early Chaldean or maybe some form of Sumerian. If that was the case, Sam's one of the only people that can read and translate these types of languages on site."

"I'm fluent in over a dozen languages, Mister G I Joe," Sam interrupted her. "There's more than muscle between my ears, unlike some-"

"Okay, Sam," Diandra intervened. "He's got a point, Dutch. If the museum realizes what it is they have, they may not even let us photograph it, let alone take it. Sam could easily read and translate it on the spot."

Pretty good advice, Dutch thought. Although he didn't want to put up with Sam's testosterone driven fascination with his wife, or soon to be ex-wife, in the middle of a mission, it seemed he had no choice.

"Okay, that makes sense," he relented.

He turned his attention to Skip, the wildcard. Dutch knew he needed his technical knowhow or it might not work.

"What do you say, Skip?"

"I'm not so sure, old boy," he hedged. "It seems a bit risky for my blood. I'm more the cerebral type you know? Command Central? This is a bit in the thick of things…"

"Come on now, *James Bond*," Dutch teased. "When have I ever steered you wrong?"

Wrong question to ask.

"Oh I don't know, Kurdistan, Athens, Libya, the list is quite extensive," Skip delivered back, deadpan. He was about to add a few more countries to the list when Dutch interrupted him in his incorrigible way.

"It'll be an adventure," he prodded. "Not like the other times." Dutch waved his hand as if to dismiss those past experiences as trivial. "We really do need you, Skip. In fact, I don't know that we can pull it off without you." This last line was delivered with a beseeching look that was designed to massage Skip's ego.

Skip sat motionless, silent with all eyes on him. He felt ridiculously trapped, sensing that respecting his better judgment would only weaken an eventual outcome. From the first moment he learned of the tablet's existence, he knew he was going, whether he thought it wise or not. Still, he stalled for a few moments… for dramatic effect. It gave him so much pleasure to make Dutch squirm, if only for a little bit.

Finally, he smiled. "Well, I suppose my face is probably on the side of every milk carton in this uncivilized country by now. And who knows? The former Eastern bloc might be nice this time of year."

"Alright then, it's settled," Dutch said. "I'm going to take the car and run some errands. Skip, you must still have a stash of your *toys* hidden somewhere, right?"

Skip nodded affirmatively.

"And a passport, since they may be looking for you at the airport?"

"Three, actually," Skip answered. "Always be prepared, say I."

"Okay. We'll pick those up and get back here around…" Dutch looked at his watch, "noon. Sam, we'll pick up whatever you need on the way to the airport-"

"Wait a second," Diandra interrupted. "When I said we should go I didn't mean in a couple of hours. How are we going to pay for this trip? We need to set things up. There are calls to be made and details to go over."

Dutch thought for a moment, aware of Diandra's need to have all in order, always. She was most comfortable in risk-aversion, which was part of their long-standing differences in modi operandi.

"Here's my theory, Di," he started. "We need to act now. I've seen things like this happen before. If we know about it, then someone else can and probably will find out about it. There's this weird sort of synergistic relationship, sometimes called critical mass.

"I've seen over and over again where the same ideas or thoughts show up at the same time to different people. So the quicker we act, the better chance we'll have to beat anyone else looking for it. We can make all the arrangements while we're on the plane. And as for the money, I've recently completed a rather profitable deal."

Diandra groaned and shook her head.

Dutch raised a finger. "*So*… I'll finance the entire mission, or trip, or whatever you want to call it. If there is a reward or anything else, you can just reimburse me, and maybe include a *small* gratuity? If not, well, that's the roll of the dice, isn't it? And as to time, I'm available, Skip seems to be unemployed and let's face it, Di, you're somewhat unemployed at this point anyway."

"I still have a job," Sam said, looking at Diandra. "I think I do, anyway?"

"I'll call Margaret and get you a week off," Diandra told him. "She owes me that much."

"Any other concerns?" Dutch asked the group.

Silence, as they looked at each other, collective breath held.

"Great. Let's get going." Dutch clapped his hands and moved toward the door.

"Hey, how about bringing us back something to eat?" Diandra dug at him, half kidding and half hungry.

"Yeah sure. I'll stop by Nathan's and get something to go," he said with a wink.

"Come on, Skip," he yelled, motioning with the keys.

As he exited the door, the three looked at each other.

"What's with his sudden interest in archeology?" Sam asked Diandra.

"He read my book," she answered, shaking her head. "He knows the completed tablet is rumored to lead to Alexander's tomb and the treasure within it."

"Ah," Skip and Sam nodded as Skip hurried out the door to catch up with Dutch.

* * * * * * * *

Vatican City

Conducting mass, Cardinal Assanti was dressed in the traditional choir dress of a Cardinal: scarlet cassock, mozetta and birreta covered by a white rochet, trimmed with lace and a pectoral cross. He reverently walked up to the ornately carved altar of the Vatican's smaller private chapel and genuflected. Opening the golden doors of the 13th century golden tabernacle, he pulled out the Eucharist chalice and a small glass vessel trimmed with gold full of red wine.

He carefully picked up a Eucharist from the chalice, raised it and spoke.

"Benedictus Deus. Hoc repraesental corpus domino nostril. Panis et spiritum et vitam fidei."

Placing it in his mouth, he bowed before the effigy of Christ hanging on the cross. Next, he picked up the vessel of wine and poured part of it into the chalice.

"Benedictus Deus. Hic est sanguis Domini nostri Jesu Christi, Panis et vinculum fidei nostrae confirmationem"

Drinking it, he set the chalice down and gave a sign of the cross, his hand outstretched. Turning to offer the small congregation of priests and brothers a blessing, he gasped, grabbing his chest. His face went ashen as he fell to one knee, struggling to stay erect. Priests ran up to help as he slumped over and hit the ground.

From the shadows of a confessional, Lilne observed the entire incident, as shouts for help and confusion reigned.

* * * * * * * *

Scarsdale, New York

After Dutch left, Diandra remembered something; she had received three letters from a patient in a private sanitarium in Spring Valley, New York, about five years earlier. Writing them off at the time as ramblings from a troubled mind, she nevertheless filed them away and thought nothing more about them. However, what jarred her memory was the fact they had included some symbols within them that made no sense. In thinking about it, she thought she remembered them being similar to the ones that were contained in McIntyre's letter.

Searching through her files, she found the letters. They were from a D.R. Werner. *Funny*, she then thought. *I wonder if he is related to the Dr. Werner from the Lower Honduras site*. She'd never connected the two.

Sure enough, two of the symbols matched. She called the hospital to confirm he was still there, and asked if she could see him. He was in lockdown, but they would get back to her if he should be able to take visitors.

When Dutch returned, she told him the story and suggested they stop by the sanitarium on the way to the airport. Sam and Skip took a separate cab and agreed to meet up with them in front of Virgin Airlines.

* * * * * * * *

Chapter Fifteen

Spring Valley, New York

Dutch pulled up to the gate of the Spring Valley sanitarium in Diandra's black Ford Explorer. An overweight guard with his shirt barely tucked in greeted them from the guardhouse, clipboard in hand.

"Names, please?" he asked.

"Doctor Diandra Weiss," she replied, authoritatively, leaning over from the passenger's side.

Looking through a list of names on the clipboard, he looked up. "I don't see your name here. I am going to have to ask you to turn around and-"

"Yes I know," Diandra interrupted. "But we just drove from the city to see a D. R. Werner. I believe he is a patient here."

Dutch pulled out a cell phone and started dialing.

"Sorry. Can't help you there," the guard said, gesturing. "If you'll just pull up past the gatehouse and turn around-"

"I'll take care of this," Dutch said raising his hand as the cell phone rang. "Hi. This is Pete Vorhees. Is he in?"

"Who are you calling?" Diandra asked.

"Hey, sorry to bother you, sir," he said, holding up his finger, "but I am in front of," he looked out the car's window to see the name of the facility clearly, "the Spring Hills Sanitarium in Spring Valley. Yes sir. It is really imperative that I be admitted. You mind speaking to my 'guard' friend here? His name is," looking at his badge, "Johnson. Barry Johnson."

"I'm not talking to anyone on that phone," the guard's face reddened in anger. "Now get moving!"

"You hear that?" Dutch spoke into the phone. "Yes sir." Dutch hung up.

The phone rang in the guard's booth. Sauntering in with a full cup of attitude, he set down his clipboard and picked up the phone.

"Hel-lo," he answered. "Excuse me? Uh…" He stood to attention. "Yes sir. No problem sir. Uh, it's a little cold out here but not too bad. Thanks for asking. You too, thank you sir." The guard slowly set the phone in the cradle and turned his attention to Dutch,

"Sorry to delay you," he said. "Drive to the first building on the left.

The gates creaked open as Dutch hit the gas and proceeded through.

"How did you do that?" she asked.

"Low friends in high places," he smiled back.

* * * * * * * *

Tiers of metal doors with paint peeling off them surrounded by cold cement walls greeted Diandra, Dutch and Dr. Matsui as the security door slammed behind them with a loud clank. They followed the railed walkway past dozens of metal doors. Sobbing, screaming and dry heaving echoed throughout, with guards and nurses scurrying about without acknowledging the visitors. Diandra was unsettled by the scene.

Dr. Matsui, a forty something psychiatrist with close cropped hair, read through a chart as he strode down the grated walkway. Dutch noticed that the doors had small windows in them, although he was unable to see behind them.

"Apparently, he is the same Werner you suspected he was," Dr. Matsui stated. "Doctor Everett Werner. He first came here in… Hmmmm… 1948." He seemed surprised at the date. "It says here," he continued, "that he was committed by the courts for having dynamited an archaeology site somewhere in Central America… And that when he returned to the US he also tried to destroy various artifacts in New York's Natural History Museum, and was subsequently arrested. After a psychiatric exam, he was found to be incompetent and committed by the courts to Bellevue in upstate New York.

"Released in 1952, he was arrested again in the mid-west after he tried to desecrate an American Indian holy site. His family had him committed with us at that time, and he hasn't left since. A trustee for the family that handles the estate of his parents has been funding his stay here."

"Why is he still here?" Diandra asked.

"Paranoid schizophrenia. Delusions that the world is coming to an end and that he can stop it. Every subsequent hearing has found him either a danger to himself or others. That's the criterion for involuntary inpatient treatment."

The doctor looked up from the chart and stopped. "This is it."

He peered in the window, reached for a set of keys attached to his belt by a chain and unlocked the door.

"I must warn you, he is considered violent. Watch yourselves." He followed Diandra and Dutch into the room. "Doctor Werner, you have visitors."

As the door squeaked open, a silhouetted man could be seen sitting upright against the wall on the single bed in the corner of the ten by twelve foot room. A television flickered static lines opposite him against the wall.

Overhead, a lone dim fluorescent bulb in a wire cage cast a feeble light. The man on the bed slowly turned and raised his head to reveal a black eye-patch over his left eye. He appeared to be seventy or so years old. Gaunt, grey haired and sallow faced, Dr. Werner slowly smiled, revealing half a mouth of teeth.

"I've been expecting you, Diandra."

Startled, Diandra gazed at him.

"How did you know my name?"

No answer.

Dutch and Diandra glanced toward each other before surveying the cell. The walls were covered with symbols, thousands of them, carved and drawn into the cement. All sizes and shapes, many of them the same as the symbols contained in McIntyre's letter. Dr.

Werner's eye followed them as they viewed the ceilings and walls. Diandra looked to Dutch who raised his shoulders; he was just as dumbfounded as she was.

"Interesting, yes?" Dr. Werner asked.

Diandra turned to Dr. Matsui.

"Would it be possible to be alone with him for a few minutes?" Diandra inquired.

"It would be a breach of security protocol-"

"I will be able to handle any problems, Dr. Matsui." Dutch interjected.

Matsui looked at Dutch, sized him up and nodded affirmatively.

"As you wish. Five minutes. I'll be right outside the door," he said, gesturing.

As the door clanked shut Diandra pulled out a group of letters from her purse.

"I'm here about these."

"I know, he replied. "I've been wondering how long it would take for you to seek me out."

"What do you mean?"

"I mean," he continued, sitting up straight in the bed, "that the time is now. The unearthing."

"I'm not sure I understand," she said, moving a little closer toward him.

"Of course you don't. Yet."

He pulled out a cigarette, slowly struck a stick match on the wall and lit it with nicotine-stained fingers. After a long inhale, he stared at Diandra.

"I hold all the secrets to the world, right here," he said, pointing to his head. "They say I am mad. Delusional." He laughed. "Perhaps I am." He took another inhale and blew the noxious smoke toward a vent in the ceiling.

"At first I couldn't handle it. The knowledge. Almost lost my mind. But I beat them. Came back. And I know."

"Dr. Werner, you're not making sense. I came here to ask you about the symbols you sent me-"

"The world must be warned!" he shouted.

Diandra took a step back as Dutch moved in closer until he was nearly between them. Placing a hand on Dutch's arm, she took a breath and then asked softly.

"Warned about what?"

"You saw part of it."

"A part of…" Diandra gave Dutch a quizzical look. He shrugged.

"At the Rejaunto Phantasma site in Lower Honduras," Dr. Werner continued. "I saw you on TV. I could tell that you felt the energy, just like I did. Only I learned too much. I did not understand. I was not worthy."

He sat up straighter in the bed and licked his lips.

"Humans have always been rather easy to deceive, Diandra… because they want to believe. In something. Anything. This has been exploited by those in power, the *real* people that control everything from behind the curtain, since the beginning of our race, in order to obfuscate our discovering who we really are. Our true nature. Our possibilities."

Swinging his legs over the side of the bed, he rose and began pacing, waving his cigarette for emphasis. "They even tried to manufacture a major calamity, supposedly predicted by the Maya."

Diandra moved out of his path. "Are you referring to the two-thousand and twelve Mayan calendar?"

"Yes, yes," he interrupted her with a dismissive swing of his arm. "As we now know, they made a fundamental dating error. The true date is two thousand and sixty-seven. But that is not important. It's all smoke and mirrors. It was designed to fool us until…"

"Until what?" Diandra asked.

"Until it is too late," he answered with a sigh.

Diandra gathered her thoughts. "What has this to do with the symbols in your letter?"

Dr. Werner stopped pacing and smiled. "Unlocking the truth. They can help lead you. You see, every monument, every ancient society, every thread of knowledge that has been handed down speaks of an end of days. An apocalyptic event. So let me ask you this, Doctor Weiss; how would they know? And, more importantly, what is it that awaits us… and when?"

"Do you know?" Diandra asked, skeptically.

"No," he answered, dropping the cigarette to the floor and squashing it out. "Or, rather, yes, but it is not up to me anymore. I can only help guide you."

Silence.

"Don't you get it?" he continued. "You are the key now, Diandra. I'm not sure why, but you have been chosen to warn the world. I tried. They laughed. I told them about the guardians, the keepers, about the…" He checked himself, frowning.

"About the what?" Diandra put one hand to her head, overcome with a sudden wave of dizziness. "I don't know what you are talking about!"

Dutch reached for her as Werner's eye went wide and his body lurched into spasm. He fell back onto the bed, writhing.

Checking to make sure Diandra was okay, Dutch moved to Werner and bent over the bed. "Doctor Werner?" No response. As he touched the man's chest, Dutch was thrown back into the wall as if by an electric shock.

"Aaaah!" Dutch shook his head to clear it. "What was that? Jesus!"

"Leave him alone!" Diandra shook off her dizziness, knelt and scooted nearer the bed, still on her knees but not touching him.

"Enuma, elish la babu shamua," Dr. Werner began to babble.

"W-what the--" Dutch stuttered.

"Shhh!" Diandra cocked her head, listening as Werner repeated the phrase over and over, his single eye rolled back into his head.

"It's some version of Sumerian," she whispered finally. "I think he wants me to… break the part… you must break something."

A key scraped into the lock as Werner's convulsions became more violent, rocking the bed.

"What's going on here?" Dr Matsui demanded to know as he entered the room then raced to the bed, pushing a panic button on the wall as he passed by. "He's having a grand mal seizure."

An alarm began to sound from the hall.

"Dr. Werner!" Diandra screamed.

"We can't have him swallow his tongue. Move back out of the way." Dr Matsui rolled him to his side on the bed. "It's time you leave," he stated authoritatively. "Guards," he shouted.

Footsteps were heard in the distance rushing toward the cell.

"Come on Di, we need to get to the airport," Dutch urged as he grabbed her arm to pull her out the door.

"Wait a minute," she said as she wrenched away.

His convulsions subsiding, Werner murmured incoherently, slowly opening his teary eye and focusing it upon Diandra.

"What did you mean, Doctor Werner?" she asked, watching him with worried eyes. "What were you saying about breaking something?"

Werner motioned for her to come closer but Matsui put his hand against her, holding her back

"Everything is connected," Werner struggled to tell her. "You've got to… find the link to who we are and our destiny. Listen to the music, it will lead you." His breathing became more labored and he lurched toward Diandra, falling off the bed despite Dr. Matsui's hold on him.

"Don't be fooled by appearances!" he screamed, arm outstretched toward her. "You must discover the knowledge on your own to understand it."

"Guards!" Dr Matsui yelled again as he stood and pushed Dutch and Diandra into the hall. They watched as two burly men in white uniforms rushed into the room, one with a straight jacket, the other with a hypodermic.

He struggled against the staff, voice strained in desperation..

"They knew this information could fall into the wrong hands, Diandra!" he shouted. "They planned for it. Listen to the music. Break the code. Remember... there are nine sides to this riddle."

The doctor plunged a needle into Werner's arm.

"Break the code!" echoed throughout the ward as Dutch and Diandra were escorted forcibly through the locked doors.

* * * * * * *

"What was that Yoda-like moment all about?" Dutch asked, shaken, as they walked to the car. "And what about that shock I got? Was that from him? What—"

"I'm not sure," Diandra interrupted. "I... I just don't know what's happening Dutch. But he obviously knows about the symbols, and perhaps even what they may mean."

"I admit seeing them on the wall was pretty spooky. But if you ask me, he's a sandwich short of a full picnic basket." Dutch said. "Earth to Werner! Come in, come in!" he mocked with an invisible phone to his head.

Diandra shook her head and forced a laugh as they reached the car.

"So what exactly was he talking about with you and that site in the Honduras?" Dutch asked.

"Nothing," she lied, looking back at the sanitarium. "Crazy or not, he gave us a clue."

"What was that," Dutch asked.

"A date," she answered. "Although I am not sure how it is connected, I'll pass it on to Skip and follow up with Doctor Werner when we get back."

* * * * * * * *

Chapter Sixteen

Queens, New York

Even on its best day, Kennedy International Airport was a nightmare. And since 9/11 the congestion had multiplied ten-fold. The group of four elbowed their way past the mobs of people staring like deer in headlights up at the arrival and departure screens, blocking the unrelenting flow of foot traffic that rushed by. Dutch headed toward a ticket counter while pointing the group to a waiting area.

* * * * * * * * *

Skip was busy typing away as Sam sat next to him, looking over his shoulder while also texting on his smart phone. Diandra had sunk into a chair across the aisle from them and had taken out a book to read. Dutch made his way to the group, carefully avoiding the current of people crossing the walkway in hurried non-awareness.

"We're booked and ready to go," Dutch informed them as he handed back their passports.

"First class, I presume?" Skip sarcastically asked without looking up from his laptop.

"Skip, that really hurts." Dutch feigned. Now *he* waited a moment, just for dramatic effect. "Of course we are."

"You are still full of surprises," Skip quipped, without missing a stroke on the keyboard. Dutch pulled out a ticket and a passport, looked at it with amusement and handed them to Skip.

"So are you, Mr. Jed Clampett. I suppose you think that's funny?"

"Well, you must admit, your TSA agency isn't staffed with the brightest light bulbs in the lot now, are they?" Skip replied as he looked up at Dutch. "Yobbs and wanks the lot of them. Seems they're best qualified to feel up the family jewels, if you know what I mean."

"Nor are they old enough to get the joke. But if they do, your family jewels will be the least of your problems," Dutch said. Skip appeared nonplussed. "So what are you two up to?" Dutch asked as he positioned himself to get a better view of Skip's computer screen

"We may need to access and crash our way into various sites and systems along the way," Skip started. "Seeing how we don't have any government cover for this rogue operation, I'm setting up a ghost account and name to run it all through. But I tell you, Dutch, I don't like for one moment we're using this airport's crappy ass Wi-Fi encryption system. Bloody hell, Helen Keller could crack it wide open. But it is safer than using a 4G system from our phones – especially given the NSA's proclivity to monitor everything that's ever been spoken or written."

Diandra looked up from her *German for Dummies* book.

"What do you mean, Skip?" she asked.

"He means it is using a rather unsophisticated codec and wireless range in here," Sam chimed in, putting down his smart phone. "Anyone with a modicum of hacking skills could tap into it and grab information from your computer. For instance-"

"Very good, laddy," Skip said, cutting him off.

"Is that the same as kid in American?" Sam wanted to know. "Because if it is, like I've told Dutch-"

Dutch wasn't going to let this go anywhere.

"Skip, it's not like anyone is after us, so it's no big security threat at this point. And I doubt if the *Federales* here would appreciate your putting up a mini-satellite dish in the middle of the airport, just for *our* security's sake" Dutch added.

"You're right about that," Skip agreed. "But I'll feel a lot safer when we are able to encrypt everything onto our own servers."

He moved the computer so Dutch could get a good view of the screen. "So what do you think about this website name I've created?"

"Seek and ye shall find?" Dutch questioned, smiling.

"That's what I based it on."

Diandra looked up again from her book.

"Based what on?" Diandra asked.

"It's from the Torah," Sam said. "It's what Professor Standhead would tell us whenever we started a new dig."

"I like it," Dutch said. "It describes us perfectly."

"Does seem pretty appropriate, doesn't it?" Skip added, obviously pleased with himself. "I did end up spending a large chunk of your money on the name."

"Nothing ventured, nothing gained," Dutch responded.

"What?' Diandra asked again. "What are you calling us?"

* * * * * * * *

Simultaneously, at another location, a laptop computer emitted a loud beep and up popped an urgent message on the plasma screen from ICANN, the international registry for domain names.

Fingers typed away on the keyboard as the message was opened and displayed on the screen:

'Your search and inquiry has resulted in one result. One of the names you submitted has just opened an account. If you would like to see it please press 'enter'. A finger hit the key and up popped:

www.TheSeekers.com

On another laptop a billing record was displayed showing a credit card transaction from American Express for Pete Vorhees. Four one-way first-class tickets were purchased for a flight to Berlin, Germany. The names were all listed.

A smile gleamed on Shadowman's face. In a sinister low-pitched voice he whispered to himself:

"Credit cards. Don't leave home without them."

* * * * * * * * *

Chapter Seventeen

Vatican City, Rome

A black Mercedes S-600 limousine scattered pigeons from its path as it glided through the back alleys of Vatican City and effortlessly screeched to a stop. The impeccably dressed driver exited and hurried to the rear of the car as the gull winged rear door opened upward. Whirring noises emanated from under the car as a platform extended and plopped onto the wet cobblestone street. An umbrella sprang open from the driver's hand as a man in a wheelchair descended the short ramp, rolled over the cobblestones and entered the large wooden door that opened before him. Identical Swiss Guards stood at attention and eyed the mysterious stranger as he wheeled past both of them and into the Vatican.

Flanked by two additional Swiss Guards, he was quickly ushered down a long hallway covered on both sides by dimly lit 16th and 17th century old masters' paintings of various styles. At the end of the hall they turned left and approached two more Swiss Guards standing in front of a large, gothic carved wooden door with a gargoyle sitting atop the door's header, carved out of stone. Large candles attached to the walls cast shadows over the entire scene.

The Swiss Guards stood at attention as the wheelchair bound visitor was whisked through the door and into the room.

Inside, hundreds of votive candles of various colors sat on myriads of stadium type rows of wrought iron against the walls. Incense burned from a solid gold goblet sitting upon a small wooden altar, graced with a mural of Jesus behind it. In the far right corner stood a raised poster bed with stylized lions' heads atop the four posts, peering out like lighthouses. Cardinal Assanti was lying on the bed; gaunt, pale and with dark circles underlining his sunken eyes.

Assanti weakly motioned the guest to come toward him, holding out his hand. When able, the man grasped it gently and kissed his ring.

"Thank you for coming, my old friend," Assanti mumbled with difficulty.

"I came as soon as I heard about…" the stranger's voice trailed off. For a split second, a slight smile graced Assanti's face.

"Have they discovered what happened?" the stranger asked.

"They know nothing, and yet they try to cure me, in vain I am afraid. If I am correct in my guess, there is no hope for me." He coughed laboriously.

"There is always hope, as long as there is life-"

Assanti motioned for silence with his hand. Moments passed.

"How long has it been, forty years?" Assanti warmly asked.

"And then some, your grace."

Assanti eyed the man and motioned. "Come closer, my friend, for it labors me to speak."

The man leaned in from his wheelchair. Assanti grabbed his hand.

"I am going to ask my first and only favor of you. There is much to share, and I've not much time." He coughed again. "I need your help."

"Anything you ask," he replied.

"It is not for me. The fate of humanity may depend upon what I am about to tell you."

* * * * * * * *

Lilne's private phone rang as he sifted through papers on a desk in his sparsely furnished office within the Vatican. He picked up the receiver.

"Yes?"

"I have an update for you on that matter we spoke about a few days ago," a low gravelly voice spoke.

"Hold on," he told the caller as he pressed the hold button.

He rose and walked around his desk to close the office door. Returning, he sat down while hitting the speaker button.

"Continue," he said.

"I had no luck in finding any trace of our primary target. My men inform me that the trail has grown cold. But I have had some success with the secondary target. It seems they have created a web-site and-"

"They?" Lilne interrupted, impatiently.

"Yes. In addition to Vorhees there are three other people. I will email you their bios in a few minutes. As I was saying," his gravelly voice continued, "they created a web site, which I was able to penetrate. There was an encrypted file containing a copy of an old KGB list of artifacts confiscated near the end of World War II, that now apparently reside in a museum in Dresden. One of the items on that list was highlighted."

"Which one?" Lilne demanded to know.

"A tablet fragment. The item number on this list is NTR0497. Mean anything to you?"

"Indeed, it's the missing half of the Macedonian tablet." Lilne sat back in his chair and took a deep breath. *It did exist!*

"They will undoubtedly be headed to Dresden," Lilne continued.

"It's where they *are* headed right now," the gravelly voice continued. "They just purchased tickets to Berlin for the four of them."

"I see." Lilne said, pinching the bridge of his nose in thought. Then, leaning forward, he picked up a pen and made a note. "Meet them there. They must not get hold of that tablet under any circumstances."

"I understand."

"Perhaps they are also meeting McIntyre, and you can kill two birds with one stone."

"Your meaning?"

"I know about you and Vorhees," Lilne stated.

"It is of no concern of yours. Nor will it compromise the mission. I will take care of your problem and even up the score on mine. No charge to you."

"What about these three other people?"

"If they get in the way, then you'll really be getting a bargain."

There was a moment of silence while Lilne digested this, then he nodded to himself.

"This situation is escalating rapidly. I need to be assured it will be resolved, quickly," Lilne told him.

"Do not worry, Monsignor," the gravelly voice assured him, "I am personally going to take care of this matter. There will be no mistakes."

The phone line went dead.

* * * * * * * *

"There is something I have never shared with you," Assanti continued, "and it is critical that you understand what I am about to say.

"The church became aware, hundreds of years ago, that something catastrophic would befall the Earth. We are not sure what it is that will happen. Only that it has happened before in the past, and that it will come to pass again."

"Are you sure?" asked the stranger.

"Yes. Tantalizing clues tell us of it. We still have millions of tablets and scrolls from our Christian Crusade excursions into the Middle East that have not been studied, which may hold answers. But certain things we do know. Whatever the event, it will be witnessed by the entire planet. It is extremely disruptive and devastating. No doubt the flood of our Bible was connected to it, although that was an account of the *effect* of the cataclysm, not the cause.

"Is there anything else?"

He struggled to catch another breath as his eyes searched for his next thought.

"I am not sure how to preface this," he stated, struggling for breath. "Whatever I say, and whatever you learn, your faith in the church must never waiver."

The stranger nodded.

"We have shared a love for archeology and truth for many years, yes? And the questions of the anomalous discoveries found that cast doubt as to its accuracy have been many. There is a reason for this. However, even on my deathbed I am sworn to secrecy as to why. What I can say is the history we believe… regarding mankind and creation, is not true. Our understanding of the theological aspect of our life on Earth is completely wrong. Once you understand why, then you can start to appreciate the predicament the church is in, and why it needs your help."

Assanti's face grimaced as he moaned in pain.

"We are the Shepherds of mankind's soul," he finally continued, grabbing another labored breath. "That will never change. As a church, it must be our main focus. As to the question of how we were created, that is another matter." He coughed and struggled for another breath, holding up his hand for the stranger to be patient. "You can be the instrument of the gods to make that happen," he continued.

"Gods, your grace?"

"I have said too much, and I grow weaker. There is a Cardinal, McIntyre, who may now hold the key; a book that may shed light on all that I have shared with you tonight. He has been working for me to help parse out this information to one of the archeologists whose career we have been supporting. She wrote the book I suggested you publish.

"Doctor Weiss?"

"Yes. In that regard, I have used you to help further my plan. It is possible he may try and contact this woman, so keep a close eye on her and continue, as in the past, to fund her digs. It is very important that you protect McIntyre and his discovery, and to get it released to the world."

"Yes, of course. Is there anything else I can do?"

Struggling to roll over on his elbow, he turned to face the stranger.

"There is one more thing. By coming here, you are now in great danger. There is a man…" He started to cough hoarsely and struggled to catch his breath. "That is funny," he continued. "He is not a man… at least, not as we think…"

His coughs had turned to convulsions as the stranger shouted for help from outside the door. Assanti's breaths shortened as two medical personnel followed by Swiss Guards rushed into the room and reached him. Blood spurted from his lips as he stretched out his right hand and tried to make the sign of the cross for the stranger. A slight smile, followed by blank eyes, appeared as the final breath left his body, and all movement ceased.

* * * * * * *

Chapter Eighteen

Dresden, Germany

Plush reclining first class seats supplied some much needed rest for Diandra and Sam – they slept most of the way from New York's JFK to Berlin's airport. Skip made use of that time to access Dresden's city plans and digest what information was available about the museum -- its floor plans and other details using the spotty international internet service the airline provided for first class passengers.

Diandra noticed that Dutch seemed to be pretty tired when they were deboarding the plane and making their way toward customs. She remarked more than once about it. Casually brushing it off, he told her he had a lot to think about, which was true. What he didn't tell her was more worrisome.

His first major concern at that moment was getting their belongings through customs. Skip had a few tricks up his sleeve – most of the cases were MI6 issued and had hidden compartments for some of the items he brought. On the way to the airport they had stopped at a courier service that Dutch had used many times before, and dropped off *his* package. They specialized in highly sensitive shipments, used mostly by government officials and the CIA, and had promised it would arrive at a warehouse near Dresden about six hours after they arrived in Berlin. But those six hours seemed like an eternity to Dutch.

When they reached the customs officer Dutch asked to see a supervisor. The burly mustached former Georgian grudgingly obliged and led him to his boss's office. He then returned and asked, in a heavy Russian accent, for Skip and the group to wait while he motioned them aside and started to process an elderly couple that was next in line.

Dutch was pretty sure he could strike a deal with the supervisor, whom he immediately assessed as a pre-cold war politburo relic who clearly was not concerned with what was happening under his supervision. Dutch barely got two words out when the man cut to the bottom line and asked what he was offering? After a not so dispassionate bargaining session ended with an exchange of banknotes, Dutch returned with the supervisor who briefly winked at the customs officer and spoke softly in Russian to him. The officer smiled, nodded his head a little and asked for their passports. He stamped them and then said in perfect English, "Please, have a nice day," and then waved them through.

That was one less thing to worry about. Dutch was thankful that relations had thawed and governments had merged and changed drastically since the wall had come down, or they'd have been jailed for a stunt like that. He was also thankful they weren't familiar with Jed Clampett and the Beverly Hillbillies, although he admitted to himself that it was pretty funny.

The cab ride to Dresden, which was about thirty kilometers southeast of Berlin, passed through the rainy suburbs of three different townships and usually took about thirty minutes. But today was an exception. The traffic police were on strike, so the military had taken over the duties and clearly were out of their league - massive traffic snarls resulted in chaos near the center of the city – jamming up Prager Straße. Although the group's spirits were riding high, their voices became echoes in the background as Dutch repeatedly replayed the events of the last four days in his mind, like an old World War II newsreel, over and over again.

What disturbed him, and what he hadn't shared with Diandra, was Skip's pulling him aside about an hour before they landed. He had never seen Skip out of sorts regarding technical things. Fieldwork? Yes. He was actually a coward at heart. But when it came to surveillance, computer systems, microphones and cameras – almost anything electronic, Skip was his man. What Dutch especially enjoyed was his fanatical attention to detail and security – what his underlings at MI6 used to call his *anal* attention to detail.

But that attention had saved Dutch's butt on more than one occasion, and he had no qualms about it.

But there Skip was, almost uncomfortable in having to tell Dutch what he had just found out, running his hand nervously through his sparse hair. Apparently, someone had hacked their way into the server they were using and accessed the KGB file that was stored on their website. Skip couldn't run his own personal encryption program to save it when he sent it back from the airport because of the limitations and potential conflicts it would create using the airports' WI-FI network. So when he sent it back, it was not security encrypted. And now somebody had a copy of it.

Unfortunately, he was unable to determine what else had been accessed with any certainty, including who they were and where they were going. He was mortified that someone had gotten into the account, and worried as well.

But that wasn't the worst of it. Skip ran a reverse tracker program to find out who or what organization had broken in, hoping in his heart of hearts that it was either some stupid government spider system looking for terrorist info like Carnivore, which was no big deal, or some goofball hacker kid making his bones by proving he could crack into some site randomly.

Neither of these was the case. His search dead-ended at a server in Turkestan that was primarily used by the Russian mafia and rogue terrorist groups. A very sophisticated setup of Trojan horses and phantom sites and servers. Skip had known about the existence of these servers since before he left the Queen's service, but as far as he knew, no one had been able to find out who ran it and where its central headquarters were located.

This meant that now, Dutch had a real problem. He was going into the field, with two untrained operatives, assuming Skip would remain in the background as he normally did, and he had no idea what he might be up against – if anything. This was exactly what he hated. Not enough intelligence to assess the risks and dangers of an operation. He had to assume that somebody was interested; that was established. And it was probably not some academic group, or the source wouldn't have been using that server in the Middle East.

But who, what and why are deadly questions if left unanswered. Dutch reviewed dozens of different scenarios and came up with a hundred different outcomes. Bluntly, he confronted the facts as he knew them.

Fact number one: The incident at Mali's. If he looked back at the whole event with McIntyre under a different lens, it could have all been about the tablet. Taken on its own, it was no big deal. *Oh well*, he had thought at the time, *maybe it was about a bad debt or a lover's quarrel, who knows?* It didn't really matter to him, and he dismissed it at that point. But now it was time to revisit the whole incident in light of this new development.

Fact number two: Their site was hacked, and whoever did it knew about the existence of the other tablet. They *might* not know where yet. That's the only good news.

Fact number three: If someone or some group is after the tablet, and they now know where the other part is, well, men have been killed for a lot less than the Treasure of Alexander.

Dutch looked at his watch. Four more hours until he could get to the shipping company and pick up his only sense of security at that point, his Smith and Wesson chrome plated .45, and a rapid fire .45 Uzi he had shipped before leaving. He'd only included a couple hundred rounds, more than enough he thought at the time. Now, he was not so sure.

He hadn't mentioned to Diandra about the fight with the other men in McIntyre's room when relaying the story to her at dinner, preferring instead to edit the story to both make the point and lighten it up a bit. *It wouldn't have mattered in the end,* he reasoned, *because she still would have wanted to go and get the damn thing anyway – danger or no danger.*

He rubbed his eyes, rolled his shoulders and tried to clear his head. All this thinking and no rest had given him a headache, and he knew he'd be no good to anyone if he didn't get some sleep, and soon. He was going in blind and would need one hundred and ten percent of his attention in order to anticipate what may happen and protect the group.

Maybe I'll be able to catch a few hours at the hotel, he assured himself. That was all he would need to recharge.

* * * * * * * *

Entering the city of Dresden, the cab made its way toward the Zwinger Museum, located near the center of the city. The cab driver explained in labored English how the city had been almost completely destroyed by the allies in February of nineteen forty-five. It had subsequently been rebuilt into the quaint little township it had now become – the city planners retaining the aesthetic of the original architecture designed and constructed under the auspices of the 18th century ruler Augustus the Strong. The museum was now home to many fine treasures including Raphael's 'Sistine Madonna'.

The cab wound its way around and through small cobbled streets and passed directly by the Zwinger, turning right and stopping in front of the City Herberge, a three star hotel that sat directly across the street from the museum. Dutch got out and bee-lined to the front desk. After some spirited haggling with the manager, and the surrender of some American greenbacks, he succeeded in procuring them a couple of rooms on the northwest side, directly facing the Zwinger.

* * * * * * * *

Skip opened his assorted suitcases and other cases while Dutch took a shower. Diandra and Sam were in the adjoining room, Sam getting unpacked and Diandra showering in the other bathroom. Skip pulled out a large can of Lysol and started spraying the desk area, and also his hands, wiping them with a paper towel. Satisfied with his disinfection protocol, he reached into one of his cases and lifted a false bottom, pulling out a satellite dish attached to another one of his Rube Goldberg boxes. Out of another case came different sizes of headphones, cameras, miniature boxes and battery packs, along with various types of glasses. From yet another case he carefully lifted out plasma flat screen monitors – three of them. Dutch came out of the bathroom rubbing his hair with a towel and wrapped in the KMart special bathrobe the hotel had *generously* provided.

"What exactly have you brought, Skip?" Dutch asked.

"Just the usual sort of, you know, spy stuff," he replied, deadpan while continuing hooking everything up. Straightening, he winked at Dutch.

"Okay. I get it," Dutch laughed back. "We'll go over it when we-"

"Wow, look at this stuff," Sam blurted as he entered the room. He visually soaked up every centimeter of Skip's 'control central' like a kid in a toy store. "What is all this?" he asked, moving one hand toward the table.

Diandra walked in behind him toweling her hair in the same chintzy robe. Dutch shot her a 'what are you doing in a robe like that with Sam here look' which she quickly dismissed by rubbing her hair a little harder and looking away. Skip peered around at Sam and Diandra.

"So you like my toys?" Skip asked them, gently guiding Sam's questing fingers away from his bailiwick.

"Man, it's like Mission Impossible on steroids," Sam replied, wide-eyed.

"You're not too far off," Skip answered. "In fact, the producers of that movie checked with MI6 as to what the latest gizmos were they were working on and added some of them into the film."

He reached for a seemingly normal pair of gold wire rim glasses.

"This is the main type of support we'll use for this *mission*," he began, the reference being obvious to all. "At the end of this arm, the part that goes around your ear, is a low frequency emitter that sends signals to your eardrums – basically a headset that no one can hear but you. I can talk to you from here."

He pointed to the junction where the glass frame met the arm.

"Up over here, we have a micro camera and transmitter, black and white unfortunately, since I didn't have time to get my newest stuff. Still, all in all it will send a wonderful picture up to a half-mile away, and I'll be able to hear you clear as a bell. And in this other arm," he pointed, "is the antenna that sends it all back to me."

He set the glasses down and let his explanation sink in, proud of his lesson 101 in spy school.

"Oh, by the way, I forgot," he paused for dramatic effect. "There is a GPS locator in there for good measure that will let me know exactly where you are within fourteen inches."

With that he smiled at Dutch, who returned his smile in spades. *As always, a job well done, Skip,* he thought.

"Just like old times, eh Dutch?" Skip added, "Only this time without wondering whether we're going to be killed or not."

"You know, I don't want to hear about stuff like that," piped in Diandra.

"I do," Sam said enthusiastically.

Diandra shot him a 'knock it off' glare and Sam's shoulders sank a bit.

"So what's the plan?" Diandra asked.

"Room service would be a nice start," Skip suggested.

"*I'll* break in and secure the tablet," Dutch started in, ignoring Skip's remark. "Then I'll-"

"That won't work, Dutch," Diandra interrupted, hands on her hips. "We need a plan. P-L-A-N. The museum has dozens of rooms, each containing thousands of tablets and artifacts. It would take you years – and that's if you even knew what to look for."

"She's got a point there, old chap," Skip chimed in.

Dutch shot Skip a 'button it up' look. He disingenuously nodded.

"You have a better idea?" Dutch asked Diandra.

"As a matter of fact, I do," she replied with obvious satisfaction. "I say we call the director of the museum and see if he'll extend a professional courtesy and let Sam and me in the front door. I checked with Jack Woods at Penn State and got his name. I could have him call this director and set it up."

That was what Dutch was afraid of. He didn't want them going in, but could not tell them why. And, she did have a damn good point about knowing what to look for. If this was going to work, he had to assume they had a fair jump on whoever it was that may be looking for the tablet. So time now really was of the essence. He raised an eyebrow at Skip.

"Sounds good to me," Skip offered. "Always better to go in invited, I say."

"Okay," Dutch relented, looking back and forth into both of their eyes. "But you're going in completely wired. And, you'll do exactly what we tell you to do. Is that understood?"

Diandra nodded.

"Are you kidding? This is the coolest thing ever. Just like James Bond, dude," Sam proclaimed. "I can't wait to post this on my Facebook and twitter!'

"After the mission," Skip interjected. "We're in top secret mode right now. By the way, to whom are you talking on that smart phone?

"My relatives in Iran," Sam replied. "It's how I keep in touch with them." He tapped a few more keys on the phone and looked up. "Did you know that 'Q' is the only letter that does not appear in any of the United States?"

"That a fact?" Dutch answered as he looked at his watch and made a mental calculation.

"It is," Sam answered, raising his eyebrows up and down.

"The museum opens in a few hours, and we'll want to get right in," Dutch continued, ignoring him. "Skip, get them accustomed to the equipment. Diandra, make your call to this Jack guy."

"Sam..." he thought for a moment while Sam beamed waiting for his assignment. Dutch smiled.

"You go and get a cup of this establishment's finest tea for our central commander here," he said, gesturing toward Skip, who gratefully inclined his head.

Sam's entire body deflated upon hearing the menial assignment.

"And what about you?" Sam shot back in irritation.

"I'm going out to pick up a package we need and hopefully, when I get back, grab a couple hours sleep." He stood up, stretched and added.

"I'm going to be with you every step of the way, even if it's from command central here."

* * * * * * * *

Chapter Nineteen

Zwinger Museum,
Dresden, Germany

Diandra and Sam, looking like two college geeks wearing wire-rimmed glasses and carrying briefcases, were not sure what to expect as they were met at the front door by the museum's director, Mischa Chubrinsky. Diandra had managed to get hold of Jack Woods, who in spite of the late hour in Philadelphia, was able to call and track down the director, even working out a deal to get them both in an hour before the museum's opening hours.

Herr Doktor Chubrinsky fumbled at, and then opened the glass door. With a robust and infectious smile he greeted them with enthusiasm.

"Zis is such a pleasure to meet with some koleags from the United of States. Pleze to come in," he said.

He motioned them through and into the lobby. He was a fifty something portly man whose crumpled shirt didn't quite fit into his suspendered pants. This left a belly button gap with hair sticking out of it at the bottom of his shirt that Diandra didn't even want to glimpse on a good day. A futile attempt at a comb-over with a few straggling hairs and a big bushy mustache that seemed disproportionately oversized for his face completed his look. He locked the door and motioned them down the steps toward a hallway.

"You must excuse pleze, the mess. Ve are, er, how you say?"

"Remodeling?" Diandra filled in.

"Exakly. I must say Professor Weiss, that I wuz most zurprized that you were ze author of 'Unexplained Archeology.' I read it cover to cover and enjoyed it vedy much. Although much contoverzy, yes?"

"Word travels fast," Diandra noted. "And thank you for the compliment, Mr. Chubinsk, inskie…?"

"Pleze, to call me Mischa," he offered.

"Mischa, your English is very good," she told him almost sincerely.

"Danka. I sink I have a little bit of an accent still, nein?" he joked with a wink.

Dutch and Skip looked on and listened to the conversation through both Diandra and Sam's glasses on two different screens.

"No kidding," Dutch piped in to Skip. "You sound like an extra out of 'From Russia with Love".

They heard Sam chuckle on the computer screen.

Diandra nudged Sam to shut up.

"Well, maybe just a little," she noted wryly.

"Oh, you are much too kind," he beamed. "Pleze to follow me to ze rooms zat Profezor Woods mentzoned you are zo interested zin."

"Where are they now?" Dutch quizzed Skip.

Skip scanned over the blueprints he had printed earlier and then focused on a small area on one of the screens that had a miniature version of the museum with two green dots on it, moving slowly – the GPS indicators.

"They're heading toward the basement as far as I can tell. These plans are pretty old, and I assumed that they were still current. This remodeling revelation is a surprise," Skip said with a frown.

From force of habit, Dutch grabbed his binoculars and crossed over to the window to scan the street below. He was not sure what he was looking for. Having picked up his package with his armaments inside, intact and accounted for, he felt back in control having his Smith and Wesson in its holster next to his heart. He also managed to get a good two hours sleep, leaving him feeling awake and refreshed. Now it was just a waiting game. *But waiting for what*, he wondered?

Skip eyed him over at the window and smiled. He typed some commands into his keyboard and up on the third plasma screen appeared a video feed of the exact view Dutch was seeing.

"Why don't you come sit down and relax, my boy. You can watch from here," Skip noted dryly.

Dutch swung around and observed the screen.

"How'd you do that?"

"I hacked into their city's street camera system," Skip calmly told him. "Dresden, it seems, is a very traffic conscious city."

"Thank God for the cold war." Dutch added, walking over and sitting down to view the screen.

Diandra, Sam and Mischa had already walked down the stairs into the lower basement of the museum. Mischa fumbled to find the old twist and turn style light switch that was popular when this part of the museum was refitted with electricity almost seventy-five years ago.

"Down here is ze area zat we keep all of ze, what you zay… uncatulogged?"

Diandra nodded in an encouraging way – gently prodding him along.

"…items in ze Museum. Due to ze budget costs and all, ve have no been able to do anyzing for almost thirty yearz. Ze offizials vant all funds to go to bringing in ze tourist dollars, yez?" He looked to his companions for understanding nods.

They reached a door, where Mischa pulled out a key from his pocket, inserting and twisting it with force. It didn't budge. Obviously chagrined, he made a face at the others then turned to put his whole substantial body weight into it and – click, clonk. It turned. Mischa beamed at his success while pushing the door open.

"If zis tablet you are interezted in iz in our muzuem, zis is where it would be, yes?"

He pushed the door open, and they were met by a large room lit by a small grilled window in the corner which cast prison-like striped shadows over the hundreds of wooden shelves lined up in rows, each containing an assortment of boxes, crates, artifacts and statues. The floors were covered with more wooden boxes, many partially opened, and reams of loose papers were scattered everywhere. A thin layer of Dresden's finest dust topped everything in a half-inch blanket.

"Man, I thought my room was a mess," Sam whispered.

Mischa reached over and twisted another light-switch that flashed a spark. A large light bulb in the central light fixture flickered once or twice before fully illuminating.

"As I zaid, ve vere not expecting compony," he apologized.

Diandra looked around, overwhelmed, trying to make some sense of how the storage room was organized but came up clueless. Scribbled on the sides of the boxes were descriptions in various languages. There was no apparent organization to what was there, and she didn't have any idea where to start. This was more than the proverbial needle in a haystack. Try adding finding one blind. She put on her best face.

"If it's okay with you, we'll just take a look around," she said.

"But of course. Az I zaid to your American profezzor, we are happy to eztend mutual courtesies," Mischa replied.

Sam and Diandra slowly walked around and surveyed the seemingly endless shelves of archeological artifacts. *Truly amazing,* she thought to herself. *One could spend years in here just cataloging all of this. Who knows what's here.* Sumerian god statuettes, small Egyptian sphinxes, stacks and stacks of tablets lined in rows – she wasn't sure what language they were written in. She pointed them out to Sam, who looked at them a moment and responded.

"These are Mesopotamian," he said. "These, here, are early Sumerian cuneiform. Not sure what those are over there, Diandra."

"Skip and Dutch had been watching the scene and were not hopeful either. They watched in silence as the two cameras beamed back slightly different views of the same scenes. Skip had an idea.

Leaning in closer to the screen, he spoke.

"Diandra, why not ask Doctor Zhivago if he knows where the oldest section of items are stored. If they plunked them in sequentially after the museum was rebuilt, maybe we'll get lucky. They should have been the first ones brought back."

"Mischa," Diandra asked, "do you know where the oldest of the artifacts are kept? By when they were brought in, I mean?"

He thought for a moment, his eyes darting back and forth at the shelves.

"Ve had zum vater damage a number of yearz ago. I beliefe zat ve plazed ze earlier itemz over zere for zafekeeping." He pointed toward the northwest corner of the room.

"Thanks," Diandra replied graciously as she and Sam made their way over to the area he pointed toward and started looking around. On the top shelf were mostly small cuneiform tablets – two by four inches in size.

"Probably Mesopotamian," she whispered. Sam took a closer look.

"Babylonian, first era," he replied. Next down were small paintings, early Christian era. "In pretty good shape too," she noted. She squatted to check the boxes and small wooden crates stacked on the floor, tilting her head to read them. Sam elbowed Diandra so hard in the ribs she jumped, startled.

"What?" she said to him.

He pointed to one of the crates with Cyrillic numbers stenciled on the side. Below, they could read the letters KGB in Russian script.

"This seems *very* interesting," Diandra said to Sam, giving him an exaggerated wink and a smile.

"That's the sign, Skip," Dutch shouted so loudly that Diandra and Sam could hear him through Skip's microphone, followed by Skip's equally loud, "Stop there! That's it!"

"Ow!" Sam cried as they both grabbed their ears. Mischa looked at them curiously.

"Sorry about that, I do apologize," Skip said as he realized how loud he had been and turned down a knob on his box. "Just hold still so I can get a close-up on that crate."

He right clicked his mouse and freeze-framed Diandra's image. Typing in some commands, he put a box around only the Russian text and kept enlarging it until it filled the screen. Hitting control C, he went to another screen and pasted it in.

"Okay, step one complete," he murmured to himself.

"What are you going to do?" Dutch wanted to know.

"First, run it through Google language translator, and then I'm getting into the Queen's servers and letting my old buddies at MI6 confirm the work for me – sort of a retirement perk I use once in awhile."

He typed more and a highlighted green line scanned the text symbol by symbol. A few seconds later a loud beep emanated from the computer and up popped the translation in a separate window on the screen. He quickly scanned it, while looking down at the old KGB document copy he had on the table.

There, in the middle of the list, was the number NTR0497. He grinned and leaned back in his chair.

"You've got a go there, dearie. Congratulations," Skip told Diandra.

Diandra and Sam beamed at each other.

"We're ready when you are," Sam said to Skip.

"Exkuse me?" Mischa asked.

Dutch paced around the room thinking that everything had gone very well. In fact, almost too well. He was getting that feeling in the pit of his stomach he'd learned not to ignore. Reflexively he started to rub the back of his neck. Maybe he was just being a pessimist, like the proverbial guy who, whenever something good was about to happen, ended up thinking the worst and sabotaged it. *No matter*, he reasoned. He just wanted them out of there as soon as possible.

"Skip, make the call," Dutch said.

"Okey dokey."

Skip fumbled for the phone, dropped it and got it back in his hand. It was an old rotary dial type with a handset, maybe fifty years old. He inserted his finger, turned it to the number and let the dial spin back to its original starting point with agonizing slowness. Six more numbers to go. They both watched the screen, hearing Diandra's reply to Mischa.

"I didn't say anything. I was just, um, marveling at all of your treasures here. Quite impressive."

"That is zo kind of vu. Az I said before, ve get very few viziters."

Come on, come on, Diandra thought to herself. *When will you guys-*

Riiiinnnggg.

The echo of a distant phone ringing bounced off the stone walls of the hallway and made its way down the stairs and into the artifacts room.

"Oh my. Vill you be so kind as to pleze excuze me? I must get zat." Mischa looked from one to the other in consternation. "Pleze to not think I am so rude and unthinking of your importance…"

"No problem," Sam replied. "We'll just wait right here," he said, pointing. "Don't worry about us."

Mischa waved his apologies while backing through the door, then turned to scurry up the hallway. The ringing continued to echo softly in the background. He could be heard grumbling to himself something about they don't pay him enough to be a tour guide there *and* answer the phone.

Once he was out of the room Sam and Diandra quickly hurried toward the crate. Sam dropped his briefcase, popped open the lock tabs and pulled out a crowbar. Diandra stood back as he inserted the snake tongue end of it under the lid of the box and lifted up. A loud creak shattered the silence of the room, and they both froze.

"Let's get this done quickly before Mischa gets back." Diandra whispered. The phone stopped ringing. *Finally, he picked up the thing,* she thought. "Hurry Sam."

Sam nodded as he pushed down again on the crowbar. The old nails gave way as the lid fell over the side onto the floor with a resounding thud. Dutch glanced over at Skip and the monitors, which flickered slightly for a moment, then cleared up again.

"Nice job, Skip. Keep that old guy talking."

Skip looked at first perturbed by the 'old guy' comment and then quizzically over toward Dutch with the phone in his hand.

"I can't, Dutch. It's not me that he's talking to."

He held up the phone while Dutch rushed over to listen to the 'beep beep' of a busy signal. Dutch frowned, rubbing the back of his neck. *Well then, who the heck would be calling him?*

* * * * * * * *

Tires squealing, a black Amadeo 500 limousine wove through the intersections and side streets near the outskirts of Berlin. Traffic was still snarled due to a transit union strike. The driver gestured wildly and yelled various German profanities while three men facing each other who looked like Eastern European participants in Wrestlemania sat calmly in their seats, checking their shotguns and handguns. Shadow Man sat next to one of them speaking on the car phone.

"I understand you have a very large collection of Sumerian tablets at your Museum?" his voice rasped in fluent German.

"Yes we do," Mischa answered back in German. "This is very coincidental that you should ask about it."

"How so?" Shadow frowned.

"We have some archeologists from America right now looking at these same-"

Shadow Man hit end call on the phone and threw it down.

"Step on it!" he yelled to the driver and then rubbed his scarred throat at the strain.

* * * * * * * *

Chapter Twenty

Dresden, Germany

Dutch paced the room while Skip laboriously re-dialed the archaic rotary phone.

"Something's not right, Skip. I can feel it," Dutch said, running his fingers through his hair in frustration.

Out of the corner of his eye Skip glimpsed some movement on the plasma screen cued into Dresden's street camera system. Swiveling his chair, he watched a black limousine skid to a stop in front of the museum.

"Dutch, you better come see this," he warned.

Dutch looked over and observed the back of Shadow Man and his three cohorts piling out of the car. A flash of sunlight glared on the screen, reflecting off something metal one of the men was hiding under his overcoat. Dutch leaned closer. A shotgun.

"Diandra! Sam!" Dutch shouted into the computer's microphone. "Get the hell out of there, now!"

A static buzz was the only sound coming out of the speakers. Quizzically, Dutch looked to Skip.

"What's wrong with this thing?" he demanded to know.

Skip pounded the keys. Nothing. Both Sam and Diandra's images were moving toward a table. Suddenly, both of their screen images started to turn to static and fade in and out. Dutch leaned in closer, his eyes darting between the two screens.

"Skip?"

"I'm not sure, Dutch. There's some sort of electrical interference. I can't find the source." Skip exclaimed.

Diandra searched through the box and found the missing piece, wrapped in an old newspaper with a number hand-written on the outside. Holding it reverently, she walked over to a table with Sam closely at her side. Sam touched and then tapped on his glasses, frowning at the static noise. Looking up, he spied an antique black metal fuse box three feet above their heads with wires running out of it, humming and sparking away.

"Can you hear anything?" he asked Diandra, tapping his headgear.

She was so focused that she ignored his question while carefully removing the newspaper surrounding it. Holding the fragment in her hand, she felt tears come to her eyes. Her body was tingling as if an electric current of excitement were running through it. In fact, she never remembered feeling that way before. In all the rush to find the tablet, she had never really thought about how she would feel once they did. And she found it was glorious. Hands shaking with excitement, she gently set the tablet down on the old linoleum covered table.

"Hand me the other piece, Sam, and let's have a quick look."

Sam reached into his briefcase and took it out.

"Talk to me, Skip," Dutch implored, as he scooped up a pair of glasses and slipped them on. "What's the quickest way to get in there?"

He pulled out his Smith and Wesson and dumped the clip into his hand.

"I'm looking, I'm looking," Skip said, his voice tight. He wiped the sweat from his forehead, then hurriedly pulled up an older version of the museum's blueprints on the third screen and scanned them, searching for a miracle.

"There!" he shouted, pointing his finger at the screen. "The west side has an old access door that leads directly down into the basement."

He looked toward Dutch, then back to the computer. "You'd be coming in the back door, on, um… Banhoffstrasse."

Dutch counted his clip and made a mental note – sixteen plus one in the chamber - and re-holstered it.

"This is the real deal Skip. Watch my back."

"Always do, old boy," he said as he reached for another Handi Wipe and nervously began his finger-cleaning ritual as…

Dutch sprinted out the door, down the hall and to the back exit of the hotel. After scaling two flights of stairs he burst out of the ground floor doorway into traffic.

A small Peugeot swerved and skidded to a stop, slamming into the curb and missing Dutch by a hair as he bobbed and weaved through the traffic toward the front parking lot of the museum.

* * * * * * * *

Shadow Man and his three goons met Mischa at the door and told him they were also researchers, there to meet the Americans.

"More ezteemed colleagues!" Mischa was effusive in his greeting but obviously confused. "Ve are very honored, but zo zurprized zat theze vaz not mentioned before. But my English ez, vell, not so gut, may not understand—"

"An oversight, I'm sure," Shadow Man interrupted in English, then reassured him in German with a slight smile. "Where are they now?"

"Down there in the basement," Mischa replied reverting to his native language with relief while pointing the way to the stairs.

Shadow Man nodded to one of the men who pulled out a shotgun and butted it straight into Mischa's face, violently pushing him against the wall. His body fell limply to the floor, blood running from his nose and mouth as a crimson pool formed around his head.

Dutch ran full gallop to the west side of the museum, looking for the entrance as he rounded the corner.

"About fifty meters further, Dutch," Skip relayed on the microphone. "Look on your lower right. There are probably stairs that descend from street level to the basement, like an old storm cellar door."

Skip viewed his progress on the third plasma screen while he typed furiously trying to get picture clarity and communication back with Diandra and Sam. The images were still flickering on and off on both of their screens – static the only sound he heard.

Dutch located the street level entrance and could see a temporary plywood door at the bottom of a flight of stone stairs. Jumping down, with one violent kick he bashed in the flimsy wooden covering, splinters flying everywhere. Metal scaffolding from the remodel blocked the door, causing Dutch to lose his momentum and trip over the threshold falling down. He scrambled to his feet and surveyed the situation.

"Where do I go, Skip?"

Skip eyed the monitor, located two green dots representing Diandra and Sam, and then down at the paper floor plans.

"They're still in the artifacts room, Dutch. Looks like you take a left at the next hallway and follow it down about thirty meters… and then right. It'll be the first door on your right at that point."

"Okay, Skip. I'm going non-com until I get there."

Dutch pulled out his .45, checked again to confirm his chamber shot was in place, and listened intently. His back against the wall, he cautiously snaked his way toward the main hallway.

Sam gingerly handed Diandra the missing fragment. She set them both down on the table. The overhead continued flickering and she found her shoulder casting a shadow over the tablets. She moved them down toward the further end of the table where the light was better.

Diandra and Sam's images became a little clearer on Skip's computer screens – less static. Skip immediately typed in commands to lessen the distortion. Simultaneously on the other screen, he watched Dutch's green dot from his glasses' GPS slowly edge toward the main hallway and then make the first turn. He hit a key on the computer.

"Diandra, Sam – can either of you hear me?" he pleaded, wiping his forehead on his sleeve.

Only static greeted his request. He typed more commands and reached over to his wire filled contraption and adjusted various knobs.

Diandra slowly manipulated the two pieces around until they were about one inch apart and lined up perfectly. She looked to Sam.

"Any idea what type of glyphs these are?" she asked.

Sam had been studying them in earnest while rubbing his brow with one hand. He made notations on his smart phone app.

"This looks turbo tough, Diandra. I thought at first it was an early version of Sumerian, but these other symbols make no sense. Do you see this one" he said, pointing. "It looks almost like one on the bottom of McIntyre's letter."

"I agree," Diandra nodded as she pushed the two pieces toward each other.

"Welcome back together you two," she whispered. "It's been a long time since you've seen each other."

At first she thought the flickering light was playing tricks with her eyes. Or maybe it was the excitement of what she was doing. But no, she saw it again. Purplish sparks jumped between the two pieces. Startled, Diandra jerked up her hand and stepped back from the table. She glanced at Sam whose eyes were as wide as saucers. Together they watched in amazement as a magnetic-like force took hold of the fragments and locked them perfectly into place.

Then it started.

Ever so slight at first.

A vibration.

A slow, sand-like ripple of concentric rings emanated from the center of the newly converged tablet. Like rings rushing out from the center of a pond after a small stone was thrown in. The ripples seemed almost translucent as the tablet vibrated faster and faster atop the table.

The sand swirling above the tablet rose and then descended again, sinking back into the tablet, and there, before them, the surface of the tablet morphed into a completely different set of symbols and lines. Drop-jawed, Diandra looked to see a mesmerized Sam.

"Skip?" Diandra had to clear her throat. "Skip, are you getting this?" "Skip?"

Skip was trying everything he could to get a clear channel to override or go around the interference. He correctly guessed the problem must be Electro Magnetic Frequency blockage from an old two-forty electrical box, and was moving their frequencies to a lower bandwidth on his magic box. He finished adjusting it when he heard Diandra.

"Skip? Skip are you there?" Diandra pleaded.

Skip could hear the concern in her voice. He quickly grabbed the mic and observed the static lessening, revealing the tablet on the table.

"Diandra," he shouted. "You have to-"

"Skip! Are you getting this?" she interrupted. "This is incredible. I've never in my life…" Diandra stopped and swallowed, for once at a loss for words.

Skip hit a key and digitally photographed the screen shots from both hers and Sam's cameras. His screen displayed: *images captured.*

"Skip. Please tell me you've got this," she again implored. Finally the static diminished.

"I've got it, okay. Now get the bloody hell out of there!" he shouted.

"What's going on?" Quizzical looks passed between her and Sam when they heard someone burst into the room.

Skip could see Dutch's camera sweep the huge room, looking for Sam and Diandra. His drawn gun showed at the bottom of the screen like an action video game.

"Hey, where are you guys?" Dutch said in an intense stage whisper, peering around stacked boxes.

Diandra whirled around, dazed by what she just witnessed and startled by both Skip's urgent plea and Dutch's voice. Her arm knocked the tablet off the table and onto the floor. She'd always seen those shots in movies when something bad was about to happen and it went into slow motion… she was experiencing it right then. In horror, she reached out too late to keep it from slamming onto the floor, shattering into sandy fragments. Only the piece they brought was still intact.

"Oh, God, no!" Diandra screamed, falling to her knees. She narrowed her eyes, and bent more closely. Among the remains she glimpsed three little chrome-like cylinders about half the width of the tablet. They were vibrating, surrounded by a glowing purple aura.

"Over here, Dutch!" Sam shouted kneeling beside her and reaching toward the broken tablet. Diandra pushed his hands away.

"Not so loud, guys," Dutch implored as he made his way toward them through the maze of shelves and boxes.

Diandra was still transfixed by the sandy mess on the floor that was once the complete tablet. Then, the sand began to swirl again, moving like liquid mercury until it returned to the tablet's original shape with the exact same break as before. Only this time, no glyphs appeared. A blank slate.

Shaken, Dutch witnessed the end of this last transformation but knew they had no time to waste.

"We've got to get out of here, now!" he told them, checking back toward the entrance. Diandra was still staring at the floor. He grabbed her shoulders and turned her to face him.

"What?" Diandra finally spoke, shaking off her trance.

"Come on!" Dutch pushed her toward the door.

Sam reached down and picked up the original fragment just as Shadow Man and his three henchmen entered the room, guns drawn and ready for a small war: two shotguns, an AK-47 and a two-inch barrel UZI with a hundred round circle clip attached.

Shadow Man slowly rounded a desk and saw the tablet fragment on the floor near the table. Walking toward it, he squatted on his knees and peered down, motioning for the others to spread out and start searching.

Skip watched the scene through Dutch's glasses as he hid behind a crate with Diandra and Sam near the middle of the room against the back wall. Snatching the blueprints from the desk, he desperately scanned them. He turned to a new page, ran his finger along some lines and tapped it on the paper.

"Dutch… Listen. There's an air vent above you, maybe a meter to your… left. If you can get up in it, the ducts lead directly to the rear of the museum. I know you can't speak, just nod your head if you can hear."

His computer screen image moved up and down.

"I'll try and create a diversion," Skip said. "Wish me luck."

Through the eerie silence and shadows of the artifacts room, Dutch looked around and sure enough, five feet to his left and maybe six feet up, he saw the ventilation grate, painted the same color as the walls. *Thank god for Skip*, he reminded himself. Motioning for Diandra and Sam to follow him, they crept along like waddling ducks to a pond. Dutch could hear the light footsteps of the men looking around, trying to not make a sound of their own.

Fortunately, crates still surrounded the area below the vent, and Dutch looked up to assess the hinged grill. *Another miracle,* Dutch noted. One bottom screw and it should open, he observed with relief. Stealthily climbing up on a crate, he took out a small pocketknife, unscrewed it and got back down. He let his breath out. *Okay, so far so good.*

But how to get three people up and in it before being discovered? This was one of those moments when he had to trust someone else. The kind of moment he hated. But since he had to put his faith in someone, he was glad it was Skip.

Looking over at the other two, he took in Sam's scared expression and grabbed him just as he was starting to get up and run. Dutch pushed him back down and motioned him to wait. It was an act of faith on Dutch's part. He wasn't sure of anything at this point. Reaching into his pocket he pulled out an extra clip of sixteen bullets and held it in his hand, next to his Smith and Wesson.

The gunmen had begun their search at the two exterior walls of the room and walked methodically down the first row of shelves, sweeping their weapons side to side. They were trained professionals and knew how to stalk their prey. *Another two or three minutes and they will have worked their way to our position*, Dutch assessed.

Skip watched in horror, piecing the whole situation together in his mind from the three camera angles. He felt the seconds ticking away, the group's lives in his hands. He tore through drawings, blueprints and diagrams, simultaneously typing frantically on the computer's keyboard.

"Come on, Dresden. Come on. Please tell me it's still working."

Dutch had to make a decision. They couldn't wait there like sitting ducks for too long. He knew that the crates wouldn't stop the inevitable barrage of flying bullets that he was sure would follow their discovery, and there was no defensible position from which to shoot. Then, there were Diandra and Sam to consider, who were more than likely scared shitless and unpredictable as hell. He'd be lucky just to get them walking, let alone stealthily climbing into a vent six feet above. He decided to reach up and remove the vent cover to save a few seconds when they most counted. He stood up and grabbed it with one hand, fingers through the grill, and pulled. Nothing. He looked it over. No other screws could be seen. *Painted shut?* He forcefully yanked again and it gave, but not before letting out a screech that reverberated throughout the room. "Ah, shit… that's definitely not good," he whispered to himself.

Shadow Man and crew froze. Slowly they turned, trying to determine the origin of the noise. One of the men pointed in Dutch's general direction, and the others nodded.

RIIIINNNNNGGGG.
RIIIINNNNGGGGG.
RIIIINNNNGGGGG.

The fire alarm went off, reverberating everywhere. Skip nearly fainted with relief, thunking his forehead against the keyboard.

Dutch tapped Sam on the shoulder and motioned with his thumb jamming upward. Sam jumped up on the crate and hiked into the vent. Dutch reached around and saw by the fear in her eyes that Diandra was frozen. He grabbed, pulled her toward him and then hoisted her straight up. Sam reached out, grasped her hand and pulled while Dutch pushed from below and in she went.

"Search this place!" Shadow Man's raspy voice could barely be heard over the fire alarm's bell, veins bulging in his neck as he grasped his throat to support his vocal cords. "Block the exits. I want them found." Furious, he pushed boxes full of priceless artifacts crashing to the ground as he ran from aisle to aisle.

Dutch was the last one up on the crate. He turned around and from his vantage point could see a profile of Shadow Man in the flickering of the main light.

The hair at the back of his neck rose as he tried to place where he might have seen him before but realized he had neither the time nor inclination to ponder any further. Skip had provided them with their moment and he had to seize it. He turned back around to pull up and crawl in when he had a thought.

Dutch aimed his Smith and Wesson at the ceiling above Shadow Man and fired off three rounds. Blam. Blam. Blam.

Plaster flew off the ceiling and dusted Shadow Man, causing him to crouch low and search for the source of this firepower. He was only expecting two of them – Diandra and Sam, according to Mischa. This display of firepower caught him by surprise – just the response Dutch was hoping for.

Shadow Man felt a vibration by his foot as he looked down and saw the remaining tablet fragment start to ripple, almost imperceptibly. Slowly, the original glyphs started to appear. He shook his head in disbelief.

Dutch's penlight lit the way ahead of Sam as he crawled on all fours. They came to a 'T' in the vent system. Dutch called out.

"Skip. Thanks for the diversion," Dutch said. "Now, which way do we go?"

"Turn left and follow it to the end," Skip said, "and you're welcome."

"Good to hear your voice again, Skip," Sam added.

"Yours too, laddie," Skip quipped.

"Pack up shop, Skip. We're outta there as soon as we get back."

"Affirmative, Dutch. Already in process."

They made the turn when; blam, blam, blam, blam. A flurry of bullets punctured the metal duct where they had just been resting.

"Come on… let's get out of here," Dutch shouted, pushing Diandra forward by her feet.

Sam reached the end, spun around with his back into Diandra, braced himself with his two hands pressing outward, and with all of his strength kicked the grill separating them from freedom. Off it flew into the parking lot. Daylight flooded in. He jumped out and reached back to help Diandra down. Dutch followed quickly turning around feet first, covering their rear with his gun. Once he hit the ground, they all heard the clicking sound of shotguns as shells ratcheted into their chambers. Turning around, they confronted three men who looked like they stepped out of the 'Men in Black' movie – complete with coats, ties and sunglasses.

Dutch knew they were caught, but he was more upset about the fate of his charges than for himself. He wouldn't mind going down in the blaze of a high noon shootout – he'd have a chance, maybe. But they wouldn't. He needed some time, if only a few seconds, to figure out a plan.

"Hey guys, I can explain all of this," Dutch stalled.

"Give me your gun, Mr. Vorhees," one of them stated while holding out his hand.

Dutch was caught off guard by the man calling him by name. He was at a total disadvantage, but knowing that it would buy a few moments to think, he decided to give it up. Holding it by the barrel, he reluctantly handed it over. A large Mercedes limousine rounded the rear of the museum and pulled up next to the group. The rear door opened.

Suddenly two of Shadow Man's men sprinted around the front corner of the museum and opened fire with a shotgun and .45 caliber Uzi. One of the men in black quickly grabbed Diandra and threw her into the back seat of the limousine, with Sam voluntarily diving in right behind her. Dutch fell to the ground and crabbed over behind the limo's door. Two of the men in black returned fire with their shotguns. It was World War III. They were pumping out metal buckshot as fast as they could pull the triggers.

Shadow Man's men returned it with the same venomous determination. Bullets bounced off the limousine as the men in black made their way toward the back door. One of them was hit in the shoulder and went down behind the limo's door, clutching his side and dropping his shotgun.

Dutch picked it up and continued the assault, hitting one of Shadow Man's men in the hip and spinning him around to the ground. The other man in black grabbed his downed partner, picked him up and pushed him into the car. He turned and grabbed Dutch by the shirt, tossing him inside too, while grappling the shotgun out of his hands.

He turned and fired at Shadow Man's other goon who had retreated behind the museum's corner wall for protection. Plaster and brick flew in all directions.

The man in black pounded twice on the roof of the limousine with his fist, jumped in, and the Mercedes squealed off. Shadow Man and the third gunman appeared from around the corner and sprayed the car with as much firepower as they could direct at it. Sparks flew off the side panels and windows of the obviously bulletproof vehicle as it sped away.

Shadow Man looked down at his injured man, bleeding and lying on the ground, aimed his gun at the injured man's head and pulled the trigger.

Having witnessed the entire scene on a street cam aimed at the parking lot of the museum, Skip wasted no time. Trembling, his sweaty finger hit a key on his computer that downloaded all his files, pulled out the digital flash stick and pocketed it. After entering a destruct data code on his computer, he picked up his backpack, threw in his magic box and was just about to reach for the door handle when the door was kicked in, throwing him back a couple of steps.

Two Federal looking agents dressed in suits, guns drawn, entered the room. They quickly searched the bathroom and adjoining bedroom, and then came back into the main room where Skip was standing, legs shaking and wondering if Dutch had gotten him into his last mission on Earth. One of the men nodded to the other, who addressed Skip in a monotone voice.

"Would you grab what you need and come with us, Mr. Duffin? Now."

* * * * * * * *

Chapter Twenty-One

Berlin, Germany

Dutch had gotten the time he needed to hatch a plan, but it didn't help. He was totally confused. True, they weren't dead. But they were trapped in a car traveling eighty miles per hour with two armed men and another man wounded and bleeding. He could feel his backup small caliber .38 Smith and Wesson strapped to his leg with a fourteen shot clip, but trying something in close quarters like this would be a recipe for disaster.

Plus, he reasoned, these guys had just saved their bacon back there. Or did they? Maybe it's all a ruse – some elaborate trick to find out what they knew. Or maybe this trio was another group competing against the first bunch. Their stonily silent glares pretty much assured he was not going to find out anything from them. No, he had to wait for the opportunity he needed to either get his team out of there, or strike a deal.

The limousine raced back into Berlin, entering via highway 114 and heading toward the Reichstag building located in the financial district –the German equivalent of Wall Street. Since the wall had come down, over fifty of the world's major conglomerates had opened offices as a stepping board to the entire eastern bloc.

They wound their way down Otto-Braun Strasse, turned left on Alexander Strasse and turned sharply into an underground cement garage beneath a tall black-glass building that had a steel gate blocking its entrance. An overhead video camera's red light blinked and the gate slowly opened, descending again as they passed through and headed toward the rear of the garage. Dutch made a note that his options were quickly going from escape to deal mode at that point.

The limo pulled up to a group of service elevators and stopped, where a uniformed medical team was waiting. Paramedics helped the injured man out of the car and onto a gurney, quickly inserting an I.V. into his arm and taking his pulse. They wheeled him into a service elevator and the doors closed.

The other two men exited the car and motioned toward the trio.

"If you would please follow us?" one of them requested.

They walked toward another set of elevators and pushed the up button. Dutch was intrigued at this point. *They're awfully damn nice*, he thought to himself. He was reasonably sure they were not in immediate danger, which gave him more time to devise a plan. Until he knew who or what was behind this little incursion, he could be risking all of their lives if he took the wrong action at that point.

And then there was Skip. *They may have him too. It costs nothing to wait and see what happens,* he reasoned. *It was the same odds – he with fourteen shots against whatever they came up against. Maybe he could parlay those to better odds once he found out where and why they were being brought there*. He looked at Diandra, who seemed oddly preoccupied, while Sam fidgeted nervously. None of them had said a word to one another since being captured.

The elevator doors opened to the lobby of the penthouse suite where they found an uncharacteristically disheveled Skip sitting in a chair, hugging his backpack. He seemed as pissed off as Dutch had ever seen him. Skip tacitly acknowledged the trio with a frown, stared for a moment at Dutch, and then turned straight ahead.

Diandra smiled for the first time since they left the museum. "Skip, thank God you're okay," she said as she rushed over to him and put her hand on his shoulder. He abruptly shrugged it off.

"Skip... what's wrong?" she asked.

He looked up at her and then over at Dutch.

"What's wrong? Oh, I don't know," he stated, pointing at Dutch. "Maybe the fact that every time I get involved with Rambo there I almost get killed?"

He looked back down at the floor, steaming. He was still pissed, but as much at himself as he was at Dutch. He had planned for what he thought was every contingency, but this one had caught him completely off guard. Now the group was in trouble and he felt more than partly responsible for it. He looked back up at Diandra, sighed and shrugged his shoulders.

"I'm sorry. Where are my manners? Are you okay?" he asked.

"Yes, Skip, we're *all* fine." She sat next to him and whispered.

"Any idea what's going on?"

Skip started to reply when an impeccably dressed man in Brooks Brothers' finest entered the lobby through a pair of beautifully hand-carved teakwood doors.

"Would you all be so kind as to follow me," he requested, smiling politely and motioning toward the inside of the doors.

Skip stood up, still hugging his backpack and walked in, followed by Diandra and Sam. The man eyed Dutch, who had paused before deciding to see what awaited them on the other side of the doors. He cautiously followed the others in, shadowed by the two men in black who had brought them up there.

Paintings by Old-World Masters lined the walls, beautifully spotlighted museum style - Monet. Raphael. Michelangelo. Rare statues and archeological reliefs populated the floor, walls and teak bookcase shelves. Sam and Diandra stopped dead in their tracks, stunned by all the rare and ancient artifacts they saw, while Skip made silent note of the positions of cameras and electronic equipment, which, although discreetly hidden, blanketed the entire room. Dutch noticed them as well, catching Skip's eye to acknowledge that fact.

Dutch's scrutiny took in a man sitting in the shadows behind a large teak desk in the center of the room. His only light was a small Tiffany stained glass and bronze lamp sitting on the desk beside him. One of the men handed him some paperwork and a computer flash drive. The man at the desk glanced at it as two of the men who accompanied them left the room. *Now the odds were getting better,* Dutch mused. *There were the four of them, plus Mr. Smiley-face, and the stranger behind the desk. Things were looking up for a change.* The ticking of a large grandfather clock in the corner of the room was the only sound piercing the silence.

The man behind the desk leaned forward, coming into the light. Dutch sized him up. Graying hair, very distinguished looking, maybe in his late fifties. His perfectly trimmed goatee added an almost Raleigh debonair look to the package. But his deep gray eyes gave him away. He was a businessman to the core, and from the looks of it a tough negotiator. He reminded Dutch of a couple of three star generals he'd had the misfortune of running into.

The man gave a curt smile to the group. "Thank you for joining me," he intoned. "Can I offer you anything to drink?"

"Like we have a choice?" Skip flippantly replied. "But a cup of Earl Grey would be nice."

"Hey, what's going on here?" Diandra finally blurted out, coming to her senses. "We just about got killed back there and you're serving drinks? What's this about and who the hell are you?"

Dutch was as much surprised by Diandra's outburst as their mysterious host appeared to be, and he gently squeezed her arm to silence her. She shook his hand off, holding her stare at the stranger.

The man pressed an intercom button.

"Did you get that, Maria? Cup of tea for Mr. Duffin."

"Yes sir," answered the female voice at the other end.

The man leaned back and observed the obviously overwhelmed Sam, who'd been dazedly admiring a statue on his desk. Dutch never loosened his gaze at him, trying to figure out what he was up to.

"This looks like the god Anu," Sam excitedly murmured, reaching one finger toward it but stopping short in awe. "Although… I've never seen an unbroken statue like this before."

"You're quite right, Sam," the man answered, nodding, "and you are as knowledgeable as I've heard you are. It's the only one in existence." He leaned forward on his desk. "May I call you Sam?"

Sam beamed at the recognition.

"Okay mister, you've made your point. You're in charge," Dutch said, then demanded, "Now, why are we here?"

The man motioned toward the big overstuffed chairs surrounding the desk.

"Please, take a seat," he offered, his tone a little lighter.

Maria came in rolling a cart with a steaming cup of tea and teapot along with a tray of biscuits. Skip walked over and got his tea, while Diandra and Sam sat down. Dutch remained standing. The host acknowledged his defiant act with a shrug.

Skip walked back sipping his tea, surprised.

"P G Tips. I am impressed," he said while slipping into a chair, feeling a bit calmer.

"Now, to answer your question, Doctor Weiss, my name is Robert Tanner. And, as you can see," he motioned with his arm without moving from behind his desk, "in addition to my various enterprises, I collect treasures. Throughout the years I've noticed that many of them, in addition to their value and beauty, speak about gods, myths and legends. All of which I've considered fodder for the weak-minded. The blind 'believers' if you will, who will turn any idea into a cult or religion. Although my faith in a personal God is strong and grounded, I've always believed that if I couldn't see it, feel it or touch it… it didn't exist."

He paused a moment, while considering each of his listeners in turn and carefully choosing his next words.

"But now… I am not so sure."

He picked up a remote control and a wooden panel rose against the wall to his right revealing a large flat theater screen. He turned toward it as the lights started to dim in the room. Clicking the remote, images appeared on the plasma surface.

"We all know about the Pyramids in Giza, the statues of Easter Island and the ruins of Machu Picchu in Peru. These are well-documented tourist attractions, yet they comprise only a few of the hundreds of mysterious structures built around the world that leave many questions unanswered. Why were they built? Who built them? How did they do it?"

He pushed buttons on the remote and an ornate crystal skull appeared.

"Here is one of a handful of crystal skulls that have been found all over the world. My engineers tell me that they couldn't replicate the precision and perfection of these today without cracking the crystal. What purpose do they serve? How were they created and why? What were they used for?

He pushed the button again.

"And this is the largest hand-carved stone block on Earth, resting in the quarry where it was created, estimated to weigh over two thousand tons. There's one just like it that was moved more than five miles away to use as the foundation for the city of Baalback in Lebanon…. six thousand years ago. We couldn't even move it a foot today."

Images appeared in quick succession as he punched the remote.

"Giant stone balls in Costa Rica, a city composed of more stone than the pyramid of Giza, located in the middle of the Pacific Ocean, a pyramid in Bosnia, a twelve thousand year old city called Göbekli Tepe in southern Turkey, not to mention the hundreds of thousands of tablets worldwide that haven't been deciphered. And yet many of the tablets we have deciphered cryptically mention great civilizations of the past that have been destroyed. Lemuria and Atlantis, for instance. What happened to them? Where did they go?"

"You know," interrupted Dutch. "This 'Unexplained Mysteries' history lesson is all very interesting. But what's the point?"

Tanner hit a button and the wall panel descended while the lights slowly brightened.

"The point, Mr. Vorhees, is that I now have reason to believe that all of these mysterious structures, tablets, and more, are somehow connected."

He looked to Diandra.

"You see, Diandra, I believe you were absolutely right in your book. There is a great deal more to many archeological finds, more than we ever dreamed. Yet, because the present archeological establishment refuses to question its own assumptions, there is very little chance of discovering the truth about them."

Tanner let that sink in for a moment.

"There seems to me to be a thread, if you will, running through all of them," he continued, "a hidden message or secret knowledge of some kind. A message, which, from all indications I've found, was left as a *warning* to us by our ancestors. Unlocking its meaning is becoming more urgent every day."

"What is," Sam began, and then had to clear his throat. "What's it about?"

"I wish I knew," Tanner said, raising his eyebrows.

"What makes you so sure this knowledge or message even exists?" Diandra challenged. "This sounds farfetched, even to me."

"I have been given information from a reliable source that leads me to believe it is true. Let's leave it at that for now."

"So, as Dutch just asked," Skip questioned, emboldened and slightly irritated, "what's the point and why are we here?"

Tanner looked again at the four of them, one by one. The tapping of his fingers on the desk competed with the ticking of the grandfather clock. Leaning forward he continued.

"I need your help. I believe the answers to all of my questions may reside within the Tomb of Alexander. But the Macedonian tablet, without its other half, has always mystified archeologists as to where it may lie buried."

Eyeing the copy of Skip's printout on the desk, he picked it up.

"And today, I believe, you saw why," he added.

"In all fairness," Diandra said, "I don't know if *I* even believe what I saw today."

"I'm down with that," Sam added quietly to himself, shaking his head.

Tanner picked up a red savings passbook from Credit Suisse, reached over the desk and handed it to Diandra.

"If you do choose to help me, I believe this will take care of your expenses."

She opened it as Dutch viewed it over her shoulder. The name in the space after the account was 'The Seekers', followed by all four of their names. The amount deposited: ten million US dollars. Diandra took a deep breath, momentarily stunned.

"This is a lot of money," she whispered, wondering if her eyes were playing tricks on her.

"How much is it?" Sam inquired, leaning over to see. "Wow."

"In addition, you'll have access and free rein over all of my company's resources." Tanner added. "Which, I assure you, are indeed, quite vast."

"A bottom line kinda guy, I see," Dutch stated with a skeptical expression. "But I still don't get the whole picture here."

"I'll take that as a compliment." Tanner sat back and crossed his arms. "Yes, I am a *bottom line kinda guy*, and I have the resources to achieve my ends. It's really quite simple, Dutch. I want you and the others to decipher the tablet and find Alexander's tomb."

"Uh huh," Diandra responded. "And exactly what would you like to do with the contents of the tomb if we do find it?" She looked around the room full of artifacts and narrowed her eyes.

"I know what you're thinking, Diandra," he answered. "I like to collect treasures. But this is different."

Tanner turned to address the group.

"This time I don't want to keep anything for myself. I only want to be the first to see, to interpret and understand whatever it is that you find."

"So, you'll bankroll this expedition, and you just want a *first look* at the findings?" Skip asked in a sarcastic tone. "Hmmm. I believe I'm with Diandra on this one. A wee bit…shall we say, dubious?"

"I'm sorry to make this so painless," Tanner responded, drily. "But that is it in a nut-shell. Whatever money is left at the end of your adventure is yours to keep."

"Why us?" Dutch wanted to know.

Tanner turned to Diandra. "It may surprise you to learn, Doctor Weiss, that I've followed your career for the past few years," he started. "In fact, I've funded most of your expeditions, donating the money directly to the museum through various foundations that I own or control." He smiled at her look of astonishment. "It may also surprise you that it was one of my holding companies that published your book, which by the way, was brilliant.

"I've been waiting for someone with the same passion and commitment to finding the truth as I have, and I believe that you are that person."

He reached for and opened a manila folder in front of him, looking at typed pages. "Now, as to the rest of you…"

Quickly scanning the first one he started reading.

"Ebrahim Hasim Zahed," he said looking up smiling, "or Sam, as you like to be called, IQ exceeding 180."

Sam looked at Dutch on that note and smirked. Dutch rolled his eyes.

"Born in Iran. Smuggled out and into the US when you were eight years old. Graduated MIT at sixteen. Familiar with Middle Eastern and Asian cultures, and fluent in twelve modern and ancient dialects."

"Fourteen, actually," Sam amended.

"Impressive," Tanner replied. He turned to another page and focused his attention to Diandra.

"Diandra Marie Weiss: Two doctorate degrees, one each in archeology and ancient civilizations. Supervised over twenty archeological digs around the world. And a recently disclosed expert on what is known as 'forbidden' or 'contradictory' archeology by the revelation of your being the author of *Unexplained Archeology*. A best-seller, I might add," as he gave her a quick wink.

"Geoffrey Alan Duffin, or 'Skip' as most of your friends call you. Served forty years in Britain's MI6, electronics expert extraordinaire, specializing in breaking complex coding, retired with honors," he smirked, "and infamous computer hacker."

Skip took a slight bow as he got up and walked back toward the teacart. Tanner moved to the next page.

"And Peter James Vorhees. Graduated number one in your class at West Point, Special Forces for seven years, took early retirement a few years ago, as a lieutenant colonel. Since then you've completed twenty-one successful missions as a freelance agent for the US government."

Diandra gave Dutch a quizzical look at that revelation. She had no idea he still worked for the government. All this time she thought he was working for, well, bad guys or something. He held his hand up for her to let it pass. Tanner looked up.

"So, to answer your question, Dutch, I couldn't have picked a more synergistic team if one even existed. And I've tried."

"I don't know about you guys," Skip said as he bit into a biscuit from the cart, "but I'm impressed."

Dutch was still wondering what Tanner's angle was. Ten million dollars is a lot of dough for just finding something, no matter how you cut it. Maybe to him it's pocket change. But even so, he must know what it meant to them. There must be more to it.

"So who were those guys back at the museum that were trying to kill us?" Dutch asked.

"Good question, Dutch. We're trying to find that out now. We've been monitoring your progress since you arrived here in Berlin, and were tipped off about this other group by the limousine company. We're not sure who they are or what they know. I'm assuming we'll find that out and take care of it."

He looked toward Diandra.

"I'm sorry we couldn't have gotten our men there sooner, and that you had to go through that."

"She was in good hands," Dutch piped in, feathers ruffled. "We would have been okay even if your men hadn't intervened."

"Well… of course, Dutch. I didn't mean to imply otherwise." Tanner said.

Men, Diandra thought. *Do they ever stop competing?*

"When do you need a decision, Mr. Tanner?" Diandra asked aloud.

"Now. This is a one-time offer, my *bottom line,*" Tanner replied, acknowledging Dutch. "Take it or leave it. Your choice."

The ticking of the clock was the only sound in the room. The four of them looked at each other while pondering what they would say.

"I say we do it," Sam offered. "This is everything we could ask for."

"I've got some legal problems," Skip informed him, "that may preclude me from-"

"They've already been taken care of," interrupted Tanner with a slight smile.

"Oh." Skip liked that. "You can do that?"

"We have certain influences in various governments," Tanner stated matter-of-factly. "Sometimes they come in handy."

"My only concern is that whatever we find reaches the general public." Diandra stated. "I don't want another Dead Sea Scrolls fiasco. If you can guarantee that, then I'm in."

"It's done." Tanner answered.

Tanner turned to Dutch.

"And how about you, Dutch? As you've already found out, the road ahead will be dangerous. This plan of mine only works if you're in too. Are you up for it?"

It was more of a taunt than a question. They all turned toward Dutch, waiting for his decision. He saw the excitement in Diandra's eyes, the same eyes he fell in love with when they first met. He looked back at Tanner, returning his unblinking gaze. They were on even ground. Tanner needed him, and Dutch knew it.

"We have full control and say so on what we do and how it's done?" he asked.

Tanner slowly nodded yes, without breaking the stare between them.

"Well then… I guess we'll be doing business together," Dutch stated.

For the first time, Tanner broke into a big, boyish smile. He turned and came around from behind his desk in a wheelchair, reaching out his hand to seal the deal.

"I guess we will," Tanner said.

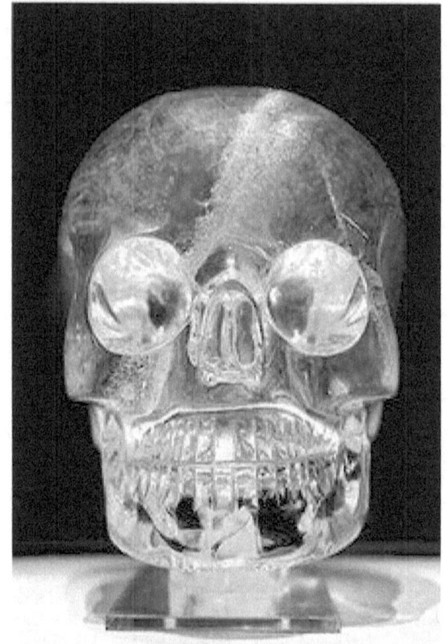

Crystal Skull

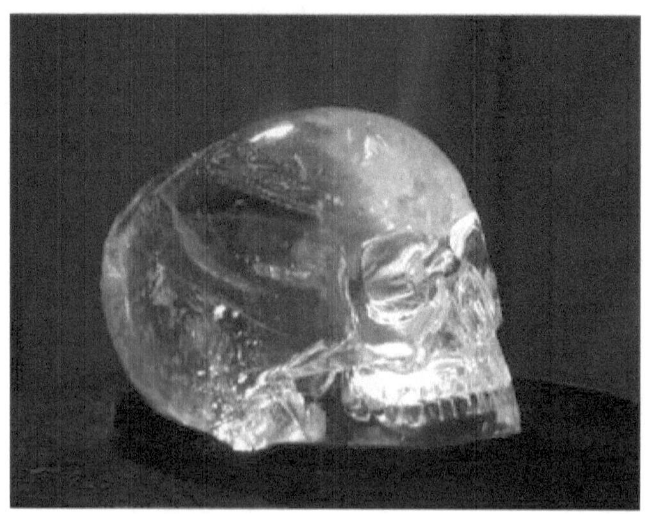

Mitchell-Hodges Skull

Baghdad Battery

Temple of Baalbek – Lebanon

Largest carved stone on Earth

Vimana spacecraft found in a tomb in India

Helicopter and Spacecraft depicted in Egyptian Hieroglyphs

An example of one of the giant Stone Balls of Costa Rica

Ancient Stone ball in front of the
National Museum of Costa Rica

Pyramid of Giza, Egypt

Göbekli Tepe – Located in Turkey
Considered the world's oldest temple

Nan Madol – Pacific Island city

The Lost Tomb of Alexander

Part Two

Knowledge is the true organ of sight, not the eyes
Panchatantra

Chapter One

Tanner Enterprises,
Berlin, Germany

Brushed steel elevator doors silently glided open. Dutch, Diandra, Skip and Sam, who was fidgeting quite nervously and appeared sweaty, were met by a strikingly beautiful black woman in a white lab coat. Her perfect oval face was framed by a short, chic hairstyle. She appeared to be in her early thirties and wore rimless glasses and an unobtrusive Bluetooth device inside her left ear.

"If you will all kindly follow me," she pleasantly said, motioning, "my name is Zoë. Mister Tanner has instructed me to assist and furnish you with whatever you require."

* * * * * * * *

The previous twelve hours had been a whirlwind for the Seekers. After meeting Tanner they were whisked away to the Kempinski Hotel Bristol on Kurfürstendamm Boulevard in downtown Berlin, accompanied by a new 'Men in Black' security team. The entire top floor had been reserved for them; everything they could want was provided. Dutch noted the men in black remained by the elevators while others waited watchfully outside the hotel.

Diandra phoned her mother Katheleen to catch up. Dutch checked with his contacts in Switzerland and confirmed that the money was indeed in their account. He also placed an ad in The World Herald Daily. Skip enjoyed a hot bath accompanied by a special complimentary tea service that had been provided by the hotel, while Sam was on his smart phone checking worldwide soccer and baseball scores.

Dutch also had Skip research Tanner Industries. It was a private holding company that managed hundreds of smaller companies worldwide. Everything from fiber optics to shipping. Skip discovered that, in addition, they were a major contractor along with Blackwater in supplying services in Iraq and Afghanistan. *Could be bad or good depending on the circumstances*, Dutch noted.

Although officially incorporated in Delaware in 1947, the company had, in fact, been in existence since the 1850's when Tanner's great, great, grandfather emigrated from Kentucky to California, spurred on by the gold rush. After a modest find, he and his family then opened a string of supply goods shops that prospered tremendously during that period. They also procured lucrative contracts to supply the US Calvalry and army with foodstuffs and other staples.

When the Pacific railroad was finally connected at Promontory Point, Utah, in 1869, the Tanner family procured the exclusive lease for space on the trains for cargo traveling east and west, cementing the continuation of the family's fortune.

Robert Tanner took over as head of the company in 1969, having left the Marines after a devastating crash in an A-35 trainer jet, which left him a paraplegic. Under his guidance and vision, Tanner Industries, had it gone public, would have become one of the fifty largest companies in the world.

Dutch wondered why he had never heard of them before and made a mental note to follow up with his contacts about that when the time presented itself.

* * * * * * * *

Zoë led the team down a stainless steel hallway to another burnished steel door. Placing her hand on a piece of glass, a green bar scanned it while a red laser quickly flashed and read her eye's retina. The door whooshed open to a balcony overlooking a football field of floor space below. Security cameras, although unobtrusively placed, were present everywhere. Dozens of white-coated and gloved personnel were milling about at tables photographing, measuring, x-raying and testing what appeared to be ancient and not so ancient artifacts – tablets, vases, small statues and paintings. The environment was spotless. Zoë directed them toward a flight of stairs.

"What, exactly, is this place?" Diandra asked as they proceeded down.

"Tanner Enterprises, among many other things, is the world's largest transporter of ancient and collectable artifacts. An ancillary benefit for us," Zoë tilted her head and her brown eyes warmed, "is that everything we transport is brought through here, or one of our other sites like this around the world, for examination, research and analysis before being shipped on to its final destination. We get to see some truly amazing things."

They reached the bottom of the stairs and walked along the perimeter of the processing floor giving Sam and Diandra a close view of the operation. Their close proximity to the artifacts surprised and thrilled them both.

"This is amazing," Sam whispered to Diandra, pointing. "Do you see that statue of Amenhotep over there?" he marveled, gesturing to the idol. She nodded, wagging her eyebrows.

"Our operations allow us access to pieces that we otherwise would not be able to view," Zoë said. "We are trusted implicitly by even the most secretive of collectors and governments."

"Why is that, Zoë?" Dutch asked.

"Because we *never* ask questions," she answered, not missing a beat.

Skip looked to Dutch with a smirk and leaned in.

"Oh, I like her," he whispered with a sly smile.

"You said there are facilities like this elsewhere?" Diandra asked, clearing her throat and shooting Skip a look.

"At least one in every major country. We have three in America," Zoë turned to Diandra. "One very near your home city of New York."

Reaching another door, Zoë gracefully repeated the hand/eye security process and the door retracted, revealing a huge octagonal room over nine stories in height. She ushered them inside and the door clicked shut behind them. Polished white marble slabs protruded from the walls, with metal shelves recessed within them. Three sets of robotic arms picked up books from a conveyer belt and moved them to various designated shelf locations on the walls. It seemed there were millions of books visible.

"Welcome to the Berlin Book Repository," Zoë said.

Standing there viewing the scope of the operation, the four of them were awestruck.

"What is this place?" Sam murmured.

"My thoughts exactly," Skip remarked crisply.

"It looks like every book ever printed," Diandra said wonderingly.

"Actually, it is merely *every book ever printed* in Russian, German and most languages of the various Eastern bloc countries," Zoë stated matter-of-factly. "This is part of our Archival and Retrieval of Knowledge, or ARK initiative, for short."

"Isn't Google doing something like this?" Sam asked.

"They are trying, in an amateurish way," she responded coolly, guiding them deeper into the repository.

Zoë stopped as they reached a shallow alcove. Diandra noticed it was bare except for a lone planter box and a hand scanner on the right wall.

"This is where you will be working on your research. Everything you need to decode the tablets should be in there. If you should need any help-"

"Unfortunately, Zoë, not only is my German and Russian a little rusty," Skip said, "I don't work on paper."

"Where are we supposed to work?" Diandra asked.

Zoë gestured to the scanner.

"Would you be kind enough to put your hand on that reader, Mister Duffin?"

"*Please*, my good lady, call me Skip," he said, chiding her with a wink.

She motioned again with her head and hand, showing no reaction to his obvious attempt at flirtation. Moving up to the scanner, Skip placed his right hand and watched as the green light scanned it, while a red light quickly flashed in his eyes. Instantly, two doors opened before them.

Skip gave her an impressed look "How did you do that?"

"All of your biometrics were taken during our walk from the elevator," Zoë stated. "Each of you is now cleared to go anywhere in this and any other Tanner Enterprises facility."

"That's some pretty sophisticated technology," Sam noted.

"Really?" Zoë replied, bemused. "We've had it for quite a while."

Stretching beyond the doors was a spacious NASA style command room. Four wall-sized computer screens, various terminals, keyboards and scanners hummed imperceptibly in the background. Skip grinned and rubbed his hands together like a kid in a candy store. "Ah!" he said happily. "I've missed this since leaving MI6!"

Behind one of the glass walls towered a large steel bookcase containing thousands of metallic CD size discs organized in rows. A dormant robotic arm sat nearby.

"Every book you see in our facility has already been laser scanned onto titanium memory discs," Zoë continued. "Each has been translated into fifteen major languages, cross referenced and key-worded for search. This main terminal is connected to all of our other repositories worldwide. Additionally, we are connected to Internet two and three, which means you now have access to all academic material, worldwide. These have also been translated."

Skip surveyed the room, drew a deep breath and then stared at Zoë, letting the air escape in a thin, low whistle.

"I must say, Zoë, this is a brilliant set up you have here."

"Thank you… *Skip*." She smiled at him and then eyeing the group inquired. "I trust the accommodations are to your liking?"

They nodded as Skip tried to hold Zoë's eye contact for a split moment. Smiling, she continued. "Anything additional you may need, please ask either me or the special concierge at the hotel. I can be reached through any computer in this facility simply by speaking my name." She tapped her ear device. "Now, if there is nothing else…"

"Actually Zoë, there is one thing," Skip said, slightly raising an index finger.

"PG Tips I assume? A pot is in the room to your left, steeping. By the way, there is a suite of small sleeping rooms and a lounge to your right. Our executive chef will cook anything you order. When you are ready to return to your hotel, just-"

"Call out your name?" Skip spoke out in a singsong.

She laughed as she walked to the doorway.

"*Something* like that. By the way, Jeff Steinberg, our CTO, will be here in a few moments to go over the architecture of the computer system."

Skip's eyes trailed after Zoë as she left the room. "What a *beautiful* woman," he sighed.

"You can say that again," murmured Dutch, "and smart too."

"She's a babe," Sam confirmed.

"Men!" Diandra groused. "I hope there's a shower in here." Then, looking through the doors toward the book repository, a puzzling thought occurred to her. "I don't get it," she wondered aloud. "Why has Tanner gathered all of these books? It's like he is storing the entire world's history of knowledge."

"Maybe he just likes to read?" Dutch chimed in.

* * * * * * * *

Vatican City, Rome

"What happened in Dresden?" Lilne demanded to know, pacing about his desk.

"Someone helped them escape," Shadow Man's voice scratched coldly from his cell phone. "An unforeseen circumstance."

"Do we know who?"

"Unknown at this time. I am making inquiries."

"Do I need to find someone else to handle this matter?" Lilne taunted.

A few moments of silence passed.

"I will complete the job as promised. It is a game of chess, and we are only in the first moves. We do not know all the players yet."

"I have neither the time nor patience for a game of chess… or your excuses," Lilne fumed. "We have recovered the stolen tablet. Now we need McIntyre and the *other property* in his possession. That is where your attention must be focused."

"And it will be," Shadow Man responded calmly. "I am making inquiries in Morocco. We'll soon know if our quarry is still there."

Lilne disconnected the call. Thinking for a moment, he pushed a button on his desk.

"Send me an update on known independent contractors operating within Berlin and elsewhere in Germany," he demanded.

* * * * * * * *

Chapter Two

Tanner Enterprises,
Berlin, Germany

"So where do we start?" Diandra queried luxuriating in her ergonomically designed rolling chair. She scooted a few feet to the left, experimenting.

"We will start with what we know," Skip replied as he lovingly considered his new oversized Oriental tea mug with its clever matching lid to keep the liquid hot.

"We know that the laws of physics took a holiday back at the museum," Sam offered while studying the metal repository with the titanium discs.

Skip removed the lid by a tiny gold knob on top and sipped his tea pondering Sam's remark.

"There is *always* a cause Sam," he said. "It is how the universe works. We just don't understand the mechanics of it yet. My guess is it is based on some kind of electromagnetic energy. We'll find out once Tanner's people finish x-raying and testing the tablet fragment we have. But that hardly seems credible given the antiquity of the thing."

"Not really," Dutch offered. "There is that three-thousand year old Baghdad battery that produces electricity."

Diandra threw him a surprised look.

"I told you I read your book," he informed her with a smile.

Shaking her head in mock disbelief, Diandra picked up a copy of the photo image captured by Skip revealing the transitioned tablet in Dresden.

"Well, it was no magnet like I've ever seen, Skip," she said. "More like a…, I'm not sure what. It looked like a soft wave or transformation of sand. The detail is astounding."

"Indeed," Skip said. "Such intricate formations and images: lines, circles, symbols. It is surprisingly complex."

"Are you saying you can't crack it?" Dutch challenged.

"Now, I did *not* say that, did I?" Skip replied, eyebrows raised. "I was simply letting you know that I will be earning *my* share of our new-found fortune."

"Then you'd better get to work. Looks like it will be a long night," Dutch said, glancing at his watch and thinking for a moment. "Speaking of which, I need to check for a message I've been waiting for." Pulling out his smart phone, he dialed and was greeted by a recorded message.

"No coverage here," he grumbled, pocketing the phone.

"I am sure this whole facility is Faraday protected from electrical magnetic frequency interference, Dutch," Skip assessed. "You can call through this computer."

"I'd rather not. I'll be back in a few minutes."

"What is the call about?" asked Diandra.

"Earning *my* part of our fortune."

Dutch nodded as he passed a middle-aged suited man entering the room.

"Good day, Mister Duffin. I am Doctor Jeff Steinberg, Chief Technology Officer for Tanner Industries, and I am at your service."

"How *lovely* to meet you, my good man," Skip replied, rising to shake hands. "And by the way, my name is Skip. I've been taking in this facility you have provided and must say I am *very impressed*."

"Coming from you sir, I am honored." Dr. Steinberg replied with a small, good-natured bow.

Skip beamed as Diandra and Sam reacted with approving looks at the kudos for their friend.

"Do you have any questions?" Jeff continued.

"Mainly about parallel processing and how many simultaneous functions the system will handle."

Jeff smiled slightly as he walked up to the keyboard and leaned over it, entering keystrokes. His diminutive frame and slightly graying temples gave some gravitas to his mid-forties age.

"This is a dual xenon processor based terminal you will be working on, Skip. We already have one thousand two hundred of these processors up, running and coded. That should give you a terabyte of processing per second."

Skip slurped his tea on that note.

"Oh, pardon me. Indeed. That is… very fast."

"One trillion operations per second, Di," Sam offered in response to her look of confusion.

Jeff grinned. "We will be adding more as you need it. I'll keep an eye on your usage and adjust accordingly."

"How much can you add?" Skip asked, more for his own benefit than need.

"I am quite sure you will not max out this system anytime soon. As to your question, given enough time, unlimited."

Jeff typed a few more keystrokes.

"Here are your access codes." He straightened up and addressed the group. "Is there anything else you need?"

"I have another question," Skip said. "What about a firewall?"

"We are a fully secured facility, Mister Duffin," Jeff answered.

"I mean *from* Tanner Industries."

"I am not sure I understand?"

"We want the research we do to be off-line and on a separate password protected server. Can you provide that?"

"Interesting," he answered, pursing his lips as he thought about it. "I will have a dedicated server delivered here in fifteen minutes. You can download everything to it with full access. Will that be sufficient?"

"Lovely, Jeff."

Sam half-raised his hand.

"Is there a terminal where I can access..."

"This should work nicely for you, Mister Hussein," Jeff said as he handed him an iPhone.

"Wow. Version 6.0. I didn't think they offered that yet." He cradled it as if it were spun glass.

"They don't. It is connected to the mainframe and will get you anywhere you want to go on the Internet. It has been a pleasure meeting you," Jeff said, eyeing each one warmly, "and if you should need me, you can-"

"Call out your name near the computer?" Sam and Diandra spoke out simultaneously.

"You already know," he responded with a slight laugh.

As Jeff left, Skip slid into a rolling chair before the array of screens and set down his tea, replacing the little golden lid. He reached for the handy wipes left for him and started his ritual, finishing with the fingernails. Raising his hands as a conductor would before his orchestra, he spied the access codes Jeff left on screen.

"Well, my dear. Time to see what you've got."

* * * * * * * *

Chapter Three

Cafe im Literaturhaus
Fasanenstrasse 23

Early morning sunlight started dissipating the dew left from the previous night. Newspaper vendors, business people rushing about and the hubbub of an embryonic workday were in full view on Western Berlin's skyline. Brick buildings appeared storybook like with ornamental cement arches and canopies of various colors overreaching the cobblestone sidewalks. Dutch sat in front of Cafe im Literaturhaus, sipping a cafe Americano to which he had strategically added some Jack Daniels.

A newspaper dropped onto his table with a big red circle around an obituary, startling Dutch to attention. He turned to see a familiar dark, sweaty face. Navarro quickly slipped into the chair opposite him. Dutch checked his watch.

"What kept you?"

A waitress promptly appeared and asked if she could get Navarro anything.

"A triple shot cappuccino, two-percent milk, please," Navarro answered.

She moved over two tables where the three familiar *gorillas* in Navarro's employ were once again failing to be discreet.

"The grocery bill on those three must be huge. How do you afford to keep them fed?"

Navarro laughed. He always enjoyed his banter with Dutch, and especially taking his time to answer.

"Work pays well," he finally responded, taking off his hat and running his fingers through his slicked back hair. "Speaking of which, to what do I owe the pleasure of traveling two thousand kilometers overnight? And, first class I might add."

Dutch leaned in closer and lowered his voice.

"Somebody tried to take out my team on a small job in Dresden three days ago. I want to know who was behind it and why. They were definitely Special Ops trained and probably entered Berlin within the preceding twelve hours."

"I'll check around," Navarro said, pulling out a case of Cigaronne Blacks. He extracted one and lit it slowly, blowing the smoke away from Dutch.

"Also," Dutch continued, "What do you know about a Robert Tanner?"

"The industrialist?"

Dutch nodded. "Can I trust him?"

Navarro took another drag from his cigarette, a thin trail of smoke exiting his nostrils as he spoke.

"You know me, Dutch. I don't trust anybody. But if it is any consolation, I hear good things about him."

Navarro smiled as the cappuccino arrived. The waitress also set down a bag of pastries for Dutch.

"Dankashe," Navarro offered. Focusing back on Dutch he asked if there was anything else he needed.

"I think there may be a connection with a fellow named McIntyre."

A slight twitch above Navarro's left eyebrow told Dutch he hit something.

"Are you sure about that?" Navarro asked.

"No, I'm not. That's why I am mentioning it."

Navarro took a long sip of his coffee. He slowly set the cup down, rattling it slightly in the saucer. Quickly he stilled it with his other hand.

"I have heard things. Rumors really. Some parties very high up want him found and are offering a substantial reward. Alive. Very bad people, Dutch. Not to be crossed."

"Can you find out more?"

"Perhaps."

The waitress brought a tray of food to the gorillas; piles of sandwiches, a gigantic basket of fruits, and large cups of coffee. Dutch shook his head and smiled.

"On another matter," Navarro continued, "are you interested in a new mission?"

"I told you, I'm through."

"Pity," Navarro stated. "Have you seen today's headlines?"

Dutch looked down at the World Herald Daily and opened it to the front page. The headline read:

Long Forgotten Servicemen Returned Home. Accompanying the article appeared one of the pictures Dutch had given Navarro in Turkey.

"I'll be leaving Berlin soon," Dutch said without looking up, still reading. "When you have the information, send it to me via this website."

A card tossed to Navarro read *JPV@TheSeekers.com*. Navarro pocketed it. Standing up, Dutch left the paper on the table, donned his coat and started to pick up his pastry bag. Navarro grabbed his forearm.

"Now who is embarrassing whom?"

Dutch smiled as he dropped an envelope onto the table.

"Shall I count it?" Navarro asked.

"Up to you."

Navarro smirked. It was always the same game. In the twenty years they had known each other there had never been a shortage of funds delivered. Trust or no trust, they always kept their word.

"We'll be in touch soon, my friend," Navarro told him. Grimacing and shaking his head at the salutation, Dutch turned to go up the street, passing the three gorillas on his way.

"Hey," Dutch said, holding up the bag as he passed them. "You guys should really try the pastries here. They're very good."

Navarro laughed as he slipped the envelope into his pocket.

* * * * * * * *

Morocco

"Yes?" a voice answered on the other end of the telephone.

McIntyre had patiently waited for a week to hear from Cardinal Assanti. They had devised a system where he would check the Vatican website and a cryptic message would be left for him, after which he would contact Assanti. None had appeared.

"Is his Excellency Cardinal Assanti there, please?" McIntyre timidly asked.

"Who is this?" the voice requested.

"A friend from the Sarmoun Monastery," he replied.

Silence for a few moments.

"I am sorry to report that his Excellency has died."

"Excuse me?" McIntyre's voice stumbled out. "Ah, whom am I speaking with?"

"Father Daniels, his personal secretary. If you need information as to the time of the wake, I can send it to you."

McIntyre hit end call at the Internet cafe and sat there, dumbfounded and unable to process what he had just heard.

* * * * * * * *

Chapter Four

Tanner Industries,
Berlin, Germany

Dutch entered the lab carrying the pastry bag while gingerly balancing a tray of steaming, lidded Styrofoam cups. He found Diandra and Sam browsing through books, while Skip sat fascinated and consumed at the computer. A white Plexiglas screen against the wall covered with electronic writing from Sam and Diandra revealed it had been a productive morning.

"Anyone up for some pastry and a caffeine rush?" he asked, motioning with the bag and tray.

Dropping them on a small table, the three took a welcome break and joined him, each grabbing pastries from the bag and a cup. Skip removed the lid from the one Dutch handed him.

"Oh my goodness, coffee?" he grumbled.

Dutch smiled and pulled a different cup from under his jacket, a tea bag label hanging from the lid.

"Gotcha," he smiled.

"I see some civility has finally rubbed off on your less than couth nature," he said, grabbing the cup and savoring the aroma. He carefully poured it into his new mug.

Dutch studied the Plexiglas board for a few moments.

"How is it going?" he asked.

"Slowly would be a fair word at this point," Sam responded in a frustrated tone.

Dutch studied the board again, noting the layers of cross outs and do-overs.

"So that's it, huh?"

Sam chomped down his cherry croissant and gestured roughly with his hand, spraying bits of buttery flakes toward his computer.

"So far we've managed to decipher very little," Sam said. "We keep thinking we're getting close to what it means, but then nothing pans out."

"Skip?" Dutch asked.

"Quite right at this point," he agreed. "This is one tough bugger."

Dutch thought for a moment. "How about running what you know fresh by me, and see where it goes," Dutch suggested.

"At this point, that sounds like an excellent idea," Diandra concurred, sipping her caffeine fix. "Maybe if we all listen to what we have, it will help jar something loose."

She remained standing by the board while Sam and Dutch took seats.

"Skip, can you pull the tablet up on this screen?" she asked.

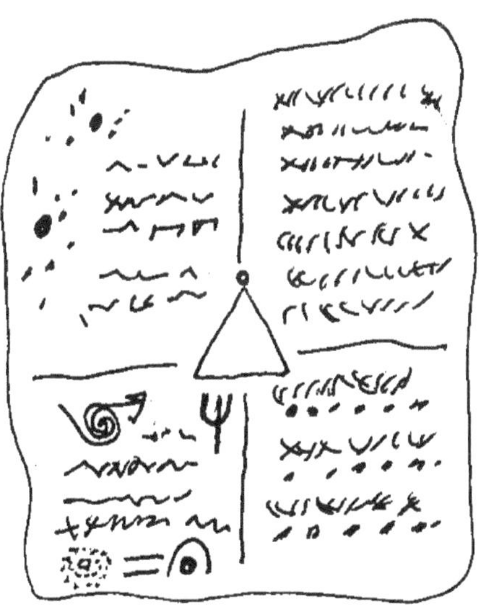

Without answering he turned and pressed some keys. Diandra pushed a switch on the wall, which lowered the lights.

"The tablet is divided into four quadrants," Diandra stated once the picture displayed, "with this triangle shape as a center to the crossed lines. We know there are two stars, or systems, in this upper left quad here," she continued, pointing. "What they mean is unknown at this point, although one of them is reminiscent of Sirius. Also, the symbols in this area appear to be mathematical, but of an unknown script. The next quad to the right is pure symbol lettering, and we think it is a version of Sumerian, perhaps precedent to their cuneiform. If we are right, we should be able to break this portion very soon."

She took another drink of coffee and replaced it on the table.

"The lower left is really interesting. This drawing resembles one of the glyphs in Nazca, Peru. The other one is completely unknown. The trident is a close replica of the one carved into the mountains leading to the Nazca plateau and visible from both the ocean and the sky. All these signs indicate it may have something to do within or near present day Peru. There is also this drawing, here, that may indicate a cave or opening. Skip, can you pull up the Mayan Symbols?"

Skip typed a few keystrokes and they appeared on the screen to the right. "Notice here the resemblance of the glyphs to Mayan," she said, pointing again. "Maybe pre-Mayan? And, it looks like mathematical symbols and words here, and here."

"This last quadrant is perplexing as well," she explained, stepping to the right and pointing to an area on the lower right of the tablet. "It contains lettering, and these dots in clusters under each of what we are, for now, considering to be word groups."

"Anything at all we can tie into Alexander or where he is buried?" Dutch asked.

"That's the odd thing about this," Sam broke in. "Our original tablet fragment clearly mentions Alexander and his sepulcher, but so far, nothing on this new version that appeared seems to correlate with him in any way."

"We've run Alexander's name through various programs. Nothing matches up," Skip added.

"Skip," Diandra, asked, "Will you pull up the various Sumerian-based translations we've worked on for quad two?"

He nodded, typing for a few moments. Different Sumerian glyphs appeared beneath some of the strange cuneiform letters.

"Gibberish," she muttered. "We've run this through every translation program we can find, and it is still not complete. Even these are still a guess. We've tried various programs that apply values, like here, and here…"

Diandra stopped, becoming absorbed in thought.

"Di?" Dutch said.

"Hold on," she replied, motioning with her hand. "Skip, maybe this runs right to left."

He spun in his chair and typed.

"Interesting," she said mostly to herself.

"What?" Sam asked, "What have you got?"

"An article I read a few years ago while researching my book. It postulated that when God confused man's language after the tower of Babel incident, he not only changed their language symbols, but also their direction of writing and reading. I'm thinking maybe this tablet is using that same sort of thinking," Turning to the group. "In other words, the different languages go toward the direction of the central point from which they were removed."

Complete silence from the group communicated their thoughts that Diandra was doing an excellent job of holding their attention.

"Present day Iraq," she continued enthusiastically, "is where Babylon and Sumer were located. So, for instance, China is north of Babylon. Hence, Chinese characters go from top to bottom, or south *toward* it. Persian writing reads right to left, or west *toward*-"

"Bingo, Diandra, we have a hit!" Skip shouted. "Take a look."

The image on the large screen changed and the symbols from the quadrant appeared with a translation into Sumerian below them. Sam studied it.

"Holy cow," gasped Sam, moving closer to the screen and mouthing words to himself.

"What does it say, Sam?" Diandra pleaded.

"Okay, just a moment." He grabbed a pen and paper and started writing. It took a few moments to discern how the symbols were related. "This is unbelievable."

* * * * * * * *

Umbrian Region,
Northern Italy

"We've found no leads as to who helped Dr. Weiss and the others escape," a man in his early thirties dressed in Armani from head to toe informed Lilne via his holographic computer screen. "All local operatives have been contacted and accounted for."

"Is there anything more?" Lilne impatiently demanded to know as he leaned forward in his chair.

"There is also no record of anyone being treated for gunshot wounds in any Berlin hospitals that match the intel you provided. It may be they were treated privately, or perhaps died."

Looking through pages he held for a moment, the man continued.

"However, we were able to trace the license plate of the vehicle they escaped in. It is registered to an Isle of Man corporation, which is wholly owned by a Netherlands company called Archival Retrieval Knowledge Systems. The majority shareholder of that corporation is Tanner Industries."

He stopped and caught Lilne's eyes on screen. "Perhaps not coincidently, Tanner Industries has a large presence and headquarters in Berlin."

"This is getting interesting," Lilne said.

"Indeed," he replied. "It is a private holding company headed by a Robert Tanner, and wholly owned by him and his family. A very secretive man. In fact, the only picture we could find of him was in our own archives. I have forwarded it to you."

"I need everything you can find out about Tanner and his companies. Dig deeply. I want no surprises at a later time."

"As you wish, your Excellency," he said as the holographic screen disappeared.

Lilne tapped on his keyboard and a new screen appeared before him. He motioned at it with his finger and sat back while a picture of Tanner appeared. It was a Catholic charity function. Tanner sat in his wheelchair with Cardinal Assanti at his side. Leaning forward, Lilne's eyes narrowed as he realized the connection.

"So, who exactly are you, Tanner?"

* * * * * * * * *

Chapter Five

Tanner Industries,
Berlin, Germany

Skip finished typing in the translation Sam had given him. The golden letters starkly contrasted against the jet-black wall screen. The group drew closer, mesmerized, and began reading out loud, as one.

The key to all knowledge is contained within.
Three times three have we placed it.
Follow the markers left for you.
Only the worthy will discover.
The future of our planet is in the balance.
Those with the wisdom will survive.

"Skip?" Jeff's voice projected from the computer. Skip hit a key and Jeff appeared on a small screen near his desk, while the others continued focusing on the inscription on the big screen.

"Yes, laddie," he replied.

"I have uploaded an update to the UPP program we discussed earlier. A folder is on your screen to monitor it."

"Thank you, Jeff. It appears we'll need this more than ever at this point," Skip replied as he cleared the screen.

"What was that about?" asked Dutch, breaking his focus on the inscription.

"Fantasy land program, really," Skip replied. "Proprietary algorithm and all. Seems Jeff and crew have created the mother of all pattern recognition systems, and can now run a program that finds relationships and similarities without first programming any search parameters. In our case, for instance, it will look for relationships to any historical symbols based on the markings on the tablet. And who knows what else it will find. Give me a moment here."

Typing furiously, he finally hit enter and turned back. "This is really interesting," he explained. "We've been running it on the tablet since we arrived. A program like this was the Holy Grail we were trying to create at MI6. Never thought I'd see a working version of it in my lifetime."

"Can we get back to this inscription and its meaning?" Diandra requested impatiently.

"Good point," Sam added, absently rubbing his hand over the top of his head until his dark hair stood up in dry gel-tufts. "For starters, this message is radically different than what was previously on the surface of the tablet. The original definitely stated that following some sort of keys would take us to Alexander's tomb and his *treasures*," he reminded the group, smiling and winking at Dutch. "However, now I am not so sure if they are related. The reference to our planet's future and three times three don't seem to add up."

"Reading it from a totally non-archeological perspective," Dutch extrapolated as he stood up and paced, "it seems to be telling us that there may be nine locations that contain all knowledge, and that only those who are *wise enough* will be able to find them." Looking to Diandra he added, "And by the way, that was the same thing your buddy in the hospital said too."

"My thoughts echo yours," Diandra added, nodding in his direction as she walked to the screen. "And I do remember what Dr. Werner said. But why or what is this about?" she added, tapping the screen where it said *The future of our planet is in the balance*. "Some cataclysm that happened eons ago? Or is it a warning for the future?" Her eyes searched for an answer. "And what is meant by *all knowledge*?"

"Could be its related to the Mayan prediction of the end of the world in two-thousand and twelve," Sam broke in, catching Diandra's bemused look. "Well," he continued, "those Mayan-like symbols on the tablet could have something to do with it, right?"

"Getting back to reality," Diandra said, shaking her head, "let's just take the message literally. Whatever is on the tablet leads to some sort of repository of knowledge. Isn't that what the Library of Alexandria was in essence? The center of the world's knowledge? Maybe that's how the two are connected."

"The big problem with that supposition is the age of the tablet," Sam countered, breaking from his smart phone's screen, "At the very least it is pre-Sumerian, and I am guessing much older, which puts its creation at least three-thousand years before the library even existed."

Hold onto that thought, young man," Skip interjected. "We have an urgent update coming in."

Spinning round in his chair Skip typed away. Images appeared on the main center screen. His eyes studied the stream of incoming images while simultaneously asking for someone to get him a fresh tea. Sam volunteered and returned in a few moments, a steaming porcelain cup with lid and bag in hand. Skip continued typing, holding them all in suspense, while he silently counted. Finally, he pulled the tea bag out of the cup, took a sip, and leaned back.

"Do you have something for us?" Dutch asked, his patience wearing thin.

"Just a moment," Skip teased, holding up his finger while taking another sip, ecstasy gracing his face.

"Well then," he started, "we now know two rather important additional bits of data." He typed a couple of commands, single-handed. Images appeared on both sides of the center screen.

"One, the upper left quadrant contains two star groups, Orion and Sirius, each with a particular star larger than the rest. The UPP program indicates they could be target stars, or more precisely, points we can measure from. And two, there are also potential angles of degrees that are attached to each one."

"Coordinates?" Dutch offered.

"Probably," Skip answered.

"Like a manual sort of GPS locator?" Sam asked.

"Very good," Skip said while taking another coveted sip of tea. "However, with a GPS you have satellites sending angles to a receiver on the ground, which then extrapolates the data and establishes your location. Two data points would be sufficient for that operation. In this case, you need two additional data points: an observation point located on the ground in reference to the sky from which the angles flow down, and the time frame during the night sky it is taken. Without them both, we won't be able to pinpoint the location."

Skip spun round in his chair to a smaller computer screen, typing while speaking.

"However, there is also something really interesting about this that *I* just figured out. The two angles from the predominant stars also lead, on the tablet, to the tip of the triangle shape in the middle."

"The pyramid at Giza!" Diandra shouted, unable to contain herself.

"Exactly. Unbelievably clever." Skip hesitated a moment for effect. "But not too clever for G A Duffin, code breaker *extraordinaire*."

"Do you know approximately where these coordinates lead?" Dutch asked.

Skip typed a few moments. A map of the Middle East appeared.

"The best I can narrow it down, if we are to assume that the pyramid is the ground reference point, is in this area here." A yellow highlight flashed on the screen and covered a large region. "Somewhere within the areas of southeastern Turkey, northern Syria or Kurdish Iraq. I am pretty sure it is between thirty-six and thirty-seven degrees latitude, and maybe forty-three to forty-five degrees longitude."

"That is one *large* area, Skip," Dutch observed.

"Agreed," Skip acknowledged. "However, I do have an additional bit of good news."

"What's that, Skip?" Diandra asked.

"The UPP program suggests that one of the two symbols on the lower left quadrant may correlate with a known symbol located on the Nazca Plateau. The other one is even more interesting. It turns out there is a picture in a book by Professor Standhead, whom I believe you knew, Diandra?"

"Hero of mine," she acknowledged.

"Yes, well, anyway," Skip continued, "he has a photograph in one of his books that matches it *very* closely. But here is the interesting part. It is a picture of another group of markings south*east* of the main Nazca markings. And up until Standhead found them, they were completely unknown."

"What are you saying, Skip?" Dutch asked.

"I'm saying that this tablet is referencing a landmark that was only discovered five years ago." He let that sink in for a moment. "As amazing as that seems to be, there's more. Since the tablet used coordinates in the upper left quadrant, I actually entered the request in the UPP program to determine if these Mayan-like signs and glyphs could be distances, and sure enough, part of them are. They are based on the Mayan *vigesimal* system, meaning a base unit of twenty in the second placeholder. Same problem as before, only in this case we only need to know the direction of each one.

"Fortunately, the tablet actually shows us and confirms it with the remaining glyphs," Skip said. "Although, it's complicated as hell. There are four dots that seemed to be random on the tablet, two each beside the glyph and the drawing of the structure, and two in the body of the symbols. They look like they are not really part of the tablet, but they are. When we connect the two dots, they form a line at a very specific angle from each one." He turned to type on the keyboard and studied the screen. "Approximately one hundred degrees from the center of the Nazca glyph drawing, and about forty-five degrees from the center point of the rock structure."

Typing, a map of southern Peru appeared onscreen.

"When these lines are extended using these angles and lengths, we have a very particular spot where they intersect."

A small green circle covered a specific area of the map.

"You mean like 'X' marks the spot?" Dutch asked.

"In this case, Mister Vorhees, I believe so," Skip winked and laughed. "Whatever it is the writers of this tablet want us to find there, we have a pretty good idea where to look. It is about seventy-five kilometers northwest of Sascahuarman near Cuzco."

"Near Machu Picchu?" Sam asked.

"No. More inland toward the rainforest area," Skip answered, looking at his computer. "Although I will use that landmark and see if there is a correlation later. And Diandra," he continued. "As we thought, those final symbols and drawing strongly indicate it may be in or near a cave."

"I'm getting chills," Sam said. "This is the bomb."

Silence reigned for a few moments as they digested the information.

"Skip, can you put a whiteboard onscreen?" Diandra asked.

Once it appeared, she stood up and started writing.

"Let's go over what we know," she started, slugging down the rest of her coffee. "First, there is some sort of knowledge hidden by, whom?" She looked to the group. No response. "Okay, we don't know who left this. Next, we believe it is in Northern Turkey-"

"Around latitude thirty-seven and longitude forty-three," Skip said, studying more figures on his screen.

"Okay, somewhere near there. By the way, Sam, that area is near the ancient city of Harran. Let's follow up on that."

Sam nodded and entered it into his smart phone.

"Next, we believe that there is a piece to this puzzle in southeastern Peru near, where is it Skip?"

"Northeast of Cuzco about seventy-five kilometers," he answered.

"So, we have a very good idea where that is located." She set the light pen down and rubbed her hand through her auburn hair, shaking her head.

"So here is the million dollar question. *Why so complicated*?"

"Indeed, although I, for one, relish the challenge," Skip noted.

Dutch jumped up and walked to the main screen.

"It tells us right here why," he said pointing. "It's why no one has found it yet. Only the *worthy* will know. *Wisdom* will prevail. Seems like they, whoever they were, made damn sure it was complicated." He started laughing to himself. "Think about it. They were advanced enough to not only make this tablet, but also to separate two clues by an ocean. A hundred years ago no one would have been able to figure this out. Amazing."

"More than that, it seems impossible," Sam added.

"This whole business seems impossible," Diandra stated, rubbing her eyes. "How about we take a break and eat something."

"I'll catch up with you later," Skip told them. "I still have a lot of work to do."

* * * * * * * * *

Chapter Six

**Tanner Industries,
Berlin, Germany**

While Dutch, Diandra and Sam sat silently eating, the phone on the table rang. Dutch pressed the speaker button.

"Yes?" he answered.

"I spoke with Tanner," Skip relayed, "and he wants to meet with us in his office in fifteen minutes."

* * * * * * * *

Diandra was examining a fourteenth century Portuguese Madonna with Sam looking on while Dutch gazed out at the Brandenburg Gate through the large window. Skip and Tanner's wheelchair almost ran into each other getting to the door.

"Sorry about being late," Tanner stated as he wheeled over to his desk. "I was making some arrangements that will hopefully help. Skip reported that you have made some great progress and filled me in earlier. It is both amazing, and *startling* to say the least."

"I think the Peru piece of the puzzle unlocks the rest of the tablet," Diandra said. "The Rosetta Stone to unlocking the location to… what we're hoping is Alexander's tomb."

"It appears so," Tanner agreed. "Seems like there are two places you have to be in at the same time."

"We've been talking about that, Tanner," Dutch responded, "and think we should divide up; Sam and Diandra to Peru, and then Skip and I can get everything ready in Syria."

"That would have been my suggestion exactly, Dutch. In fact, one of the reasons I am late is because I've been overseeing the retrofit of one of our G10's for your use. I've had Jeff installing state of the art satellite uplinks and computers for *you*, Skip; while there are a couple of special features I am sure *you* will appreciate, Dutch.

"Diandra," Tanner continued, "I think it will be more expedient if we send you and Sam over on a commercial flight. Do you agree?"

"I do," she answered. "Seems like a pretty easy situation to wrap up. Then we can rendezvous with Dutch and Skip in Syria."

Tanner looked over to Skip, noticing the Cheshire grin spreading across his face.

"Is there something else, Skip?" he asked.

"Actually, I hadn't a moment's time in which to inform you all. Just before I arrived for this meeting we made further progress on the fourth quadrant. It seems to be a hymn or song of some sort, just as we originally suspected. We are proceeding on that assumption with the UPP program."

"Good news," Tanner added while turning his attention to the rest. "How soon do you anticipate you'll be able to depart?"

"Twenty-four hours for us," Dutch replied. "There are a number of logistical challenges we have to consider, especially getting in and out of there."

"What are they?" Tanner asked.

"For starters, it is a very dangerous region. Not real high on the American tourist list, if you get my meaning. We don't exactly blend in." Noticing Sam's crestfallen look. "Well, apart from you. There is still an undeclared war going on. It is a disputed territory with the Kurds and Turkey, and NATO runs patrol and training exercises intermittently in that overall area. If I were picking a place I would *least* want to go into stealthily, that area would be first on my list. Even *with* a professionally trained team.

"Given the tensions in the region, and the potential for an uprising starting at any time, I believe rendezvousing in northern Syria and taking local transportation is the best way for us to get close enough before we go in on foot. I am thinking we get as far as Tali Kujik and then recon a way to get in and out without bringing much attention… maybe somehow appear as locals. As I said, Skip and I have some work to do."

"I have some cousins still living in that area we can contact," said Sam. "They may be very helpful."

Dutch nodded. "Great, Sam. Let's connect with them once we have our plan in order."

"Anything else?" Tanner asked the group.

"That's it for now," Dutch replied.

Tanner wheeled out from around his desk.

"I would say this is going to be quite the adventure. I wish I were going with you… but as you see," tapping his wheelchair, "I don't think my ATV here would be much help. You'll need to be my eyes and ears. But I will stay apprised and Zoë will be available twenty-four seven whenever you need anything. She has full authority to make any necessary decision."

"Thanks for everything, Mister Tanner," Diandra said.

"You're welcome. And good luck to you all," he said emphatically, smiling.

"It's going to take a lot more than luck to get us through this one," remarked Dutch sarcastically. "Planning and execution is critical for any mission to be successful."

He got up and headed toward the door, then stopped short.

"But to be on the safe side, I'll take luck whenever I can get it," Dutch said.

Tanner smiled slightly and looked down, absorbed in reading some papers. Dutch started to leave again.

"Oh, by the way, Dutch," Tanner responded without looking up. "I hope I checked out okay."

"So far, so good," Dutch replied without hesitation. "I'll keep you apprised if anything changes."

* * * * * * * *

The Seekers spent the next couple of hours planning their rendezvous in Syria after Diandra and Sam finished up the details of their itinerary to Peru.

"Can we take a break for a minute, guys?" Sam asked, pushing his chair away from the table and stretching his arms up. "I've been thinking about something. Is it only me who's wondering about how much money, people and time is being thrown at us? I mean, it seems really out of proportion to what we might find."

"I've been thinking the same thing, Sam," Diandra concurred.

"Well, there's a surprise," Dutch said.

Diandra's look stopped his train of thought in its tracks.

"Seriously," Sam continued, undeterred. "We have unlimited funds and resources to find what, the tomb of Alexander? Other ancient sites? And it is *only* for Tanner's curiosity? To just be the first to see what we find?"

"Sometimes guys with no balls and a lot of money do strange things, kid," Dutch said. "Who knows why people like that do anything? Look at the Amazon guy building the spaceport in Mojave. They have way too much money and time."

"I don't know, Dutch, I think the lad's on to something." Skip shook his head. "There may be more to this than we suspect, but at this stage I find myself unable to speculate."

"We don't have time to speculate or care at this point," Dutch stated. "Tanner is paying for everything, and we'll get the fame and glory." Looking to Diandra. "I mean you'll get it."

She withheld comment for a few moments. *Same old Dutch*, she thought. Some things never change.

"I *know* what you mean," she finally said.

"What I *mean* is this," Dutch continued. "We're being paid for a job. He is our employer, we're his lackeys. Very well paid lackeys, I might add. At the end we are all very wealthy, win, lose or draw. So I say we get it over with, do the best we can and enjoy the challenge. Case closed."

Diandra clapped her hands together and motioned them upward.

"Case opened, Amsterdam," she started. "This is more than a job to me. So let's not make it so black and white. Sam has a valid point we need to address. What are Tanner's real motives?"

"Well, well, children," Skip interjected, "unless we're going to call your famous psychic hot line and get a definitive answer, I believe we'll have to defer this conversation until we have more data."

He sat back and ran his hand through his thinning gray hair.

"I will say this," he continued. "We do need to be careful. And keep each other informed of anything we notice. If there is an ulterior motive, which I admit there bloody well could be, we need to know if it is in our best interest or not. His actions will let us know."

"Hopefully not before it is too late," Sam added.

"Okay gents," Diandra interjected. "Let's table this and get on with our plans."

She thought for a minute and added. "And for the record, I have no intuition or inkling that he is telling us anything but what is true. If there *is* more, I believe it has nothing to do with us."

* * * * * * * *

Diandra and Sam were scheduled to leave Berlin on Iberia Airlines flight 3540 at 7:30 am the next morning for Lima, Peru. Planning and arrangements were minimal – they would only need topographical maps, local assistance and such. It made sense for them to leave as quickly as possible.

Dutch and Skip, on the other hand, needed the full twenty-four hours, and more, to prepare for their excursion. Skip was busy finding and generating satellite images and maps, topographical surveys, weather data, historical records, and local language *cheat sheets,* while Dutch planned the route and inspected their new Gulfstream. He learned that the special feature Tanner had provided in the jet was a secret hermetically sealed compartment that would hold weapons and ammunition. Almost impossible to find in case of a customs search, which Syria was famous for.

Catching only a catnap's worth of sleep, Diandra knocked on Dutch's door and came in to say goodbye. He was awake reading Skip's reports.

"I wish I were going with you," Dutch looked up and told her.

"I'm a big girl now, Dutch. I've got a few digs under my belt since we were kids," she answered.

"That's not what I meant-"

"I know what you meant," she interrupted softly, smiling. It was another of those moments she feared; alone with him, tired and vulnerable. Shaking it off, she headed for the door.

"I'll see you when I'm looking at you, Dutch."

"Yeah, yeah. I'll keep some baklava on the table for you too."

After she closed the door, Dutch thought about what he wanted to say to her. To be extra careful. But, he knew it would both alarm *and* piss her off. For the past couple of days Skip had been searching to uncover who it was that tried to kill them at the museum. So far, he hadn't been able to come up with anything of substance. The man killed at the museum was a faceless, nameless assassin – no fingerprints on file anywhere, but of obvious eastern European heritage. Tanner came up with goose eggs as well. It was as if they never existed at all. *Very strange, to say the least*, Dutch thought. His red flag alert system was going full force.

Without knowing who those adversaries were, or more importantly, their motives, Dutch felt vulnerable, especially being responsible for the group's protection. He vowed to err on the extreme side of caution until he knew more.

He and Skip were scheduled to be wheels up at 2:00 pm that afternoon for the little over four-hour flight to Damascus. After clearing customs, they would fly up to Aleppo's International airport.

Sam had given Skip the contact information for his relatives in that city. Dutch was happy to have some trusted locals to call on without having to bring in contract help, which may tip off others to their location. *The fewer people involved the better,* he reasoned.

Onboard the G10, Skip and Dutch continued strategizing as to different scenarios and options they might use once they landed. In his researches, Skip learned of a particular religious sect that was revered and respected by almost all groups they were likely to run into once in the field, including Shiites, Muslims, and Kurds. His idea was to see if they could dress in a particular fashion and pass themselves off as members of this sect and travel relatively unmolested.

Additionally, once in Aleppo they would need transportation, food, and logistical support for the mission, plus a number of other items more easily purchased locally. Skip started making a long laundry list of supplies they would need once there.

Finally able to lie down on the Gulfstream's luxurious couches, they grabbed a few extra winks.

* * * * * * * * *

Chapter Seven

Aleppo, Syria

Pushing a cart loaded with four large bags, Skip and Dutch exited Aleppo International Airport to find an animated, skinny middle-aged Syrian man excitedly approaching them.

"So pleased to meet the friends of my most cherished relations," he jubilantly greeted them with a thick Arabic accent. "My name is Farouq, and I must say your pictures look just like you."

He walked up and gave Dutch a customary left/right cheek kiss, then turned to Skip who instinctively held up his hand as a stop sign.

"I do not do hugs or kisses, thank you very much."

"Ah, an Englander, yes?" Farouq smilingly noted. "Please let me help you with your bags. My vehicle is just over there," he said, pointing.

Dutch and Skip followed his finger to a seriously rusted 1987 Saab 9000 T16; a four-door model with a broken taxi light atop. It was impossible to tell what color it might have been.

"You're daft, right?" Skip asked as Farouq took over steering their cart and motioned them to follow.

"Oh no, this is Saab. Designed by jet fighter engineers, you know. Best car in world."

Reaching the trunk, he popped it open and Dutch set one bag in. Farouq motioned for him to stop and shushed them around toward the back seat. Dutch watched as he tried to get the next bag off the cart. No luck. He redoubled his effort, let out a grunt, and it barely moved. Dutch laughed and stepped forward to grab it and the remaining bags, tossing them in. Farouq then dusted his hands together with evident satisfaction of a job well done, before slamming the trunk. A loud clanging sound confirmed that the front left fender had fallen off onto the pavement. Farouq's shoulders drooped as he grimaced.

"I do hope those jet fighter engineers work for the other side," Skip noted dryly.

Dutch thought that cab rides in New York were the most harrowing he had experienced until Farouq took them careening through Aleppo, where people jumped out of their way, screaming, and curbs were considered passing lanes. At the end of Mr. Toad's Wild Ride he skidded to a stop in front of the Beit Salahieh Hotel Aleppo, located in the Al-Mustadamiyah Quarters.

Skip and Dutch tried to ignore the fender duct-taped to the top of the cab as they exited and looked around. Skip surveyed the hotel, focusing on the fact that it looked as if it hadn't been painted in years, if ever.

"Well then, Mr. Vorhees, I now know where you'll be staying," he said. "You can have Farouq here drive me to the Mandarin or its equivalent in town."

"Afraid not, Skip," Dutch answered, while helping get the bags out of the trunk. "We're deep low-key and non-com here until the mission starts. Then we'll go to plan B as we discussed."

"Unbelievable," Skip retorted shaking his head, watching Dutch empty the trunk. With a visible shiver of disgust he pulled a container of Handi Wipes from his backpack in preparation.

"Please, please, you insult me," Farouq pleaded. "You are my guests. Allow me to do this for you. You go in and relax," he said pushing them away from the car with exaggerated hand motions.

"My wager is they neither have room service nor tea here," Skip grumbled to Dutch as they walked through the front door and into the tiled-floor lobby.

"I wouldn't bet against you on that one," Dutch replied humorously.

After some negotiating with the proprietor and a discreet exchange of cash, Dutch procured a group of adjoining rooms on the second floor. They climbed the stairs while Farouq struggled to get the first bag up behind them. Skip was right about the lack of room service. However, Dutch surprised him by relaying he had managed to have Zoë pack some tea in one of their bags.

Farouq finally dragged the bag into the room and plopped onto the couch.

"American bags are very heavy," he noted, huffing and wiping his brow with his sleeve, almost out of breath.

"Do you see a hot water pot anywhere in here?" Skip asked Dutch while opening and closing the various cabinets.

"Not really," Dutch replied. "Hey Farouq, I'll tell you what. You find my friend here a nice hot water pot and I'll bring up the rest of the bags. Deal?"

"Oh, these is such a good deal, I will take it right now." He jumped up and exited the room, calling over his shoulder. "I will be back in one hurry."

* * * * * * * *

Skip sat transfixed on the electric water pot while it slowly heated up as Dutch entered the room with the final bag, setting it down gingerly. Farouq, in much better shape than earlier, sat on the couch with an empty teacup in hand.

"That's the last one," Dutch noted loudly.

"Oh, these is good, I am waiting for my new English friend Skip to make his tea. I am in charge of the cup." He set it down and stood up. "Friend of my cousin's cousin, if there is anything more which you should need while here… do not hesitate to call on your new eternal friend, Farouq."

"Thanks Farouq," Dutch said, pulling out a piece of paper, handing it to him. "You can help us with some of the supplies we will need."

Farouq slowly unfolded the paper and read intently, his forehead creasing markedly as he moved down the list.

"These is very difficult items to procure. What with the Syrian rebels in Damascus, the fighting and all, everything is hard to come by. Very much expensive." He looked up and raised his shoulders. "If you had come a few days ago, maybe…"

Dutch pulled out a wad of Syrian lira, opened it and looked at Farouq.

"I will need these Thursday."

Farouq was mesmerized by the cash as Dutch started to peel off hundred lira bills, slowly.

"I could possibly be managing, with the greatest of extreme effort, to have them by Sunday, late evening."

Bills continued peeling off.

"I was thinking more like Friday afternoon," Dutch responded.

"Oh no no no no, these is quite impossible. On Saturday later day will be the most earliest before such a list as yours could be fulfilled."

More bills unfolded.

"Saturday morning?"

"Middle day noon?"

"Done," Dutch agreed as he peeled off a few more bills for effect and handed them to him. Farouq quickly placed the cash into his pocket, smiling.

"Also, Farouq, we are going to be doing some exploring east of here, so we will need local transportation."

"Where exactly east of here?" Farouq inquired with a slight frown.

"Could be as far as northern Iraq."

Farouq paled and backed toward the door a few steps.

"Is very dangerous there, very dangerous indeed."

More bills peeled off the bankroll.

"Can you make the arrangements?" Dutch asked.

Grabbing the new cash, his demeanor quickly changed back to the old ingratiating Farouq.

"But of course," he gave a little bow. "Anything is for my new kindred relations. I will be back with these supplies you request on Sunday, noon."

Dutch reached over and grabbed his fist full of money.

"Oh, did I say Sunday?" Farouq squeaked. "Excuse for my mistake. Saturday at middle day noon Farouq will be here."

"Are you two through yet?" Skip chimed in. "Because you're beginning to sound like you're enjoying this little tête-à-tête, and I need to start work here."

"Remember, my almost blood brother, anything else you need, Farouq is your man." He hugged and kissed Dutch goodbye and headed toward Skip, stopped himself, and with another bow, left the room.

The electric teapot started whistling.

"Finally," Skip exclaimed.

* * * * * * * *

As Farouq exited the Beit Salahieh Hotel and jumped into his cab he noticed a rather heavy-set man lurking in the shadows of an alley beside the hotel. He adjusted his rear view mirror and made note of what he looked like as he sped off, almost hitting a pedestrian in the crosswalk.

* * * * * * * *

Chapter Eight

Central Peru, near Cuzco

"So far, so good," Diandra softly thought out loud as she studied the photos and maps of the area in which they hoped to find the Seekers' first physical clue mentioned in the enigmatic tablet.

Their flight into Lima was uneventful, allowing them time to plan the excursion. It was not lost on them how traveling first class had helped make that experience more enjoyable. However, the thunderous rainstorms in the southern Peruvian mountain regions prevented them from flying directly into Cuzco, where the local 737's aerobatic maneuvers to land there, even on a clear day, made most passengers lose their lunch. They decided to fly into Ica airport near Nazca in a Cessna 208 Caravan and take the three hundred plus kilometer bus ride up to Cuzco.

Thanks to Zoë's efficiency they had extensive satellite imagery, maps and location grids to aid them in their quest. She had also made arrangements for a local driver with a four-wheel drive vehicle to meet them when they arrived in Cuzco, where they would head north on highway 3S until reaching Urabamba. From there, they would continue northwest until they needed to go off the road and head toward the general area indicated by the tablet. They would hike in by foot the rest of the way.

She and Sam were travelling aboard a decades-old Bluebird bus from the Ica airport up the bumpy and curvy Carretera Interoceanica Highway, along with a few caged chickens and a full load of Peruanos. The bus's windshield wipers barely kept ahead of the torrential rain as they alternately sped, slowed, and lurched around decrepit farm vehicles and small herds of cattle and their rain-soaked caballeros as the bus headed toward the J. Manuel Seoane exit into Cuzco. Diandra continued smiling her apologies at the woman sitting in front of her as the maps and charts she unfolded brushed the back of the woman's head.

Sam, using the GPS on his smart phone, calculated it would be less than twenty minutes before they arrived, even with the heavy downpour that had been battering the roads since they started their journey almost seven hours earlier.

As the bus made a slight left turn onto Avenida Prado Alto, three black Land Rovers with flashing blue lights appeared directly ahead, blocking the road. Machine gun bearing men in green army fatigues stood at full attention front and center, drenched, except for one carrying an umbrella above one of them. Shouting out a curse or two in Spanish, the bus driver threw up his arms in frustration and screeched to a stop.

Diandra half looked up while grabbing the sliding papers and maps she had spread out, unconcerned and assuming it to be a security check point.

"Do you have your passport ready?" she asked Sam, who was staring ahead through the rain-spotted windshield as the men approached.

Sam held up one hand to shush her as he strained to hear what they were saying. The soldiers were shouting to each other and toward the driver, in Portuguese. His face went ashen.

"Trouble, Diandra," he urgently whispered.

"What?" she said turning to him and suddenly concerned by his ghostly pallor.

Two of the rain-soaked military-dressed men entered the bus, machine guns in hand, and stood at attention on either side of the aisle. The driver had turned in his seat and was shouting at them. The closest man rammed the butt of his weapon into the driver's head, slamming it back into the side of the bus. He slumped down into his seat, bleeding from his nose and mouth.

A third man, dressed like an officer, slowly walked to the bus door, closed his umbrella and jumped up the three steps to enter. The two saluted and called him Commandant. He slowly took off his gloves while surveying the passengers, his red beret barely dripping water on his shoulder pleats. Silence reigned while the downpour continued pounding atop the bus. Slowly he started walking down the Bluebird's aisle, looking left and right at the passengers, all trying to avoid his steely glare. Diandra quietly put the maps and pictures under the seat and out of view. Reaching their aisle, he stared down at her.

"Passport?" he demanded, with outstretched hand.

Diandra pulled it out from her purse and handed it to him. He looked to Sam, who quickly handed his over. Opening them, the commandant's eyes darted over the blue booklets' contents.

"Americanos?"

Diandra and Sam nodded.

A slight smile etched his scraggily bearded face as he lasciviously eyed Diandra's body from head to toe. She noticed a twitch under his left eye.

"You both will come with me," he ordered in English, motioning with a jerk of his head.

"What is this about?" Diandra demanded to know.

"Guardias!" he shouted while waving his arm. They quickly headed down the aisle as the commandant moved away from their seat. One of them grabbed Diandra and yanked her up.

"What are you doing? Hey!" she shouted defiantly, trying to shake loose from the man holding her. "We're American citizens. We've done nothing wrong."

Forcefully he pulled her toward the front of the bus. Passengers' eyes purposely ignored the entire scene. Sam was grabbed next and forcefully pulled out of his seat.

"We need our bags!" Diandra screamed at the commandant.

"I am afraid you will not be needing them," he snarled back..

"Let me go," she pleaded to the soldier holding her. "This is illegal. You can't do this to us."

"Ah, but we can," the commandant laughed from behind them as they were dragged off the bus and into the pouring rain. He shouted some orders while raising his umbrella and two more military men ran to help drag Diandra and Sam toward the SUVs.

After being searched and forcefully thrown in the back seat of one, the commandant spoke with two of the men outside their door. They laughed as he kicked shut the Land Rover's rear door and walked away.

"Who are they and what were they saying?" Diandra quietly asked Sam.

"Red Guard rebels," he answered. "I heard them speaking before they got on the bus."

"Oh my god," Diandra breathed. "What have we gotten into?"

Sam shrugged his shoulders. "I don't know," he replied, visibly shaken.

The two men jumped in and started the Land Rover, still laughing. The entourage sped east onto the main highway and then north toward the inland jungles.

* * * * * * * *

Chapter Nine

Aleppo, Syria

After settling Skip in at the hotel, Dutch left in search of a local souq the manager had told him about. He took a cab to the jdaide quarter of the old city, home to the great mosque. Armed with a color printout of the type of fabric he would need, he headed south on Al-Khandak Street and turned on one of the unnamed streets where he hoped to find the bazaar. Their plan was to purchase some material at one location and have it sewn at another.

Finally reaching the end of the block, he found what he was looking for – vendors lined up for as far as the eye could see, in the same way they had been since the days of the Byzantine Empire. He loved the sounds and smells of these local businesses. Putting on his best *I am an idiot tourist* face and dressed in non-descript clothing, he headed into the thick of it. After a few minutes of declining everything from incense to cooked sheep heads, he found what he was looking for – a booth that sported hundreds of rolls of fabric in every color imaginable. After the usual and expected five to ten minutes of negotiating, where he purposely paid more than double what he knew the material to be worth, he not only ended up with the material but also the name of a trusted tailor where he could take it and have it sewn.

After dropping the fabric off and supplying pictures and measurements, Dutch returned to the bazaar in search of the next items they needed – prayer boxes. This quest involved finding a half dozen of them that fit the measurements Skip had provided for carrying their equipment. He'd noticed some when there earlier and quickly found a vendor with the right size boxes. After lengthy and, for Dutch, spirited negotiations - which included the use of the owner's teenage son - the two of them carried the boxes back to the hotel, where the final modifications would be made.

Skip, meanwhile, had fired up one of his computers to begin testing their equipment. He first set up a small satellite uplink dish on the sill of a north-facing window. Within a matter of minutes, encrypted communication was established with the main bank of computers at Tanner's Berlin headquarters.

Through Zoë's contacts, they were able to acquire the latest in 'gadgets' as Skip would call them. In this case, the most critical were the personal communicators the Seekers would use in the field – the model 358 made by Lintronics. Small, nearly invisible, the miniature Personal Video Device, or PVD, was placed in the ear with a tiny protruding fiber optic cable the size of a human hair. Heat activated, it would perform for almost twenty-four hours before needing to be recharged. Skip had never worked with these particular models, and wanted to thoroughly test them. A small uplink box would receive the PVD's signals within a distance of thirty feet, and then send those signals to a geosynchronous satellite. Random encryption coding would assure the security of their transmissions.

However, for the three of them to be working simultaneously, Skip needed to add some additional coding to make sure they would work together without stepping on each others' frequencies. He first tested the video and audio and was pleasantly surprised at the quality. Not quite hi-def, but very clear. In color mode they lasted only about twelve hours, so he dismissed that as an option. Black and white it would be. He noted that the time delay from satellite uplink from the relay box to his computer downlink was less than a second. *Very decent,* he thought.

The PVD also came with an extension device that lengthened the tiny fiber optic cable to reach another four inches. It attached to the temple, giving access to video in case hair or some obstruction should present a problem. These worked as advertised.

To maintain power to the units in the desert, Skip had a small solar panel and converter made at Tanner's that would recharge the liquid crystal lithium micro batteries. About the size of a pack of cigarettes, the solar device at their latitude would take about ten minutes to accomplish a full recharge.

Satisfied that everything worked to his specifications, Skip sat back and took a breath. He was an expert in this sort of equipment and mission, and he had proved to himself that the equipment's viability was a perfect match for this mission. Of his skills, he had no concerns. He was prepared for every eventuality he could think of. However, he, like Dutch, was concerned about what they didn't know.

"Nothing is going to go wrong on my watch," he assured himself.

Swatting flies off his cup, he carefully wiped the edge with a Kleenex, then took a swig of tea and almost spit it out.

"Bloody hell!" he shouted, realizing he had been consumed for hours and forgotten about his tea growing cold. "How uncivilized," he muttered.

Dutch walked in with the teenager from the bazaar, and after dropping the boxes off and giving him a small *baksheesh*, the young man left.

"What's the shouting about?" Dutch asked.

"Nothing you'd understand," Skip replied as he got up, poured the contents of his cup into the sink and turned on the hot pot.

"How does the equipment check out?" Dutch asked.

"I am going to go over it again, but so far, so good," he said.

Looking up he swatted another fly while waiting for the hot pot to boil. "Damn dirty beasts!" He grimaced.

"Next time, Dutch, we really do need to get a hotel with room service… and more sophisticated sanitation, I might add."

* * * * * * * *

Chapter Ten

Eastern Peru

Two hours passed before the trio of Land Rovers came to a stop amid a makeshift rebel encampment consisting of a dozen tents and lean-tos encircled by thick jungle foliage. Although the rain had subsided, it had made the red clay soil muddy and difficult to walk in. Diandra and Sam were forcibly removed from the SUV and taken into a ten by twelve foot army camouflage green tent, guarded by two rebels. The commandant stood outside the tent speaking with an unseen man. From the sounds, it was a heated discussion.

"Do you know where we are?" Diandra asked one of the rebels.

He looked at her menacingly and grunted.

"You?" she directed the question toward the other.

He ignored her.

"What are they saying outside?" she quietly asked Sam. Taking in his glance at the rebels, she added. "I don't think they understand English."

He nodded, and then answered.

"They're arguing about how much to ask for our ransom. They think from the ID in your purse you still work for the museum. Me as well. They're hoping to get more for the both of us."

"That's a relief. At least we'll get out of here when they get their money."

Sam looked away, silent.

"Right? Sam?" she said, searching his eyes for a positive response.

"We're in some deep shit here, Di. They're saying that they're going to kill us after the ransom is paid.... at least me."

"What do you mean at least you?"

Silence.

"Sam?"

He avoided her eyes. A moment passed while she processed the implications. Grabbing his shoulders, she shook him.

"Look Sam, once they make the ransom demand, everyone will know we're captive. Dutch will get us out of this."

"I have calculated he and Skip are in Syria by now. I'm not sure we have that long. *Dick for brains* out there is telling everyone he's going to…" He started tearing up, unable to look at her again.

"What is it Sam?" Suddenly, a chill shivered down her back and through her body. She released her hold on Sam as she remembered the commandant's lecherous smile.

"We've got to escape, and quickly," she said.

"That won't be possible, I am afraid," the commandant interrupted, peering into the tent flap now half open. "You have an appointment."

He shouted some orders. The rebels in the tent forcefully pushed them out through the flap door. He barked more orders and two more rebels grabbed hold of them on each side. A small bearded and bespectacled man approached with a newspaper and digital camera in hand. He shoved the newspaper toward Diandra.

"Hold this so your friends can see it clearly," the commandant ordered her. "Your life will depend on it."

"Give it to him," she replied defiantly nodding her head toward Sam. "I'm not going to hold it for you."

The commandant nodded his agreement to the little man as he pulled a ski mask from his side pocket and donned it. Sam yanked a hand loose, grabbed the paper and held it in front of him. The dogs across the compound started barking and growling at the strangers. One of the rebels went to the kennel and ordered them quiet.

"This should speed up the payments," the commandant laughed as he unholstered his silver-plated .45 pistol and touched it to Diandra's temple. The cameraman focused the Canon digital S1 and snapped five flash pictures in quick succession. He studied the LCD screen and nodded an okay to the commandant, who ripped off his ski mask and replaced it in his pocket.

Rain dripping from the side of the tent was the main distraction offered Diandra and Sam as they sat cross-legged on the dirt floor, handcuffed to each other and the central tent pole. Judging from the hours that had passed since they arrived, and the diminishing light outside, they guessed it was getting near nightfall. Both were lost in thought. Sam tapped a non-existent tune with his foot.

The tent flap flew open as the commandant and an aide sauntered in.

"You will be interested to know that we have sent word to your embassy of your situation. We expect a reply very soon as to when you will be able to leave."

"Can we get something to eat?" Diandra demanded.

"But of course. We would not want our guests starving while in our care, yes?"

"We are your prisoners, not your guests. And you will pay for this," Diandra shot back, raising her hand shackles high into the air.

He stared at Diandra with a smirk.

"Actually, we will be paid handsomely for *this*."

He turned and spoke Portuguese to his aide. They laughed.

"Some food?" Diandra again asked.

He barked an order to the aide who quickly exited the tent. The commandant bent down on his knees and leaned into Diandra.

"You let me know if there is anything else I can do for you, yes?"

His nostrils flared as he spoke, while his hand gently touched some strands of her hair.

"There isn't," she said icily, locking eyes with him while shaking the hair out of his touch.

He stood up, smiled and left.

"That guy is one big asshole," Sam said.

"No shit. He's a horny, short Napoleonic coward," Diandra replied, shuddering his touch and energy off of her. "Like all bullies, he's all talk, no action."

"I wouldn't bet on that," Sam cautiously replied. "We, *you,* need to be very careful around him."

Diandra reflected on their situation for a few moments.

"We'll be okay. All we have to do is keep our wits about us. Dutch and Tanner will do everything they can to get us out of here. I am sure of it."

"Agreed," Sam said, valiantly trying to lift their spirits. "And I sure wouldn't want to be Pancho Villa out there when he runs into Dutch."

He got quiet for few seconds. "*If* he runs into Dutch." He looked to Diandra. "Who are we kidding? He and Skip are halfway around the world."

"Believe me, Sam, I know Dutch. He and that commandant will meet someday. Hopefully sooner rather than later."

The thought made both of them feel a little better.

"By the way, what did he say to that other guy?" Diandra asked.

"Something about getting two rewards…"

The tent flap opened and plates with beans and pork were brought in. One of the guards removed one side of the handcuffs from each of their hands and clasped it around the tent pole, allowing one arm free movement. No utensils were provided. They dug into the food with their fingers, knowing that they had to keep their strength up for whatever was ahead.

Finally finishing, Diandra leaned her back onto the pole.

"How are we going to sleep?" Sam asked.

Diandra looked around for an answer.

"I guess back to back, with the pole in the center. She shuffled so that she could lean against the pole.

Silence mixed with the newly pounding rain hitting the tarpaulin tent.

"Diandra?"

"Yes."

"I'm wondering… how we are going to go to the bathroom?"

"I was just thinking that myself," she replied.

"Any ideas?" he asked.

"Let's call out to them. Maybe they'll take pity on their guests."

Berlin, Germany

Tanner appeared on the LG forty-eight inch wide screen that rose before Zoë in her office. He turned around from his desk and faced her. His corporate jet windows framed the background.

"Yes, Zoë."

"Mr. Tanner, we just received word from the Lima Federal Police that Diandra and Sam were forcibly taken off a bus going to the pick-up point we arranged in Cuzco."

"Are we sure about this information?" He frowned with concern.

"The injured bus driver reported it from the hospital. He stated the men were armed. We have been unable to contact the driver we arranged for them to meet. No cell coverage out there."

"Any idea who is involved?"

"At this point, our guess is Red Guard rebels, or some faction thereof. We don't know for sure. We have contacted our embassy and they are checking on it."

He leaned back in his chair, tapping his fingers.

"Any ransom demands?"

"Not yet."

Zoë waited while Tanner digested this news.

"Should we contact Vorhees?" she asked.

Leaning toward the screen, Tanner's features got steely.

"No. We don't know for sure what happened, except for this one report. Send a team there immediately and get some feet on the ground. I want solid, confirmed data that they have, in fact, been abducted."

"I don't think he will-"

"Zoë, it is my call. When and *if* we get confirmation, or a ransom demand, we will bring him in. At this point, as far as we know, they are simply un-locatable."

"Yes sir," Zoë responded, unhappy but resigned to the decision.

Tanner shook his head in frustration.

"This was supposed to be the easier of the expeditions. Hell of a way to start this thing," Tanner noted. "I'll be there," looking at his watch, "in about four hours. Have Cantwell briefed and ready to meet with us then."

Pushing a button, the screen went black.

* * * * * * * *

Eastern Peru

"I don't like what I'm hearing out there," Sam said.

"Like what?"

"Nothing I can put my finger on. They laugh a lot, like this is a game. But no talk of when or how they will be letting us go."

Diandra straightened and sat upright.

"I think it best if we keep our minds on what is going on here. This is a business deal for them. They have us. They want money. They'll get their money. They need to keep us happy and healthy."

"And alive, hopefully," Sam added, tentatively.

"You scared, Diandra?" he asked, trying to keep the tremor out of his voice.

"No. Yes. Well, maybe a little. The point is, Tanner will make sure they get paid, and we'll be out of here."

"I hope this isn't an ominous sign about our future adventures."

"Look, Sam," Diandra said turning to him, "if we need a dour assessment of this situation, we can call Skip, okay?"

Despite himself, Sam laughed.

"Okay, okay, I understand. Glass half full, stiff upper lip, look on the bright side of life and all," he replied irreverently.

Diandra half laughed back.

"Come on let's see if we can get some sleep," she said while rubbing her neck with her free hand. "I am sure Dutch knows what is going on. I can feel it."

* * * * * * * *

Aleppa, Syria

Empty containers of food littered the table as Skip and Dutch finished cleaning their plastic plates of *kibbeh, ba'lawa* and goat cheese. Dutch set down his plate and went to the sink to wash his hands. Drying them, he looked to Skip.

"Let's see if we can get hold of Diandra and the kid on Skype," he said.

Skip fired up the computer, pulled up a screen and they could hear the phone ring, followed by the deflating onscreen sound of not being connected.

"Unable to get through, Dutch," Skip said.

"That unusual?" he asked.

"Not really. Coverage there is spotty at best. I would be surprised if we did get them."

"Yeah, I suppose so."

A few minutes later, Dutch started pacing the floor, then stopped by the computer.

"I don't like it, Skip," he said, rubbing the back of his neck. "You know how I don't like being non-com with my team. It gives me a bad feeling."

Skip smiled, knowing by 'team' he meant Diandra.

"Really, Dutch, other than a few mosquito bites, what could possibly go wrong with them over there?"

* * * * * * * *

Chapter Eleven

Eastern Peru

The next morning Diandra and Sam were fed breakfast and allowed a short walk around the grounds, handcuffed. A break in the rain had left a mist in the area. As they neared the dog pen the two akbash dogs started barking and growling. The rebels laughed as the dogs tried to climb the chain link fence and tear into them. After being forced to take another picture together, the commandant approached them and spoke softly to the near-sighted cameraman Jorge, and then laughed.

"Ah, now to business of pleasure," the commandant said, following up with orders to the rebels guarding the tent.

"No!" Sam shouted as he understood what was said. He furiously tried to break loose from their grip. The commandant backhanded him across the face. The two rebels laughed.

"So, you understand, yes? Then you can stay out here and listen to our fun."

Gesturing to the man holding Diandra, he pulled her back into the tent while the commandant followed. Stopping, the rebel grabbed and held both of her arms straight down from behind. Walking up to her, the commandant ripped open her blouse, exposing her bra. She struggled to pull away, to no avail. He grabbed her bra and tore it apart, exposing her breasts. The rebel holding her laughed.

"Very nice. I will like this, and so will you," the commandant said.

He started unbuttoning his shirt. His lips broke into a smarmy grin while his left eye twitched more furiously. She continued struggling to break free.

"If you like it rough, I can arrange that too." He ordered the guard to release her. Diandra shook off his touch, immediately closed her blouse with her left hand, and swung her free hand around to slap him. He grabbed it with authority and bent it backwards, causing her to buckle and fall on her butt atop the cot, grimacing.

"Rough is to my liking. It is your choice," he stated in a husky voice, obviously aroused.

He released his grip on her hand; her wrist now throbbing with pain. Her shoulders slumped in resignation as she cradled her arms. The commandant ordered the rebel to leave while he slowly unbuttoned his camouflage shirt, exposing a forest of chest hair.

"Why not let us both enjoy this, since it is to be, yes?" he said.

She looked up at him, and gently opened her blouse to expose her breasts. He quickly removed his shirt and walked toward her, unzipping his pants. Standing up to meet him, she wrapped her arms around his sides, pulling them closer, skin to hairy chest, while turning her head away from his lips. He leaned in and licked her cheek, causing her to cringe.

"I hope you do like it," Diandra whispered.

As he pushed her back toward the cot, she jerked up her right knee between his legs, grabbed his buttocks with both hands and arching her body backward while falling. The descending force of his weight pushed her knee full force into his groin, and by the time they stopped moving she'd made a direct frontal assault.

He groaned and bent over as his pupils raced toward his nose. She swung her right elbow around in an arc and drove it into the side of his head, connecting with the temple just above his eye. Going limp, he collapsed on top of Diandra, stunned and bleeding from the blow. Struggling, she was finally able to push him off to the side, where he slowly slumped onto the muddy clay floor, out cold.

Quickly, she un-holstered his .45 and grabbed a couple of clips from his belt. Looking around the tent she could see nothing of much use to her. Running on pure adrenaline, she needed a plan. Any plan. She knew there were too many rebels for a John Wayne style shootout. And she wasn't that good of a shot anyway. *What to do?* she kept asking herself as she paced the tent, thinking and praying for an answer. Finally, she came up with an idea. Walking to the tent flap, she opened and peeked out just enough to barely show her breasts.

"Sam, tell that guard the commandant wants him to get us a bottle of tequila."

You want me….What?" Sam hesitated, forehead creased in worried confusion.

"Tell him now."

He nodded and then relayed the message in Portuguese. The guard looked alarmed, pushing Sam aside and rushing toward Diandra. She backed up, letting her blouse open fully as he entered the tent. His eyes failed to see the commandant on the floor before she slammed the pistol from behind her back into the front of his head, causing a bloody gash that spewed blood. He slumped to the floor, the machine gun falling from his hand. Sam followed him in and also glanced at Diandra's breasts as she quickly buttoned her blouse.

"Grab his machete," she ordered Sam, pointing. "And take your mind out of the gutter."

Embarrassed, he fumbled while pulling the machete out of the guard's sash.

"I am so glad you are okay," he said.

"We're going out the back way," she said motioning with her thumb.

"Where to?" Sam asked.

"Anywhere but here," Diandra interrupted him. "Let's go."

Sam grabbed the machine gun off the floor and slashed the fabric at the back of the tent with the machete. They ran full speed out of the opening and into the jungle.

* * * * * * * *

Rome, Italy

Lilne stood before his desk studying a three-dimensional hologram with images and cuneiform letters floating above it. A purplish hue lit his face. Using his fingers, he moved the images around. A knock on the door interrupted him.

"Quid est?" Lilne responded

A man poked his head in.

"We've intercepted a message that may interest you," he stated.

"Go on," Lilne replied while continuing to move the images.

"It appears Diandra Weiss, the archeologist you are interested in, has been kidnapped in Peru. They sent a ransom demand to the US Embassy a few hours ago."

Eyebrows rising in surprise, he slowly sat down, turned the swivel chair toward the man and leaned back.

"That *is* interesting. How much are they asking?"

"Two million US," he replied.

Lilne laughed to himself, shaking his head.

"Who is behind this?"

"We believe the Red Guard."

Picking up a thin tablet computer, he tapped in some data and scanned it.

"That is one of our funding projects. Contact a General Herrara. Level one security. I'll send you his information. Tell him we want her for questioning. We'll pay his ransom as a bonus."

Setting the electronic tablet on his lap, Lilne looked up at the man who now stood in the doorway.

"Make sure he understands. Under no circumstances is she to be harmed."

He raised and input more commands into the tablet. A picture of Diandra appeared. He hit send and set it down on his desk.

"At this point, she is our only lead in locating McIntyre," he continued. "We need to know what she knows. Continue to monitor all relevant communications."

"And if she won't cooperate?"

"I just sent her information to one of our top Cuban trained interrogators," Lilne said.

"She will talk. Or die."

* * * * * * * *

Eastern Peru

Holding a bloody bandage above his swollen left eye, the muddied and half naked commandant sat on the edge of the cot, fuming. The cameraman Jorge entered the tent with some additional gauze and a bottle of pills. The commandant grabbed the bottle, opened it and quickly swallowed several of them down. Jorge handed him the new bandages.

"I want them caught and executed, do you understand, Jorge?" he spat out angrily, teeth clenched in pain. "Take the dogs and track them down, now!"

Jorge bent down and lifted the bandages to view the wound beneath. He reached for the iodine that sat on the nearby table, swabbed some onto a piece of cotton and started to clean the gash Diandra had left. The commandant groaned and slapped his hand away.

"What of the ransom money?" Jorge inquired, gently resuming the dabbing of disinfectant.

"We have already sent the picture with yesterday's newspaper," the commandant answered. "We have another to back it up. When they pay, we will give a suitable excuse for the deaths."

"And you're sure about… the woman?" Jorge asked, half looking up from dressing the wound for a reaction.

The commandant defiantly stood up, wobbling for a moment, and then grabbed his groin area, grimacing.

"Kill them both. And get me some ice!"

* * * * * * * *

Diandra and Sam raced through the jungle, dodging around and jumping over dead trees and broken branches. They were in panic mode, knowing neither where they were nor where they were heading. Only that they had to put some distance between themselves and certain death.

"Diandra," Sam finally managed to blurt out between pants. "Let's stop and rest a few minutes. The altitude is getting to me. My lungs are killing me."

She stopped, took in Sam's exhaustion and nodded okay. Her breath was labored too, and she welcomed the chance to catch it --- and her wits. Sam sat down on a tree trunk lying on its side, while Diandra leaned up against a Huarango tree and wiped off the sweat running down her face. They looked at each other while collecting their thoughts. A few moments passed, silently.

"We've got to somehow get word to Zoë and Dutch about what is going on," Sam insisted.

"Agreed," Diandra concurred, using her sleeve to wipe more sweat, now dripping from her face down to her neck. "But first we need to know where we are. I'm not even sure where north and south are at this point. The clouds and rain…"

She looked up at the forty-foot canopies towering above them, and shook her head.

"Unless we can see the sun, we're out of luck. For all I know, we could be circling back to their camp."

Sam shuddered at the thought, and then froze.

"Diandra, don't move," he said emphatically, eyes wide.

"What, Sam?" Diandra started to look around.

"Don't! Don't move your head, whatever you do," he whispered, motioning with his hand like a stop sign.

Her eyes followed him as he slowly reached down, fumbled for a thin tree branch, picked it up and gazed to her left.

"Oh my god, Sam, what is it?" Diandra pleaded without moving a muscle on her face.

"Naka naka. It's about a foot from your left side, above your head."

"In a tree?"

Sam nodded. Diandra understood he meant a Peruvian coral snake, and was aware of its deadly venom. She held so still she could hear her pounding heartbeat, and fought with her instinct to run, aware that this snake could strike within milliseconds of any movement to escape.

"What are you going to do?" she whispered through her clenched teeth.

"I think I can pin its head against the trunk with the end of this branch… at least for a moment. That should give you enough time to get away."

"Sam, you know what will happen if-"

"Diandra, it is heading down the trunk toward you." The branch trembled in Sam's hand. "What do you want me to do?"

"Just do it," she said, her fear overridden by expediency and resolve.

Rising slowly, Sam gingerly walked toward the tree. He raised the branch like a fencing sword, ready to thrust.

"On two, Di."

"What happened to three?"

"We don't have time." He counted one, aimed the branch, and then a forceful two as he thrust it and pinned the snake before the branch snapped. Diandra lunged away as the snake struck with deadly accuracy the spot where her head had been, and quickly fell out of the tree.

"Oh my god," Sam shouted as he dropped the branch and quickly backed away so fast he tripped and fell. Luckily, the snake slithered off in the opposite direction. Feeling something touching his shoulder, Sam screamed and scrambled back toward the tree.

"Sam, it's me." Diandra yelled, withdrawing her hand.

"Thank goodness," he said, visibly relieved. "I was afraid he had some relatives."

"Sure it was a he?" Diandra quipped, nervously.

"Not really," Sam laughed, getting the joke. "Let's get out of here," he continued. Looking around, he asked "Which way do you think?"

"I'm making this up as we go along," she replied. "But I would say-"

"What's that noise?" he interrupted, touching her arm.

They listened for a moment to the unmistakable sound of dogs barking in the distance.

"Holy sheep shit," Sam exclaimed. "This is going from bad to worse."

"Let's go!" Diandra shouted, motioning with her arm.

They ran in the opposite direction of the distant howls.

* * * * * * *

Aleppo, Syria

Skip had one more job to do before he could relax; security of their hotel room and its perimeter. He carefully unpacked the Testronic model 618 micro cameras that Zoë had procured for the mission at his request. About the size of a cigarette filter, they were the latest state-of-the-art fully self-contained cameras and wireless transmitters. He tested them and, once satisfied they were working properly, he proceeded to install one on the first floor stairwell, another at the top of the stair landing and then another two on top of the room's doors. They were held in place by the paste equivalent of bubble gum.

He also placed wireless contact devices on the windows and finally, a motion detector in both rooms. Once everything was in place, he sat back and relaxed.

No one was going to get to his mission control room without his knowing about it.

* * * * * * *

Chapter Twelve

Eastern Peru

It seemed to Diandra that no matter how fast they were running, the barking continued to grow louder – meaning the dogs were gaining on them. Minutes seemed as hours. They slogged through boggy areas, vines clutching at their legs and branches whipping their faces. Finally, jumping over a downed atlas cedar trunk, they landed in a shallow river.

“Let’s follow this upstream,” Diandra suggested. “Maybe if we stay in the water they will lose our trail.”

“Sounds like a plan,” Sam replied as he waded in.

Carefully stepping around the more jagged rocks located underwater for fear of slipping, they made good progress up the slow flowing water. They were heading into a valley, the walls rising higher on both sides. The dogs’ howls started competing with the emerging sounds of a waterfall ahead. A turn in the river’s path revealed a large cliff face of rock, rising over fifty feet high and jutting off in both directions. The waterfall exited an aquifer below a large cave and added volume to the flowing water. Soaked and out of breath, they stood knee-deep in the river, staring at the cliff. The echoing howls and barking of the dogs grew closer.

“We’ve no choice, Sam. We’ve got to go in that cave,” Diandra said, pointing.

“I don’t like it,” he replied, shaking his head. “What if there’s no other way out?”

“Hopefully, they won’t know we’re in there.”

“I still don’t like it.” Sam looked exhausted and panicked at the same time. “What if they do figure out we’re in there? They can wait us out, or worse.”

“Look Sam,” Diandra’s voice took on renewed strength. “Dutch and Tanner are bound to be looking for us now. We’ve got to trust this is going to work out. Besides," she pulled out the silver plated .45 she'd taken from the commandant, "they know we have this and the machine gun you have. I don't think they will be too keen on running into a dark cave looking for us."

"Right." Sam replied, his heart beginning to pound. "That sounds entirely logical… and it's what we need to do." He paused and swallowed, eyes growing wider. "There's, uh, oh God…There's just one problem."

Diandra was checking her gun's clip before entering the cave. Slapping it back in, she turned to Sam. "We need to go. Now!" She noticed his hesitancy. "What is it?"

"I, I don't like small… confined… areas," he croaked out a hoarse whisper, clearing his throat as she looked at him in horror.

"You're claustrophobic?"

He nodded, avoiding her eyes.

"You're telling me this now?" she cried out in disbelief. "Ohmigod, that's just perfect."

"It never came up before, Di." Sam replied. They both turned as the braying dogs suddenly sounded louder, closer. "It's a little embarrassing, you know?" he continued, staring down at his feet.

"How bad is it?" she asked.

"Pretty bad."

She took a deep breath then scanned the cliff face, bracketed by the steep vine-covered sides of the narrow valley they'd followed in. "That's okay. We can just climb out of here."

In tandem, they tipped their heads back to look all the way to the top, then back at each other.

"Or maybe not," Sam offered, grimacing. "Okay." He threw his shoulders back and straightened. "I, I can do this."

"You sure?" Diandra asked, concerned and frantic at the same time.

"We don't have a choice," he said, resigned but not convinced. "I can't be a dickwad about this the rest of my life." He gave a rueful grin. "As my psychologist would say, it's an opportunity for growth, right?"

Diandra nodded and took his hand. "We'll go in together. Can you do that?"

"Yeah, well," he startled at the renewed barking getting closer. "I'm scared shitless, but the sooner we get in there, the harder the trail will be for those dogs to follow. And the truth is… I'm more scared of them than that cave."

They splashed through the water to the cave's six-foot entrance, climbed up the cliff face and dove inside.

"I wonder how far it goes back?" Sam asked in a faint voice. He cowered inside the dark entrance, panting.

Diandra pulled an LED mini flashlight out of her pants' lower side-pocket.

"We'll just have to find out," she said, grinning at Sam's look of thankful amazement. "Always be prepared."

Sam nodded as they disappeared into the cave.

* * * * * * * *

Three armed rebels arrived in front of the cave about ten minutes later. The two dogs were not fooled and pulled at their leashes, barely being restrained by the rebels holding them. One of the rebels shouted toward the cave. No response. The other two rebels debated as to their next move. One of them pulled out a walkie-talkie and dialed Jorge back at the camp.

"What shall we do, sir?" he asked, after filling him in on the events to that moment. "It appears they are in a cave, and quite frankly none of us wants to go in there and find them."

"No need to do that," Jorge answered, "The commandant has ordered their immediate execution. Use whatever means you have to do so."

"The rocket launcher?"

Jorge laughed, knowing they had been itching to try this new piece of equipment since acquiring it two weeks earlier.

"If you wish," he finally replied.

The rebel pushed power off and relayed the news to his comrades. They grinned at having been given permission to play with their new toy.

The second rebel swiftly pulled the thirty-two-inch barrel off his comrade's back. A nine-inch long rocket canister was carefully inserted into the rear of the tube as the man with the dogs forcibly pulled the beasts back and down-river away from the cave. The first rebel shouldered the camouflaged three-inch wide tube, flipped open the safety switch directly above the trigger and pressed the arm button. A light whir and high-pitched electrical noise pierced the air. The red LED light next to the trigger changed to green.

Aiming for an area directly over the cave's entrance, he gently squeezed the trigger. A plume of smoke spewed from the rear of the weapon as its projectile screamed toward the target, a smoking trail in tow. With a roar the projectile exploded violently, causing a shock wave that pushed the two rebels backwards in the water. Rock, sand and smoke erupted in every direction from the cave opening, while the entire front landscape collapsed. Moments later, as the smoke began to dissipate, the rebels observed the cave's entrance buried and sealed off under tons of rock and rubble. They cheered and laughed, high fiving each other. The dogs were cowering, finally silenced by the painfully loud noise.

The group's leader pulled out his walkie-talkie and pressed redial.

* * * * * * * *

Light mists of rain continued to provide a welcome relief from the constant downpours of the previous few hours. The commandant limped through the middle yard of the compound, mud up to his socks. A white bandage graced the left side of his head just below his beret. Jorge rushed up with a satellite phone in hand, frantically gesturing. The commandant grabbed the phone.

"Yes?" he answered in Portuguese.

His eyes narrowed as he listened to the conversation on the other end.

"That is true, Gen-er-al. We have, or rather had, the woman you speak of."

Impatience clouded his face as he digested the general's words.

"They escaped over an hour ago, sir. We have dogs and men tracking them as we speak."

His brows wrinkled, Jorge could hear the angry voice on the other end. An explosion rumbled in the distant background.

"It was on my authority that we proceeded with this-"

Visibly annoyed, he continued listening intently.

"Yes, yes, I understand sir. I will call you as soon as we have word."

Hitting end call, he threw the phone at Jorge, who nearly dropped it. Jorge's walkie-talkie started buzzing.

"What did he want?" Jorge asked, ignoring the interruption.

"He said something about how imperative it was this Diandra woman not be harmed in any way. Seems she has friends in very high places." Shaking his head he added. "What a *bendejo*."

Lightning flashes followed by the roar of thunder startled them as sheets of rain began to pour down. The commandant shook his head and cursed as he walked back toward his tent. Stopping, he thought better about it and turned around.

"Contact the men," he ordered. "Tell them, *if* possible, to bring them back alive."

Jorge held up his hand while he finally answered his walkie-talkie and listened. His eyes widened as he slowly lowered the phone, clearly upset. The rain intensified. Large droplets pounded down on the two of them.

"What?" demanded the commandant.

* * * * * * * *

Chapter Thirteen

Tanner Headquarters,
Berlin, Germany

"Alright people, what do we have?" Tanner asked slapping his palms on the table, commanding the group's attention. His expression was stern.

Four men and Zoë were seated around an oblong glass table in the starkly furnished ninth floor conference room of Tanner Industries. A large glass wall overlooked Berlin's downtown skyline. Mike Cantwell, head of worldwide security, stood before a wall-sized flat screen with a remote in hand. Tanner sat at the opposite end of the table.

"A digital photo with a note attached was received by the US Embassy about forty-five minutes ago," Cantwell answered. "They forwarded it to us as soon as they realized what it was."

Clicking the remote, a picture of Diandra standing with the commandant holding a gun to her head, and Sam holding the newspaper, filled the screen. Tanner frowned, while Zoë sucked in her breath at the image.

"We've already downloaded it into our database," Cantwell continued. "We think the man with the gun is Pedro Morales, a lieutenant under General Dominic Herrara. They are part of the Red Guard rebellion in Peru. We are unsure why they are so far north. Our contacts in their government are surprised as well. They are considered a very dangerous group."

"Can we learn anything from this photo as to where they might be?" Tanner asked.

"Jeff is running it through UPP now," Cantwell replied. "The foliage suggests they are in a jungle environment, and the speed at which the ransom note and photo were received leads us to believe they are within a few hours of where they were abducted, although in which direction is unknown."

"What about tracking cell phones, Mike?" one of the men asked.

"We're working on that," Cantwell continued, shaking his head. "But it seems they, along with every other terrorist group, know because of all the press with US Homeland Security and Afghanistan, that their phones can now be tracked. Maybe they are using walkie-talkies or direct satellite uplinks."

A beep interrupted Cantwell. He pulled out and answered his smart phone, nodding his head affirmatively as he listened through his Bluetooth earpiece.

"Got it," he uttered while replacing the cell phone in his jacket and facing the group. "That was Jeff. Not much data to glean. The newspaper is legitimate. Facial recognition confirms they are in fact Diandra and Sam. His team is working on telemetries of sun and shadows. But he wants us to look at…" he turned to study the picture, moving closer to the screen and pointing with his pen. "Diandra's hands."

All eyes of the group focused on that area. Her arms hung straight by her side, being held there by the rebels. However, her fingers were not all straight. On her left hand three fingers were extended, on her right two.

"He believes they are not natural," Cantwell added.

"Did he have any idea what that meant?" Tanner asked Cantwell.

"Could be a number of things," Zoë interrupted, standing up from her chair at the table. "If she were trying to leave us a message, it would have to be something we could all understand."

"Agreed," Cantwell continued. "Her fingers total five. Or maybe three and two. Thirty-two? Would that mean anything?" He looked to the others, eyebrows raised.

"Could also be twenty-three. She is facing the camera," one of the men suggested.

"Miles? Kilometers? What?" Tanner exclaimed, patience waning. "We need some answers and quick."

Silence greeted his demand.

"Okay," Tanner answered as he blew his breath out, sat back, and then continued. "What else do we know?"

"They want two million dollars, with all the usual ransom BS; small denominations, unmarked bills, non-sequential numbers, etc." Cantwell answered.

"These brain surgeons need to stop watching Hollywood movies," one of the other men remarked.

Nervous laughter followed.

"What is the history of this Red Guard group, and Morales in particular, as far as returning their captives unharmed after being paid?" Tanner asked.

"Unfortunately, spotty," Cantwell replied. "Mostly they acquire local mayors and government politicians. Small ransom amounts. Some are returned, some not. This, however, exceeds anything they have done before. A very brazen act, grabbing American citizens in broad daylight near a tourist destination. They've raised the stakes."

He clicked the remote and a copy of the note accompanying the photo appeared.

"The message also says to wait for instructions to deliver the money."

"Okay, then, let's move on this." Tanner declared, pushing back in his wheelchair and racing around to the front of the room where Cantwell stood.

"Mike, you're in charge of this operation. Make it happen, and successfully. Keep them honest. Demand full proof of life every step of the way."

"Understood," Cantwell replied.

Tanner turned to a non-descript military man at the table.

"Jim, I also want a concurrent operation to see if rescuing them is a possibility. You coordinate with Mike. I mean full use of all our resources, internal and external, understand?"

Jim nodded, expressionless.

"Her book," Zoë shouted. Startled, they all looked at her.

"What?" Tanner said, confused.

"She must be referring to her book with her fingers," Zoë grinned. "That is something we would all know about."

"She may be right," Cantwell said to Tanner. "Do we have a copy of it?"

"Wait here," Zoë said as she raced out of the conference room to her office, grabbed the book and raced back, fumbling through the pages.

"Page thirty-two," her eyes scanned the page, "is about the pyramids." She read for a few more moments. "Nothing much here, really." Slightly deflated she turned back to page twenty-three and started reading. "I'll be damned," she blurted out.

"What is it, Zoë," Tanner demanded to know as he wheeled near her and craned his neck to see the page

"Listen to this. It is about her South America dig in Argentina. 'It was a hot humid day when we started the two-hour journey *north* to the dig site'." She looked up at the group. "Is that wild or what?"

Tanner read along with her, then nodded. "Mike, Jim, you've got your hint which direction to go. I want you on this and I mean now!"

There was a scraping of chairs as everyone got up and hurriedly left the room.

"Zoë," Tanner called out. "Stay for a moment."

Once the room emptied, Tanner looked at her and smiled.

"Good job."

"Thank you sir, but it is still my responsibility. I was their contact and set up the operation."

"This was unforeseeable, so don't beat yourself up too much." A slight nod solidified the genuine nature of the assurance. "Can you get Dutch on this screen?"

Picking up the remote, she punched in a few buttons. A phone rang. Skip's image appeared on the screen with a surprised look. He set down a cup of tea.

"Oh, hello there," Skip answered. "To what do I owe the pleasure of this call?"

"Skip," Tanner started, "I need to speak with Dutch."

"So do I. But he's not here. Took off this morning for a mysterious meeting."

Tanner suppressed a groan. "Did he say when he would be back?"

"No, why?"

"We've got a situation, Skip. I need to speak with him as soon as possible. Have him contact me on a secure line the minute he can."

"What's this about?"

"Skip, just have him call. I need to tell him personally."

Concern overrode Skip's normal doubting Thomas expression on the screen.

"Everyone okay there?"

"Have him call."

* * * * * * * *

Chapter Fourteen

Eastern Peru

"Sam?" Diandra coughed out.

No answer.

Picking up her small flashlight she searched amid the cloud of dust. Barely visible, Sam was crouched in a fetal position near the wall, hands over his ears, moaning and half crying. The earthen cloud created ominous shadows as the light peered through it like a searchlight.

She stumbled over to him. "Are you hurt?" She scanned him for blood. "Can you hear me?"

"Yes. I. Can. Hear. You," he said in between gasping breaths. "I'm just hyper…hyper-ventilating. Arrgghh! I hate this! What a frigging baby!" He sat up. "Breathe! Breathe! God!" Looking around he commented. "What did they do, call in an air strike?" he asked hoarsely, bursting into a fit of coughing. He wiped his mouth with the back of his hand and then covered his nose and mouth in the crook of his arm.

"I'm not sure… but we're going to have to find another way out." Diandra took a red kerchief from her pocket and ran it over her face before tying it on as a mask to filter the air. The flashlight's beam spotlighted tons of rock blocking any possibility of returning through their original entrance.

Sam stared past the light's beam in Diandra's direction and frowned.

"Crap," he commented, voice muffled through his shirt. "How does that saying go… be careful what you're afraid of?"

He sat thinking.

"I think this would be called 'immersion' by my shrink."

"What?"

"You know, like if you're afraid of snakes, you go into a room full of them and keep handling them until you're desensitized," he explained. "She wanted me to go up and down in an elevator in her office building with her until I could deal with it and stay relaxed. I tried it."

"Sounds like a good idea, actually."

"Yeah," he smiled and coughed again. "It started to work. That would've been a piece of cake compared to this." Shakily, he forced himself to his feet and started to dust off. "Okay then, onward and upward with my opportunity for growth."

"Can you walk?" she asked.

"What?" He stuck one finger in his ear and dug it around.

"Can you walk, Sam?"

"Oh yeah, I think so. Seems everything is working, although I'm not sure my ears will ever stop ringing." He shook his head.

"C'mon then," she said, motioning with the flashlight's beam. "Let's follow this stream and see where it leads."

They dusted their clothes until realizing it was making it even harder to see.

Diandra's light found the end of the narrowing cave after a few minutes. A pool of water stretching almost ten feet wide and half again as long marked the beginning of it. They exhaled their hopes in a deep sigh. Diandra searched the small cavern with the light. No openings. Leaning up against a rocky outcropping, she tried to keep her growing sense of panic from showing on her face. Sam was scared enough for both of them. Reluctantly, she allowed her mind to wander. *What had gone wrong? What could they have done differently? What could they do now?*

"Diandra," Sam coughed, unknowingly interrupting her thoughts. "There seems to be water pushing up at the end of that pool. I can see ripples from it."

Snapping back to the present, she shined her light directly on the water, observing the ripples as well.

"Yeah?" she asked.

"Yeah. Give me the flashlight and I'll try and see what is going on."

Sam grabbed the light and slowly waded in about a foot, taking care not to disturb the gray limestone silt lining the bottom of the pond. He stood still and directed the beam into the crystal clear water.

"There is a ledge all around this pool. Then it drops off pretty deep. I can't see the bottom… but it looks like," he directed the beam toward the end of the cavern, "it's coming from a pretty large underground stream. Can you see it?"

He swung the light around and shined it on her.

"Get that thing off of me, Sam," motioning with her arms, "especially if I look as bad as you do."

She did. The dust had settled on them like Casper the friendly ghost. They laughed together in gallows humor before they broke into renewed fits of coughing.

"So what do you think?" he asked finally, wiping gritty tears from his eyes.

"About what?"

Climbing out of the water he met her at the far end of the pool.

"Reality check here, Di. We're trapped in a cave with tons of rocks blocking that way out," he stated, gesturing. "Even if… I mean *when* Dutch and crew get here, they have to force those goons to say where we are, *if* they are captured alive, and then, *if* they find the entrance, there's still the matter of removing all that rock in the middle of the Peruvian jungle. Realistically speaking, those aren't good odds."

"Okay Sam. Now I'm getting scared," she said, thinking. "Any ideas?"

Sam's eyes reflected a plan he was forming.

"Look, you're always kidding me about watching my testosterone-laden movies, but maybe one of them can help us. There was this one where a guy was trapped in a cave. He found a pool like this and there was a cavern on the other side of the wall. He swam under the water until he reached it."

She snorted. "It was a movie, Sam."

"I know. But seriously, it might be our only chance."

"What if there is no other side?"

"What's the alternative?" Sam shrugged his shoulders.

"We could just wait," she suggested.

"One big additional problem," Sam said. "Air. There's only so much volume of it left in here. I calculate there is maybe twelve hours of air by volume, although I really don't want to focus on that. I mean, really." He shuddered while grabbing Diandra by the arms and facing her.

"Listen. I know you're older and wiser than me." That elicited a smile out of her. "But that water is coming from somewhere. I'm willing to see where. If I'm wrong, we're no worse off than now. Sitting here is not an option, at least for me. I'd rather die trying."

Diandra looked into Sam's eyes, sensing a growing maturity there.

"We're a team, Sam. We both go."

Toeing her tennis shoes off, Diandra reached down to pull off her socks. Sam did the same.

"We better hang onto our shoes," Sam suggested.

Diandra put hers in her cargo pants' large thigh pockets. Sam tied his to his belt.

"Let's just walk into it and see how deep it is first," Sam said. "If there is a tunnel, it will probably be in the same direction as the cave runs."

Diandra nodded as Sam focused the light onto the water. Carefully, he waded up to his chest, then stopped and looked from the flashlight to Diandra, questioning.

"It's supposed to be 'waterproof'," she said, her fingers making air quotes.

He moved farther in and sank, yelping.

"Man, this is deeper than it looks, and cold!" He shivered, treading water. "Somehow I thought it would be warmer."

Sam swam over to where he could touch the back wall of the cave and started treading water. With the flashlight underwater casting an eerie bluish glow, he lowered his head into it and opened his eyes. Splashing back above water he was grinning ear to ear.

"Holy crap, there is a tunnel."

He swam back to Diandra, who was standing up to her chest in water, smiling back in amazement.

"I'll go first," he suggested. "I may be claustrophobic but I'm not afraid to swim," he said in a confident tone. "You follow my light. I can hold my breath pretty long, so I'll turn us around if there is nothing …"

He looked into her eyes, and quickly gave her a kiss on the lips, startling her.

"For good luck," he said. Spinning around, he started his dive. "Follow closely," he shouted while disappearing into the water.

Filling her lungs with air, Diandra clamped her fists, steeled herself and dove toward the light. The throbbing in her head became more pronounced as the silence of the cold water engulfed her. Even with the light ahead it was difficult to see. She used arms and legs full throttle to propel herself forward, then realized she would need to keep some in reserve. *Don't panic,* she told herself. *Make sure you have enough air to get back.*

Thrashing, she moved forward another five, then ten feet. The light ahead was dimming. *Am I going in the right direction?* she wondered. Her lungs started burning, and she fought against the instinct to gasp for air. Numbness started gripping her arms. Continuing forward, she realized she didn't have enough strength or air to get back. *Where is Sam?* She screamed to herself, flailing her arms. Her lungs ached for air. She felt like throwing up. Fear griped her thoughts as she started to lose consciousness. *Is this it?* She cried inwardly. *Is this how I am going to die, never to be found in a hole in a-*

A wrenching on her left wrist startled her. *What is this?* she thought. A bright light flashed at her. Suddenly she was yanked violently, feeling herself being pulled above the water.

Then, all went black.

* * * * * * * *

Careening through Vatican City onto Via Gregoria toward the Allessandro Carravilani highway, Lilne sat in the rear of his limousine, immersed in thought. Unseeing, he stared out the tinted window. A beep signaled the flat screen monitor's descent from the ceiling.

"Your Excellency," the man on screen said, "one of our contacts within the Red Guard just informed us that the hostages were killed a few hours ago."

"Continue to follow the situation and confirm this is so," he replied, emotionlessly. "Find out who was responsible for this action. In the meantime, we need to find out where the other team members are located. Proceed on that track immediately."

"Yes, your Excellency."

Lilne thought for a few moments.

"One more thing."

"Yes?"

"Once you confirm they are dead, terminate everyone who was involved. I will not have my direct requests disobeyed."

* * * * * * * *

Chapter Fifteen

Eastern Peru

"Diandra. Diandra, come back."

She felt herself rolled from her stomach onto her back. Slowly opening her eyes, she could barely make out Sam's face staring down at her in the dim light.

"Are we dead?"

"No," he said sweetly. "We're in another cave." He shifted to cradle her head in his lap, gently brushing the wet strands of hair from her face. She struggled to sit up, then vomited water onto the floor of the cave.

Sam eased her back down to her side. "Just stay there and rest for a moment, Di. I thought you were a goner. I pumped a lot of water out of your lungs."

"I feel like we've been living some bizarre, Kafkaesque nightmare," she uttered, rubbing her eyes. "I was hoping, I don't know, to maybe wake up and find it was over."

"If only," Sam acknowledged, touching her cheek again.

Gently, she pushed his hand away and gazed, still woozy, at the surrounding walls of the cavern and the darkness that reached beyond, still attempting to shake off the reality of the situation.

"Give me a few moments to rest up before we get going," she said.

"According to my watch, *we've* been *resting* for almost thirty minutes," he smiled.

"I'm sorry Sam, I just…"

"No need to explain," Sam replied. "By all accounts it's been one hell of a day."

He cleared his throat, grabbing Diandra's attention.

"I was just thinking," he clumsily started, making circles with his finger in the gravel between his legs.

"About?" Diandra asked as she groggily ran her fingers through her hair, trying to straighten it out, and then forced herself to sit up again.

"Remember that party on Frank's boat a few years ago?"

She did. An argument had erupted between her and Dutch about their new house. Truth be told, he had been drinking way too much, and she wasn't totally sober either. Running downstairs to one of the staterooms she'd bumped into Sam in the hallway. Bursting into tears, she told him she and Dutch were through, and that she needed to find someone as nice to her as Sam was. He'd encircled her with comforting arms as she sobbed her heart out. Diandra had then lifted her face to his, and in a moment of passionate weakness, kissed him.

"Diandra!" Dutch had startled them both. She quickly pushed past the two men, slamming the stateroom door and locked Dutch out. She didn't see Sam again that night.

"I'm sorry about that Sam," she said. "It never should have happened."

"Well, *I'm* not," he replied in a heartfelt tone.

She stopped fumbling with her hair and turned toward him.

"We can't go back there, Sam," she said, shaking her head in compassion.

"I'm always back there, Di."

Shakily, Diandra stood up and let the water, stress and moment drip off of her.

"We really need to get moving, Sam," she insisted, changing the mood and subject.

"Are you sure you're okay?" Sam asked, standing and brushing off, taking a few moments to pull himself together and change his focus to the present.

"I will be," said Diandra, reassuringly. "And you??"

"Me?" He barked a wet laugh and then blew his nose in his sleeve. "That last part was so freaking scary it seems like it scared the claustrophobia right out of me. I'm just glad it wasn't snakes like that Indiana Jones guy," he added, trying to lighten the moment.

"Okay, then, Sam the man. Give me the light and let's see where this leads."

This cave was larger than the previous one. A wider stream fed the sinkhole from which they'd just emerged

A hopeful sign? Diandra wondered. She turned and eyed Sam standing there, hesitant. She held out her hand. "Coming?"

He smiled, grabbed her hand and followed. After about twenty minutes Sam noticed the walls started narrowing. Soon they were almost walking single file next to the stream, Sam behind Diandra.

"I wonder," Sam whispered, looking around. "Did we jump out of the fire into the frying pan?"

Another ten minutes of walking over craggy rocks brought a new nervous moment.

"Did I just see-" Sam started.

"Yes." Diandra interrupted him. "It's the flashlight."

Subtly, it flickered. No end of the cave could be seen with the light beam.

"We may have to go Braille here pretty soon," Diandra nervously quipped as the walls continued to move inward. Sam didn't answer.

"I can see it's getting narrower ahead, Sam. You're thinner, so I think you should go in front."

Sam nodded and started to squeeze past Diandra to take the lead. Very tight quarters. Diandra put her hand on his shoulder, then took his chin and turned it toward her. She gave him a kiss on the cheek.

"For luck," she whispered.

He smiled sheepishly as he took the light from her.

"I'm going to try something," he said.

Reaching his hand behind for Diandra to grab, they moved forward a few feet. The light went off.

"Sam," Diandra yelled.

"It was me. I'm sorry I didn't tell you first. I figured I could see where we need to go, then I'd turn the light off and back on every few minutes. I saw it in a MacGyver episode. Should give us more time on the batteries."

They continued making their way in the shallow water, the rock roof narrowing slightly with each forward step. Sam turned on the light, got his bearings, and then turned it off as they moved forward.

At last, they observed a wide clearing to the right with dirt on the floor. Sam turned off the light and they made their way there.

He pressed the button to examine the area. It didn't turn back on.

"Let's sit down on this dirt area for a while," Sam suggested. "I've heard that sometimes the batteries will recharge a little bit if left off longer."

They both knew there was little chance of *that* happening, but felt their way to the clearing. Exhausted, they sank to the ground against opposite walls. Pitch black. Silence reigned, except for the continual ringing in each of their ears from the earlier explosion.

Sam ran through his mind the best of all the things he'd wanted to do but never had done. Finding his true love, marrying her and having a family. He reflected on the irony that now he had made strides in his claustrophobia he might be dead before he could investigate the Roman Catacombs, try spelunking, or explore *inside* the Pyramids. And he'd always wanted to learn to fly. All these experiences and more he reviewed in his mind in milliseconds.

Diandra was silently doing the same. She was too tired, sore and wet to be angry. Only sad. *Sad* she was the one who suggested they go ahead. *Sad* she was about to fail. This was not the way she wanted her life to end. No glory in dying an unknown death. She missed Dutch, and felt frustrated with herself for having those feelings. He'd find them a way out of here, she thought. Somehow, he always did. At least, he would say he could. That might be enough.

"Diandra," Sam whispered, derailing her train of thought.

"Yes," she answered, smiling in the dark, thinking of her last kiss.

"Do you feel anything?"

"You mean like, being scared of dying or something?"

"No, I mean, do you feel a cool breeze of some kind?"

She hadn't focused on her physical feelings. When she did, she could feel a coolness blowing on her wet arms.

"I do, Sam!" Diandra responded. "Can you tell where it's coming from?"

She heard him stretch and feel his way to stand up.

"I'm going to find out. Careful that I don't-"

He did – run right into her.

"Sorry."

"Never mind that," she answered. "Try the light again."

Two clicks confirmed it was dead. Reaching out, he found a wall and began feeling his way ahead, stopping to lick his finger and hold it up, then walking toward the slight breeze. He finally felt it on top of his head and slowly looked up. Faint blurry light was all he saw at first.

Then… heaven.

* * * * * * * *

Chapter Sixteen

Aleppo, Syria

Skip's attention was diverted from his computer screen by a beeping as Dutch opened, slammed and locked the hotel door, throwing what looked to be bags of clothes onto the couch. He punched hibernate on the keyboard and spun round in his chair.

"What have you in that suspicious little bag in your hand there, Dutch?" he asked.

"Nothing you'd be interested in… only some sweets or other," Dutch replied nonchalantly as he tossed the bag toward him, a corner of his mouth twitching upward.

Skip caught, opened and spied the bag's contents.

"Lovely, Mister Vorhees, perfect for my afternoon tea."

Dutch took off his jacket and threw it onto the bed while Skip carefully dusted off his desk with a paper towel before gingerly placing the bag on it.

"Any news from Diandra?" Dutch asked off handedly.

"No word yet," Skip replied. "But Tanner has a bug up his arse for you to get a hold of him right away."

Dutch's concern antennae went on high alert as Skip spun back around and opened up another of his screens on his desk.

"I'll patch you through on a secure line."

A phone rang through the speakers. Moments later Zoë appeared on screen.

"Skip?" Zoë asked.

"Hi my dear, did you miss me?" Skip said, pouring on what he perceived as charm.

"Is Dutch there?" she asked, ignoring the question.

"I'm here," Dutch replied, moving into range of the computer's camera. "Anything wrong, Zoë?"

"Hold while I link us up with Mister Tanner."

The screen turned black as Dutch and Skip traded looks.

"Any idea what this is about?" Dutch mouthed.

Skip shrugged. Their attention swung back when Tanner and Zoë appeared split screen. Tanner's serious expression sent hairs rising on Dutch's neck.

"Dutch, I'll get right to the point. Diandra and Sam have been kidnapped and are being held for ransom."

* * * * * * * *

Eastern Peru

Jorge entered the tent and stopped near the commandant's table, waiting silently. His superior looked up after he finished with his writing.

"We've received word the ransom will be paid," Jorge reported.

The commandant's pained look turned to smug, the muscles in his face curling into a satisfied smirk.

"Ah. Have you sent the instructions for delivery?" he asked.

Jorge hesitated.

"Something wrong?"

"They want to speak with each of the captives before proceeding any further."

"I see," the commandant muttered as he rose slowly and began pacing the area behind his desk. He turned back to Jorge.

"That is a problem…"

* * * * * * * *

Aleppo, Syria

"When did this happen?" Dutch asked.

"We received the first report last night around-"

"Why wasn't I notified about it then?" Dutch interrupted aggressively.

"That was my call, Dutch. I wanted to make sure before getting you involved. I reached out as soon as we confirmed it was an abduction. You were unavailable."

Dutch looked to Skip who nodded and mouthed *'this morning'*. Zoë's look onscreen didn't seem in concert with Tanner's response. Dutch grabbed the back of his neck and rubbed it, thinking.

"Are they okay?" he demanded to know, concern evident in his voice.

"As far as we know, yes."

"What do you mean *as far as we know*?"

"They've sent a proof of life photo showing they are unharmed," Tanner answered. "Zoë, put it on screen."

Zoë hit a button and the picture of Diandra, Sam and the commandant with the gun pointing at Diandra's head appeared full screen. Dutch's stomach turned at the sight. Skip's face went ashen as Tanner and Zoë reappeared on screen.

"Who took them?" Dutch demanded to know.

"A revolutionary guerilla group called the Red Guard," Tanner answered.

"And the son-of-a-bitch that has his gun on Diandra?"

"We have teams on the ground both in Lima and Nazca, where they were taken," Tanner continued, ignoring the question. "The money is there and waiting. We also have a good idea about where they are being held, and we're making arrangements to extract them if necessary. I've also contacted the Peruvian government at the highest levels. They are waiting to help in any way they can, including militarily. We're handling it as a top priority, Dutch."

"Who's heading the team?"

"Cantwell, head of our world-wide security."

Dutch shook his head in disgust.

"Tanner, I warned you," he shouted, motioning with his hand. "I am in charge and I call the shots. We had a deal."

"We don't anticipate any problems, Dutch," Tanner stated dispassionately. "It seems to be a simple random kidnapping. We'll pay the money and get them back. It's going to work out."

"Nothing is simple when you're dealing with gorillas with room temperature IQ's. *Especially* when they're wearing military uniforms, Tanner. I know."

Dutch paced about the room, running a hundred different scenarios through his mind. Stopping, he turned back to the computer screen while scanning his watch.

"I want a long range jet at Aleppo field in," looking at his watch, "forty minutes. Have it cleared direct for Peru. Send me *all* the intel you have including every bit of communication. I'll read it on the way."

"Zoë?" Tanner said.

She typed away at a keyboard in front of her. "Taking care of it right now."

"Anything else?" Tanner asked.

"Yes. From this point forward, anything you learn gets to me at the same instant. I want to be kept in the loop on everything as it occurs or there will be *no* 'from this point forward'."

"Agreed," said Tanner.

"One last thing," Dutch continued. "Anything happens to Diandra, and anyone involved won't be able to find a rock big enough to hide under. You get my meaning?"

"I am going to assume you are referring to the rebels."

"Assume what you like. And Tanner," Dutch intoned, moving closer to the screen. "You pull another one of your *calls* like this, and we're through."

"Are you speaking for everyone on the team, Dutch?"

Dutch just stared into the screen.

"Dutch," Tanner finally broke in, his expression softening. "We're on the same team here. I want them back and safe as much as you do. Let's focus on *that*."

"Just make sure I'm kept in the loop. I'll call once I get to the jet."

Tanner nodded. Dutch eyed Skip and motioned with his finger to cut the transmission. The screen went black. Skip turned his chair, frowning his concern.

"Bloody hell, Dutch, what do you think happened?"

"I don't know, Skip. Probably some dick-head jungle jock who decided to become an entrepreneur."

He paced the room while Skip's computer continued beeping with incoming downloads that he immediately started printing out. Dutch stopped in mid-stride with the charge of an idea.

"Skip," he said while jotting down a telephone number. "Get hold of this number in Langley on a secure line. Run it to the phone over there," he said, pointing to the room's landline.

Skip took the number, recognized the area code as originating in the Pentagon, and looked up at Dutch, questioningly.

"Just *do* it, Skip."

He input the number and routed the call. The phone rang in the room. Dutch picked up the receiver, listening for a moment.

"Vorhees here, sir."

A moment later he cut in and interrupted the other party.

"Sir, I have a serious problem and need your help."

* * * * * * * *

Chapter Seventeen

Eastern Peru

Focusing his eyes, Sam realized what he was looking at. Those faint blurry lights, those speckles of hope, were stars. Bright little stars shining down at him. Elated, he turned back toward Diandra.

"We've made it, Di," he shouted. "We have a way out!"

The charge of joy he experienced sparking through his body was almost too much to bear. Using his hands to feel the walls, he found his way back to Diandra, who was already standing up. Fumbling with his hands, he embraced her as close as he could.

"Stars, Di! I can see stars."

She returned the embrace as they stood there. Sam started crying.

"I, I love you," he blurted out.

"I know you do, Sam," she gently replied. She paused a moment, thinking.

"And I care very deeply for you, too. But we can't let these past twenty-four hours cloud our judgment." She gently pushed him back. "Now, how about we get out of this place?"

Sam didn't respond except to murmur okay. They shimmied against the rock walls to the opening above them. Sam took the lead, reaching out and hoisting himself up to the first ledge. From there he slowly made his way toward the opening, being careful to feel each step along the way while trying to stay out of the trickling water's path. Finally, he reached the top.

"Come on," he called down to Diandra. "It's easy,"

Up she climbed, using the outcropping rocks as steps. Constant slipping slowed her ascent. After slowly rising nearly ten feet, Sam was able to reach in and pull her the rest of the way out. They stood and observed that they were against a cliff that opened to a large field. The quarter moon was near the horizon, and the sky twinkled with billions of stars.

Sam whooped, "Yeah, we *made* it! Isn't that the bomb!"

He grabbed Diandra and danced her around. Stopping abruptly, he looked at her and their eyes locked. Feeling the awkwardness of the moment, he looked away in embarrassment.

"Friends, Sam?" Diandra asked, smiling.

"Friends," he echoed, looking at her and nodding in affirmation.

He drew a deep breath, unlocked his hold and faced the quarter moon, arms outstretched.

"Damn, that was sure close!" he yelled.

"I thought we were done, too," she replied, glad their moment had passed uneventfully.

Sam surveyed the landscape.

"My God, I feel so alive." He did a little post-goal victory dance.

Diandra laughed. She felt alive too. She also felt tired, sore and giddy at the same time.

"How about we find somewhere to get some rest, Sir Sam?" she suggested in a royal British accent.

She held her hand in the manner of a fair maiden, and he bowed low.

"Lead the way, will you, kind sir?" she continued with the accent.

"Certainly, me lady," he replied, taking her hand in his own as they headed toward a nearby grove of Huarango trees in search of a spot to bed down for the night.

* * * * * * * *

Morning light seeped through the canopy tops in luminescent rays trailing down to the ground. Birds' and howler monkeys' morning rituals echoed about them as Diandra and Sam trekked through the jungle. Sunrise gave them a clue which way to go. They were heading west, and as far away from the rebels as possible. Other than that, they had no idea where they were.

Sam had left the machine gun in the first cave. Diandra, however, still had the .45, although they couldn't wager whether or not it would actually fire, having gotten wet. Tropical fruit abounded, and they gorged on *lucuma*, *huito* and *pepinos*. Water was everywhere they looked, but they were careful to only drink from clear springs that bubbled directly out of the limestone. Their mood was upbeat and hopeful. After two hours of traveling, Sam stopped dead in his tracks and squinted.

"I think I just saw a reflection of some kind over there," he said, motioning.

"What do you mean?" she asked.

"I'm not sure, something about it seemed unnatural. Let's go check it out."

They cut east and headed toward a limestone bluff. Reaching it, they located the object Sam had observed at the bottom: a broken piece of Plexiglas from what appeared to be the window of a small passenger plane. Picking it up, Sam studied it a moment. Craning his neck, he looked up and observed the tail of an airplane sticking out about five feet from the bluff's edge.

"Look," he said.

She followed his arm, shading her eyes.

"Amazing! This really is like Indiana Jones," Sam said. "Maybe there's something up there we can use."

"Well then, let's go see," Diandra agreed.

After a half hour of concerted searching they discovered a pathway up the bluff and reached the wrecked plane a full hour later. The Piper Seneca III turbo was balanced precariously at a thirty-degree angle, the left wing broken off. They approached it cautiously. Sam made his way to the passenger door, brushed aside the vines and yanked it open. Inside, he found the skeletal remains of the pilot still upright in the seat, dressed in a faded Hawaiian shirt and shorts. Next to him was an Enquirer magazine. *Two years old,*

Sam noted eyeing the cover's date. He got out and opened the rear passenger door.

"Come on Diandra," he shouted, motioning. "Let's get a closer look."

She joined him as he grabbed a large duffle bag from the rear seat and pulled it from the plane. She observed the skeletal remains and shuddered. *Things happened to people in this place*, she thought. *And they weren't free yet. Not by a long shot.* Together they opened the bag and discovered cocaine neatly wrapped in dozens of kilo bags, all clumped together. Two rusted guns and a box of .38 ammo lay at the bottom.

"Must have hit the ridge, flying too low," Diandra suggested.

"Or, maybe he ran out of fuel. Judging by his flying outfit he may have been high while on the job." Sam added.

"Any idea how long this has been here?"

"At least two years, according to his reading material," Sam thumbed toward the front seat. "I'm going to check the cooler there in the back."

He climbed over the rear seat and pulled it out. Opening it he found Pepsi soda cans and a box of Twinkies. Ripping open the cellophane wrapping, he broke one of the yellow treats in half and stuffed it in his mouth, showing her the creamy white center.

"Man, these things really do last forever," he managed to say with his mouth full. "Yum! Try one!" He tossed a bagged Twinkie to Diandra who pried it open and took a bite. She checked the plane's dashboard, reached over the co-pilot's seat and flipped the power switch from on to off and back again. Nothing happened. Sam could only shrug his shoulders, working on his third Twinkie.

"Wishful thinking," she told him. "Probably crashed with full power on. The alternators won't be much good either," she lamented, moving to the window and observing the bent three bladed propellers.

"I saw a MacGyver once where he made a battery generator out of some orange juice and then used it to power a radio," Sam said, licking his fingers.

Diandra laughed.

"How about we check his flight bag back there," she pointed. "You never know. He could have been very conscientious," although she doubted it.

Sam pulled the bag from the passenger seat floor, opened it and pulled out a handheld radio/GPS unit. A package containing a Duracell 9 volt battery followed.

"Aloha! I guess looks can be deceiving," Sam observed. "I think we hit the mother lode here," he said, holding them up to show her. Diandra broke out in a smile.

"Is there a knife or something I can use back there?" she asked.

Sam searched through the flight bag and pulled out a Swiss army knife.

"Like this?"

"Perfect."

Opening the knife she used it to jimmy out the in-dash mechanical compass. Finally it gave up its hold and plopped into her hand.

"Look what else I found," Sam said, holding it up. "One man's crash is another man's pleasure."

He opened a brown paper bag with hundreds of thousands of dollars in hundred dollar bills, neatly wrapped and marked in ten thousand dollar increments wrapped with clear cellophane. Excitedly, he pulled out a handful of the packages and held them up.

"Too bad *he* won't need that anymore," Diandra observed wryly. "Let's get to higher ground and see if those batteries work. And bring that writing pad on the seat."

"What about the money?" Sam asked.

"It's weight to me. You want to carry it, *fine*."

"Seems like a waste," Sam lamented. "Although, we may need it in case we have to bribe someone."

"That is a good point. Grab a couple of them and let's get going," Diandra stated as she saluted the pilot goodbye and slammed the door shut. Sam grabbed two of the packaged hundred dollar bills and unceremoniously tossed the rest of the money back into the plane and shut the door.

"You hang onto this," he said to the mummified pilot.

* * * * * * * *

Tanner Headquarters, Berlin

Zoë hesitantly pushed the button on her keyboard and waited until Dutch appeared on screen from the jet heading toward Lima.

"Any word, Zoë?" he asked.

"There's been no communication from the kidnappers since we made a request to speak to them before the exchange would be completed," she answered.

"Seems they're stalling," Dutch noted, frowning. "I wonder why?"

She sat there staring at the screen.

"Zoë?"

Shaking herself back to the present moment, she made a decision.

"Dutch," she started, "I'm really sorry. I hope you know I had nothing to do with keeping their abduction from you. I wanted to-"

"I get it, Zoë," he interrupted. "It was Tanner. I could see it when you called the first time."

She nodded slightly at the confirmation.

"I'm not blaming you or anybody, Zoë," Dutch continued. "This mission has gotten away from me, and I hate it. Believe me, I won't let it happen again."

He fell silent for a few moments, then added.

"I think it will all work out okay, Zoë," Dutch shared. "These guys, as stupid as they are, have no reason to blow a two-million-dollar deal. Let's just stay positive unless we learn otherwise."

* * * * * * * *

Chapter Eighteen

Eastern Peru

Diandra and Sam bludgeoned their way through the jungle for a good hour before reaching a small clearing. Breaking open the battery pack, Sam replaced the old ones for new in the handheld radio. He flipped the power switch. A green LED light confirmed its status.

"Now *that* is a commercial," he said, laughing.

"Hand it here," Diandra requested as she reached for it.

Looking it over, she pushed the location button, and the LCD screen beeped and placed a plane icon over a jungle – with longitude and latitude readouts. Then she pressed the nearest airport location icon. The screen widened and listed Lima at three hundred and eighty-six kilometers ENE. She studied the screen for a moment.

"This is very… strange," she said to herself, lost in retrieving a memory.

"What's strange?" Sam asked.

The question jarred her back to the present.

"I know this sounds weird, but I think we are less than three or four kilometers from the cave area we were here to find in the first place." Excited, she looked up at Sam over the handheld radio and started laughing. "Who would have thought?"

Sam burst into laughter with her. "What is it they say? Life has a funny way of getting you where you want to go?"

"Something like that," Diandra responded.

"Next time I vote for the *easier* way."

"I'll make note of that," she quipped, using her index finger to mark an imaginary chalkboard. "In the meantime, I'll plot a direct route to the coordinates I remember from our maps. We'll need to use the compass to navigate our way there. This only gives direct air routes."

After plotting their course for a few minutes, they started off in a southeasterly direction. Diandra also set the radio transponder to 121.5 MHz and left it on broadcast while they trekked along, hoping that if a commercial jetliner flew anywhere overhead and was monitoring that frequency, they could transmit an emergency message to them.

Slogging through the muddy jungle forest, it took almost four hours to reach the area Diandra remembered from the map. Twice, they took much-needed breaks to eat and regain their energy. Another hour of arduous searching passed before they came across a large hill that aroused Diandra's interest. It was a huge mound, much like the American Indian mounds in Oklahoma. Although looking natural they were, in fact, man-made and usually contained some sort of burials. This was huge by comparison.

After some preliminary discussions about what to look for, they split up; Diandra circling to the right while Sam went the opposite way, searching for any indication of a cave opening or glyphs. Halfway around the mound, Sam spotted something.

"Diandra, come quick!" he yelled.

Gathering steam, she sprinted to the spot where Sam was standing and stared. He excitedly pointed to an outcropping of large granite stone with an intricate gear meshing carved into the inside top corner. She rubbed her hand over it.

"Well," she observed. "*This* is definitely not natural,"

"That's where my head was going too," Sam added, looking at a half dozen other carved stones lying nearby – all with intricate etchings. "Reminds me of the pieces of rock in Puma-Punku."

She nodded and moved to examine the entire piece of rock. Noticing something near soil level, she dropped to her knees and cleared away the vines, discovering a symbol carved into the stone that looked familiar.

"Sam, check this out!" She motioned for him to join her. "An enneagon star. Nine points. But it's different from anything I've seen before." She ran her finger over various size circles and dots on the outside of it next to each point. A winged globe was in the center.

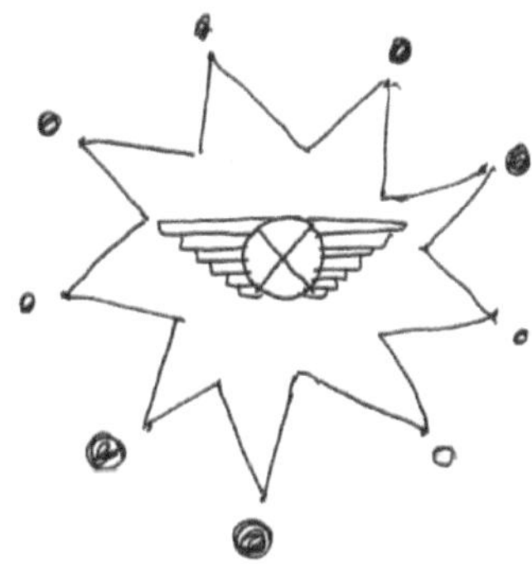

"It is similar to a couple of the symbols at the bottom of McIntyre's letter," Sam commented.

Looking closer at it, Diandra agreed.

"However, these different sized circles on the star tips are a mystery," she noted while pointing. "Why don't you draw a copy of it while I make a rubbing of these petro glyphs next to it," Diandra suggested. Moving more vines out of the way, she froze. "Sam," she shouted.

He followed her eyes to where she was staring. Next to the symbols was the Neptune fork from the tablet. "I don't believe it," he said.

"I think we've found our clue," Diandra exclaimed. "Go ahead and draw while I make a rubbing." She grabbed a couple of pages from the paper tablet Sam had taken from the airplane and put it up against the rock. Then she picked up a handful of dirt and carefully rubbed it over the paper, being sure to get the outlines of all the glyphs. Sam started sketching with a pen on another piece of paper.

Shrill beeping, followed by static coming from the handheld radio, suddenly pierced their concentration.

"This is United two-five–five-seven heavy calling. We read your emergency responder transmission. Are you okay? Repeat, this is United two-five-five-seven calling whoever is transmitting responder code-"

"We are *not* okay," Diandra shouted after picking up the ICOM IC A4 and pushing the transmit button. "This is Diandra Weiss. Please call Tanner Industries and inform them of our location. We are in great danger and unable to get out. Please help us. Are you getting this message?"

"This is United two-five-five-seven. Loud and clear. Please repeat your name and the contact you want us to make, over."

"Diandra Weiss. Repeat. Diandra Weiss from the Natural History Museum in New York. Our lives are in danger. Contact Robert Tanner of Tanner Industries immediately. She gave them Tanner's phone number.

"Our coordinates are-"

"We've got them, Miss Weiss. We're making the satellite call right now. You hang on and take care of yourself. Over and out."

"Thank God, Sam," she said turning to him with tears of relief in her eyes. "We're gonna make it. Let's get this tracing finished and…" she chuckled to herself. "I guess we'll just hang on, like the man suggests. I feel like we've been running forever."

Sam nodded, relief flooding his entire body for the first time in what seemed like years.

* * * * * * * *

Jorge answered the satellite phone's incessant ringing. It was a call from Lilne's number one man.

"Our contacts have been informed that your captives are still alive and well," he said.

"Are you sure?" Jorge barked disbelievingly.

"Affirmative. We monitored a recent communication from the woman."

Jorge looked to the commandant and frantically motioned for him to come over.

"Where are they?" he demanded, grabbing a note pad from his pocket.

"Not far. Here are the coordinates…"

Jorge wrote them down and hit *end call*. Looking up, he swallowed before answering the commandant's questioning eyes.

"You won't believe this, sir."

* * * * * * * *

Tanner Jet

The monitor before Dutch lit up while he was speaking on the phone. An excited Zoë appeared on screen.

"Dutch, we've just received word. Diandra is okay," Zoë said.

"*Great* news," Dutch exclaimed, hanging up the phone.

"Somehow, she must have escaped," Zoë continued. "A call was received on an emergency transponder frequency. The plane that picked it up forwarded us their GPS coordinates."

"What about the kid?"

"Unknown, Dutch. They said only Diandra spoke."

"What's the plan?"

Tanner joined the call on split screen.

"Dutch," he said, "I just heard. We have teams on the ground in Lima and near Cuzco. They are about two hours northwest. We'll be at those coordinates shortly."

"Damn, I wish I was there," Dutch said.

"Cantwell is a good man. He'll make it happen," Tanner assured him.

"Dutch," Zoë said, her voice warm, "I think this is a very good sign. We know where she is, and we have people on the ground to go in and get her."

Dutch pushed a button on the console.

"Yes Mister Vorhees?"

"How long till we arrive in Lima?"

"Another four hours."

Dutch searched for options, running scenarios over in his mind.

"I want real time updates, Tanner. Zoë, can you patch me through to Cantwell and his team?"

"I believe so," replied Zoë.

"Make it happen, Zoë," Tanner said.

* * * * * * *

Chapter Nineteen

Eastern Peru

"What's that noise?" Sam wondered aloud, waking Diandra from a fitful sleep.

They had been hanging on for the past two hours, waiting for word on the radio. None had come. After eating some fruit, they had unintentionally dozed off, fatigue overtaking them. Diandra sat up and turned toward the low humming frequency.

"I'm not sure, Sam," she said, shaking herself awake. "Maybe we should get in this overhang area until we see what it is."

Within moments two large black helicopters raced above the tree canopy. The noise from the blades was deafening. Continuing past them at first, the choppers turned around and crossed back overhead. They continued flying off into the distance until their hum was no longer discernible.

"Are they ours… or theirs?" Sam asked.

"I don't know," Diandra said, shaking her head, her forehead creased with worry. "I think I'll wait a few minutes and then transmit a message. I've heard black helicopters are usually bad news."

"That's what I was thinking," Sam added, "at least in all the movies I've seen."

In the distance they suddenly heard vehicles driving through the jungle. Their revving engines were getting louder and heading in their direction.

"Maybe I'm getting paranoid, but do you think it could possibly be-"

"They don't even know we're alive, Sam. That has to be our guys. How else would they know we're here? Let me send out a message on the radio just to make sure."

She pushed the button to transmit and noticed the screen was black. No power.

"Crap. It's dead."

"They're getting closer Di."

She paused before trying again. "I'm not sure, Sam. I don't want to miss them if they're rescuers, but…"

Her expression cleared as she made her decision "It has to be them. Let's just get out there and make sure that the helicopters don't see us first." She motioned for Sam to follow and they walked toward the oncoming vehicles. They could hear the vehicles stop, the doors being opened and then slamming closed.

"Over here," Diandra and Sam shouted, waving.

They could see the jungle brush move as the visitors got closer. Suddenly, they spotted a rebel in uniform with a machine gun pointing their way walking toward them from the left. Another rebel quickly joined him. More of them appeared to their right.

Directly ahead, the commandant broke through the foliage, with bandaged head beneath his red beret and blood curdling malice on his face. Slowly and deliberately he closed the distance separating them, stopping less than four meters away. Raising his hands to his hips, his steely glare rested first on Sam and then Diandra.

"Well, well. I was afraid you forgot about our date, Miss Weiss. And now I see you have not."

"How did you find us?" Diandra demanded.

"It is irrelevant, yes?" he replied, leering. "There are very important people that need to question you, and whether or not you are good, or bad, I still get you after they are through."

Diandra felt herself go on full adrenaline alert. No time for fear or regret. She calculated how much time it would take to grab the .45 from her back waist-band and fire off a shot before… well, whatever was going to happen was inevitable, she reasoned. She looked over at Sam, whose hopelessness sparked the courage she needed to make her move. Either die there in a rain of gunfire or suffer a slow death at the hands of that monster. The choice was clear. All she needed was a slight distraction. She glanced again to Sam.

"Rogant et boare," she said in Latin.

Sam got it. Turning to the commandant…

"Please, don't kill me, please I beg you," Sam shouted at the top of his lungs. Dropping to his knees, he continued pleading. "Don't kill me. I don't want to die, I beg you."

The men started laughing as he ratcheted it up a notch each time he repeated the request. In one fluid motion Diandra reached back and pulled out the .45, taking deadly aim at the commandant, one hand beneath the other supporting the gun. Everyone froze; their eyes back on Diandra.

"Oh, I see you still have my gun." The commandant raised one eyebrow. "I am glad for that, for I missed it almost as much as I missed you. If you will be kind enough to drop it," he said, pointing, "I will be taking you on your way."

Diandra cocked her head, smiling ever so slightly. Sam rose from the ground, dusting himself off.

"You seem to have lost the seriousness of the situation, *Commandante*. I have this aimed at *you*, and as you know, I never miss what I aim for." Her teeth-baring smile widened slightly.

"Perhaps you are right," he continued smugly, slowly pulling off his gloves. "But I have six men with machine guns trained on you, and you will surely die. You can not kill them all, yes?"

"Yes," she agreed. Her eyes narrowed slightly as she steadied her aim. "But I only intend to kill you."

Her gaze locked with his. No reaction on his part. She reasoned that if the people who wanted to speak with her were important enough to make him track her down, she was betting they wanted her alive. Otherwise she would already be dead. It was the only card she held, and she hoped it would be enough to come up a winner. The next move was his.

He broke her gaze and surveyed his men, all of whom were awaiting his orders, guns trained on Diandra and Sam.

"You are putting me in a very awkward position, Miss Diandra Weiss," he said refocusing his attention on her.

"Not as awkward as the one you put me in. And, it's Doctor Weiss, especially to you, you ignorant bastard."

She could clearly see that annoying twitch start to flare under his left eye. Sensing a blink, Diandra took a step toward him. The rebels shifted position, took aim and made ready to fire on her. The commandant raised his hand to stop them.

Diandra took another step, and then another while holding the gun aimed directly at his head. Finally, she reached him almost standing toe to toe, the gun barrel inches from his nose. She could see the nervous sweat pop out on his brow and smell its odor on his body. It sickened her.

Time to double down, she reasoned. *All in.*

"Order your men to back off," she ordered him. "Now!"

"That would be impossible I am afraid."

"Then we both die. Here… now…"

His eyes darted back and forth as he assessed the seriousness of his situation. The twitch spread to the entire left side of his face.

"Perhaps you have a point." He put his palm against the twitch to hide it. "But as I have already stated, that would be-"

Suddenly a blur of men in black flak-jacketed fatigues and helmets with dark tinted facemasks rushed in. Shouting in Portuguese, they forcefully hit the rebels from the sides and behind with rifle butts, stomping them to the ground. Within milliseconds all was quiet.

"What the hell?" Sam surveyed the scene with astonishment, eyes wide. Turning to Diandra, he saw that she hadn't flinched.

A dozen men trained their rifles on the rebels, who were on the ground in complete submission. One of the men spoke into a microphone on his collar. Sam heard the low frequency hum of helicopters as they returned in their direction and held about two-hundred yards away, blades whopping at slow RPM.

Diandra was still holding the gun directly in the commandant's face. One of the men carefully walked up to them and lifted his tinted helmet plate. GI Joe was written all over him.

"Doctor Diandra Weiss?"

No reply.

"Doctor Weiss, I am Colonel Jennings. We're here to help you."

Rivulets of perspiration ran down the commandant's face. Diandra held the gun and her gaze steady and true.

The colonel eyed her for a few more moments.

"We were sent by Tanner."

At that, her hands started shaking. Tears welled and spilled down her cheeks. Sam ran over, stopping next to her. Silent. Staring.

"We have a helicopter ready to evac you and Mister Zahed, Doctor Weiss," he said calmly, gently.

She took a breath and slowly lowered the gun to her side. The colonel smiled at her.

"You're going to be okay. Dutch wanted me to let you know he's on his way. He will meet you in Lima in a couple of hours."

Still mute, she nodded her head.

"If you'll both follow me, we can have you out of here right away."

"Sam," Diandra said in a flat tone of voice, breaking her silence, "you go ahead. I want to do one more thing."

Sam looked at her, bewildered.

"I'll be right there, okay?" She shooed him away with her free hand.

Sam took off with another man in black, disappearing into the jungle.

"Can you give me a moment with this animal?" Diandra asked Colonel Jennings.

"Yes ma'am. I'll be right over there if you need me," he said, motioning with his gloved index finger. He reached over, pulled the gun out of the commandant's belt and walked away.

Once out of range, Diandra leaned in on the commandant.

"I want to leave you with something to help you remember our *date*," she said icily, slowly raising her gun.

Sam reached the hovering helicopters. A yellow line dangling from a brushed steel platform awaited him. While placing one foot on it, he heard a shot from Diandra's direction. A man jumped on, held onto Sam and gave a thumb up toward the chopper. The two were whisked skyward by a winch. Sam entered the cargo area and made his way forward around the gunner who was manning a fifty-caliber machine gun.

Looking down, his eyes followed Diandra and the colonel as they emerged from the jungle and reached the staging area where the winch line reached the ground. They both jumped on the platform and held on while it hoisted them up. Once aboard the colonel spoke into his radio microphone and the helicopter's jet engines revved up full power. The CH-53E Super Stallion lurched forward, banking hard to the left for its trip to Lima.

"Doctor Weiss," one of the men in the helicopter said. "I am Michael Cantwell from Tanner Industries. Are you alright?"

"Yes," was her terse reply, staring straight ahead.

"I'm okay, too," Sam shouted to Cantwell. He smiled and nodded.

"What happened back there?" Sam asked Diandra over the roar of the blades. "You didn't kill him did you?"

"No, Sam," Diandra shouted back matter-of-factly. "I just neutered a mad dog."

Colonel Jennings smirked and whispered something to his comrades sitting next to him. They grimaced.

"Remind me, Doctor Weiss," Colonel Jennings said wryly, "to never get on *your* bad side."

Sam finally got it.

Ouch!

* * * * * * *

Mysterious stone structure – Puma Punka, Peru

Gate of the Sun, Cuzco, Peru

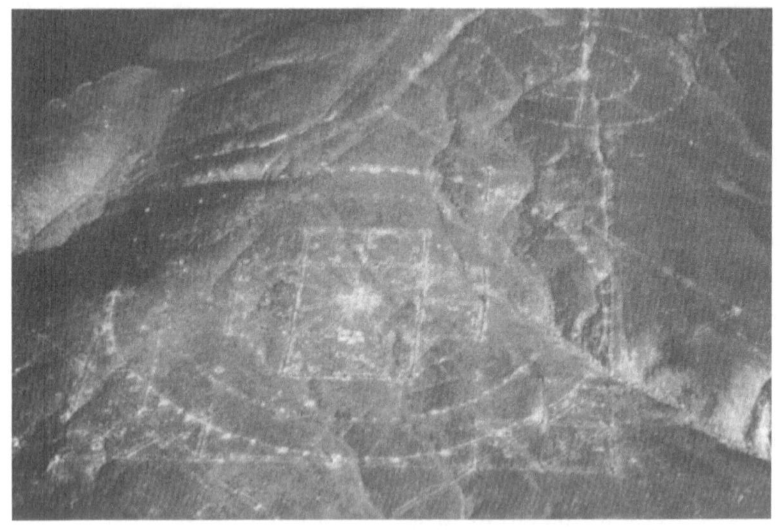

Previously unknown site Southeast of Nazca

Machu Picchu, Peru

Nazca Drawings, Peru

The Lost Tomb of Alexander

Part Three

The important thing is to not stop questioning
Albert Einstein

Chapter One

Tanner Jet

"Dutch, we've just received word that Diandra and Sam are safe," Zoë relayed from the plasma screen located in the jet's business area. "They'll be in Lima within the hour."

Dutch's breathed a huge sigh of relief and slumped back into the padded leather chair.

"Is she… alright?"

"*Neither* one of them was injured," Zoë replied. "We will have a full report from Cantwell in a few minutes. However, the rescue operation went as planned."

Leaning toward the screen he asked, "Did you pass on to Diandra that-"

"She knows you're on the way, Dutch," Zoë said smiling.

Try as he might to look at the positive side of life, the reality of past experience plus years of training and planning for possible mission failures and contingencies had jaded his outlook. When he had learned of Diandra's abduction, he'd found it difficult to shut out the images flooding his mind of her lying injured or dead. Intellectually, he understood what was going on, but it didn't help much to quell his fear for her safety. He knew, though, that for the Seekers to succeed, he'd need to be able to push those types of feelings aside. That was his role as their leader. Both the mission and their lives would depend upon his ability to do so. However, it had been difficult to shake the feeling that something had gone terribly wrong. And he'd felt powerless to do anything about it. A situation he abhorred, and vowed never to be placed in again.

This unexpected but welcome news from Zoë hit him like a ton of bricks. The fear he was harboring drained and, along with it, his final energy reserves. Struggling to focus on his watch, he made a mental calculation.

"I should be there in about two hours. Let her know-"

"I'll have a car ready at the airport," Zoë interrupted in a softer tone. "I know you'll want to see her, them, as soon as possible. This is such good news, Dutch. I couldn't be happier they are safe."

Her last comment went unheard. Dutch had pressed the off button and slumped back in the chair, tears welling up. Rubbing his eyes, he thanked God, and made a promise to himself.

* * * * * * * *

Lima, Peru

After landing in Lima, Diandra and Sam were taken under guard to the Sonesta El Olivar Hotel on San Isidro Street where they were able to shower and clean up. Juan Danieles, head of Peru's domestic anti-terrorism agency stopped by and debriefed them

Meanwhile, troops were dispatched to the rebel's campsite where they found smoking cinder piles, deep craters and a scorched forest. Searching through the destruction, they uncovered the charred remains of bodies, both human and canine, but found nothing else of any value for intelligence. The consensus from those at the scene was that the area had been hit by an air strike, although how and by whom was not known.

The rebels captured in the rescue of Diandra and Sam were taken to the nearby small city of Abancay by military troops where they were formally arrested, jailed and charged with a number of crimes. Within hours of the troops leaving, however, a local judge granted bail and the rebels disappeared.

The commandant was airlifted in the other helicopter to a hospital in Cuzco, where emergency surgery was performed to try and repair his injury, to no avail. When authorities arrived to question him, post surgery, they were informed that he had committed suicide -- in a most unusual way: suffocation by pressing his pillow against his face. When questioned further, the hospital staff was unable to explain how this was accomplished given the fact that his arms were restrained in the hospital bed.

Dutch arrived at Jorge Chavez International airport at about 4:30pm and was whisked by armored transport to Diandra and Sam's hotel, where they had been able to catch a few hours sleep after the interrogation. The three of them, along with a host of government officials, shared a quick meal together and were taken back to the airport where Zoë had arranged for the refueled jet to fly them back to Syria.

* * * * * * * *

Tanner Jet

Dutch was nursing a cold coffee, lost in thought, when Diandra walked into the galley area of the jet to fill her cup. They hadn't been able to speak much since Dutch had arrived, mainly because other people always surrounded them, until they took off from Lima. By then, Diandra had made it clear that she was beyond her reserves and badly needed to get some sleep. It had been three hours and now she was awake and ready to get her java fix.

Setting down the pot of joe, she noticed her right hand trembling, the full mug vibrating dangerously side to side. Steadying it, she sat down and placed the cup on the table. Dutch looked up.

"You okay?" he asked, taking in her creased, puffy face and exhausted posture.

She nodded half-heartedly while sipping her coffee.

"That was some wild adventure you and the kid had," Dutch said.

"Tell me about it," she replied hoarsely. Despite using both hands on her coffee cup, it gave a telltale rattle when she set it back down on the table.

Dutch looked down at her hands. "And he came up with the idea of going under that pool of water to the other side?"

"Said he saw it in a movie," she said, nodding.

"Well I've got to hand it to him," He raised his eyebrows, "That was both brave and dumbass stupid. Either way, I owe him for it."

"You owe him a lot, Dutch. He saved our lives."

Silence reigned while the two assessed one another.

"I had a chance to briefly speak with Colonel Jennings," said Dutch, breaking the silence. "Worked with him once in Iraq."

"And?"

"And…" Dutch smiled and took a sip of coffee, "he told me you left that jungle G.I. Joe wannabe a little parting gift." With a perplexed smile, he set the cup down and leaned in. "Is that how it happened?"

"I'm not proud of what I did, Dutch," she replied, taking a deep breath, "but that son-of-a-bitch…" The words caught in her throat, unable to finish the sentence.

"I would have done worse," he assured her, reaching over and touching her hand. "So in my opinion you let him off easy."

Tears spilled and rolled down her cheeks as she grasped his palm in hers, entwining their fingers.

"I was so scared Dutch, I didn't know what to do," she wept. "I kept asking myself 'What would Dutch do?' And then I would just do it." She reached for a napkin and wiped her tears, then sat up straighter, shaking her head. "And you know what? I'd do it again."

Dutch nodded and swallowed the lump in his throat while holding her hand tighter, waiting for an opening.

Moments passed.

"Di, I had a lot of time to think about things on the way over here."

She acknowledged him with the tilt of her head. He stood up and started pacing the floor.

"The thought of something happening to you… I… I just couldn't stand it."

Her eyes followed him. He stopped to rub the back of his neck with his hand.

"So I'm thinking… maybe…"

"Maybe what?"

"You know, maybe we should reconsider this divorce thing."

She stared at him, eyes widening.

"Well, aren't you going to say something?" he finally asked. "Anything?"

Straightening her spine, she started.

"How do you see that working, Dutch? Us going back to…" she ran her fingers through her hair, "Opieville in the suburbs, I think you called it? Me putting on the June Cleaver power pearls and the two of us pretending all is well? You think that will work? Get serious."

"I am being serious here." Dutch answered.

"So am I," she responded.

The silence grew.

"We can go anywhere in the world, Di. Create a life that makes us happy – invent it as we go. We don't need to waste our time with Tanner and-"

"Wait a second," Diandra interrupted, standing up. "Are you suggesting we not go ahead and look for the tomb? Is that what this is all about?"

"Exactly, we can-"

"Just hold it right there," she shouted raising her hand for him to stop while turning away to gather her thoughts. Finally, she sprung back around.

"You know I almost died a couple of times in the past forty-eight hours, right? And honestly, Dutch, the thought of not seeing you again…crossed my mind a lot."

"See?" he said, smiling and holding out his hands as a way of further explanation.

"What I see is that you *still* don't get me." She pointed at him for effect. "Jeez, Dutch! This is my life's work. And now I've been given the opportunity of a lifetime. Can you imagine?" she continued, pacing about the jet's galley. "A fully funded expedition to discover one of the world's greatest archeological mysteries. This is my chance to rub it in those assholes' faces that I can do scholarly work as well as the next guy... gal."

She walked over and grabbed his upper arms.

"This is the most important thing that has ever happened to me, Dutch," Her eyes pleaded with him. "I can't… won't give it up… not for anything."

Dutch shook loose her grasp.

"And how am I supposed to protect you, Di? In case you haven't been keeping up, things have gone from bad to worse over there in Syria. The president and his neocon lackeys are funding rebels and trying to topple their government. There's no telling what we'll be up against."

"You can back out if you want. I can protect myself."

Moments passed.

"Are you sure about that, Di?" Dutch questioned. "You want the glory but you'll have to survive in order to enjoy it. What good will the discovery do you if you-"

Diandra groaned in frustration. "Did you not hear what I just told you? I'm going. With or without you."

Dutch shook his head. Years of experience taught him there was no use arguing any further.

"Case closed?"

"Case closed," she steadfastly replied.

"And us?"

The question hung in the air as Sam walked into the galley.

"Skip is on the computer. Says he has some important info for us," he informed them.

Dutch and Diandra continued staring at each other.

"Guys?" Sam said.

"We'll be right there, Sam," Diandra said, motioning with her arm.

"It's not lost on me what you're trying to say, Dutch," Diandra finally said softly after Sam left. "It's just bad timing." She reached for his hand and gave it a squeeze before leaving the room.

Dutch leaned back against the table and rubbed his face with his hands before following her out the doorway. "Well, at least we've still got that going between us," he muttered.

Tanner Headquarters,
Berlin, Germany

Jeff entered Tanner's office and was acknowledged with a nod by Tanner.

"You wanted to see me?" he asked.

"Yes Jeff. I have a quick question for you," he replied.

Setting down his pen he sat back in his wheelchair.

"I know Skip had you create a firewall within our system for their work. Can you create a backdoor way to get in? Some sort of Trojan horse?"

"For what purpose?" Jeff asked.

"In case anything happens to them and we need to know what they know," Tanner responded.

Thinking for a moment, Jeff replied.

"Skip is very good at what he does, and he has it locked tight. I'll see what I can do. When they send their next encrypted communication I'll capture it and see if I can create an algorithm that will allow me in. But it's questionable whether I can do it without Skip knowing."

"Give it a try, will you?"

"Yes sir," Jeff replied. "Anything else?"

Tanner thought for a moment.

"Can we monitor their satellite communications?" Tanner inquired.

"That's no problem."

"Why is that?"

"Because we built them."

* * * * * * * *

Chapter Two

Aleppo, Syria

Skip was startled by Diandra, Sam and Dutch as they entered the room. Lost in concentration watching news reports onscreen, he had failed to notice them coming up the stairs on his computer's remote cameras that he'd placed throughout the hotel. Diandra rushed over as he stood up and embraced him, quickly followed by a kiss on his cheek.

"Now, now, let's not get too mushy here," he stated, flushing with pleasure.

"I'm so glad to see you," Diandra said pulling back from the hug.

"And I you, dearie," he replied. "Seemed a bit dicey there for awhile."

"We were okay," Sam said, feathers slightly ruffled.

"I knew she was in good hands, laddie." he added, turning to Dutch. "How was the ride in with Farouq this time?"

"Let's just say no one had to go to the hospital," Dutch replied, "but the city is going to need some serious sidewalk repairs soon."

"That ride was sick," Sam grinned. "Way better than Space Mountain at Disneyland."

Dutch set down two bags and plopped onto the couch, while Sam examined Skip's computer set up.

"Got any tea ready?" Diandra asked.

"Do I," Skip replied, beaming. "Does the Pope wear a funny hat?"

"Well, I'm not sure how funny it is, but I'll take the tea," she answered, winking.

After pouring hot water into a cup, Skip gently set in a teabag, a ritual perfected over the past fifty years. Counting under his breath to precisely thirteen, he pulled the bag out with a spoon, gently squeezed out the remaining drops and handed the cup to Diandra, who watched this familiar ritual with renewed fondness.

"What's the situation here in Syria, Skip?" Dutch asked, nodding toward the video footage on the plasma screen.

"It is getting quite serious," Skip answered. "The news reports aren't giving the half of it. I've been monitoring embassy cables and they are quite worried. The fighting is starting to seep over from Damascus into the city here. Fortunately, most of the rebel activity is relegated toward the south near Damascus. However, there have been reports of rebels roaming the outskirts of Aleppo and I've heard scattered gunfire."

"Embassy cables?" Dutch smirked.

"What can I say," Skip replied. "Old habits."

"I was surprised at how calm it was at the airport," Dutch mentioned.

"That's for now," Skip said, "things could change any minute. Now, if you are all up for it, I have a lot to go over with you regarding the equipment you'll be using - as well as our overall plan."

* * * * * * * *

The next couple of hours were filled with Skip fitting the personal Video devices or - PVD's - on each of them, setting up and explaining the relay boxes and solar recharge system, and demonstrating how the various other 'toys' he was providing for the mission worked. In his element, Skip was a magnificent teacher, patient yet exacting, with a knack for knowing how to language and convey instructions so they were easy to understand.

While the three of them were flying back from Peru, the images Diandra and Sam had captured from the cave wall had been uploaded and sent to Tanner Industries mainframe as well as Skip's computer. Analysis by the UPP program confirmed Skip's original hypothesis: the hieroglyphics they'd found gave a very specific date and time. Written in a hybrid form of Mayan glyphs, the ancient writers based the date upon the arc degrees of the sky's zodiac star systems. Every thirty degrees represented another astrological period, totaling two thousand, two hundred years, or revolutions of the Earth around the sun. All twelve signs totaled twenty-six thousand, four hundred years. Based on the sign and years from the glyphs, the computer backtracked the date of the glyphs' message. It appeared the coordinates were made thirteen thousand, two hundred and eleven years prior on the night of the winter solstice, present day December twenty-first. It also showed the final time was six hours, or one-quarter day past the setting sun from the pyramid's position. This was enough data for Skip to get a location plus or minus twenty-six feet in all directions; a virtual bulls-eye in everyone's opinion, considering how vast the area was.

Satellite images revealed the location to be in a very dangerous area in the Middle East, one whose ownership was still being disputed by Turkey, Syria and Iraq. The images they had were unable to produce a very clear picture of the area, which was riddled with cliffs, canyons, caves and crevices much like Petra to the south. It was about sixty kilometers west of the Tigris River, and thirty-five kilometers south of the Turkish border. Diandra noted that it was only one hundred kilometers from ancient Harran, a very important center when Alexander the Great was alive.

Based on the topography and the availability of water sources, the most expeditious route to the destination was carefully determined and laid out on computer as well as produced on a paper map.

* * * * * * *

Farouq had made good on his promise to deliver the items Dutch and Skip requested, including food, local cell phones, and tools. He also arranged for local transportation by one of his relatives who owned a transportation business right near the northwest border of Syria.

Pulling Dutch aside after their ride from the airport, Farouq had mentioned his concern about the heavyset man he'd noticed outside of the hotel the day he had left. Checking around, he had determined the man was a low-level arms dealer. Dutch confirmed that he'd noticed a suspicious man matching that description while he was at the bazaar. The two devised a plan that should take care of the problem.

Dutch and Skip had worked furiously preparing the prayer boxes for carrying their sensitive equipment, including padding, double walling and desert proofing them for safe transport.

* * * * * * * *

Location Unknown

A phone rang in a non-descript room. A speaker button was pressed on the phone.

"Yes," Shadow Man's gravelly voice answered.

"I understand you may be looking for certain persons of interest."

"Who is this?"

"It is unimportant at the moment. Is this true?"

"I have no time for games," he snarled.

"Nor have I," came the reply. "My sources tell me you are seeking four people who may be in the Middle East. I believe I have found them."

"Where are they?"

"Ah, that is the question," the voice responded. "My sources also tell me there may be a substantial reward for them."

"If the information is accurate, you will be rewarded."

"Substantially?"

"Yes."

"Good. I will have more information within a few hours. We can work out the arrangement then."

"Who is this?" Shadow Man demanded to know.

A dial tone answered his demand.

* * * * * * * *

Aleppo, Syria

Even after her fifteen-hour flight back, Diandra urgently wanted to leave as quickly as possible. The ride to the border would take about eight hours, so they decided to depart at five the next morning. Despite retiring early that evening, none of them had been able to get much sleep, especially Dutch, who was continuously running over their plan, contingency plans and escape routes, if they should be needed. He was grateful for Tanner's foresight in giving him the ability, via the secret compartment, to bring in the ordinance he felt was the minimum needed to protect the group: his Glock .45 with ten clips of pre-loaded titanium tipped bullets, a special short barreled pump action shotgun that carried fifteen rounds, and his trusty .38 Smith and Wesson with ankle holster, three extra clips attached. A twelve-inch multi-purpose serrated Bowie knife rounded out his arsenal. He purposely kept this part of the mission away from view, especially from Diandra.

Diandra was also having difficulty sleeping, for a much different reason. Lying in bed she reflected how Tanner had been right when he described this as the adventure of a lifetime. One she had dreamed about and trained for her entire career; the chance to discover one of archaeology's greatest mysteries – the location of Alexander's tomb.

But it was more than that. It would be vindication of her academic worthiness with her peers within the archeology community. In her mind, she reviewed the protocols she would use once the tomb was found: precise measurements, pictures, preservation of artifacts, cataloging. Smiling in the dark, she thought over dozens of different scenarios and possibilities, each one more tantalizing than the last. Her process and Dutch's ran in parallel; she planning her next steps and Dutch vigilantly devising ways to protect their asses.

Sam, although trying to stay awake to play the latest Game Boy he'd found on the jet home, had dozed off and was snoring wildly in his room.

Only the light from Skip's computer screen gave evidence that he continued working late into the night.

* * * * * * * *

Chapter Three

Aleppo, Syria

Farouq was prompt, knocking nervously on the door at five a.m. Four people exited the hotel and helped him load the beaten-up Saab. Dutch smirked upon noticing a new primer-painted fender in place. Overflowing bags and boxes were put onto the roof rack. As they were getting in, the hotel manager came out and wished them a safe drive to the airport, thanking them for their patronage.

Squealing tires marked the beginning of the ride to the airport, another hair-raising adventure punctuated by screaming pedestrians and street vendors clamoring to get out of Farouq's way. Dutch watched in the side mirror as a dark green Mercedes, driven by the heavyset man, followed discreetly behind. As the Saab exited Highway 4 and entered the Aleppo airport entrance, the man followed them in as they pulled up to the terminal. He slowly drove past, exiting the airport.

After Dutch observed the car exit the airport, they bid adieu to one of Farouq's cousins, Amwat, who was standing in as Skip's double for the expected surveillance. They waited another five minutes before the three of them left the airport with Farouq and made their way to Highway 4 North for the six-hour trip that would eventually put them east of Al Hawakuh near the border. So far so good, Dutch thought, confirming they had lost the man tailing them. The unmarked Tanner Industries jet would be taking off in another ten minutes back to Damascus, giving final credibility to the ruse that he and Skip had concocted to throw off whoever was following them.

They settled into the cab for the eight-hour drive and fell asleep while Farouq wound his way east, humming softly to himself the entire way.

Farouq skidded the Saab to a stop on the gravelly area in front of a large tent flanked on both sides by several corrals of camels. A sign in front read:

'Sand Dune Kamel Rides every 15 minutes!'

As they got out of the cab they heard Ahmed telling half a dozen tourists, "The way out there is hard," as he pointed dramatically toward the desert with a shaky finger. "There will be many dangers, and not all of us will survive." His deep baritoned Charlton Heston voice ratcheted up in volume.

"Death lies in waiting behind every dune." One of the younger children grabbed his father's hand and tried to pull him away.

Ahmed, a fifty-something portly Arab with short cropped black hair and a two day old beard, acknowledged the Seekers' arrival and excused himself from the tourists, letting his younger assistant take over.

Farouq and Ahmed embraced warmly while exchanging platitudes in Farsi. Farouq pointed to Sam, and Ahmed quickly went over and greeted him with a hug, kissing him repeatedly on either cheek in standard male-to-male Arab fashion.

"It is so good to see the cousin of my niece's husband," he shouted enthusiastically.

"Close family," Diandra wryly noted as Dutch laughed.

"Hello my friends," Ahmed finally said, turning to the others. "Welcome to my humble establishment. My lifelong friend Farouq has informed me of your needs, and I have your camels waiting and loaded over there," he said, pointing while barking some orders in Arabic. Two small boys appeared. "They will help you finish loading up the animals, and while so doing," he nodded toward the tent, "we can perhaps complete the business end of our arrangement, yes?"

Dutch nodded as he walked with Ahmed toward the tent. Farouq, the two young men and Sam moved the boxes from their bags on the cab and placed them on the camels. Diandra supervised. Dutch returned shortly to observe.

"Everything okay?" Diandra inquired.

"We will be traveling a little lighter in dough, but out there I doubt we'll need it," he said, smiling. Diandra could see Ahmed in the background putting a wad of money into a cash box.

"I will discreetly take the bags back to the hotel as we arranged," Farouq said to Dutch. "If there is anything else that you will need-"

"Is there a secret as to how to ride these things?" Sam asked.

"Ah yes, there is," Farouq answered. "You must always, and I mean always, not fall off. They are very high." He smirked at Dutch and waved as he walked to the cab. "But seriously," he called over his shoulder, "try not to let them think they are in charge. They are already beginning to suspect." He stopped and turned back toward the three of them.

"May Allah watch over you," he added. "I look forward to your safe return."

Two hours later Ahmed's young assistants had secured the boxes and other baggage to the camels, including the one with no rider. Ahmed came out to inspect the job.

"This is very good. My boys are expert in this area, yes?" He surveyed the three and pulled out a cigarette.

"I was not kidding with those tourists," he stated, a slight concern in his tone. "It is very dangerous out there." He lit it and took a long inhale. "I, too, will wish Allah to keep a protecting eye on you."

"Thank you, Ahmed," Diandra responded warmly. "We will be fine. It is a simple archeology dig. We should be back in a few days."

Raising an eyebrow, Ahmed exhaled the smoke through his nostrils. "Ah yes. A simple digging matter. Well, I must be attending to the tourists. *Ma-sah-lama.*"

Dutch returned the salutation and helped Diandra up onto the recumbent camel, which almost threw her off as it first straightened its forelegs, then lurched up onto all four. The two boys helped Sam onto his camel. It groaned and spit on him before his mount, while

Dutch vaulted onto his like a professional bull rider. Once all three were up, Sam grabbed the pack camel's rope while Dutch took out a Garmin 3000 GPS and punched some buttons. A slight beep and arrow appeared pointing a route southeast from Ahmed's tent.

* * * * * * * *

Chapter Four

Al-Jazira Desert, Northern Iraq

It took the better part of six hours for the intrepid group to reach the first point they had marked on the map – a small wadi known locally as the Kush Badi. Dismounting the camels was a lot more challenging for Diandra and Sam, since they had no idea how to do it. Dutch jumped off and pulled the ropes that ran through their nose rings and yanked on them, causing them to first kneel forward and then set down on all fours. *They were obstinate animals on a good day*, Dutch noted. *And this wasn't a good day.*

Once they dismounted, they changed into their new clothes; Dutch and Diandra cloaking themselves with the outfits that Dutch had made for them in Aleppo that resembled a particular religious sect, the Kwajagan, and Sam into the style of a typical nomadic Bedouin. Dutch and Skip had reasoned that by dressing as religious seekers, they would be able to travel unhindered within the region, since all the various religions gave wide berth to these particular holy men. And therein lay a serious obstacle. They had to make sure that they were covered up as much as possible, since it would be a serious crime for an unmarried woman to be caught traveling with two unmarried men. Punishable by death.

The outfits had to convey the impression that two men were traveling with Sam. To accomplish this, they wrapped material around their heads and faces, mummy style, and then topped it off with winding the material into a turban. Additionally, Dutch and Diandra applied a darkening makeup on their face and hands to more closely match a Persian complexion. The wrapping from the headgear they chose would cover everything else up.

Placing the PVD's into their ears, they activated the relays in one of the boxes and extracted and opened a small satellite dish. The dish was placed in a compartment within one of the boxes under some silk scarves. A light meal of dates and unleavened bread finished the stop.

Once they resumed their trek in the open desert, they kept in constant contact with Skip. Back at the hotel, Skip was monitoring three screens that were up and running in his room. The screen farthest to the right showed the cameras' images coming in real time, which Skip had neatly labeled with each one's name. The left screen showed a full color topographical map of the desert with three green GPS dots giving their exact location in longitude and latitude. The center screen he would use to pull up individual cameras and conduct research.

"Establishing mobile uplink, Skip. Are you getting voice and images?" Dutch asked.

"Okay, gents… and lady, everything's working," Skip confirmed, "but you're making me seasick!" The right screen's images were bobbing and weaving in three different directions.

"Yeah, right," Diandra responded with a groan. "You should feel it from my end, literally."

Skip chuckled. "Diandra, your image looks a bit fuzzy."

She adjusted her headband and tucked her hair behind her ear and the image cleared on Skip's screen.

"Perfect my dear, except for your camera jutting about like a drunken sailor. Hope you remembered the Dramamine. They don't call camels the ships of the desert for nothing you know."

"That's funny Skip… NOT." Sam replied, obviously not enjoying the swaying. "And you should smell these things," he added.

* * * * * * * *

Unseen by any of them, a lone Bedouin was high atop a ridge to the south. A high-powered AK-47 rifle slung across his back, he followed them with his Nokia binoculars while his camel snorted and spit in the background.

* * * * *   * *

"Do holy people wear these outfits for pleasure or penance?" Diandra wondered aloud, squirming to make herself comfortable while gyrating in the camel's saddle.

"What is our ETA for the first campsite, Skip?" Dutch asked, ignoring her comment.

A red dot on the first screen's map appeared as Skip typed some commands. He studied it.

"About three hours if you continue your present speed, which is about five miles per hour. I'll follow you from here. However, your GPS should-"

"I packed it away Skip," Dutch said. "Too hard to read while moving. We'll need your eyes on this one."

"You've got them, my boy."

"How come he's boy and I'm laddie?" Sam broke in. "Sometimes I don't understand why you-"

"Laddie," Skip interrupted, cutting off his mike, "the next step up for you is bucket-assed kid. Then it is whipper-snapper and then, if you work really hard, it is boy. Does that help?"

Diandra and Dutch broke out laughing as Sam shook his head in disgust, giving a very universal one-finger salute to Skip in front of his camera.

The desert was flanked to the north by rose and purplish colored sandy cliffs with tamarisks, hawthorns and juniper bushes jutting out between the sand dunes that led up to the snow capped mountains. In the far distance Mount Ararat could be seen, home to the supposed remains of Noah's Ark. *At least that's what some archeologists believe,* Diandra thought. She was still unsure. All of this was in stark contrast to the vast expanses of vegetation-free areas spread far off in the distance toward the south and east of the Euphrates River.

The trio continued forward following Skip's continuous directions until their jovial mood was interrupted. Up ahead they spied something protruding from the sand. Approaching it they observed two half-buried camouflage-painted military jeeps, blown apart and burned. Beside one of the jeeps laid a partially buried mummified body – missing its head.

"Jesus, you getting this Skip?" Dutch asked.

No answer.

"Skip?"

"Yes, yes my boy, I am getting it in gruesome detail. I was switching your frequencies using my random number generator. Needed to sync us all up. Can you hear me?"

"Yes," they answered in unison.

"Seems a bit dodgy out there," he continued. "If you want, you can head north from there and we'll get you a little more off the beaten path, so to speak, referring to the gentleman I just viewed."

He studied the map and tapped a spot on the monitor.

"Do you see a ridge about two miles from you to the north?" Skip asked.

"I do," Dutch answered, looking in that direction.

"Only another hour or so and you can be there on the higher plateau. It will offer better visibility to the south and east, and be easier to defend-"

"Look over there!" Sam shouted.

In the distance, a cloud of dust followed two military jeeps heading full speed in their direction.

"Too late, Skip," Dutch shouted. "Damn! Get your face-covering in place, Di. I hope your Arabic is as good as you say, kid."

Dutch pulled out his silver plated Smith and Wesson .45 and checked for a chamber load, then grabbed two clips of ammo from his saddlebag and tucked them into his belt loop beneath the robe. He held the gun in his hand, under a flap of his garment.

"Real deal here, Skip. Keep me informed of what they are saying. They may be speaking a dialect I don't understand."

"On it," was Skip's reply.

They watched as the jeeps bounced closer and finally skidded to a stop ten yards from them. A red-bereted soldier jumped out of the lead jeep while two military soldiers in camouflage uniforms with black berets leapt out of the rear jeep and stood with weapons in hand. The one with the red beret motioned with his hand, and the second jeep with two men in it circled behind them and stopped.

He strode up to the four camels and surveyed the group. Dutch avoided eye contact but managed to aim his temple toward the man, giving Skip a clear view.

"I am Captain Abdul Aamir. Who are you and what are you doing here?" the leader's rough voice demanded to know in Arabic.

"They are Sikhs from the Kwajagan Monastery on their annual trek to Mosel," Sam replied." He motioned a finger across his lips. "They have taken a vow of silence in respect to our almighty lord, Allah."

Abdul studied Dutch and Diandra carefully; both looked down in submissive postures and avoided eye contact as they had practiced.

Skip whispered, "He wants to know what you are doing there, Dutch."

Dutch moved his head slightly to acknowledge. He understood Abdul perfectly.

"Do you have any papers for identification?" the captain demanded.

"Again, as Sikhs from Uzbekistan, they do not. I am their guide to reach the monastery-"

"And your papers?" he growled.

Sam reached in and pulled out a Syrian passport. He leaned down to give it to the captain.

"I do not reach up for such things," the captain snarled.

Sam pulled back the single rope attached to the camel's nose ring, dug his toes in and tapped it with his whip, forcing the animal to its knees. It lay down with a loud groan, spitting and snorting, barely missing the captain.

Sam dismounted from the saddle and handed the passport to him with a respectful bow.

"Disgusting animals," the captain murmured as he thumbed through it, then eyed Sam suspiciously before closing and handing it back.

"What is in those boxes?" he demanded to know, motioning to the pack camel.

"Prayer mats and offerings for the Mullah," Sam replied, not missing a beat.

Skip typed away on Google translator as the man talked.

"Bloody hell, Dutch, he wants to know what is in the boxes," Skip's voice tightened.

Dutch shook his head as he tightened his grip on the gun while curling his finger on the trigger and assessing the situation. He was aware of the two men, kids really, behind him, but was unable to determine their exact position. The soldiers in front, although armed, were not locked and loaded. He could take them out very quickly. The captain had a handgun on his belt in addition to his rifle and was close quartered. The odds were not in Dutch's favor. He needed to see what was behind him.

As if intuiting Dutch's dilemma, Skip asked Sam to try and train his camera on the second jeep. Sam moved and turned slightly to give him a clear view.

"Dutch, the two soldiers in the back are standing outside the jeep, weapons in hand."

Captain Aamir slowly walked toward the pack camel and studied the boxes.

"Open this one, immediately," he demanded of Sam, pointing.

"I hope our ruse works, or get ready for some serious trouble," Skip spoke into his microphone at the hotel, his leg tapping furiously against the desk. He reached for a Kleenex to wipe away the sweat that was dripping down his face onto the keyboard.

Sam pulled on the pack camel's rope, shouted some curses and finally got him to the ground again. As he started to open one of the boxes, Captain Aamir pushed him aside and looked in himself. He pulled out dozens of brightly colored silk scarves, carelessly throwing them to the ground while he reached in to tap the bottom of the box.

"Sir!" one of the men in the jeep cried. "A rider is approaching."

Leaving the box and camel, the captain rounded the jeep to get a better view of the approaching camel. "At attention," he said to his men. They locked and loaded their rifles.

"This is going from bad to worse, Dutch," Skip whispered. A nod of Dutch's head confirmed his thoughts exactly.

"Subhan Allah! Subhan Allah!" the Bedouin rider shouted as his camel came to an abrupt stop and he jumped off. Captain Aamir crossed his arms.

"And who would you be?"

"I am an emissary of his holiness, Alar Ad Jamal," the rider answered. "These are the Seekers he is expecting. He sent me to personally help make their journey most pleasant."

He ran to the camels that held Diandra and Dutch, bowing profusely.

"Oh, the highest regards have been sent from his holiness," he spoke in Arabic. "You are truly most welcome by him and will be his special guests of honor."

Skip loosely translated as the Bedouin spoke. They acknowledged him with a slight bow.

Reluctantly, but with obvious respect, the captain backed away from the group. Then, shaking his head in exasperation, he turned on his heel and walked back to his jeep. Hopping in, he signaled with a flip of his hand to get moving.

Breathing a deep sigh of relief, Dutch watched them leave. The driver of the jeep looked familiar to him, but he quickly looked away as the captain swiveled in his seat and surveyed them one last time before disappearing in a cloud of dust. The Bedouin watched in silence with the rest of them.

Dutch whipped out his gun and trained it on the man.

"Who the hell are you and what are you doing here?" he demanded to know in Arabic.

"Please, please, there is no need for weapons," the Bedouin replied in perfect English, raising his hands. "I am Shamash Abmar. Farouq asked me to keep an eye on his Seekers."

Dutch digested his response, released his gun's hammer and placed it back in his waistband.

"Another of Sam's relatives?" Diandra asked, loosening her head covering with obvious relief.

"I am afraid not," Shamash answered as he looked toward the jeeps disappearing in the distance. "They will not be back," he laughed. "I will travel with you until I head north to my village. From there you are on your own again. Is this okay?"

Dutch nodded as Sam walked over to Shamash and thanked him for helping them.

"Dutch, I need you to switch to channel two," Skip said.

Reaching under his robe he flipped a switch. "Done."

"I just received an email from your friend Navarro," Skip said.

"He's not my friend, Skip," Dutch stated tersely.

"That's between you two, Dutch. Seems the man from the museum is a contract killer who is known only as Shadow Man. Apparently it is a handle he picked up while in your armed forces."

"His specialty was jungle ops," Dutch replied, nodding. "Had over two-hundred confirmed kills before being court-martialed. They said if you saw his shadow it was too late… you were already dead." He frowned, lost in thought for a moment.

"So you know this guy?"

"Know him?"

He paused, and then continued in an icy response.

"I'm the one who gave him that name."

* * * * * * *

Chapter Five

Al-Jazira Desert, Northern Iraq

The Seekers followed Skip's advice and trekked more northerly for another hour before finally making camp against a bluff overlooking the upper Tigris River valley. The wind was picking up.

Sam had no problems getting off his camel, having mastered the proper amount of swearing and kicking to do so. Diandra, sore from the day's ride, gingerly dismounted hers and started helping Dutch get the supplies off the pack camel. Shamash gathered dried tamarisk tree branches and camel dung to start a fire while Dutch and Sam set up the tent. It was a pretty quiet affair as everyone went about his or her assigned task.

Sitting around the fire after a warm meal of *dawalyeh* and *coobebe* stew, they relaxed against the padded camel saddles, watching the sun set in a glorious progression of gold to orange to purple. It was so clear they could see the stars before the sun faded behind the mountains. Even at that time of year, the nights tended to get cooler, and they all had wraps around them. A speaker box allowed Skip to participate in their conversations.

"What did you think of the recipe?" Sam asked the group. "It was handed down to me from my great grandfather."

"It was really… hot," Diandra noted, fanning her mouth with her hand for effect.

Dutch and Shamash laughed.

"What was in it?" Dutch asked.

"You really don't want to know," Shamash answered, winking at Sam.

Diandra laid back and gazed at the merging stars. "It seems like the sky goes on forever. Absolutely majestic."

"Yes, quite beautiful," Shamash answered.

The wind picked up and they leaned toward the fire.

Diandra rubbed her hands together. “I’m not sure what we would have done if you hadn’t shown up, Shamash.”

“I had everything covered,” Dutch stated.

Diandra smiled slightly.

“I know that Dutch,” she replied. “I only meant-”

“It was with Allah’s grace that I was able to get there in time to avoid any unnecessary violence,” Shamash volunteered. “The Iraqi and Syrian forces have been very aggressive near these borders ever since a group called the Kurdish Worker Party was formed. Very violent. They probably thought you were moving weapons in the boxes.”

“I’m sure glad we took the time to create those false bottoms,” Skip’s voice came through the speaker box.

“Me too,” Dutch added, nodding his head.

“Well, for whatever reason they hassled us, I was sure scared,” Diandra said.

“I wasn’t,” Sam boasted, looking at Dutch. “What about you?”

“You bet I was scared, kid,” he answered as he stirred the fire and threw in a couple of more tamarisk branches. “No matter how good you are, something can go wrong. Overconfidence is deadly.”

“Quite right,” Skip added. “More people get killed by accidents than-”

“I think we get the point Skip,” Dutch interjected. “By the way, what are you doing there?”

Skip had his feet on the desk, watching the scene through Dutch and Diandra’s PVD’s. A hot meal and tea sat perfectly balanced on a tray in his rotund lap.

“Nothing, Dutch. Just struggling with the terrible lack of room service at this fine establishment you’ve graciously set me up in,” he replied.

“Wish you were here?” Dutch asked.

“Not on your life,” Skip replied with a snort.

“Think we’ll run into any more bad guys?” Sam asked.

Dutch took a drink of coffee, measuring his words. "There are no bad guys, kid. Only *guys* that happen to be on a different political side than us. People think it's easy to kill bad guys. Just call them something other than they are: gooks, collateral targets, rag-heads."

Realizing what he had just said, he looked to Shamash who raised his hand as if to say *no problem*. "But they are flesh and blood, just like us. Same dreams, hopes, families, futures. And when they die, all of that vanishes with them. It's not pretty. They're just doing their job, taking orders from a boss who is taking orders from some other asshole playing chess with people's lives, and who is never at risk. And right is always determined by the one who isn't dead at the end."

He took another sip of coffee and poured the rest in the sand. "I would have killed those guys today, because it would mean that we would live." A moment passed. "I'm glad I didn't have to."

Diandra tilted her head and considered what Dutch had just said. He so rarely talked about his past in Special Forces. She assumed he had killed people. After all, that had been part of his job, being shipped to conflicts in different parts of the world. But, he had never shared how he felt about it, and after a few arguments between them when he had been in the service, she'd learned to never ask

The killing. She also thought, like most everyone else, that being in the military took the feeling out of the act, forcing soldiers to squash those emotions and pack them into a tiny compartment stored in their head. In fact, she had secretly thought that it may have been one of the reasons they were never able to get as close in their marriage as they had been as teens growing up together before he had joined the army; that maybe his ability to share other intimate feelings had been lost, too. Listening to Dutch just then, something within her tweaked just a bit. She wasn't sure what it was. A new understanding? Empathy? She sighed.

"I've been wondering, Shamash," Sam said, breaking the silence. "Who is this holy man you mentioned?"

"Ah, his most holiness Alar Ad Jamal. His lineage goes all the way back to before the time of Babylon. In spite of your government's foray into the politics of this region, the religious hierarchy has never changed. Saddam, when he was in power, was an outward ruler, dealing with effects. The other rulers in power as well.

"His holiness is a leader of what is really important; that which is within," he said, tapping his chest. "Focusing on the true knowledge and causes of existence. There is no distinction as to his teaching, and Shiites and Sunni Muslims alike equally respect him. Whoever has been in power has always paid respect to him and his lineage. It is rumored that he is over one hundred years old and has fathered dozens of children, even recently."

"Sounds like a man I should get some fatherly advice from," Skip commented from the speaker.

"I'm trying to picture little Skips running around with their tiny little teacups," Dutch mused aloud.

"Knock it off, Dutch," Diandra chimed in. "I think they would be really cute, and smart too."

"Well, well. If I get to have any say in the matter," Skip broke in, "I think we should finish the mission first and then worry about my potential fatherhood proclivities later."

"Good idea," Dutch answered, amused by Sam's look of bewilderment at the word he didn't understand.

"What is it you Seekers are looking for?" Shamash asked, changing the subject.

Diandra looked to Dutch, who nodded okay.

"Alexander's tomb," she replied.

"Ah, very famous man among my people," Shamash said.

"For good reason," she replied.

"It is rumored that Alexander followed in the footsteps of the great hero Gilgamesh, yes?" Shamash asked.

"Interesting you should say that, Shamash," Diandra said, thinking for a moment. "That could be true. Gilgamesh, like Alexander, claimed he was a demigod; that he was entitled to everlasting life. He and his servant Enkido traveled to Lebanon to seek out the god Utnapishtm and claim his divinity and right to everlasting life. Alexander traveled to the Oracle of Delphi, and then later to the Oracle of Siwa to obtain the wisdom about the same thing. Alexander had to fight his way there, country by country. Many scholars believe this was the reason for his conquests.

"I hadn't thought about it in this context," she continued. "But it could be Alexander was following exactly in Gilgamesh's steps. The biggest difference between the two is that Gilgamesh's *mother* was the goddess Ninsun, making him two-thirds divine, wherein in Alexander's case it was his *father*, rumored to be Amon the Egyptian god, dressed in disguise, making him a demigod but only one third divine."

"What would it matter?" Dutch asked. "It turns out they were both mortal and died."

"True," Diandra answered, "but not before Gilgamesh was told of a special plant that would make him young again. After getting it from the bottom of the ocean, it was stolen by a serpent. So he almost became immortal except his chance for immortality was stolen by that serpent."

"Sort of like your garden of Eden?" Shamash asked.

"Exactly," Diandra responded.

"What happened to Alexander?"

"His search for immortality didn't end well. He died in Babylon at the age of thirty-three, which is an interesting number in itself," she answered. "However, in those thirty three years he accomplished more than any one man in history up until that time. Discovering his tomb will help solve one of the greatest archeological mysteries of our time."

"Well, we better get some sleep if we're going to make that discovery," Dutch piped in. "Skip, what're those noises I hear in the background?

'"Rifle shots. A few explosions. The rebels have been taking potshots at the Syrian troops. Not really dangerous, but it could get a bit dodgy here."

"I've been thinking, Skip," Dutch said. "Let's move up plan B by a day and go into it tonight. Agreed?"

Finishing his meal at the hotel, Skip still had his legs propped up on the table while he methodically cleaned his hands. He looked around at everything in the room, exhaled, and shook his head.

"I do," Skip finally said, "although reluctantly. Good night all, I have a lot of work to do. See you in the morning."

"Seems like a perfect time for us to turn in too," Diandra noted, grabbing her outer garment and drawing it tighter. "It feels like it's getting colder and windier."

"There could be a storm coming in," Shamash agreed. "Best we turn in and get an early start."

"What is plan B, Dutch?" Sam asked.

"Insurance," he answered dismissively. Rising to his feet, he turned to enter the tent.

* * * * * * * *

Chapter Six

Al-Jazira Desert, Northern Iraq

"This is where I must leave you, my new friends," Shamash shouted, covering his face against the gusting wind and blowing sand. "I will pray for Allah to protect you on the rest of your journey… of course, along with Dutch's help!" He wrapped his turban more securely, covering all but his eyes.

Dutch pulled his camel around and stuck out his hand. "Thank you for everything, Shamash," he yelled back as they shook hands.

Shamash peered up at the sky. "It would be best if you reach your destination quickly. A big storm is going to pass this way soon."

He waved, turned his camel north and disappeared over a ridge.

"He is right, everyone," Skip said through their PVD's.

"What, Skip?" Diandra shouted above the wind's howling.

"There is a storm moving in your direction. It is not serious yet, but these types of meteorological events have a way of getting out of control quickly in your area."

"How long till we get there, Skip?" Dutch's voice was already getting hoarse.

"Well, let us see. About two minutes, in an F-16. In camel mode? Another couple of hours, at least. Unfortunately, you are heading directly into the easterly winds of the weather front. The good news is that I've been researching your mode of travel, and the camels will be able to make their way perfectly well through the sandstorm. Those nostrils that have been blowing mucus all over you—"

"Yeah," Sam sounded disgusted. "They have a major snot problem."

"Yes, well, be thankful, laddie," Skip continued, "because they can almost close their noses to keep the sand out. And those lovely long eyelashes belonging to your particular beauty will protect her eyes."

"Thank you, Doctor Wild Kingdom," Diandra laughed. "Actually, that's comforting, because I can't see a frigging thing! It's the first time I'm actually grateful for this horrible brown sack I've had to wear."

Wrapping their faces more securely in their Arab garb, they continued their trek eastward.

* * * * * * * *

Despite waking up to the mounting wind and blowing sand, the morning had gone reasonably well. After breaking camp at dawn, they were able to make good progress staying closer to the parallel bluff with coordinates supplied by Skip. Riding the camels had become less frustrating and more fun for the group, with the previous day's pointers from Shamash on how to be more confident and enjoy the beasts.

"Remember to pretend like you know what you're doing," Diandra called back to Sam as his camel refused to go forward. "Bop him on the butt with your stick!" The animal lurched forward and she laughed as Sam grabbed his turban, righting it.

The mood turned jovial as they lumbered closer to their destination, and by mid-afternoon they were racing each other, laughing uproariously and carrying on.

Skip had been following the weather reports and satellite images for most of the morning. Although not confirmed, weather service said there was a possibility of a severe weather front with winds exceeding one-hundred miles per hour in the area, stretching from Turkey to eastern Iraq, which could translate into a full blown sandstorm. He had researched these weather events and knew they were highly unpredictable, appearing with startling speed and intensity. This was part of the reason that Skip wanted the group hugging the cliffs for shelter, if it should become necessary. As an added precaution, he tapped into a Comsat five weather satellite feed and was monitoring the situation in real time.

* * * * * * * *

Within a few hours of their parting with Shamash, their worst fears were realized. The wind, and with it sand, was whipping up at almost fifty miles an hour, impeding their progress and making for a very uncomfortable trek. They were forced to communicate with each other via their PVD's.

And then Skip saw it. "Oh dear."

Moving toward them was a bright red area on his screen.

"I've got a bad feeling about this," Sam said, looking around fitfully. "I've seen this type of storm before, and it's not good, guys."

"We've got to find some shelter!" Dutch yelled. "Any ideas, Skip?"

Skip jumped to full attention, his movement startling a six-inch cockroach that scuttled from the back of his computer screen and stared at him eye-to-eye from atop the monitor.

"Ayyyyeeee!" he screamed, jumping up and swishing it away.

"Skip! Are you okay?" Dutch yanked his camel to a stop.

Collapsing back in his seat, Skip refocused on the map, putting one hand on his chest to still his pounding heart. The red dot had doubled in size and was almost to their green GPS spots on the screen."

"Skip?" Dutch asked again.

"Oh, no," Skip whispered.

"Just what does 'Oh no' mean, Skip?" Diandra asked, voice tight.

Howling wind made it difficult to hear anything. The camels started calling and snorting to each other, milling about.

"Dutch, you need to get somewhere to protect yourselves as best you can, and quickly!" Skip implored.

Dutch searched the ridge for an alcove, but the sand was obscuring any chance of seeing one. Diandra's camel started to fold its knees in preparation for lying down to weather the storm.

"No!" she yelled at it, yanking at the rope attached to its nose-ring. "Bad camel! Keep going!"

Dutch turned to see what was going on just in time to see her camel flop to the ground, throwing Diandra off to the far side. He leapt from his own saddle and raced over to help her as she laid there, her head next to a big rock.

"Are you okay?" he asked, kneeling down beside her. Gingerly he probed the back of her head and felt a growing bump. Withdrawing his hand, he saw blood on his fingers. "Shit."

"Ow! That hurts," she said, pushing him away and sitting up. "I'm fine…" She collapsed back down. "Maybe not," she added in a weaker voice.

All the camels had ignored their riders and laid down in a group, eyes closed and ready for the oncoming sandstorm.

"Get up, you stupid beast!" Sam yelled as he kicked and flailed it with his whip.

Hearing his struggle, Diandra opened her eyes again. "I'll take it slower this time." Sitting upright with Dutch's help, she tried to stand, stumbling back to her knees. "My ankle was under Mister Ship-Of-The-Desert when he decided to lie down. I think I may have broken something," she said grabbing her ankle. "Hurts like hell."

"Dutch," Skip yelled into the microphone. "Dutch, Diandra, can any of you hear me?" Static was his only response. The red area was now directly over and obscuring their position. He could only stare in horrified disbelief.

Dutch waved to Sam and pointed in the direction of the cliffs.

"Leave the damn camel! We need to get going." Lifting Diandra into his arms he started walking.

They could barely see each other. The deafening roar of the wind and stinging of the sand grew more intense as they disappeared into the swirling cloud.

Chapter Seven

Aleppo, Syria

"Zoë, I've lost communication with everyone because of a sandstorm," Skip relayed to her on his flat panel computer screen. "It doesn't look good."

"What do you want me to do, Skip?" concern in her voice.

"Getting someone in there to evacuate them would be a good start," Skip responded, shaking his head.

"Hold on," she said, pushing a button on a keyboard.

Tanner appeared on screen, sitting in his office. "What is the situation there, Skip?" he asked.

"Dutch, Diandra and Sam are caught in the middle of a sandstorm, Mister Tanner. I've lost contact with them, which means they and the camels have separated. I've got no GPS location data."

"Knowing Dutch, I am sure they took precautions-"

"You are not reading me, sir. They are non-com. I'm blind here. We need to send in a team to extricate them, now!"

"Skip, that would be impossible," Tanner said, trying to calm his voice and diffuse the situation. "They are in a NATO no-fly zone. If we did send in a chopper, it would be intercepted and be considered an act of aggression. Not to mention they would try and shoot it down. There are politics to consider here. We've got to trust that they are okay at this point."

"Damn the politics. They are in trouble," Skip retorted.

"I'd like to, believe me. But I am not going to risk an international incident or another group of people's lives at this point. Is there a contingency plan for this?"

Skip hesitated for a moment. "It was barely discussed," he confided. "We did not plan for this eventuality. But if we became totally non-com Dutch would head north in the most direct route toward the Turkish border, probably toward Simak or Ridyal."

"I see," Tanner said, pausing for a moment to think. "Let's give them a few more hours to regain communications. If not, I will try and set something up on the Turkish border for them. Short of that, there is really nothing we can do. Keep me informed."

"Right," Skip replied as the screen went black.

He sat back in his chair, pulled out a Handi Wipe and began his ritual hand cleansing.

"Where are you Dutch?"

* * * * * * * *

Farouq was in line in front of the Park Hotel on Bagdad Station Street, smoking a cigarette while waiting for his next fare. Suddenly, the rear door of his Saab opened and in plopped a man. The night prevented Farouq from being able to see him clearly.

"I am not next in line," Farouq stated.

"It is okay. Please take me to the airport."

"Shall I get your bags?" Farouq asked.

"No need, just drive," the man said.

Farouq put out the cigarette in the ashtray, started up his cab and turned onto Al Arkoob Street. Reaching the corner, he turned left and headed toward the airport.

"My name is Farouq, and I am at your service," he said.

"I know who you are," the man said.

A streetlight illuminated the inside of the cab. In his rearview mirror Farouq saw that it was the Fat Man. His heart lurched as he heard a click from the back seat followed by a gun pushing into the back of his head.

"We need to talk," the Fat Man said.

* * * * * * * *

Chapter eight

Al-Jazira Desert, Northern Iraq

It seemed to Dutch that he would never get all the sand out of his clothes. After finding a slight overhang against a cliff they had spent the next six hours waiting and praying that the sand that was slowly covering them in a drift would stop rising. The fury of the storm finished as quickly as it had started, waning to a howling wind just as the level of sand approached their chests.

With a lot of struggling and wiggling Dutch was able to extricate himself, and then helped Diandra and Sam dig out. Dutch checked Diandra's ankle and determined that although badly swollen, it was a sprain rather than a break. He tore off a piece of his robe and wrapped it the best he could.

They sat awhile, silent, while they tried to get the sand and dust out of their eyes, mouths and ears. Dutch tapped his earpiece and in a raspy voice shouted over the wind and motioned for them to see if they could communicate with Skip. Each shook his and her head after a few attempts.

Dutch figured they had about two hours before nightfall, and the bitter cold that would accompany it. Pulling out his Bowie knife, he extracted some matches from the end and gave them to Sam.

Reconnoitering the area while Sam went and gathered some tamarisk brush for a fire, Dutch's hopes were dampened when over a kilometer away, he found camel's feet extending above the ground about six inches. It would take hours to dig it up and see which one it was. He reasoned they could come back tomorrow if they really needed to.

After a search of the perimeter that lasted a half hour, he gathered his garb closer to his body and returned to the makeshift camp with a small fire blazing.

"Any luck?" Diandra asked looking up at him hopefully.

Dutch shook his head, bending down to the fire and warming his hands. "Everything is covered in sand. No sign of the camels," he lied. Sitting down he reached behind his robe.

"What are we going to do?" Sam asked.

"Shit!" Dutch yelled, fumbling around his back, startling Diandra and Sam. "My .45 is gone." Throwing his arms up in anger, he continued. "That's just perfect!" Checking his leg he confirmed his .38 Smith and Wesson was still there. "At least we have *some* protection."

"What'll we do?" he jumped up remembering Sam's question. "I'll tell you what we're gonna do. This adventure is over. Finished." He kicked the sand. "And we'll be lucky if we get out of here alive." Noticing Diandra's look of concern he continued. "I can't sugarcoat this thing. We are in some deep shit here, and it is going from bad to worse."

Looking up at the darkening sky, he rubbed the back of his neck and started pacing.

"You don't have to be so negative, Dutch," Diandra said. "We're still alive and tomorrow we can--"

"We can what? Just go on a little hike tomorrow and leisurely make our way to…? Oh, that's right. Where? Back to Syria? That's maybe two days away on foot, if we're lucky. And that's not including your limping all the way. Getting to Turkey is our only chance, except we're in the middle of a war zone. I know I can get us to the Turkish border, hook or crook. But with your gimp, it'll slow us down."

"And don't forget we'll need water," Sam added. "The human body needs one point eight liters per day for optimum performance."

Dutch stopped pacing for a moment and frowned at Sam. "Thank you for that helpful and hopeful bit of info."

Echoing in the wind, they could hear jackals howling in the distance, causing all three to look in the direction of their cries.

"What about the tomb?" Diandra asked, turning back to the conversation and ignoring Sam's comment.

"Damn it, Di. This mission is over. Get it?" Rubbing his eyes with one hand. "It's been jinxed from the start. We'll be lucky to even-"

"Well, mister glass half empty – what about never giving up?" Diandra reminded him.

"Reality check here. We're in the middle of a frickin' desert… with apparently not enough water," Dutch nodded toward Sam. "I'm not sure I remember where there is any water around here, since I lost my map too. So I repeat, this mission is over," he said, gesturing with his hands like a referee ending a fight. He stopped pacing and thought. "I don't know why I let you talk me into this in the first place."

Sam and Diandra drew their clothing tighter against the growing chill.

"You'd think these things would be warmer, being as bulky as they are," Sam noted in a total non sequitur to the tense conversation.

"We all agreed to go, Dutch," Diandra said. "Nobody talked anybody into anything." She stirred the fire and let that hang in the air. "It's not just about you. I'm not taking my toys and going home," she added after the long pause.

"We've no choice, Di," Dutch kneeled down, facing her. "It's either quit or risk dying, and I'm not willing to let that happen. We can always come back." He resumed his pacing about the fire. "I've got to think…" he said, rubbing the back of his neck.

"Dutch, what if we—" Sam began.

"Look kid, I don't need any of your ideas-"

"Don't you treat him that way," Diandra lashed out.

"Ugh," Dutch exhaled.

"I can handle this on my own," Sam said in a defensive tone to Diandra.

Dutch glared at Sam, pointing his finger. "Don't you be writing ego checks you can't cash. I'm the wrong guy to fu…" He caught himself, stopped, threw up his hands in exasperation and stomped off.

Diandra held her hand up to Sam as she pushed herself to her feet, grabbed a long piece of firewood and, using it for support, limped after Dutch.

"You okay?" she finally asked, putting her free hand in the crook of his arm

"Not really," he replied tersely, staring off in the distance.

"I'm sorry I yelled at you. I didn't mean-"

"It's not you," he said, turning around, "it's me." Blowing out his breath he shook his head. "It was up to me to protect the mission, and-"

"You can't plan for everything," she interrupted. "It was a sandstorm, for chrissakes."

"Makes no difference, Di, my watch," he said while shivering from the cold piercing wind. "Best we get warm again by the fire and figure this thing out."

He supported her as they walked back slowly and sat down. Jackals continued cackling in the distance, intermixing with the howling of the wind.

"Probably dining on our camels," Dutch said to no one.

After a few minutes Dutch turned to Sam. "Sorry, Sam, I didn't mean to, you know… What was your idea?"

"I don't remember," Sam replied. "It probably wasn't a good one anyway."

Diandra gave Dutch a frown. He shrugged, furrowing his eyebrows.

"Hopefully in the morning, the dust from this storm will clear," Dutch said, "and I'll be able to get our bearings. Being in the middle of the desert can fool you sometimes. I've been in this situation before. We'll be okay, but as I said, it won't be easy. In the meantime, I suggest we get some rest. It'll be a rough trek tomorrow."

"How are we going to get that rest, Dutch?" Sam asked.

Dutch thought for a moment. "We'll dig a shallow pit next to the fire, big enough for the three of us. Then we cover it with sand, leaving our heads exposed near the charcoals. We'll need to sleep together to save body heat." Looking around. "We'll dig it here," he said, pointing.

Sam got up, knelt at the spot indicated, and started scooping sand. Dutch followed suit.

"You know, when we were growing up in Iran, things were getting pretty dangerous," Sam said, waiting for Dutch to respond, who continued digging silently. "My father would put us all to bed and tell us that everything would be better in the morning… that the difference between hope and despair was a good night's sleep."

"That a fact, kid?" Dutch said.

"It's not 'kid', Dutch," Sam retorted angrily.

"Okay, you two knock it off," Diandra interrupted.

Dutch stopped digging and looked at Sam.

"I hope your dad was right, because right now I don't feel very hopeful." He stopped shoveling and pulled his robe closer. "We'd better hurry before it gets much colder. Di, you'll sleep in the middle. Sam and I will get on either side. Hopefully, we'll stay warm enough."

"Sounds good to me," Sam said.

"I thought it would," Dutch replied.

Diandra was too cold, tired and hungry to argue.

"Sam, you get closest to the fire. I'll stay up for awhile and keep watch. Those jackals sound-" catching himself, Dutch stopped. "They're probably fat, dumb and happy from all the camel meat by now. I'm sure we'll be safe," he continued, trying to sound reassuring. Their eyes told him they weren't buying it.

They continued digging until they had finished a sleeping area about eight inches deep. Diandra and Sam covered up with sand as best they could. It would be a long night.

Dutch had fallen asleep on watch and woke up screaming *"No!"* startling Sam and Diandra awake. Jumping up he shook it off, rubbing his hand through his hair. The moon could be seen through the light dust that remained from the dwindling storm, He walked away to clear his head.

Diandra shook off the blanket of sand and pushed herself to her feet with the stick. She hobbled after Dutch, wincing at the pain in her ankle.

"What was that about?" she asked.

"Nothing. Same old, same old," he said, shivering from the chill of the nightmare sweat.

"Patrick, again?"

He nodded. She turned and stared up at the moon.

Silence.

"It wasn't your fault," she said softly.

"That's what everyone says."

"Well, it's true."

"Not for me."

Patrick had been Dutch's younger brother by six years. As kids, they were inseparable. Traveling from one military base to another throughout their childhood, they became each other's best friend out of necessity. Dutch was preparing to take Patrick to college the summer after his graduation from high school. He even set him up on his first date, which unfortunately ended badly. In order to make up for it, Dutch planned a big bash for his eighteenth birthday at Big Daddy's in Fairfield, Iowa. A surprise party.

All of Patrick's friends were there. The music and drinks were plentiful, and before Dutch realized it, Patrick was drunk. He asked him to wait outside while he paid the bill and he would drive him home. Exiting the bar, Dutch saw Patrick pulling onto Highway 66 in his 1965 convertible Cutlass where he turned the wrong way and ran head on into a speeding eighteen wheeler barreling down the highway. When Dutch got to the mangled wreck, Patrick was already dead, his neck snapped to an impossible angle.

While it took the fire department and the Jaws of Life over an hour to remove his body, Dutch ran through his mind what he could have done differently: What if he had grabbed the keys from Patrick before he told him to wait outside while he paid the bill? What if he had cut him off from drinking earlier? These and a thousand other questions ran through his mind.

Since then, he had been haunted with the constantly recurring dream of running toward the wreck in slow motion, never being able to reach it; never being able to save his brother.

"You'd better get some sleep," Dutch finally said to Diandra. "I'll be back there in a few minutes."

"Sure you're okay?" she asked, shivering too.

"I said I was," he replied.

She sighed, realizing that talking any further would be fruitless, as it always had been when she'd tried to offer him emotional support. She returned to the dying fire, added a few more branches, and lay down, covering herself as best she could with sand.

* * * * * * * *

Chapter Nine

Al-Jazira Desert, Northern Iraq

Dutch was deep asleep when he felt something blowing softly on his cheek. He opened his eyes to see a huge camel nose above him. Startled, he pushed the camel's head and scooted a foot away in one fluid motion.

"What the hell?" he shouted as the camel followed him and kept licking while Dutch shooed it away as best he could.

Sam woke up in time to watch him jump up and get eye to eye with one of the beasts. The camel's snotty nose blew, and was a direct hit. By then Dutch realized what was happening.

"They're back!" Sam shouted with joy.

"What's all the ruckus about?" Diandra asked, rubbing her eyes.

"The camels, they came back!" Sam said as he jumped up and ran toward the other two animals lying placidly nearby.

"I'll be damned," she said with a huge grin.

Sam petted one of the camels and looked over to Dutch.

"I guess my dad was right, huh!"

"I guess so, Sam," Dutch said, smiling, "although what they probably want is food."

Dutch went over to the pack camel, opened one of the holy boxes and pulled out a new headset and put it on.

"Skip, are you there? Skip?"

Skip was sound asleep when he heard Dutch's voice. Jumping out of bed he ran to the desk and answered.

"Dutch, is that you?" he said. "Thank god you are okay. Do you have any idea how worried I was about you?"

"We're fine, Skip. Just a little worse for wear."

"I'm not kidding, Dutch, almost had Tanner bring in the army, navy and the marines to find you. You gave me a hell of a scare-"

"Skip!" Dutch interrupted him.

"Yes?"

"We are okay," he said, smiling at Sam and Diandra while pointing to his ear. "Diandra and Sam need to replace their PVD's and all will be right."

"Bloody hell, Dutch, you had me worried to death."

"Yeah, well, fortunately, it ended well," Dutch noted. "Although it does bring up a point I'd like to discuss with you at another time. In the meantime, let's check all of the equipment and take an inventory. Seems we lost one of the beasts in the storm. One of the pack camels."

"Any idea what else you lost?" Skip asked.

"If I remember, it carried most of our camping supplies and part of our food, but I'll have to make sure. In the meantime, plot us the most direct course to the Turkish border."

After taking inventory, they found Dutch was right. Their camping equipment and most of their food supplies were on the camel that died. Although Dutch knew where the camel was buried, he decided it was not worth the effort to dig it up. They had enough food to get back, and that was good enough for him. Most of their electronic gear was on the other pack camel, as well as his shotgun, which gave him a little more confidence.

Skip had mapped out the nearest route to get out of there. It would take less than half a day to reach the Turkish border.

After using some of their drinking water to clear their throats and devouring a fresh meal, a more hopeful mood swept over them. It was as if the night before had been a bad dream; one they didn't want to discuss. Dutch was busy making plans to go to Turkey when Skip came back online.

"Dutch, you realize you are now only a few kilometers from the site," Skip informed them. "Fortune is smiling upon you, I'd say."

Both Sam and Diandra heard Skip and eyed Dutch.

"As bad as it seems everything has been, it would be a shame not to at least have a look-see, no?" Skip coaxed Dutch.

Taking in the excited expressions on Sam's and Diandra's faces, Dutch replied. "I don't see how I would be able to stop these two, do you?"

"We're going, Skip," Diandra piped in. "So give us the coordinates and let's get on with it."

Dutch smiled and shook his head. "Like the lady says, we're going. We'll pack up and be ready in about thirty minutes. By the way, everything go okay on your end?"

"No problems at all," Skip replied, "just like we planned."

"What are you two talking about?" Sam asked.

"Nothing kid. Let's get this wrapped up and on the road."

"I am not a kid," Sam retorted indignantly before turning back to his camel.

* * * * * * * *

Aleppo, Syria

Skip noted movement on the computer screen to his left from one of the cameras he'd set up at the hotel. It was the Fat Man and two of his associates, creeping up the stairs. Sitting back in his chair he folded his arms and watched as they passed the first camera on the landing and came into view on the second camera. The system's resolution was so good that he could see the sweat running down the Fat Man's face. He was short and stocky with multiple chins. A mustache drooped over his lips, while his eyes were deeply embedded below black caterpillar eyebrows. His associates were neatly dressed dark complexioned Persian appearing men.

Reaching the second floor landing, they made their way down the hallway and came into view of the third camera, stopping in front of his door.

Skip leaned forward and frowned at the screen. The Fat Man motioned silently and the two others drew their pistols, nodded to him and rushed toward the door, kicking it in.

Skip typed some commands and the camera inside the room showed the scene as they rushed inside… to an empty room. He watched the three dumbfounded men search the room and then the bathroom before one of them stopped and looked above the door, staring curiously. Reaching up, he covered the lens while trying to pull the camera out. Skip lost the feed, his computer screen going black.

Plan B had worked brilliantly, Skip mused, rubbing his palms together with satisfaction. He and Dutch had planned on his moving to another hotel across town without informing Farouq. They felt the mission could be compromised, even with the ruse they had pulled for the benefit of whomever was watching. He had left the cameras in place at the hotel and used a transmitter relay to receive the images.

However, this new development meant that their original plan to fool the Fat Man had failed. He had to assume that since they, whoever they were, knew about *him*, they also knew the *others* had not taken off in the jet. Informing Dutch became a priority, and he made plans to adjust their equipment.

He grabbed a wipe and cleaned under his nails while continuing with this line of reasoning. The scope of the mission had changed. They were now compromised. Why were these men looking for them? Who was the Fat Man working for? Were the others in danger as well? Those questions and more ticked through his mind like interlocking cogs. Skip resumed typing on his keyboard, pausing his research only to contact Dutch.

After Skip shared with Dutch what had happened at the hotel the two agreed that they had to assume whoever was looking for them was aware of their purpose, or at least had a pretty good idea. As a precaution, Skip had the team disable the GPS feature on their smart phones, leaving only the ones in his PVD units active, so that no one could track them.

* * * * * * * *

Syrian desert, Syria

Shadow Man spoke with Lilne on his cell phone while pacing around the front of Ahmed's tent.

"We have learned that they did not take off in the jet as we thought. It was a rather clever diversion. They took a cab to a rendezvous point on the northern border of Syria and have crossed into Iraq by camel."

"Do we know where they are heading?

"We are in the process of interrogating the proprietor of the transportation business as we speak."

Turning round, Shadow Man watched two goons beating up Ahmed, who fell to his knees before collapsing in the sand. "It shouldn't be too long before we know. I believe you need to get here as quickly as you can."

"I will be there in the next six hours," Lilne said. "Meet me at Mosul airport. It is critical that no one do anything until I get there."

* * * * * * * *

Chapter Ten

Al-Jazira Desert, Northern Iraq

After loading up the camels, the Seekers made their way north, northeast toward a distant canyon. The cliffs gradually rose to form its sides from the flat canyon floor leaving a passage about thirty feet wide. They gazed up as the walls reached higher than fifty feet. The canyon made a slight turn to the left. Dismounting, they led the animals as the canyon narrowed.

"Doesn't seem to be much around here," Dutch noted.

Diandra and Sam were absorbed in studying every crevice and cranny on both walls.

"According to my calculations, you are there, Diandra," Skip said.

"And you're sure this is the right spot?" Sam asked.

"Plus or minus thirteen feet," Skip confidently replied.

"Well, seems to me you could be off a hundred feet and not find anything in here," Dutch observed. Looking around, all he could see were the smooth walls of the canyon punctuated by shallow rock outcroppings.

Sam walked up to one of the outcroppings, stopped and studied it carefully.

"Guys," he said, motioning for them to come. "Notice anything strange about this?" he asked, staring at it.

Dutch looked up at it and walked to the other side. "Looks a bit like a face if you really use your imagination."

"The rock," Diandra blurted out.

"Exactly," Sam agreed.

"What about the rock? Dutch asked.

"It shouldn't be here," Sam answered.

"He's right," Diandra concurred, rubbing her hand on the stone's smooth surface.

"This is andesitic. It is not natural to the area. In fact, it is totally out of place." Walking back a few steps she looked up. "And it is huge." Moving around to the other side of it, she felt the edge.

"It is a face," she finally said. "See the nose, the mouth and the eyes? If you weren't looking for it, you would totally miss it. You can see the erosion marks, here and here. It has barely worn down." Turning to Sam. "It has got to weigh hundreds of thousands of pounds."

"At least," Sam replied.

Dutch assessed it for a few moments. Its chin started about five feet above the floor of the canyon, rose to over twenty-five feet above that, and was perhaps twenty feet across. Although the indentations where the eyes would be were worn, he could see that it could have once been a face, with the center above the lips being a nose. The canyon's wall rose another fifty feet above the head.

"So why is it here?" Dutch asked.

Diandra stepped back and considered it from different angles.

"I'm not sure," she said as she bit her lip thoughtfully. "Maybe…"

"Perhaps I can offer a suggestion?" Skip broke in on the headsets.

"Go ahead," Diandra replied.

"There is an eye on the last quadrant of the tablet," Skip started. "I've wondered what it has to do with this whole business, since it stands out on its own with no relations to the musical notes or anything else for that matter."

Sam eyed his smart phone with a picture of the tablet. "It's the eye of the face that is important!" he shouted, looking to Diandra, who nodded.

"Exactly, laddie," Skip confirmed. "Maybe it means you have to see something-"

"Or, the face itself is staring at something," Diandra interjected.

"Brilliant. So here is a suggestion," Skip continued. "How about *someone* going up and seeing what that head is staring at? Seems banal, but what else do you have to do at this point?"

"It's pretty steep," Dutch noted, looking up. "Any volunteers?" he asked half mockingly, looking around the canyon.

"No? Okay, I guess I'll go."

"Good idea," Sam said, winking at Diandra.

Dutch shook his head as he walked back to the remaining pack camel to get the equipment. Pulling the false bottoms from one of the cases revealed loops of carabiners and spikes. Slinging them plus a rope onto one shoulder, he also grabbed a climber's pickaxe and returned to the area. Sam and Diandra started to unpack the satellite dish to get a clear signal with Skip.

Dutch surveyed the rock face. *Shouldn't be a big deal,* he thought. *Maybe twenty-five feet up, max.* He'd done climbs much more difficult than that. After mentally plotting the route he would take, he approached the cliff face and hammered in a piton.

"Wish me luck," he said as he wound the rope through the carabineer and made a loop at the bottom. Pulling the rope up about half way, he put his foot in the loop and stood up. He was then able to put the next piton in. It was slow going, as the rock was extremely hard.

He climbed up along the left side of the face in this way until he became level with the eyes. Reaching out to his right he hammered in another piton, attached a carabiner, threaded the rope through and using his foot, moved up about three feet. He repeated the process again, only this time the carabiner fell out of his hand and hit the ground below.

"Sorry about that," he yelled, his voice echoing throughout the canyon until it was a whisper.

"Just be safe," Diandra pleaded as she watched his progress.

Hammering in the piton and using the carabiner to reach the area where he believed the eyes were located, he carefully made his way toward the middle between them and stopped where the nose protruded slightly. Diandra and Sam watched as Dutch anchored himself against the stone face and carefully turned around, using his feet to precariously brace himself. It seemed a lot higher than twenty-five feet to him.

"See anything Dutch? Diandra shouted, her voice echoed.

"Not really," he replied, searching the canyon wall. "Let me get my bearings."

And then he saw it. Across the canyon, about twelve feet up from the ground and inset into the canyon wall, a piece of stone about three feet wide and about eight inches tall. The light from the sun cast a slight shadow revealing a carved glyph symbol on it. He made a note of its position relative to the stone face and ground.

"Got it!" he shouted with a grin.

"Got what?" Diandra shouted back, their two echoes intermingling and chasing each other.

Suddenly, with a rain of shattered sandstone, his footing gave way and Dutch slipped off the rock face nose. He grabbed the rope and it jerked taut, the carabineer straining under his weight.

Ping. He was weightless for a moment before falling to the next carabineer, which held for a brief jerk before giving way.

Ping, ping, ping, went the rest of the pitons as he slid down the rock face, rolled on his side the last ten feet and came to a crashing halt at the bottom.

"Dutch!" screamed Diandra as she came out of the shock of watching the scene as if in slow motion. She limped to where his motionless body laid and fell to her knees, cradling his face.

"Dutch, are you okay?" she pleaded putting her hand behind his head and stroking his face with the other.

"Whoa, that was a tough fall, dude," Sam remarked as he reached the two of them.

Diandra threw him a quick look that said *shut up*.

Turning her attention back to Dutch, she noticed a very slight smile start to cover his face.

"Does this mean you still care about me?" he asked, opening his eyes.

"You!" she yelled, releasing her hold on him and standing up. His head bonked the hard ground. "You about scared the bejesus out of me," she shouted, pointing. "You-" She turned away before he could see the tears of relief well in her eyes.

"Yes?" he said with a grin. "Bejesus? Really?"

Silence.

"I'm okay, thank you," he said as he rolled over, pushed himself up and stood, considering his scraped and bleeding hands.

"I've got to get the hang of that next time," he said looking back up at the face. He hobbled a few steps to work out the sore spots, straightened his back, and then went to stand below the wall that hid the glyph he had spotted. Checking the head's position again, he pointed above him.

"It is right here above us," he said.

"What is?" Diandra asked.

"A stone mantel and glyph."

"What was it?"

"What?"

"The glyph, Dutch, what was it?"

"I don't know, Di. It looked like… like,,," Looking around for something to draw on, he squatted and sketched it in the dirt with his finger.

"An enneagram?' Diandra asked.

"That's what is looked like to me," Dutch said, raising one eyebrow.

"That is very interesting," Sam noted, squatting beside him. "That was one of the repeating signs at the bottom of McIntyre's letter. I wonder what it means?"

Dutch raised his shoulders as he looked around. "Don't know. But I don't see any entrance here. Shouldn't there be an X marks the spot or something?"

Slowly, Diandra ran her fingers over the canyon wall directly below where Dutch had seen the symbol. Suddenly she screamed and leapt away from the wall, shaking her hands as if burned.

"What's the matter?" Sam grabbed hold of her arm. "What happened?"

"I, I don't know," she replied. "I'm not sure how to describe it… my god!" She took a breath. "It was like a split second glimpse of a movie only…only…"

"Only what?" Sam asked.

"Only it was more a feeling than anything else. There were people scared, frightened. Running. Screaming. I don't understand it." she said, rubbing her hand to get the numbness out of it.

"Maybe it has something to do with finding the entrance?" Sam suggested.

"I don't think so," Diandra replied, her heart still pounding from the disturbing images in her mind. "My god," she repeated, and sat down on the ground. "Give me a minute."

"Whether a feeling or a case of low blood sugar, we need to find a way in," Dutch said.

"The last part of the tablet contains those eighteen notes to a tune," Sam reminded them cocking his head to one side and considering the sandstone cliff. "I wonder."

Rubbing his hand over the same area Diandra had just received the shock from, he had a thought.

"Remember how when the two tablets were put together, they swirled and formed another tablet?" Sam said to Diandra.

She nodded, still catching her breath.

"The Tanner lab guys think it had something to do with magnetics. But I wonder… maybe it had to do with-"

An inspiration hit him with force.

"I know it sounds stupid," Sam continued, "but I think we should play that tune and see what happens."

"It does sound stupid," Dutch said. "What say I just get a little C four and blow our way in? It'll take five minutes-"

"Dutch, stop it," Diandra cut him off, frustrated. "Give Sam a chance, here. What I experienced was definitely not in the normal realm, so even if it sounds *stupid…*" She thought for a few moments. "Dutch, do you remember what that Doctor Werner told us?"

"Who is Doctor Werner?" Sam interjected.

"Which part?" Dutch asked.

"Listen to the music… he said it will lead you," she replied.

"The guy was a nut case, Di."

"Maybe so," she said. "But maybe… maybe he was telling us to listen to *this* music," she said, holding up her smart phone. "I have the notes downloaded on this."

"This is crazy," Dutch retorted, shaking his head.

Ignoring his comment, Diandra located the player app and found the eighteen-note tune. Pointing it toward the wall she hit play. After the notes were through playing, they stared at the wall in silence.

Nothing.

"I'm telling you, Di, I can have this open in a few minutes," Dutch egged her on, impatiently.

"I'm being serious here, too, Dutch. There could be valuable artifacts behind this wall that would be destroyed with you doing that. If we have to, and I mean when we have run out of *every* other idea, then we can consider it. But honestly, we really have nothing to lose trying again."

She turned up the volume on her phone and hit play again. The notes echoed hauntingly throughout the canyon. They stared at the wall, waiting for something to happen.

Nothing.

"Well, shoot, now I feel stupid," Diandra said.

"Maybe we should say something like… *open sesame*?" Dutch wiggled his eyebrows.

Her look let Dutch know she was in no mood for jokes.

"Diandra," Skip broke in. "Sorry to be non-com, but I have been working on a little research project here that I think may help."

"Yes Skip?"

"Well, ever since we learned about the notes on the tablet, it got me to thinking. What notes are these exactly? Are they present day notes, in a present day musical scale? I thought not.

"So I started researching, and what I found was eye opening. It turns out that a new standard for most musical scales was adopted in nineteen thirty-nine. And get this, it was spearheaded by the Nazi party *and* the Rockefeller foundation. We can go into the whys and wherefores of that later. Without getting too technical, they chose

440 megahertz as the frequency for middle A. As near as I can tell, before that, it was 432 megahertz, the same frequency used by Mozart, and Bach. Anyway, that led to the following thought: what were the frequencies used in Alexander's time?

"I have had Zoë working on that very question these last couple of days. She found a flute in the Museum of the Ancient Orient in Istanbul and had the notes tested with a frequency machine. I just now received the results. It shows that the equivalent of A on the scale is 428 Megahertz. So if my theory holds true, I can recalculate the tune and send it in that frequency. Hold on for a moment."

The group stared at one another, dumbfounded.

"Wow, thanks Skip," Diandra said, grinning at the others. "Have I told you lately how amazing you are?"

"Couldn't hurt to repeat it once in a while," Skip responded. "Sending now."

Diandra raised her shoulders, grinned and waited silently until her phone beeped twice.

"Okay then, on to plan B," Diandra said half kiddingly. Turning to Dutch, she crossed her fingers. Dutch returned it with a nod. She wiped her sweaty fingers on her pants, then carefully hit play and the tune ran through the notes.

"I didn't really hear much of a difference," Dutch said, his tone skeptical.

"You wouldn't," Skip answered, "It's barely perceptible-"

"Look at that!" Sam shouted, pointing.

All eyes focused on the canyon wall, which started softening at its center. Slowly it expanded out in ripples, increasing in speed until reaching a crescendo in a mini, swirling sandstorm. They watched in open-mouthed amazement as they heard a loud, metal-on-metal grating sound.

Suddenly, everything stopped and the sand dropped to the ground, revealing an opening. It was seven feet tall, about six feet wide and went deep into the cliff face.

"Whoa, dude," Sam whispered "That was friggin' awesome."

"More like unbelievable, I'd say," Diandra noted after a deep exhale.

"I'm getting chills about it, dearie," Skip added on their headsets.

Dutch hurried toward the pack camel, retrieved his special shotgun with the eighteen-inch barrel, grabbed a signal repeater for Skip, and returned. He set up the repeater just inside the tomb's entrance, hit the power up button and stepped back.

"What do you plan on doing with that," Diandra said, pointing to the gun.

"Lead us in."

"Against two-thousand year old dead people?" Diandra asked.

"Just making sure they stay that way," Dutch replied. "Come on," he said while motioning for the two of them to follow.

"What do you mean, come on? *I'm* leading us in," Diandra responded grabbing her support stick and hobbling ahead.

"It's either my way or the highway," Dutch replied, gently pulling the back of her shirt.

"You know what, Dutch," Diandra, said, putting her free hand on her hip. "I've missed the way you speak in bumper sticker."

Dutch feigned being hurt, stepped back and swept his arm toward the door.

"After you, then, my liege," he said.

"Children, can we just get inside?" Skip interjected. "I'm on needles and pins here."

"You okay with this, Sam?" Diandra asked quietly, looking concerned as she passed him.

"I think I'll be alright," he replied with a deep breath and confident nod.

"What is going on?" Dutch glanced from one to the other.

Ignoring Dutch's question, Diandra pulled out a flashlight, flicked it on and started in. Sam followed, with Dutch bringing up the rear.

"Why do you think that tune opened the door?" Dutch asked aloud as he brought out his flashlight and turned it on.

"Something to do with the vibration, I guess," Sam answered.

"It had everything to do with harmonic vibrations," Skip responded. "When you find the right megahertz and it parallels the-"

"English, Skip," Dutch interrupted.

"It is like a garage door opener, is that simple enough?" he answered with an audible snort.

"Works for me," Dutch replied.

Diandra laughed at the exchange as she continued down the corridor.

"I hear what you're saying, Skip," Sam said. "But it's still pretty bizarre to me…that mini-sandstorm open-sesame thing using a tune. Kinda spooky."

"Spooky doesn't begin to explain how they could have the technology to pull that off," Skip said.

"I was thinking the same thing," Diandra concurred. "But even though I don't fully understand it intellectually, it makes my gut feel that we're in the right place."

Her flashlight picked up footprints of various sizes in the dust on the floor as she slowly made her way downhill. "There've been a lot of people in here," she observed. "I wonder how long ago?" She played her light on the walls, which were smooth and without marks.

Sam came up beside her, and they stopped for a moment. "The air is so still in here." Looking down he studied the floor for a moment. "The footprints are in the style of early Greek sandals, *possibly* around Alexander's time. It is amazing they are so well preserved," he observed, "Although… I'm not sure why they wouldn't have swept the sand up before sealing the tomb."

They had to step carefully in order not to slip on the steep sandy floor, and by the time they had reached a marble archway almost forty feet in, they had descended about twenty-five feet.

Diandra placed a hesitant finger on a winged disk carved into the threshold. "The sign of Marduk," she said reverently.

"The sign of one of the Babylonian gods," Sam explained to Dutch, anticipating his question. "It means literally the calf of the sun. It is believed to refer to a god that was the son of Ea. Very unusual."

"I'd say," Diandra added with a look of wonder on her face as she turned back to him with a grin. "Especially since we are looking for Alexander, and that sign would indicate this tomb is thousands of years older."

Gazing, awestruck, at the carvings, Diandra and Sam slowly passed through the archway, and then turned a corner.

Sam bumped Diandra's back as she stopped abruptly. "Sorry!" His eyes went wide. "What the…. Wow!"

* * * * * * *

Chapter Eleven

Al-Jazira Desert, Northern Iraq

Before them loomed a huge cavern, revealed by their flashlights to be twenty feet high and at least fifty feet wide before disappearing in shadow. Inside were hundreds of wooden boxes stacked neatly in seven rows with aisles in between. They were unmarked.

Diandra's flashlight revealed large, amethyst-colored crystals embedded at two-foot intervals in the walls. As she entered the cavern, these began to glow, accompanied by a humming noise, until the room was lit with a slight purple hue.

"Jesus," Dutch commented, coming up beside her.

"What?" Skip asked. "What is going on in there? I am getting a lot of interference on your receivers."

"Um, Skip, I don't really know how to describe this," Diandra replied, stumbling over a rock as she tried to pitch her camera angle so he could see along with them. "I'm not sure I believe what I am seeing. Dutch?"

Gape-jawed, Dutch looked around the room. "I don't know, Di…"

Sam approached one of the crystals, hand extended. Dutch moved quickly to stop him, grabbing his arm.

"I wouldn't do that, kid," he said.

Sam followed his eyes to an area about three feet away where a mummified, shriveled version of a man lay on the ground, his hand still touching a glowing light.

"Better safe than sorry," Dutch added, as Sam jerked his arm back.

"Good idea," Sam said, shuddering at the thought of what might have happened. "Thanks."

"Skip," Diandra said. "There seems to be some source of energy in here that is powering up crystals within the wall. We have light." She turned off her flashlight.

"I can see that," Skip replied. "Someone needs to add another signal repeater at the beginning of the cavern's entrance to help me hold our communication."

"I'm on it," Sam said as he retraced their path through the chamber door and out of sight.

"So what do you think, Di?" Dutch asked, setting the shotgun atop his shoulder.

She paused for a minute as a grin spread across her face. "What do I think? I think this is the most amazing thing I have ever seen in my entire life. I'm not sure what we have discovered, but whatever it is will make world headlines. Oh my god…"

Dutch smiled as Diandra walked up to one of the crates, pulled out a pocketknife and jimmied open the top. Looking in, she saw hundreds of scrolls set in rows of small, perfectly carved, ebony insets. Sam came back, set up the wireless signal repeater and walked over to where she was standing with a crowbar.

"What is it?" Sam asked.

"Not sure," she answered, handing it over to him. "What does it say?"

Dutch continued walking down the aisle toward the end of the cavern, examining the hundreds of crates.

"It is written in old Greek." Sam said. He read some more as he set the crowbar down and stopped. "Diandra!" he exclaimed, looking at her, "It says 'copied by Thealamis per royal decree of our lord Demetrius.'"

Looking over at the cases she thought for a moment, taking a breath.

"We've found it, Sam. We found it!" She screamed, throwing herself at him in a big hug. Dutch turned toward her.

"So this really is Alexander's Tomb?" Dutch asked.

"Yes!" she said, glowing, as she hobbled over as fast as her sore ankle would permit and put her arms around Dutch.

"These scrolls are from the library, Dutch, the Serapeum. Demetrius was put in charge of it after Alexander left." She swept her arm. "I'm not sure how, but these hundreds of boxes contain scrolls from the Library of Alexander. It's all so overwhelming."

"And without doubt the find of the millennium," Sam said with equal enthusiasm. "Maybe even the greatest find of all time. Imagine… the lost scrolls. There must be thousands of them here."

"The implications are unfathomable." Diandra, said. "What we thought was lost, all of the knowledge of the world up to that time, is sitting right here. Do you realize the enormity of this, Dutch?"

"Sure, Di," he said, "I'm really happy for you. So just in round numbers, how much do you think all these scrolls might be worth?"

"Not now, Dutch."

"Diandra," Skip broke in. "Let me get some pictures of those scrolls."

Walking back to the box she held one of the scrolls open in front of her PVD.

"Got it," Skip said.

Carefully setting it back in, she started to open another box. Dutch wandered down to the end of the row of boxes, turned the corner and stopped.

"You'd better have look at this," he said in an urgent tone.

Sam and Diandra rushed to Dutch and followed his eyes. Before them, in a room just off the main cavern, lay a plain wooden crate, the size of a large coffin, resting atop a black granite altar. Entering through the arched doorway, they slowly approached it and stopped.

"Alexander," Diandra whispered as she started caressing the box. "We've been looking for you."

* * * * * * *

Mosul, Iraq

Arriving from Rome in a Gulfstream 350 Vatican jet, Lilne was met at the airport by Shadow Man and a cadre of soldiers. They were spirited away by limousine to a military base outside Mosul. Once inside headquarters, they were met by General Asoul along with three of his commanders.

"To what do we owe this urgent visit by so high an official from the Vatican?" General Asoul asked.

"It is imperative that I find the people I spoke to you about as quickly as possible," Lilne said.

"I understand," the general replied. "They have violated our sovereign laws by entering our country without permission. Unfortunately, we are unable to avail ourselves of satellite imagery because of the weather. But our best guess, from the information provided by your associate, is that they are somewhere in this area here," he pointed to the general area of northern Iraq between the Tigris and Euphrates rivers.

"Can we fly there by helicopter?" Lilne asked.

"Not until the storm clears."

"When will that be?" Lilne asked.

"Maybe this afternoon, if Allah wishes it. These things take time."

"Time is what I do not have," Lilne responded.

"At this point, it will be quicker if we travel by land. We can take Highway One and then cut over from there near Zummar. It will take a few hours at most."

"When can we leave?" asked Shadow Man.

"Within the hour. The vehicles are being readied as we speak," the general replied. "We also have alerted a patrol near the area that may be able to find them sooner."

"I want to make this very clear. No one is to do anything until we arrive there," Lilne said.

"As you wish. May I ask what we are looking for?"

"You may not," Lilne tartly replied.

"I see. And once we find these people?" the general inquired.

"After I question them, they are yours. You can do with them as you wish." Lilne gave a dismissive wave of his hand.

A slight smile showed on the general's wizened face.

* * * * * * *

Chapter Twelve

Al-Jazira Desert, Northern Iraq

The wooden box was larger than the black granite altar upon which it rested askew. After studying it, they decided to move it onto the ground before attempting to open it. With great effort, Diandra and Sam lifted on one end while Dutch heaved on the other. It slipped from their grasp for the last few inches and fell with a thump to the floor of the cavern.

"Careful," Diandra shouted, appalled. She ran her fingers over the surface of the wooden box, assuring herself that it was intact.

"I'll remember that next time," Dutch responded sarcastically, shaking his hand, which was almost crushed when it fell.

"I'll get your official opening tool. You know, that archaeologist crowbar thing," Sam volunteered. Diandra nodded her head as he ran out and returned with it a few moments later.

"You do the honors," he said, holding it out to her.

"Why thank you, I would be delighted," Diandra replied, grabbing it. "But I have to be really careful not to damage anything." She wiped her sweating palms on her pants, before kneeling and placing the tip of the rod between the lid and one side of the box's top.

"I'm really happy for you, Diandra," Sam said.

"Thanks Sam. You can take equally as much credit." Looking quickly to Dutch. "And this wouldn't have happened without you, Dutch. You know that, right?"

He nodded.

"I can't wait to share this with the world. Wait!" She paused. "We've got to take pictures."

"I'll go get the digital camera and some more repeaters for Skip. I can barely hear him," Dutch said, setting down his shotgun and hurrying out of the tomb area.

"What's with him?" Sam asked, motioning with his thumb.

Diandra shook her head ruefully, as she felt about the lid for the best place to start prying. "Do you see any treasure?" she asked.

"Oh," Sam replied, nodding.

Diandra stood again, leaning against the black granite altar, and stared at the box.

"What are you doing here, Alexander?" she whispered to herself. "And how did part of your library end up here too?"

Dutch returned with the camera and set up another repeater for Skip, his attitude all business.

"You getting this, Skip?" he asked, turning it on and testing the signal.

"Loud and clear, my boy," Skip replied enthusiastically.

"You're on, Di," Dutch said, motioning with his hand.

She nodded, took a deep breath, released it, and knelt again next to the box. She inserted the crowbar under the lid at one end and pushed down. The nails holding it squeaked loudly as she pushed harder, levering it slightly ajar. She removed the crowbar, limped to the other end and repeated the process. A couple more hard pushes and the lid gave way. Dutch and Sam helped lift it off and set it down. Peering in, she could see a very thin, translucent alabaster coffin lid. Through it could barely be glimpsed a male face with full beard. The remains of a white gown covered the body.

"Are you recording this, Skip?" Diandra asked.

"Perfectly," Skip said, his voice so low they could barely hear it.. "This really is like that Indiana-

"Yeah, yeah, Skip. Only I'm better looking and this is real," Diandra cut in, laughing.

She stood up and started on one of the sides. It was much more difficult, taking ten minutes to work the side boards loose, walking back and forth between the boards to loosen them so it would lie down. Walking to the other side, she wedged the crowbar in between the boards and yanked. It finally gave way after a few more attempts, while Dutch took digital pictures with the flash clicking away. Excitement was running among them like static electricity.

Setting the crowbar down, Diandra walked to the front of the coffin, noticed a small inscription, and knelt down to read it. She went ashen.

"What the… this can't be," she muttered to herself, hanging her head.

"What?" Sam asked.

Pointing at the inscription as she stood up, she stated, "It says 'Here Lies Our Lord Demetrius.'"

"What? I don't believe it!" Sam scrambled over to confirm the inscription and her translation.

"That guy at the library?" Dutch asked.

Diandra was lost in thought.

"I just don't understand any of this," she finally shared. "Thousands of scrolls squirreled away, apparently from the Library of Alexandria. The tablet and how it led us here. The sarcophagus with Demetrius entombed."

Silence hung in the air.

"There is a scenario that makes sense," Sam finally offered, a pensive frown creasing his forehead "Although it is a little farfetched."

Diandra turned her attention to him. "I'm listening."

"They knew about this location, and also knew that the tablet fragments, when put together, would eventually lead us to it. So they moved the boxes here before the library was burned in hopes it would be discovered," he stated.

"Who exactly are 'they'?" Diandra asked. "And how did *they* know about this place? And how did they move all of this here?"

"Good questions," Sam acknowledged. "I don't have the answers."

"Hmmm," she sighed in frustration, and then asked, "Any ideas Skip?"

"No, dearie," he replied. "I'm just as gob smacked as the rest of you. But for the record, this is still the find of the century, Alexander or no. And from what I am pulling up here, Demetrius was a pretty important fellow."

"Alexander put Demetrius in charge of Alexandria after he left," Diandra explained, confirming Dutch's earlier question. "He was the one who actually founded the library and made it the cultural as well as knowledge based center of the world."

"So if I am getting this right, the boxes out there and this casket-"

"Sarcophagus," Sam corrected him.

"Sarcophagus," Dutch continued, "are not really supposed to be here? So answer me this: what was this place built for? It looks like a tomb to me. What if that is not an altar," he said, pointing to the black granite altar.

Diandra was shaken out of her thoughts and dragged into Dutch's.

"You're right. Crystal lights, that granite face out there, the way the tomb opened…"

Her attention was drawn to the altar. "You know," she said, walking over and studying it for a few seconds with her hands, "this has a lid on it. The precision and joints are almost invisible." Turning her head toward Sam and Dutch, she wiggled her eyebrows. "There just might be something… or someone, inside of this."

* * * * * * * *

The light started flickering inside Dr. Werner's cell as he lay on top of the sheets. His body started to shake and shudder as his eyes rolled back into his head, causing the metal frame of the bed to rattle with a loud clanging sound.

"The truth will now be known!" he screamed.

"The truth will now be known!"

His screams were accompanied by footsteps running down the hall. After unlocking the door, two orderlies rushed in toward his bed.

Werner's body arched back so violently the force of the movement caused his body to leap off the bed and fly onto the floor, landing at the feet of the orderlies. Stunned for a moment, they quickly knelt down to restrain his arms from flailing about. Another orderly ran in with a syringe and straight jacket.

"The truth will now be known!" Dr. Werner continued screaming as a needle was stuck into his left shoulder and the light-blue liquid contents of it were plunged into him.

Within seconds his body relaxed on the cold cement floor, as the orderlies lifted his head up to fit him into the straight jacket.

* * * * * * * *

Chapter Thirteen

Al-Jazira Desert, Northern Iraq

Diandra smiled, picked up the crowbar and handed it to Dutch. "Your turn," she said.

"Thanks a lot," he replied, returning her smile. "Give me the easy jobs."

He approached the altar and looked at the sides. There wasn't much space between the lid and base, but he managed to slip the end of the crowbar into the crack and, heaving and pushing up, got it to move. All his effort caused the lid to travel about four inches. Sam pulled out a combination laser and tape measure.

"Let me take some measurements before you continue," he said. "Just in case you break it."

"I hope not," Diandra added.

Dutch nodded and stepped aside. Sam measured the lid, along with the width and height of the pedestal, noting them down in a journal. After nodding toward Dutch he was through, Dutch tried moving it again and gained another two or three inches.

"This is one heavy son-of-a-bitch," Dutch noted, starting to sweat.

He worked at it and finally got the bar between the lid and the inside of the altar, and was able to push it further as the sound of grating stone echoed throughout the cavern. Finally, he was able to push it completely off. It fell long side first and crash-landed at an angle, followed by a resounding thud that reverberated within the chamber. Dutch looked in and saw that it was empty. Crestfallen, he sat down as Diandra and Sam looked in next and groaned with disappointment.

Nothing.

"If it's not a burial sarcophagus," Sam wondered, "then why is it here?"

"This is getting very frustrating," Diandra shared as she stepped back and observed that the whole structure was carved out of a solid piece of black granite, the walls being about one inch thick. The inside walls were smooth, perfectly forming into ninety degree angles.

"Wait a minute!" She put a hand to her head. "What were the outside measurements again, Sam?"

"Ninety inches long by thirty-eight and three-quarters wide by forty-two and one-quarter high."

"After the lid was removed?"

"Subtract an inch," Sam said. "Making it forty-one and a quarter."

"Sound familiar at all?" she asked.

"Like what?" Sam said.

Silence.

"Like the king's chamber sarcophagus in the pyramid of Giza!" Skip shouted on the earpieces. "I typed the figures in and came up with it."

"Exactly," Diandra remarked. "This is getting stranger by the minute."

"So what, this is a king's chamber?" Dutch asked.

"Unknown," Diandra answered, shaking her head. "The king's chamber in the Giza pyramid was named that by Petrie simply because he could think of no other reason as to what it could be. There is plenty of evidence that casts doubts as to whether the Great Pyramid was actually a burial site built by Cheops, which I mention in my book. For instance, in studying the pyramids in the late eighteen hundreds, Adam Smyth believed that the great pyramid was, in fact, already in place when the Egyptians arrived, and that they built the two smaller ones afterwards.

"One of the latest theories, by Bauval and Shoch in their book, postulate it was built about twelve thousand, five hundred years ago. They based this on certain coordinates they discovered that line up during that particular time. But who really knows what it was used for?"

Studying the structure more closely, Diandra looked up. “Whoever built this used the same type of black granite as in Giza. Weird coincidence, huh?” She started emptying her pockets. “I am going to go inside the thing,” she said as she removed her smart phone from her pants pocket. “Here, catch,” she added as she tossed the cell to Sam and turned to climb in.

“What?” Sam startled and grabbed for the phone as Diandra scrambled inside, favoring her lame ankle. Fumbling a few times, Sam dropped the phone to the ground, where it started to play Diandra’s eighteen-note program that had opened the tomb.

The room around the sarcophagus started to rumble, followed by a loud grating noise. The stone beneath Diandra’s feet in the structure began to move. Quickly climbing out, she observed the floor dropping down and splitting horizontally. With a final loud scrape, the noise stopped. They all moved as one to peer over the edge, and saw that the bottom of the sarcophagus had descended, forming a stairway extending down into the shadows.

“This tomb is full of surprises,” Dutch declared, intrigued, pulling out his flashlight. “Did you know-”

“I had no idea,” Diandra replied, dumbfounded. “The tune opened it up. Thank you, butterfingers!” she said, turning to Sam and laughing with delight. He grinned back.

“Skip, you getting-” Dutch began to ask as he shined the light down and revealed a tiled floor.

“My god, man, I wouldn’t miss this for the world,” he replied. “I must say, you seem to be having a jolly good time there.”

“Wish you were here?” Dutch asked.

“I’m a bit torn on that one,” Skip answered. “But I’ll leave it to you professionals. Now, I am getting more static. Place a signal repeater on the top of the sarcophagus and let’s see what happens. That is, of course, if you are going down that stairway.”

“What do you think?” Dutch asked the others. “Go or no go?”

“Are you kidding?” Diandra asked.

“I’m in,” Sam volunteered.

"In for a dime, in for a dollar, or penny and pound for you, Skip," Dutch laughed. "Guess we're going in."

* * * * * * * *

Two Humvees escorted by a military jeep raced down Highway Two in northern Iraq. After passing Zak Bu they turned off the paved road and cut east across the desert, driving straight into the wind and trailing dust from a waning sandstorm. Unable to see clearly, the drivers used the vehicles' GPS to get their bearings.

General Asoul was speaking on his cell phone while Lilne looked out the window dispassionately. Shadow Man peered out the other window.

He slapped his phone shut. "My men are a few minutes from the area we believe these people to be within. I have told them to survey the area and once they are located, to await my orders."

"That is good," Lilne replied with a nod. "How much longer before we arrive?"

"The weather is not cooperating. I would say at least another hour."

* * * * * * *

Dutch stepped over the wall of the sarcophagus and descended the stairway, shotgun at the ready. Diandra turned to Sam who gave an okay sign, before following closely behind. Pulling out his flashlight, the light's beam revealed a mosaic floor at the bottom of the stairs. Reaching it, he aimed the flashlight to the right and then left. They were in a large hallway, thirty feet in either direction. The walls rose about ten feet and then curved to form an arched ceiling. On both ends were alcoves that held golden statues.

The three of them looked around in wonder as a soft, lavender light gradually illuminated the hallway. Two-inch crystals were recessed into the top of the walls about every three feet, their light growing in intensity until everything was clearly visible.

Diandra rubbed her hand against the polished marble walls. They were cold to the touch. Looking down the chamber, she could see that there were reliefs cut into the walls of scenes with glyphs gilded in gold.

"Which way?" Dutch asked Diandra, shattering the silence.

"Let's try right," she said, pointing.

Nodding, Dutch turned off the flashlight, pocketed it and then shouldered his shotgun. In the silence each of their steps seemed to echo back and forth between the ends of the chamber. Diandra reached the first glyphs carved into the wall and studied them.

Two people were depicted, dressed in some sort of heavy suits and helmets. They stood on either side of an object that was curved, came to a point and had three triangular projections attached beneath it. Above it was a simplified picture of the sun and another planet or star with a trail of flames following it. Framing the scene were various scripts written in elongated and inverted V's, intermixed with dots and dashes of various lengths.

"What the heck?" Diandra commented in surprise. "What do you think, Sam?" she asked. "I'm not sure what it is. Or, rather, it can't be what I think it is."

Studying it, Sam shook his head. "The picture could be a stylized version of some ceremonial garb of some sort. I've seen similar scenes in Sumerian seals. But this object in the middle is most interesting. I don't see how it could be anything else other than a stylized rocket ship.

"As to the script…" he continued, examining it closely, recalling and comparing it to every known script he could think of. "I've no idea."

Turning to Diandra.

"It's unlike anything I've ever seen. Maybe it's Klingon?"

"Funny," she replied as she reached in her pocket and pulled out a digital camera. Aiming it at the wall, she took a picture, the flash bouncing off the gold and almost blinding them.

"Sorry," she said as she lowered the camera. "That should get the world abuzz."

"This whole thing will get the world abuzz," Sam observed.

"Seems like a lot of gold down here," Dutch said. "Guess they figured they'd hide it here for safekeeping."

"In plain sight, I'd say," Sam said.

"Look at this," Dutch said as he motioned with his finger to Diandra to look at the mosaic on the floor. About five feet in length and four feet in width, it was a picture of a magnificent city set against lavish green hills. Graceful white houses and buildings dotted the sides of the mountain, sloping to a harbor with large modern-looking boats with no sails. The mosaic's sky was tiled in numerous subtle shades of azure, turquoise and blue, dotted with puffy white clouds.

"What is that in the sky?" Dutch asked, pointing.

In the upper left hand corner, above the clouds, they could see a flying disc. Large in perspective, it had an enclosure above it with portholes.

"Well, it looks like a flying saucer to me," Sam said.

"Me too," Dutch agreed.

"Maybe it's a representation of something like a Vimana from the Vedas," Sam suggested. "Or a fire boat from the Chinese era."

"That doesn't make any sense." Diandra stated. "I'm just guessing, but this place seems much older than either of those eras. And where is this city? It doesn't look like anything familiar to me."

While Sam and Diandra continued discussing the mosaic, Dutch turned his attention to the end of the chamber. Arriving at the front of the alcove, he stared at the golden statue, which was floating three inches above its pedestal. It reminded him of an Egyptian god, except this one had an extremely elongated head projecting up and out from the rear. About four feet in height, it was in real human proportions, not stylized in any way. The arms extended out, the left hand holding a scepter and the right supporting a globe. Dutch studied it more closely, trying to make out the symbol at the scepter's end.

Reaching out, he felt the smoothness of the gold. Trying to move it with his hand, it didn't budge. Sam and Diandra joined him.

"This is so strange... Why do you think it is floating?" Dutch asked.

Diandra put her hand between the base and the statue and moved it around. "Maybe they used magnetics... you know, like two positive or two negative plates."

"I don't see anything like that," Sam observed. "And there are no markings I can see as to who it might be." He scoured over the statue for a few moments and focused on the extended arm. "The symbol on the scepter may mean something, I don't know. But what do you think of that totally weird head?"

"Craniosynostosis," Diandra stated. "It's very unusual, although we've found dozens of examples of this around the world. In my book I mention how Tutankhamen and other members of the Egyptian royal family may have had the same genetic defect. However, this statue seems to celebrate it... and it *is* beautiful."

"And gold," Dutch said with obvious satisfaction, setting down his shotgun. He reached with both hands and tried to pick it up. Diandra stopped him with her hand.

"What are you doing?" she asked.

"Seeing how much it weighs," he answered. "We're going to have to move it at some point." Looking at it he pursed his lips. "But it doesn't seem to want to budge at all."

Shaking her head she stepped back, aimed the camera and captured another picture.

"We'll deal with that *later*," she said. "Skip, can you see any of this?"

No answer.

"Skip?"

"I'll go see what the problem is," Dutch volunteered, grabbing his shotgun and walking away.

Diandra watched him go down the hallway and then brought her attention back to Sam.

"I feel… I feel overwhelmed. This is all so amazing," Diandra confided, leaning against the cool marble wall, and closing her eyes for a moment. "I have no idea what this place is."

"Neither do I. But I can tell you this, Diandra, there is nothing like it *anywhere* else on Earth that I know about." He placed one hand on the wall by her head and leaned closer. "You've got to be beaming inside."

"I am," she acknowledged, turning away and moving toward an arched opening to the right of the statue. She pulled out her flashlight and peered in. "I get the feeling it is very important that we found this place, maybe even fated, or… I don't know… destiny." The flashlight showed a smaller hallway descending about twenty feet to a wall. She thought she could see another opening to the left at the end.

"What do you think?" she asked Sam, nodding her head down the hallway.

"About destiny?"

"No, Sam… about this hallway here," she replied, pointing with the light.

"I say we go take a look," he answered enthusiastically.

They descended the hallway, the smooth walls reminding Diandra of a jet's passenger loading ramp. Reaching the end, her suspicions were confirmed, there was another opening to the left. Shining her light within it, she fell back a step with surprise. "Whoa!"

A large room, about forty feet long by twenty feet wide with a curved ceiling stood before her. Crystals started to activate and illuminate the room. Covering the walls of this chamber were crystal tablets, laid out neatly on ledges four high. They were about eight inches tall by four inches wide. Dutch joined Sam and Diandra at the entrance.

"I put another relay at the bottom of the stairs," he said. "Should take care of the problem." He stopped to look around. "Man, what is this all about?"

"Hello all. I missed you," Skip said on their PVD's. "What am I looking at?"

"I don't know," Diandra replied, scanning the room slowly so Skip could get a clear picture of it.

"Looks like a library of some sort," Skip offered.

"Agreed," Sam said. "But of what?"

"That is the sixty-four thousand dollar question, isn't it," Diandra replied.

She walked into the room and picked up one of the crystal tablets, studying it.

"No markings visible," she observed softly, holding it to the light and turning it in all directions. "It's perfectly clear."

"Maybe they are like computer chips," Sam suggested.

"Do you realize what you are suggesting?" Diandra said, putting the tablet back on the shelf and picking up another to examine. "That would be a technology more advanced than even we have today."

"There are some sort of markings below these things on the shelves," Dutch said, studying them. "Maybe they tell what they're for?"

Diandra studied the markings for a moment. There were the same extended and inverted V's with dots and dashes below each one as they had observed in the main chamber.

"These won't offer much help until we figure out how to read them. Skip, can you get a picture of this and see what you can find out?" Diandra asked.

"Absolutely," he replied. "Hold still for a moment. Got it. Also, for your information and that of the world, I am recording everything from this point forward. Should make for great cinema."

"Fiction or non?" Diandra mused rhetorically as she walked along the wall, mesmerized by the hundreds of crystal tablets. Suddenly, she received a shock from the one she was holding, followed by a flash of a vision: people screaming, running away, babies crying for their mothers, a panic on a massive scale.

She let go and the tablet crashed onto the floor, shattering into small fragments. The echo from the crash reverberated throughout the chamber, causing Dutch to grab his shotgun and look around.

"S-sorry guys, I don't know what happened," Diandra stuttered, then cleared her throat.

"Did you hear a sort of humming before you dropped it?" Sam asked.

"No… I… I had a…" She shook herself out of it.

"A what?" Dutch asked.

"Nothing," she said, looking down at the crystal fragments and wiping the sweat from her brow. "Another one of those feelings, visions, whatever. Let's get some pictures and see what other surprises this place holds."

"Well, just for the record, I distinctly heard a humming noise," Sam noted.

After shooting pictures of the room they walked back up the hallway to the main chamber. There was another opening similar in size on the left side of the statue. Diandra led the group in and down the hallway and into a room at the end that opened to the right. It had similar dimensions as the first but the contents were slightly different. As the crystal lights brightened, they could see row after row of bronze colored metallic tablets lining the walls, the same in size and shape as the crystal tablets.

"Well, well, this is getting interesting," Dutch said. "Is this place starting to remind you of anything?"

Diandra walked along the outer wall and reached out to touch one of the metallic tablets.

"Tanner's ARK project, for instance?" she said, turning around to Dutch.

"That's exactly what I was thinking," he answered.

Picking one of them up, Diandra studied it. There were etchings on both sides.

"This has got to be some sort of repository, a hall of records," she remarked, looking at both sides of the tablet and setting it back in place.

"Like Edgar Cayce's hall of records?" Sam asked.

"Like his *alleged* hall of records," she corrected him.

"He said it was located under the Sphinx," Sam relayed to Dutch in response to his quizzical look. "It may have been discovered there already, but the Egyptian director of antiquities, Zari Hawass, blocked anyone from going any further. I saw some pictures of the supposed entrance to it on the Internet."

Turning his attention to Diandra, Sam continued, "Last I heard, Mister Hawass was perp-walked in handcuffs and then to jail with the regime change in Egypt. But nothing more on the hall of records."

"Cayce also said there were two more located in different parts of the world," Diandra added as she surveyed the room. She thought for a moment. "This may be why they… whoever *they* were," looking to Sam, "chose this place to store the Library's scrolls. They knew it would be discovered someday because of the tablet." She bit her lip as she thought.

"But what are we looking at?" she asked aloud. "The records of an ancient civilization?"

"Lemuria? Atlantis? Shangri La?" Sam suggested.

"*If* they existed, and that's a big if," she responded.

"There have always been indications that most of our modern civilizations may have emerged from some ancient single source. An alpha civilization. Maybe this is the source?" Sam added.

Placing the metal tablet back on the rack, Diandra shook her head. "Perhaps. But so far, there is no hint of who or what left this, other than those mosaics in the outer chamber."

"What are you saying?" Dutch questioned. "We've stumbled onto a mystery surrounded by an enigma?"

"Apropos, Dutch," Diandra agreed, half laughing. "Let's see if there is anything else that may help us explain this place."

"These glyphs, or symbols, do not relate to anything I can find," Skip informed them. "I ran them through everything known, and it comes up empty. I'll upload them to Tanner's mainframe and let the UPP program have a shot at it."

"Thanks Skip," Diandra said as they made their way back up the hallway and into the main chamber. Continuing down past the stairs to the other end, they passed four more recessed carvings in the wall covered with gold. Diandra curiously looked at them, but decided to continue on and study them in detail later.

In the middle of the other end was another golden statue, floating above its pedestal, this time of a woman with a flowing dress. She also had an elongated skull. In her hands was an ankh symbol held high above her head. "The Tree of Life," Diandra whispered to herself, before snapping a picture. She turned to the right, where another arched doorway awaited her.

"To the next adventure!" she playfully shouted to the others, the echoes from her voice reverberating back and forth. Down the hallway she went, reaching the end and a doorway to the left leading into a chamber. As it started lighting up it revealed thousands of clay tablets, all neatly lining the walls and stacked eight high. These were smaller in size; four inches by six inches. Written symbols were clearly visible.

Sam suggested they might be pre-Sumerian in nature, although that was just a guess. Diandra held up two of the tablets for Skip to get a clear picture and set them back down. Taking a last look around the room, she motioned for Dutch and Sam to follow as she walked up the hallway and into the main chamber.

"Did you notice the mosaic at this end?" Diandra asked the others.

Looking down, they could see what looked to be a stylized solar system, with various planets in orbit, the Sun, with the moon circling about the Earth, were clearly visible. Other planets had lines defining their orbits. Diandra made a quick calculation and frowned.

"Too many planets," she noted, perplexed.

"What?" Sam queried.

"Count them. There is one too many," she repeated.

Sam made a quick mental assessment and confirmed her observation.

"I get twelve," he said, "counting the moon."

"So do I," Diandra said. "Plus, Venus seems to be out of place."

"Maybe they were in a hurry and made a mistake?" Dutch suggested.

"So you think that whoever made this place, these crystals, these tablets, this very room made a mistake?" Diandra asked. "I'm doubting that." Pulling out her camera she took a picture both in portrait and landscape mode.

"In my book, I interviewed Professor Standhead, who claimed there was another planet. He called it the twelfth planet, and that it circled our Sun every thirty-six hundred years," she continued, putting the camera back in her pocket. "He said the Sumerians called it Niburu; and that the people of this planet, the Anunnaki, visited Earth for a few hundred years every time its apogee was nearest our planet's, and then left."

"Aliens, Di?" Dutch said. "Isn't that a bit farfetched?"

"It is," she replied. "But then again, this whole place is farfetched."

Sam had walked down the final remaining hallway and reached the end.

"Holy shit!" he exclaimed.

Diandra and Dutch joined him as the crystal lights circling the perimeter of the room reached their maximum brightness. They were greeted by thousands of round golden discs, lined up in rows six high that wrapped around the entire room.

"Hel-lo there," Dutch whispered, smiling.

Diandra was speechless. Walking into the chamber on autopilot, she gazed around, followed by Sam and Dutch, who were also lost for words. She reached out and picked one of the golden discs off its granite shelf and examined it. It felt heavy, like solid gold. On closer inspection she could see there were grooves on both sides, much like a modern CD but with no hole in the middle.

Dutch also grabbed one and held it up to look at, getting it to reflect and bounce the light off the walls.

"Solid gold, I'd say," he observed, looking around. "And there are thousands of them."

Diandra eyed Dutch. "The real treasure is contained in the grooves on these, Dutch. They must contain-"

"I get it Di," he interrupted. "But after they are read-"

"After they are read," she continued, "they will be worth a hundred times beyond the price of the gold. There is no value you can place on these. They are the most unbelievable things I've ever seen."

She placed it back on the ledge and exhaled a deep breath. "And… I'm really not sure I believe what I'm seeing here," she laughed.

"Oh you can believe it, dearie," Skip kicked in. "I can see them from here."

"This has been one hell of a discovery," she said, turning toward Sam. "Let's get some readings. We'll use whatever equipment we have left from the camels. Also, we should map this place out and get a preliminary drawing of the layout. And bring down the laser tape measure."

Sam nodded and left the chamber. Diandra turned to Dutch who was still admiring the golden disc.

"This is a real game changer, Dutch. I'm not sure what our ancestors left us, but whatever it is will be startling, and could very well rewrite history as we know it. Coupled with the scrolls from the library up there," she motioned with her hand, "it will forever-"

"Guys," Sam yelled. "You'd better come here, quick!"

* * * * * * * *

Answering his cell phone, General Asoul listened and then smiled, asking a question in Arabic and then hitting end call.

"It seems my men on patrol have found the people you are looking for. We are about," looking at his watch, "thirty minutes away."

"They are to wait until we arrive without doing anything?" Lilne asked.

"I confirmed that with the Commandant," Asoul replied.

Chapter Fourteen

Al-Jazira Desert, Northern Iraq

Diandra rushed out of the room while Dutch pocketed the golden disc he was observing and followed closely behind. They met up with Sam standing next to the stairs.

"What is it?" Diandra asked.

"Look over there behind these stairs," he said, pointing. "There is another hallway, hidden in the shadows."

Walking around the stairs, Dutch noted how cleverly they operated, using a cantilever that moved up and down with a metal cable that went through the tile floor and was attached to some sort of weight below.

Diandra and Sam walked behind the stairs and noticed a glyph of a winged planet carved into the granite above the arched doorway. Sam acknowledged seeing it as they entered the doorway and peered in. Pulling out her flashlight, Diandra quickly assessed that it descended about ten feet further than the previous hallways, ending with another doorway, this time to the left. Dutch joined them and turned his flashlight on too.

Making their way to the end of the tunnel, they turned left and entered the cavern. Their flashlight beams revealed hundreds of golden statues scattered throughout the room; pyramids, animals, figurines, temples, trees, and various other objects. Everywhere their lights flashed, more statues were observed, their golden brilliance reflecting the light with majestic intensity.

Dutch shook his head in astonishment. This was everything and more than he was hoping for. It exceeded even his wildest imagination. Walking around he shined his light on the golden treasures, focusing it on object after object: intricately carved elephants, lions, gods and goddesses similar to the statues in the alcoves above. Sam bent down and touched a golden dragon.

"Seems our ancestors had a real jones for gold," Dutch said.

Sam laughed, standing up.

"A treasure trove of knowledge and gold," he mused. "They thought of everything."

"The question still remains," Diandra whispered. "Who are they?"

Dutch's flashlight landed on a four foot golden pedestal about eighteen inches in diameter located in the corner of the room. As he raised the light it rested upon a human-sized crystal skull.

"Uh, Di? I think you should see this," he implored.

Turning toward his voice, she followed the flashlight's beam to the crystal skull. Cocking her head, she stared.

Speechless.

This was so unexpected. She had seen the Hodgkin's crystal skull displayed at an exhibition fifteen years earlier in Ontario, Canada. Her book, *Unexplained Archeology* included photographs of an additional four of them. But this was more beautiful than any she had seen. Flawlessly clear, the slightly larger than life-size skull had an elongated cranium like the statues in the main hallway, with an attached jawbone. It appeared to be carved out of one solid piece of crystal. It stood like a lone sentinel watching over the golden treasures in the room. She reached out and held her hand an inch away from the skull, as if to caress it.

"I'm getting a lot of interference from your end," Skip said. "An outside source of power of some kind."

Gently, she touched the skull.

A low-frequency hum began vibrating within the room. Dutch jerked the shotgun from his shoulder and whipped it toward the door. Pulsating, the sound grew in intensity. Dutch grabbed the back of Diandra's shirt with one hand and yanked her away from the skull, with Sam backing away from it in lockstep. A light source from beneath and inside the pedestal emanated upwards, causing the skull to glow in a pale purple hue. The eyes started glowing brighter than the skull.

"It's getting strange, guys!" Skip yelled. "Whatever that skull is doing is generating a tremendous amount of energy. I might lose you."

"I know, Skip," Diandra's voice trembled. "I can feel it."

Dutch doubted his own eyes. Even though for years Diandra had been telling him there was more to ancient history than was made public, he took it with a grain of salt, mostly humoring her and her theories. But this was real. He could see it, touch it. And it surpassed anything he had experienced before. Heart pounding, he realized he was afraid, a feeling he rarely experienced. Holding the shotgun tighter, he held his breath as the light in the skull increased.

Sam felt every hair on his body stand on end, electrified; every cell in his body was vibrating with excitement.

But it was Diandra who was affected the most. Energy coursed through her body as the light of the skull pulsed with growing intensity. Frozen in astonishment, she couldn't move if she wanted to. And she didn't want to. Whatever was going to happen, she wanted to experience it to the fullest.

The skull reached a blindingly illuminated state, and the vibration suddenly stopped.

Silence.

Greetings my children…

* * * * * * *

Tanner Headquarters,
Berlin, Germany

"Jim," Jeff said urgently as he burst into Tanner's office.

"Yes, Jeff?" he answered looking up from his desk, alarmed at Jeff's tone.

"We've just intercepted some intelligence that the Seekers' mission in Iraq has been compromised. It appears that there are military personnel on their way to their location as we speak."

"This is confirmed?" Tanner frowned.

Jeff nodded. "Intercepted satellite cell calls."

"Get this information immediately to Skip," Tanner urged. "Make sure he understands the gravity of the situation."

Tanner pushed back his chair as Jeff rushed out of the room. Rubbing his face, he thought for a minute. Pushing a key on his computer, a female voice on the other end responded.

"Get Cantwell up here immediately, and put me through to our office in Turkey."

* * * * * * *

Chapter Fifteen

Al-Jazira Desert, Northern Iraq

Greetings, my children,

If you have found this skull, you are indeed worthy of the knowledge and power we have amassed for you.

It also means there may still be time.

We have gathered all of the knowledge of our civilizations, our world, and left it for our future generations. Steps have been taken to protect and save it in seven repositories like this around the planet, above and below the mantle crust, for we are unsure of what will remain after the event.

It has been left for you in many forms to help you understand. For understand you must, if you are to have any chance of surviving.

"How is it able to know I speak Arabic?" Sam whispered to Diandra, motioning with his hand toward his ear. Shocked, Diandra mouthed she was hearing it in English. Dutch heard it in German.

Within these archives we provide the keys to avoiding the same fate as has befallen our civilization. It is too late for us. The race against time has been lost.

In the age of the water bearer, when our world has revolved around its star an additional two hundred times, the start of this planet-wide catastrophe will begin. You need to be prepared. It has already occurred once. If you are here, my children, it means it did not succeed in destroying us all. There is still hope.

Suddenly a beam of light shot from the skull. The Seekers were stunned with images of people screaming, children crying, mass destruction of cities, earthquakes and tidal waves; all within a split second. Then, the beam stopped.

It is also important you understand your true origins, your true nature and your true potential. You are children of the divine ones; those whom from heaven descended. And in that sense, you are entitled to all of the fruits of that divine kinship. You have the ability to accomplish all that you can imagine, if you but only access—

"Blasphemous idolaters!" a loud male voice screamed from behind in Arabic. Dutch spun around and saw a soldier standing in the doorway with an AK-47 rifle in hand. He squeezed off a couple of rounds that hit the skull, knocking it off the pedestal. The light beneath the pedestal dimmed as Dutch pushed Diandra to the ground. Bullets from the soldier's rifle flew everywhere, hitting the rock walls and golden statues.

Dutch crawled crab-like toward the center of the room to get a clean shot at the soldier. Rolling on his side, he pumped a shell into the chamber and fired the shotgun in one fluid motion. The force of the deadly load lifted the guard off the floor and slammed him into the back wall of the hallway, where he gurgled as the life force left his body.

Dutch fished out his flashlight and turned it on, motioning for Diandra and Sam.

"Follow closely behind me!" he whispered urgently through clenched teeth.

"Wait," Sam said, motioning with an open hand. He crawled over to the wall and grabbed the crystal skull off the ground. Swinging his backpack around, he eased it in and slung it over his shoulder. Crawling back he gave an okay sign.

Dutch jumped up and held the flashlight far away toward his left side and ran past the dead soldier and up to the entrance behind the stairs, stopping to peer out.

Sam followed Dutch, slipping in the crimson pool of blood forming around the soldier.

"Oh my god!" Sam cried out. "Is he dead?"

"This ain't the A-team," Dutch replied, slapping his shotgun. "Real bullets, kid. Stick close to me."

He didn't need to ask twice.

Peeking around the bottom of the stairs, Dutch blasted a round upward toward the sarcophagus and pumped the shotgun for the next shell. Nothing. He motioned for them to follow him up when gunshots echoed throughout the chamber. A guard came down the stairs firing away. Dutch pushed Sam and Diandra to his sides as he pumped and fired three times. The guard, a hole the size of a football in his chest, fell to the bottom of the stairs in front of Diandra, dead before he stopped rolling.

Dutch motioned to Diandra and Sam. "Move!" he shouted. He noticed Sam clutching his shoulder. Rushing over, he checked the wound. It was a small hole but seeping blood steadily

"Shit," he said while whipping out his knife and cutting a strip of fabric from Sam's sleeve.

"Am I going to die?" Sam asked, scared to death.

"Someday, kid," he answered. "But not from this." He cinched it to try and cut off the bleeding "Can you move?" he asked.

"It really hurts," Sam replied. "I'm sorry."

"Oh Sam, it's not your fault," Diandra said as she bent down and touched his other arm.

"I'll be okay," he said, braving it up. "Let me just sit here for a second. I'm a little dizzy…"

"Is he going to be-" Diandra mouthed to Dutch.

Dutch shrugged his shoulders worriedly, then said aloud, "We need to get out of here and quick."

Looking up the stairs for a moment, he turned back and rolled the soldier over with his foot.

"I recognize this one. He is one of the kids in the desert who stopped us. That means there are at least a couple of more up there," he said, hooking his thumb upward. Picking up the AK 47 rifle, he looked it over. "This may come in handy. Can you walk Sam?"

"Sure." He sounded woozy. Diandra helped him up.

"Ouch," he screamed, clenching his teeth.

"Let's get up those stairs," Dutch said.

Reaching the top he scanned over the rim of the sarcophagus with his shotgun in the lead and pulled the trigger with a deafening blast. Looking up and out again he surveyed the area. No one could be seen.

"Come on," he whispered loudly, looking left and right for any sign of the other men as he jumped out.

Suddenly, a grinding noise and rumbling started.

"What the hell is that?" Dutch wondered aloud, looking around.

Sam and Diandra reached the top step, poking their heads up over the rim.

Then Dutch saw it.

A wall was sliding closed over the room's entrance that separated them from the main chamber.

"We need to hurry up here, guys!" Dutch yelled, turning to help Sam get out of the sarcophagus. The grating grew louder as the rock wall inched its way closer to sealing off their escape.

"Come on." Dutch urged as he pulled Sam over the rim, causing him to cry out in agony as he hit the ground. Dutch checked their exit and realized they would never make it. Picking up his shotgun, he raced over and jammed it lengthwise between the moving rock and the wall. The wall kept moving, almost splintering the handle, and then stopped, slightly bending the barrel.

Running back, he picked up Sam and motioned for Diandra to follow while he half carried and then eased Sam over the shotgun to the other side. Diandra followed, carefully stepping over it. Dutch returned to pick up the AK-47 and joined them on the other side.

"I really liked that shotgun," he said ruefully, observing the deformed weapon jammed between them and certain death. "Damn."

"Why do you think that wall started closing?" Sam asked, referring to the wall moving.

"Maybe the noise from the shotgun affected it," Diandra offered.

"It doesn't matter at this point," Dutch said over his shoulder. "Follow me closely."

Turning his attention to the chamber, he reached the corner of the boxes and squatted down. No one could be seen. He snaked his way halfway through the boxes and still no one. Diandra watched in silence until Dutch waved them forward. Limping herself, Diandra wrapped her arm around Sam's waist to help him walk.

"The blind leading the blind," he said in a wry whisper. "Or rather the lame leading the… Ow," he groaned. She gave him a squeeze.

Making their way out of the tomb's main chamber and up toward the entrance of the tunnel, Dutch could see the back of a soldier standing at the top, smoking. He gestured with his hand as a stop sign and touched his lips for Sam and Diandra to be quiet and stay put. Moving sideways, his back to the tunnel's wall, he inched his way toward the entrance. He figured that if the guard was having a smoke, he must not have heard the gunfire coming from inside the tomb and would not be expecting them to come out.

Finally reaching a few feet behind the soldier, he raised the AK-47 and walked the rest of the way to his back and whispered to him in Arabic to raise his hands. Cigarette falling from his lips, the soldier slowly complied as Dutch came all the way out of the tunnel.

Instantly Dutch heard a gun's hammer pull back and lock next to him. Turning, he saw the captain holding a pistol to his head.

"It is you who will drop your weapon," the captain said in Arabic.

* * * * * * * *

Chapter Sixteen

Al-Jazira Desert, Northern Iraq

Dutch cursed himself for his stupid blunder. This was the kind of mistake he was trained *not* to make, but make it he did. A hundred scenarios raced through his mind. He could shoot the soldier, and maybe take the captain out too. But if he were wrong, Diandra and Sam would be at risk. Then a thought hit him. *Why wasn't he dead already?* It was a question he was willing to wait and find out the answer to. Meanwhile, it would also give him a chance to make a plan.

He dropped the AK-47 and raised his hands, turning toward the captain. He hadn't realized how short he was, being on the camel the last time he saw him. But looking down on him here, now, he guessed he was maybe a few inches over five feet.

"It seems your deceptions are many," the captain stated. "I will take great pleasure in learning how deep these deceptions run. It is unfortunate that I have been ordered to wait until the higher authorities arrive."

The other soldier ordered Sam and Diandra out of the tunnel and had them under guard.

The captain's eyes narrowed as he recognized Sam.

"Well, if it isn't the leader of the holy people we met the other day," he said, shoving Sam to the ground. Sam screamed in agony as he grabbed his shoulder and rolled to his side, moaning.

Casting his gaze upon Diandra, with the dark skinned makeup still around her eyes, he shook his head and turned back to Dutch.

"Where are my men?"

"Looking for their virgins, I believe," Dutch answered in Arabic.

The captain turned beet red at his response.

He was short tempered, Dutch observed. *A hopeful sign.*

"I suppose you think that is funny?" he responded, spitting out the words.

"I do, indeed," Dutch answered, smirking. "And by the way, it will take more than your sorry ass to interrogate me," he taunted. Knowing he had one shot before it would be too late, he had to take it.

"Is that so?" the captain's voice rose while looking ready to explode.

"Without that gun in your hand," Dutch added, "you're just another dumb-assed towel head."

With a shriek, the captain jumped forward to pistol-whip Dutch. Having anticipated the move, Dutch had turned slightly so it would miss his face, but the force of the blow caused him to hit the ground, hard.

"Dutch!" Diandra yelled, struggling against her captor's grasp.

"Shut her up," the captain shouted to the other soldier, while he kicked Dutch in both sides with his boot. Dutch curled up to protect himself from the brunt of the blows.

"So I am a fucking towel head, you infidel!"

His kicks grew fiercer as Dutch used his bent arms as best he could to block the kicks.

"Stop it, you animal," Diandra pleaded.

The captain paused for a moment, snarling toward Diandra. But that moment was enough for Dutch to reach into his pants leg and pull out the Smith and Wesson .38 that was hidden there. Just as he was taking deadly aim he heard a loud thud. The captain's eyes rolled into the back of his head and he fell face first onto the gravelly soil. Behind him stood the last remaining soldier, his AK-47 in hand and trained directly at Dutch. They met eye to eye.

Standoff.

Dutch stared at the soldier, wondering what his next move would be. Then a memory emerged, a feeling that they had met before; the same feeling he had in the desert at their last encounter. He had seen this man before, somewhere. But where? And then it hit him. Mali's hotel in Turkey. In McIntyre's room. The man with a long scar running across his face.

Scarred-face smiled and nodded, sensing Dutch's recognition of him.

"There is nothing here worth dying for," he stated in Arabic.

Dutch hesitated, then rose from the ground and dusted himself off.

"Go now, take your friends and leave," scarred-face continued.

Dutch took in Diandra's wide-eyed look as he replaced the gun back in his ankle holster and helped Sam, grimacing, to his feet. Touching his headset, he called for Skip. No answer. He then noticed the repeater they'd left at the entrance was smashed.

"Try yours," he said to Diandra, pointing to his head.

Still obviously shaken, she called out. "Skip, are you there?"

"Thank god, you're okay," Skip answered.

She nodded to Dutch, indicating contact with Skip. Dutch grabbed her headpiece and switched it out for his.

"Skip, we've got to make for the Turkish border, fast. What's the quickest way there?"

"Hang on," Skip answered.

"You okay kid?" Dutch asked Sam while waiting.

"I'm good," Sam replied in a weak voice, although Dutch could see he'd lost a lot of blood.

"Dutch," Skip broke in, "I have a heading. Do you still have the Garman?"

"Negative," Dutch replied. "We'll be going dead reckoning."

"Okay then. You'll be leaving the canyon you are in through the opposite side to the east. Maybe three kilometers away. After that you'll take a heading approximately north, northwest for about… perhaps four hours, I am guesstimating."

"Sam has been shot and Diandra has a sprained ankle. It's gonna be a slow go for us," Dutch informed him. "Any chance for a welcoming committee?"

"Is Sam okay?" Skip asked.

"It's a flesh wound," Dutch said aloud as he faced Sam. Then he turned and added in a lower tone, "He's hanging in there, but he's losing a lot of blood."

"I'll see what I can arrange." Skip said. "I just got a call from Jeff stating there are hostile government troops heading your way."

"We've already met them," Dutch stated. "Luckily, one of them was on our side." He glanced at scarred-face and nodded his gratitude.

"I see," Skip said. "Once you leave the canyon, I am going to lose you."

"I understand. In the meantime, you better get out of there, post haste."

"You're telling me? All hell has broken loose here. Sounds like world war three outside the hotel. Troops and rebels everywhere. Bloody hell. The Syrian army is flying fighter jets over the city, for Christ's sake."

"You be safe. Don't take any risks. Just leave."

"Dutch."

"Yeah, Skip."

Silence.

"Skip?" Dutch questioned.

"You be safe," Skip finally said with a deep, audible breath.

"I'll be seeing you when I am looking at you," Dutch assured him.

Turning his attention to scarred-face he said, "I owe you one."

"My debt is paid," he replied. "The next time we meet, we will be on opposite sides again."

"Until then," Dutch replied, giving a short salute. "In the meantime, I'll be needing your weapon."

Scarred-face threw it to Dutch who caught it, released the clip and checked for ammo.

"Ready to go?" he asked, eyeing Diandra and Sam while reinserting the clip.

"Ready," she replied, reaching for Sam with one arm and her walking stick with the other.

Dutch scanned the area, sensing something.

"We'd better be going." Turning to scarred-face man, Dutch started to ask him a question.

"I will be fine," he volunteered, holding up his hand. "You over-powered me after taking out my commanding officer. He was a jerk, anyway."

Dutch nodded and motioned for Diandra and Sam to follow him. They half ran as best they could toward the end of the canyon, reaching it in about twenty minutes. A huge expanse of desert greeted them. Dutch took his bearings, wiped the sweat off of his forehead and the three of them headed for the Turkish border.

* * * * * * *

Chapter Seventeen

Al-Jazira Desert, Northern Iraq

Two Humvees and a camouflage Jeep with four armed men arrived and stopped about thirty feet from the tomb's entrance. Lilne and Shadow Man, along with the major general, exited one of the Humvees and rushed to the tomb. Surveying the scene, they noted that scarred-face was trying to bring the captain back into consciousness.

"What happened here?" Lilne demanded to know.

Scarred-face explained in Arabic how after they arrived at the tomb two of them had gone in and tried to capture the people inside. When the people came out of the tomb, they were captured. The woman pulled out a gun, grabbed his weapon and hit the captain on the back of his head. Scarred-face related how he had barely escaped with his life.

"Tell me about these prisoners?" Lilne asked.

"They escaped about thirty minutes ago," scarred-face replied. "I heard them mention something about going back to Syria. I do not think they knew I understood their English."

"Get a helicopter out here and find them," Lilne turned and demanded of the major general.

"Very dangerous, Monsignor," the major general said. "There are Kurdish elite out here with surface to air missiles."

"How hard can it be to find them?" Lilne asked, taunting the man while eyeing the camels the Seekers had abandoned, still carrying their supplies. "They have no food, no water and are in the middle of the desert."

"Do not underestimate Vorhees," Shadow Man interjected. "He is very dangerous and resourceful."

"It is I and my patience that should not be underestimated," Lilne snapped back. "These incompetents should have waited until we arrived. Those were my orders." Looking around at the additional jeep he asked, "Where are the men from this other jeep?"

"Inside," scarred-face answered. "They went to see if either of the wounded soldiers could be saved."

"Unacceptable!" Lilne shouted at the major general. "I gave specific instructions for *no one* to enter this tomb!"

"Ambitious men," the major general stated with a shrug.

"Indeed," Lilne said coldly. "Their ambition will cost them dearly."

Lilne then turned his attention to the entrance of the tomb. Walking up he examined it, touching the outer edge with his fingers.

"Interesting," he murmured. Shadow Man, the major general and two soldiers followed him in.

Walking down the forty-foot corridor to the archway, Lilne observed the symbol of the winged globe over the door, stopping abruptly.

"This cannot be," he whispered to himself.

Two soldiers saluted as he, Shadow Man and the major general made their way past them standing guard at the cavern's entrance. His head tilted as he entered the main chamber and observed the crystal lights. Turning his attention to the hundreds of boxes stacked in aisles, he started to make his way toward the boxes Diandra had jimmied open.

"Mother of God," the major general exclaimed as he entered the main chamber.

Lilne stopped and watched silently as the man walked past him to one of the glowing crystal lights and slowly reached out his hand to touch it.

Sparks flew from his hand and spread to his body. He convulsed violently as his life energy quickly drained. Within seconds, his shriveled lifeless body slumped to the ground, while the other soldiers watched in horror as foul smelling smoke rose from his carcass.

Lilne observed the event as one would the death of a fly, completely detached. “Highly interesting,” he commented, stepping around the body. He reached the boxes that were opened, pulled out a scroll, unrolled it and read. Tossing it down, he pulled out another. After reading it, he threw it to the floor and scanned the rest of the room.

“What is this place”” Shadow Man quietly asked.

“A place not supposed to exist,” Lilne replied.

Two soldiers carried the body of one of the soldiers killed below past Lilne.

“Is he dead?” Lilne demanded.

One of them nodded yes.

“Then set him down and wait for my orders,” Lilne snapped irritably. “Where are the others?”

They pointed toward the end of the rows of boxes. Lilne gestured for Shadow Man to go and take a look. Upon reaching the end of the boxes, Shadow Man walked to where the shotgun was holding open the stone wall, and called out.

“Sir!”

Lilne walked past the two soldiers, reached Shadow Man and peered in.

“Who is in that casket?” Shadow Man asked.

“It is irrelevant,” Lilne answered. “Go and get the satchel and bring it back immediately.”

He bowed slightly and left while Lilne carefully stepped over the shotgun, walked to the casket and bent down to read the inscription.

“Hello, Demetrius,” he finally said, a slight smile covering his face. “Imagine my surprise finding you here when I thought you had already been destroyed. I will not make that same mistake again.”

A noise caused him to turn his attention to the black granite sarcophagus. Standing up, he peered in to see two more soldiers trying to bring up the lifeless body of another comrade. Lilne’s face flushed red.

"Leave him down there!" he shouted. "And stay there until I call for you."

Quickly stepping over the shotgun and out toward the tomb's entrance, Lilne met a colonel who had accompanied them to the site.

"Get all of the men who have seen anything here back *in* the tomb to guard its contents," he barked. "Now!"

"Achmed stays with me," the colonel replied, referring to scarred-face.

"And why is that?" Lilne asked.

"He is my nephew."

Shadow Man returned with a large satchel, while the colonel ushered in the remaining soldiers, including the captain who was finally awake but barely able to walk. When they had been herded into the tomb's main cavern, Shadow Man set the timer, got a confirming nod from Lilne, and threw it deep into the tunnel entrance.

"One minute," Shadow Man informed them, tapping his watch.

Lilne, Shadow Man, the colonel and scarred-face man raced back to one of the Humvees and jumped in. The driver floored it and left a dusty cloud of sand in their wake. A thunderous explosion erupted behind them, followed by a gigantic plume rising up from the tomb area and sweeping high into the sky. The ground shook, causing the Humvee to swerve as it left the canyon and raced across the desert.

"Why did you do that?" the colonel asked, looking back at the destruction.

"It is healthier not to ask such questions," Lilne replied. "I want those people who escaped found. Make that your priority."

* * * * * * * *

The smoke and debris rose hundreds of feet into the wind-blown sky. Kilometers away, Dutch, Sam and Diandra felt the ground shake from the explosion. Viewing the dusty plume in the distance, Diandra shook her head, aghast.

"Damn those sons of bitches. They just blew it up, didn't they," she screamed.

"That's what it looks like," Dutch replied, solemnly. "Di. I'm sorry-"

"Animals," she said to no one, tears welling up in her eyes. "How could they?"

Silence.

"We'd better keep going," Dutch said softly.

* * * * * * * *

Chapter Eighteen

Aleppo, Syria

After losing contact with Dutch, Skip had contacted Zoë. She arranged for him to be met at the airport by a private jet. He ran a custom program he had created that erased all of the RAM chips on the motherboards of his computers, and then removed the physical hard drives and put them in his briefcase. Taking a last sip of tea, he looked around the room and made sure nothing was left before exiting and catching a cab in front of the Ramsis hotel on Baron Street. The ride to the airport was interrupted by going around two makeshift roadblocks and intermittent gunfire in the background. It appeared the rebels were moving into the city. *Where was Farouq when you needed him?* Skip thought.

Arriving at the airport Skip entered the non-commercial aircraft terminal and proceeded to the customs area. Out of the terminal's window he could see a Tanner Industries Gulfstream G 550 taxiing to a stop and a jet-way begin its descent.

Fidgeting with his briefcase, he walked up to the customs counter and handed the smiling woman his passport. She entered a few keystrokes, and although trying to mask it, her friendly demeanor changed as she looked back at Skip.

"Something wrong?" he asked.

"I will be back in a moment," she said, taking Skip's passport into a back office.

Skip could see three men stepping down the jet stairway and walking toward the terminal.

"Would you come with us, please," a voice from behind startled Skip. Turning around, he observed two plain-clothes security men with his passport in hand.

"What is this about?" Skip asked, his hands visibly trembling.

"We need to clear a few things up. You are Mister Duffin, yes?" one of the men asked.

"Yes," Skip replied.

They smiled with obvious satisfaction, having gotten their man. An urgent cable had gone out asking for all airports to be on the lookout for Skip, based on Farouq's information that he had not yet left the country.

"It will only take a few minutes of your time," the shorter, balding security man lied.

"I, I urgently need to get going," Skip said as he grabbed his briefcase with both hands and hugged it against his tightening chest, his breaths growing more shallow by the second.

"You will come with us now," the taller, thin security man insisted, grabbing Skip just as the three men from the Tanner jet walked in the door. Skip could see one of them was Mike Cantwell, head of security for Tanner Industries. The other two looked CIA, sunglasses and earpieces included. They hung back at the entryway to the tarmac as Cantwell made his way up to Skip.

"Is there a problem, Doctor Duffin?" Cantwell asked.

"This is no problem of yours," the shorter security man told them. "He is in our custody. This is a government matter."

"Is that so?" Cantwell countered. "Since when do you treat *diplomats* with such disrespect?"

"He is no diplomat," the taller man continued. "He is a government spy and we are taking him in for questioning."

Cantwell calmly reached into his suit jacket's inner pocket and pulled out a red diplomatic passport from the Isle of Man. Opening it, he handed it to the shorter of the two.

"As you can clearly see, you are mistaken," Cantwell informed them.

The men examined it closely. Skip could see his picture and name on the passport and tried to hide his relief. The two men looked back at Cantwell.

"We must report this to our superiors and await orders on how to proceed," the shorter one stated as perspiration beaded his forehead.

"I have an idea," Cantwell countered, opening his suit jacket and pulling out a flat black .45 Uzi. The two CIA-looking men followed suit by opening their coats displaying the same weapon. "We're running late and can't wait for you to 'await' your goddamn orders. So why don't you get the hell out of the way and let Doctor Duffin come with us before we blow your sorry ass brains all over this terminal."

Physically closing in on the two men, he continued. "Is that a clear enough fucking order for you?"

Their eyes widened as they looked from each other to the two armed CIA clones. Rivulets of sweat ran down the shorter one's face. They were outnumbered and outgunned. The taller one holding the passport gave a resigned sigh and handed the red passport to Skip.

"Thank you for visiting our country," he said, voice trembling. "You may go now."

Skip grabbed it and nervously smiled as he raced through the doorway and toward the jet's stairway. The two armed rescuers backed their way out the terminal door, covering everywhere in the terminal area with their sunglass shaded eyes. Turning round they caught up with Skip at the bottom of the jet-way and walked him up.

Cantwell watched and waited until they were safely inside, then turned to the security men.

"Gentlemen," he said, bowing slightly and backing up. Once through the airport doors he turned and made his way to the jet's staircase, taking them two at a time.

"You okay, Skip?" he asked, entering the cabin.

"What a bunch of wankers," Skip said in a voice strained with false bravado. He set the briefcase down and collapsed into his seat, "Remind me to never, ever, visit this country again."

Cantwell smirked. "I'll be sure and do that."

Chapter Nineteen

Al-Jazira Desert, Northern Iraq

The weather had mostly cleared, but there was still a residue of dust and sand that Dutch, Diandra and Sam had been struggling with for the past four hours on their trek toward the Turkish border. Sam was growing noticeably weaker. Dutch kept stopping and checking the pressure bandage, compressing it to make sure he was losing as little blood as possible. These breaks also gave Diandra's painfully swollen ankle a rest.

By Dutch's estimation, they should have been within a few kilometers of the Turkish border, but he was unable to get their exact location because of Skip having disarmed the GPS function of their PDA's for security reasons. Aware that every passing moment increased their chances of successfully making it to the border without incident, Dutch started to relax. The formidable knot in his gut lessened its grip.

Then he heard it.

From the distance came the unmistakable low frequency hum of a helicopter. Raising his hand for Diandra and Sam to stop, he listened intently. It seemed to be coming in their direction from Iraq. Gesturing with his arm, they made their way up to a cliff face and leaned against it.

"Do you think they know we're here?" Diandra asked, looking to the sky.

"They know by now we are not heading into Syria," Dutch answered. "My guess is they are executing a concentric search pattern, expanding it wider and wider. It may take them a couple of passes before they get here. But they will. We've got to get over that border. It can't be that far."

"Let's go then," said Sam, gritting his teeth.

Diandra helped him the best she could, despite her limp, while Dutch took the lead. Fifteen minutes passed before the sound of the blades became noticeably louder.

"They're getting closer," Dutch observed, his expression grim but determined. "They're doing this by the book. It won't be long before they pick us up on infrared and..." He let that hang. "Let's stick by the cliffs and buy a little time."

Within minutes, a Russian-made Kamov Ka-60 helicopter flew low and directly overhead from behind the cliff. Continuing in the same direction for about three hundred yards, it stopped and hovered. Slowly, it turned one hundred eighty degrees and directly faced them.

Dutch raised the AK-47 and started firing. Bullets sparked as they ricocheted off the craft's bulletproof Plexiglas cockpit enclosure and surrounding metal armor.

"Come on!" Dutch yelled at Diandra and Sam as they scurried along the cliff's face. The helicopter opened fire with a barrage of .50 caliber bullets ten feet in front of Dutch, pitting the cliff face and causing him to crouch to the ground and halt. Another burst of fire hit five feet above, causing chunks of sand and rock to rain down on them. Shaking off the dust, Dutch paused for a moment to think.

"They're trying to stop us, not kill us," he said aloud. "We've still got a chance."

With one hand he fired his rifle while making his way along the cliff. The bullets glanced off the chopper in all directions. When the AK-47 finally ran out of ammo, Dutch threw it down. The Kamov Ka-60 moved another fifty yards closer as it released a short burst of gunfire directly in front of Dutch, causing him to back up a few steps. Bending down, he reached for his Smith and Wesson .38, pulled back the slide and started firing at the monster, moving in front of Diandra and Sam. He emptied the clip, ejecting it with one hand while pulling out another from his leg holster and inserting it with a slap. Pulling back the slide and loading, he used his left hand to steady his grip. Aiming at the transmission and blades, he methodically fired until out of bullets.

Ejecting the empty clip, he reached for the last one from his holster, inserted it and ratcheted a bullet into the chamber. This time he aimed at the cockpit and slowly pulled off rounds, one by one, knowing he only had a total of fourteen in the clip. The bullets bounced off like a peashooter against a tank. Dutch could see the two pilots laughing in the cockpit as he continued firing shot after shot. The chopper eased closer, stopping less than a hundred and fifty yards away.

After firing seven shots Dutch took aim and fired four more rounds at the rotors.

Nothing.

Checking to make sure he was in front of Diandra and Sam, who were huddling behind him, he fired the last three bullets at the chopper's mixer box. The force of wind from the whipping blades was blowing sand everywhere, the noise was deafening.

"We've got to make a run for it!" Dutch yelled as he threw down the empty .38 and reached over to pull Sam to his feet.

"Sam can't go on anymore!" Diandra shouted back over the blades' noise, then added hopelessly, "And neither can I." Her teary eyes let Dutch know she had no reserves left.

Another burst of fire from the chopper hit less than two feet above their heads. They could feel the percussion of the bullets as they whizzed by and slammed into the cliff face, chips of rock raining down over them. The Seekers could see the pilots grinning, clearly enjoying their game of cat and mouse.

Suddenly, two unmarked Sikorsky UH-60 Black Hawk helicopters rose from below a canyon about a half-mile out. They made their way slowly toward the rear of the Kamov Ka-60, whose pilots remained unaware of their presence.

Continuing toward the rear of the chopper, the Black Hawks separated and spread out, flanking them from behind at about a thirty-degree angle on each side. They remained there, hovering.

"You are in Turkish airspace," came a booming voice in Arabic from one of the Black Hawk's loud speakers. "You are ordered to land immediately."

The expressions of the Kamov Ka-60 pilots turned from jovial to serious business in milliseconds. They craned their necks both ways to see what was going on, observing the two Black Hawks on either side of them. They had a decision to make.

It was the wrong one.

The pilot in command pulled his accelerator up and quickly gained altitude while simultaneously flying backwards and turning around to get a clear shot. Before he could execute the plan, both Black Hawks released air-to-air missiles that slammed into the helicopter with a deafening explosion.

Flames from the jet fuel shot hundreds of feet in all directions as the massive wreckage fell to the ground in a thunderous crash. The concussion wave slammed Dutch and crew against the cliff face. Composite rotor blades shattered and flew in all directions. Within seconds, the helicopter had been reduced to a smoldering pile of burning wreckage.

"That's what I'm talking about," shouted Dutch as he turned to Sam and Diandra. "You guys okay?"

Diandra smiled back, nodded and turned back to Sam.

One of the Black Hawks slowly made its way around the wreckage and landed a few hundred feet away from the cliff face. Two helmeted and flak jacketed men jumped out from the side, one carrying a medical kit. They raced over to the group while Dutch rose from checking on Diandra and Sam to meet them.

"You okay?" one of the men shouted to Dutch over the choppers' deafening noise.

"He needs help," Dutch responded, pointing to Sam.

"Right," the man answered as he set the medical kit down next to Sam and started checking his shoulder and arm.

"Welcome to Turkey, Mister Vorhees!" the other man shouted with a grin.

"So we made it?" Dutch shouted back.

"Close enough," the man replied loudly. "But we better get out of here just to make sure."

Chapter Twenty

Tanner Headquarters, New York

Tanner's New York offices were very similar in taste and décor to his Berlin office. Antique statues lined the walls. Ancient artifacts were showcased in lighted glass cabinets. A large mahogany desk rested in the center of the room, backlit by a window with a panoramic view of the New York skyline.

The Seekers waited impatiently for Tanner. Dutch and Diandra sat in leather padded high backed chairs. Skip, following their now customary glad to see you hugs and kisses and his pretending not to like it routine, was absorbed with his own ritual of dropping his tea bag into a cup of steaming hot water for a silent count to twelve. Pulling it out and setting it aside, he took a seat, gently blowing to cool it down. Sam was studying a glass case showcasing Sumerian tablets.

* * * * * * * *

Ankara, Turkey

The helicopters in Turkey had taken Diandra, Dutch and Sam to Incirlik Airbase where Sam's gunshot wound was attended to by the base's medical facility. The injury turned out to be grave but by that point non-life-threatening, although he had lost a lot of blood from the bullet nicking a major blood vessel. The doctor complimented Dutch on his quick work and credited him for saving Sam's life. He was ordered to wear a sling for at least two weeks.

Dutch and Diandra were checked by military doctors and found to be in good health. Determining by x-rays that there was no fracture, they re-wrapped Diandra's ankle and gave her crutches.

Zoë had arranged for them to catch a commercial flight from the Dalaman airport to New York. After cleaning up they boarded the plane and slept most of the way. Zoë had Cantwell meet them at LaGuardia and accompany them to Tanner Industries' New York offices, where Skip awaited.

* * * * * * * *

Tanners Headquarters, New York

The four Seekers turned as Zoë entered Tanner's office, grabbed a remote and hit a button. Sam walked from the antiquities case and joined the group as a large LED screen came down from the ceiling. Tanner appeared within moments on the HD projection screen.

"First of all, I want to apologize for not being there in person. I had some urgent business in Tokyo that could not wait. That aside," he said, eyeing copies of the notes Skip had made of the ordeal, "I must say I am absolutely exhilarated that you are all safe and sound. I'm guessing it would be an understatement to say you had one heck of an adventure."

"What did you call it at the beginning?" Diandra asked. "The adventure of a lifetime? Unfortunately, it turned out to be the greatest loss of knowledge to humanity since the original burning of Alexander's Library."

"On the contrary, Diandra," Tanner replied. "It was successful beyond my wildest expectations."

"What are you talking about?" she asked, cocking her head in confusion.

Tanner set the notes aside, leaned forward in his wheelchair and steepled his fingers. "In the past few days, you have come closer to uncovering the truth of our true origins than anyone in recent history." He gave a rare grin. "My god, you were right there! You found the repository and more. I can't even imagine what a thrill it was to see and touch all that you discovered."

Diandra looked to Dutch and Sam and raised her shoulders.

"I don't get it," she said. "I thought we failed. The repository was blown up."

"True," Tanner nodded, "but remember when I told you I was made aware of some information that caused me to look deeper into the world's mysteries? It was from a high official within the Catholic Church. He said the church knows from ancient texts in the secret Vatican archives that there will be a huge event, worldwide in scale and cataclysmic in nature. He did not know exactly when, but felt it was imminent and was *very* adamant that we needed to make plans for such a possibility as soon as possible. Hence my ARK project and various other steps I have taken to save the world's knowledge.

"Up until now we've had no legitimate confirmation that such an event was even real, other than legends. Now, thanks to your efforts, we do. According to the notes you gave us, the crystal skull mentioned a cataclysmic event that happened twelve thousand years ago and is scheduled to happen again. It appears our ancestors had the same idea of saving their world's knowledge for us. Most importantly, they stated they possessed the knowledge we will need in order to avert the catastrophe this time. It is unfortunate that we don't know what it is that will happen."

"What about the Mayan prophecies about the end times?" Sam asked.

"I never did lend much credence to that, Sam," Diandra said, shaking her head. "It's based on the mistaken premise that the Mayas observed a three-hundred and sixty day calendar year. When it was first discovered, archeologists knew the Mayan calendar was based on a three-hundred and sixty-five day year, which would push the *end of times* date out another forty or so years."

Tanner nodded his agreement.

"We've preliminarily analyzed what you brought back, including the pictures and the crystal skull," Tanner said as he picked up another set of papers and scanned them.

"Here is what we do know. The skull's core temperature remains a constant seventy degrees, which is what the Hewlett-Packard laboratories discovered about the Mitchell-Hedges skull. It was also cut from a single piece of flawless crystal *against* the natural grain of the crystal, which is very unusual. I doubt if we could do that today. And, it is in one solid piece.

"The jaw," he continued, "although it appears as if it can separate, is an intricate part of the skull. Fortunately, the bullet that grazed it only chipped the lower left side. We are subjecting it to various tests to see if we can at least extract the core message that you heard."

"It's there," Diandra said. "I heard it, and so did Dutch and Sam."

"I heard nothing but static," Skip stated. "It could be something was wrong with my recording devices."

"I don't think so," Tanner said. "What you recorded is very important, Skip. It is what we believe to be the base vibrational code or algorithm to the message, and may be instrumental in helping us crack the code to their language."

"How was it we each heard it in different languages?" Diandra asked.

"Jeff thinks that what you heard was a direct vibration that translated itself into the language of your core DNA. An example would be a computer program that recognizes what language your computer browser supports and sends information in that language. If true, it is an extraordinary technological development."

"So that means the soldier who fired at us must have heard it in Arabic too," Sam noted, raising his eyebrows. "Wow, no wonder he was spooked."

"What about the golden disc I gave you?" Dutch asked.

"That is a little more interesting. They are not solid gold. Rather, they contain about ten percent platinum."

"What?" Dutch exclaimed.

"You're as surprised as I was," Tanner said. "The fact that they mined platinum, let alone used it in metallurgy, is, well, unexplainable. But there is more. The grooves you saw are actually very small texts etched into the disc. They are unable to be seen without significant magnification."

"What does it say?" Diandra asked.

"Unknown," Tanner replied, shaking his head. "It is in the same script as the other glyphs you found in the tomb. We are running it through Jeff's UPP program, but it is slow going. I believe we'll eventually crack it, but it doesn't look like anytime soon."

"I still don't understand something," Dutch said, standing up. "The original tablet gave us the impression that Alexander was buried in that tomb, when in fact it wasn't even a tomb at all. So how did the library's scrolls and that Demetrius guy get in there?"

Tanner shrugged his shoulders and raised his hands. "Theories?"

"Sam and I have been working on one," Diandra replied, looking to Sam for confirmation. "What if someone high up in the library knew about this repository and its true purpose and decided to place part of the library's contents in it, knowing that one day we would find the tablet and discover its location? We would also discover the library's contents they placed there as well. That would explain a lot."

"Hard to believe, Diandra, that someone would know that much back then," Tanner said. "But then again, we don't know all of the knowledge the library contained, so that's certainly a possibility."

"Plus," Sam added, "those crystal lights and other things we saw at the tomb. Totally rad."

"There are definitely technologies at work we do not completely understand," Tanner answered. "Fortunately, we have the recordings Skip made of your adventure, as well as the digital pictures from your camera, Diandra. We are having those analyzed as well."

"When are we going to release the footage and pictures we do have to the public?" Diandra asked.

"I think we should wait and see if we can translate them first," he answered. "If we can find another one of their repository sites, we will have the evidence we need to make a world-wide announcement. At this point, I think it is a little bit premature."

"Scholars had trouble deciphering the Dead Sea Scrolls correctly until the Huntington Library released them to the world... against those scholars' wishes, I might add," Diandra argued. "And if they hadn't released them when they did, we would still be wondering what the scrolls said."

"Good point," Tanner responded. "But I think I would feel more comfortable if we had a head start on what we are dealing with. What if they contain the location of another repository? We want to get their first, don't we?"

"I suppose so," Diandra frowned, not convinced. She glanced at the others.

"But here is what I will do," Tanner conceded. "We'll discreetly contact some trusted scholars around the world and get them working on the translations. Maybe they can help speed up the process."

"You said *we* would want to get there first?" Dutch asked.

"Yes." Tanner adamantly replied. "*We* need to follow up every lead we can… you realize how serious this is. I cannot overstate what's at stake here. We have got to find those repositories."

"We get it, Mister Tanner," Diandra said. "We were there. The visions and images we saw, if true, were absolutely horrifying." She took a deep breath, blew it out and looked to Sam and Dutch. "They showed total worldwide destruction."

Tanner sat back in his wheelchair and assessed them.

"Well then, are you up for the challenge?" he asked.

Diandra turned to Sam and Skip, who nodded, and then to Dutch.

"We're in, Tanner," Dutch said, "Although I'm not sure what we're getting ourselves into."

"So what do we do?" Sam asked, ignoring Dutch's comment.

"Continue doing what you were doing." Tanner clasped his hands together. "Seek out and follow up any lead you come across, no matter how insignificant it may seem. Our ancestors went to a lot of trouble to bury knowledge and clues around the world for us to find. We need to discover and decipher them, to search for their meanings and origins.

"We have the most advanced computers and resources available in the world at your disposal." He thumped the arms of his wheelchair with enthusiasm. "Use them! I suspect it will often be tedious, and sometimes disappointing. But I have found that success comes to those that do not give up. In order to win, you have to get up one more time than you fall."

"One huge problem with that plan," Dutch said. "We have William Lewis and-"

"Who?" interrupted Tanner.

"Shadow Man… and whoever is helping him trying to stop us from finding this information. And believe me, he doesn't come cheap. There is someone with a lot of power and influence behind him. There are a lot of questions that need to be answered."

"I agree. That is troubling," Tanner said, shaking his head. "I have a lead on that, but I feel like I am chasing ghosts, here."

"Seriously?" Sam's eyes widened. "There's been some crazy stuff on this adventure…"

"No, metaphorically," Tanner replied. "There seems to be some extremely secretive group within the Vatican no one acknowledges exists. It may take time to discover who and what this organization is, but I *will* find out. In the meantime, you'll need to be cautious. We'll create phantom accounts, new identities and do whatever else it takes to keep you invisible to the world so you'll be able to carry out your explorations.

"I've had offices set up for you here and in Berlin. You have carte blanche, anything you need, you'll get. We need to discover what is going to happen and, just as important, *when* it is going to happen."

"We're up for it," Dutch said, the others nodding their assent. "When do we start?"

"The sooner the better, because there is one more thing you should know," Tanner continued. "From the message the crystal skull gave you relating to the era beginning with the water bearer, or Aquarius, and the revolutions around the sun, we have a potential time frame for dates."

"Excellent!" Diandra said, "And they are?"

"Anywhere from twenty seventeen to twenty seventy-seven.

"That's a lot of leeway," she noted.

"It's a very accurate window when you consider that they were trying to leave us a message over twelve and a half thousand years ago that we would be able to understand today."

"That coincides with Sir Isaac Newton's predictions," Sam noted.

"What do you mean?" Tanner asked.

Sam looked to Diandra, who nodded her assent to continue.

"They found a document in his handwriting wherein he tried to work out cryptic references to the end times mentioned in the Bible," Sam informed him. "He came up with three different scenarios."

"The one Sam is referring to," Diandra cut in, "is a not earlier date of two-thousand and sixty, according to the present calendar."

"Where is this document?" Tanner asked.

"The Jewish National and University Library in Jerusalem," Sam answered. "I can send you a link."

"I see. Yes, please do that," he said, thinking for a moment. Then, changing the subject, he asked Diandra if she had heard from McIntyre.

"Not yet, and I am worried about him," she replied. "If the same people are after him that were after us, I wish him god-speed," Diandra said

"Agreed," Tanner added.

"Speaking of which," Skip interjected, "I still need to get on that translation in the letter. There might still be something we can use contained in it. Especially since some of the symbols showed up in the tomb."

"Good point, Skip," Tanner said. Leaning forward in his chair, his look turned earnest.

"There is one last thing. As I mentioned, whatever it is we need to find, you will have my full support, both personally and financially. The truth is, we need to uncover what our *true* history is, or we are doomed to repeat it. I think you'll agree the skull's message was quite clear. We don't want to repeat it.

"For now, though," he smiled, "why don't you take a couple of days off and relax. Let Zoë know what you need and she'll take care of it."

They started to get up from their chairs when Tanner continued. "By the way Dutch, I've left something for you in the top left drawer of my desk."

Intrigued, Dutch walked around and opened the drawer. An oak box lay within. He pulled it out, opened it and smiled.

"I heard you lost yours in the desert. Thought you might like it."

Dutch pulled out a silver-plated Smith and Wesson .45. Holding it up to admire, he checked the magazine and smiled.

"Very nice, Tanner. You do surprise me," he said.

"As do you," Tanner replied. "I didn't have a chance to thank you for your influence in arranging those helicopters and government troops in Lima. It seems your reach is high."

"I have my moments," Dutch replied.

"Mr. Tanner," Diandra said. "I… we, want you to know how much we appreciate all your support."

"Remember, Diandra," he responded, concern in his voice. "It's as much for me as it is for humanity." He stopped and thought for a moment.

"After all, I am on this same planet as everyone else."

* * * * * * * *

Chapter Twenty-One

Tanner Headquarters, New York

Dutch, Skip, Diandra on crutches, and Sam with his arm in a sling, exited the lobby of the Tanner building on Broadway and breathed in the air.

"I don't know about you guys," Dutch said, looking up and down the street. "But I could use a beer."

"Let's have Tanner's driver take us to a nice Italian restaurant and get something to eat with a couple of bottles of good vino," Diandra suggested. "Except for that food on the plane, I haven't had a decent meal in a week." Looking over to Sam she saw she'd hurt his feelings. "Excepting of course, the wonderful meal you cooked for us in the desert," she continued, winking at Dutch.

"I am so glad you liked it. As I mentioned, it was my father's recipe and I…" He realized Diandra was yanking his chain. "Okay, I get it. The recipe needs a little tweaking to cool it down."

They all laughed.

"That's an understatement," Diandra said.

Dutch's phone rang. Picking it up he held his index finger up to the others and walked a few feet away.

* * * * * * * *

Across the street high atop a rooftop Shadow Man was using a listening device to monitor their conversation. A man with a headset held the two-foot dish with a microphone in the center. Dutch was in the crosshairs of a sniper kneeling below Shadow Man with an M-40 silencer-equipped rifle. Setting his earpiece down, Shadow Man dialed his cell phone.

"They have just finished their meeting with Tanner and agreed to keep searching," Shadow Man's gravelly voice relayed. "We have Vorhees targeted and can take out the rest of the group. We're awaiting your instructions."

"Wait until I give the word," Lilne ordered. "We are waiting to acquire our primary target first."

* * * * * * * *

"Vorhees here," Dutch answered.

"My sources tell me that the man you mentioned, McIntyre, has been spotted in Morocco," Navarro stated.

"Is there more?"

"Mostly background. Very costly information."

"I am good for it."

Silence greeted that last comment.

"Navarro?"

"Maybe not, my friend. It seems you and your Seekers are also wanted with a very substantial reward for any information. I could make much more turning you in than helping you."

"Do you have any idea who's behind this?"

Silence.

"I've never seen this much worldwide chatter. All the usual suspects and more, including their respective governments. I will send you what I know about McIntyre through our normal channel. In the meantime, you be careful, my friend."

"Navarro?"

"Yes?"

"Thanks."

"Do not mention it. I mean to anyone, Dutch. It would be bad for business if word got out that I should have a conscience."

* * * * * * * *

Tanner Headquarters, New York

A black limousine pulled onto Broadway in front of tanner headquarters and stopped. Getting out the driver circled the rear of the Crown Victoria and opened a door.

"Everything okay?" Diandra asked, referencing the phone call.

Dutch nodded slightly. "Sure thing." He eyed the limo and driver waiting. "So, we'll get something to eat in mid-town?" he asked the group as they walked toward the car."

"I'm really excited," Sam said. "I feel like we're on a grand adventure."

Dutch laughed. "Yeah, kid, what more can possibly go wrong."

* * * * * * * * *

Casablanca, Morocco

Walking through Casablanca's Mohammad V's airport, McIntyre sensed that two men walking behind were following him. Surreptitiously checking behind him via a shop window, he tightened his backpack straps and walked faster.

"We have located him," one of the men said on his cell phone to Lilne as they picked up their pace to overtake McIntyre, dodging around and pushing people in the terminal. "We are in the process of picking him up."

Lilne had both cell phone conversations up and playing through his computer's sound system. "Get ready," Lilne leaned in and said to Shadow Man.

Tapping the gunman on the shoulder, Shadow Man held up one finger in a wait signal. Almost there.

Gaining on McIntyre, the two men were ready to grab him when three non-descript Bedouins moved to insert themselves behind McIntyre. They were holding cages of chickens and opened the doors, releasing them. Travelers jumped aside, screeching and laughing, as chickens and feathers flew everywhere. Swearing, the two men pushed through the pandemonium to find that McIntyre was nowhere to be found. The three men with the chickens had also vanished.

"We have lost our target! I repeat, we have lost our target," one of the men screamed into his cell phone over the squawking chickens.

"Stand down," Lilne shouted to Shadow Man on his cell phone.

Shadow Man tapped the sniper on the back twice. The sniper misinterpreted this to mean it was a go and slowly squeezed off a kill shot. Shadow Man quickly grabbed the barrel of the gun, yanking it up and causing the bullet to hit a ledge twenty feet above Dutch as he was about to enter the car. Pigeons scattered, their wings creating a fluttering crescendo, while chunks of dust floated down. Dutch looked up to observe the commotion.

"What happened?" Shadow Man shouted as he pulled the sniper's rifle out of his hands, knocked the man in the face with the barrel, and tossed it. He angrily circled the rooftop, cell phone to his head.

"We lost our target in Morocco," Lilne informed him. "Those Seekers are my only connection to him. We will follow them and wait for McIntyre to make contact."

"It's your dime," Shadow Man growled as he hit end call and pocketed his phone. "Mission over," he snapped to his men. "Time to wrap up and leave."

Turning to the street below, he shook his head.

"I'll be watching you, Vorhees," he whispered, teeth clenched. "Our time will come."

* * * * * * * *

Chapter Twenty-Two

Location Unknown

The Guardian council were gathered in a darkened room lit only by torchlight. Twelve men sat around a rough-hewn wooden table, many with cowls over their heads.

"I have learned that there are repositories hidden around the world that contain the knowledge we have endeavored and committed to keep secret all these centuries," Lilne informed them from the head of the table.

Murmurs and hushed tones of disbelief erupted from the council. "What are we to do?" asked one of the eldest members.

"Nothing," Lilne continued, holding up his hand for silence. "These *Seekers,* as they call themselves, will be the ones whom we will follow. Their searches may lead us to these repositories. Let them do all the hard work. We will not be disappointed."

"This is a dangerous game we are playing, Lilne," a hooded member said. "What if these Seekers, as you call them, are successful and the world finds out that which we are sworn to protect?"

"There is little chance of that," Lilne replied. "However, if they should come close to succeeding in their quest, they and all they find will be destroyed."

Lilne stood up and moved slowly around the large wooden table.

"We do not know how many of these repositories may exist," he continued. "Nor their locations. We need our Guardian book to search for clues. Without it, we are at a disadvantage. Therefore, we must still locate McIntyre and retrieve our property. These Seekers may be helpful in that endeavor as well."

"I pray that you are right Lilne, for the world is not yet ready to find out the truth," another member stated solemnly.

Lilne stopped pacing.

"They will never be ready for the truth."

* * * * * * * *

South of France

Finishing copying and making notes from the ancient book onto a sheet of paper, McIntyre set down his pen and closed the book. He pulled out a FedEx envelope and carefully placed the pages inside and sealed it. Extracting a piece of paper from his pocket, he studied it for a moment and then copied an address onto the front.

Exiting the front door of his rented cottage, he walked down the street and stopped in front of a postal office. Entering it, he handed the package to the clerk along with the shipping paperwork.

"Ah, you are sending this to the United States, yes?" the clerk asked in French.

"Oui," McIntyre replied.

"And this address is correct?"

"Oui."

The clerk, a short, fat, jovial looking man with a perpetual smile gracing his triple chins, typed it into his computer.

"It should be there day after tomorrow," he informed him.

"Very good," McIntyre replied in French as his attention was directed to some children passing by the shop's facade, laughing and playing.

"Contents?"

"Excuse me?" McIntyre asked as he turned back around.

"The envelope. What are its contents?" the clerk asked.

"Just papers," McIntyre replied. "Nothing important."

"Au contraire," the clerk said. "Everything we treat as important," he said, beaming.

McIntyre returned the smile, paid for the package and left the shop. The clerk finished the paperwork and threw the envelope on a pile, address side up.

It read:

Dr. Diandra Weiss
C/O The New York Museum of Natural History
125 E. 56th street
NY, NY 10056

* * * * * * *

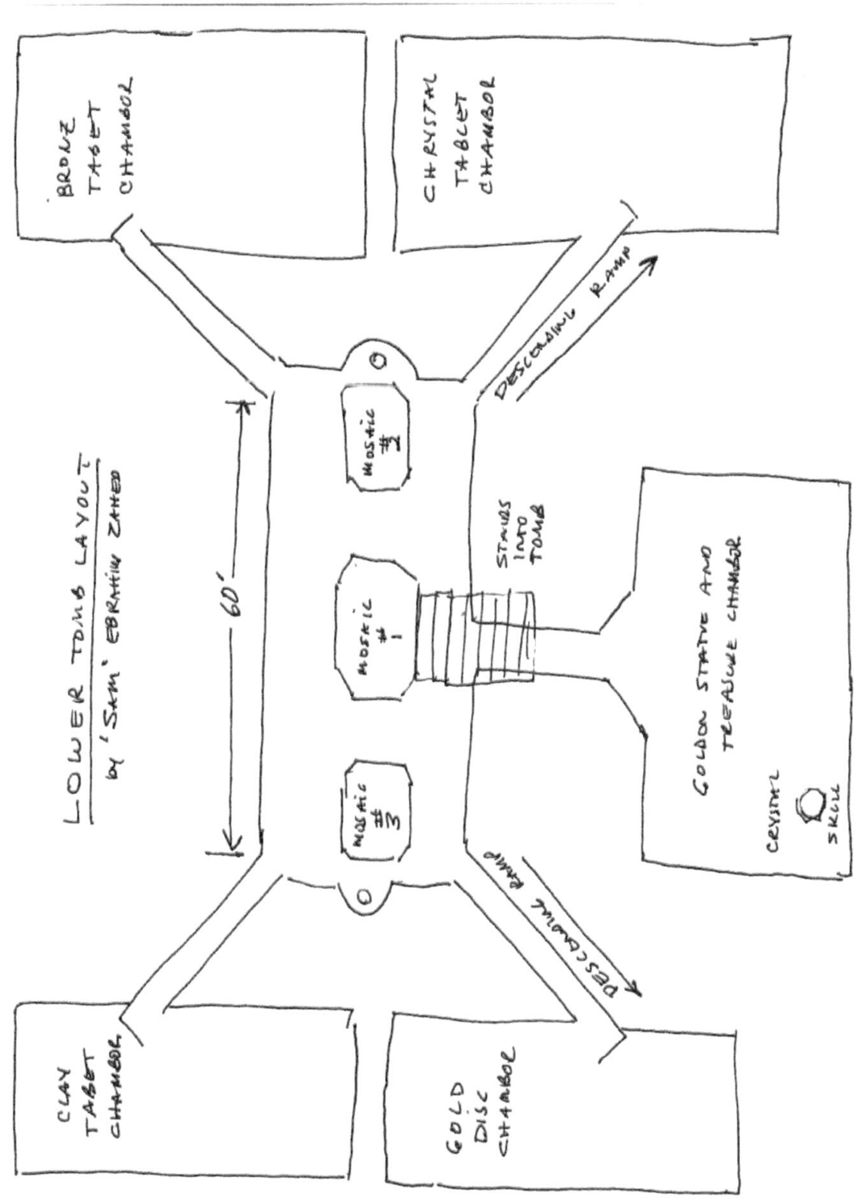
LOWER TOMB LAYOUT
by 'SAM' EBRAHIM ZAHED
BRONZ TABET CHAMBOR
CHRYSTAL TABLET CHAMBOR
DESCENDING RAMP
MOSAIC #2
MOSAIC #1
MOSAIC #3
60'
STAIRS INTO TOMB
GOLDON STATUE AND TREASURE CHAMBOR
CRYSTAL SKULL
DESCENDING RAMP
CLAY TABET CHAMBOR
GOLD DISC CHAMBOR

Winged Discs or Planets

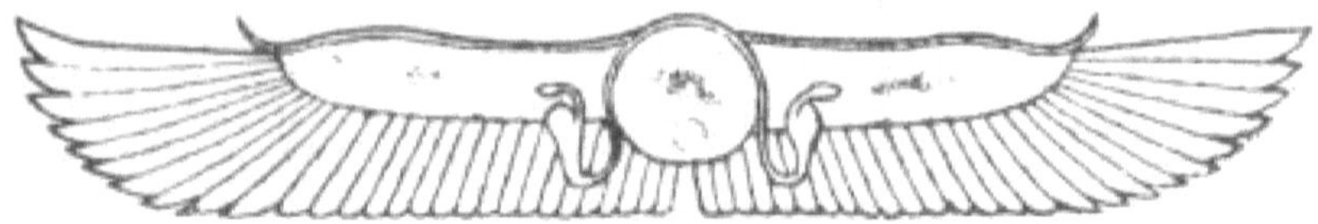

Ahura Mazda

John O'Melveny Woods is the Award-winning author of several books and resides in Fairhope, Alabama.

Lost Tomb of Alexander is the first release in *The Seekers* book series.
www.LostTombofAlexander.com

John may be reached through his website at
author@JohnWoodsAuthor.com

Additional titles:

Return to Treasure Island
www.R2TI.com

Jesse James Secret
www.JesseJamesSecret.com

The Crusaders
www.TheCrusadersBook.com

Now Available at

amazon.com

www.ingramcontent.com/pod-product-compliance
Lightning Source LLC
Chambersburg PA
CBHW021624030826
48979CB00036B/2095/J
* 9 7 8 1 9 4 5 1 9 0 1 2 4 *